# CURTAIN OF DEATH

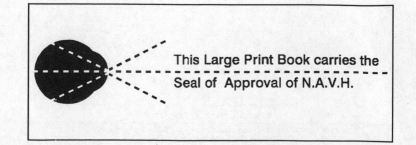

This Large Print Book carries the
Seal of Approval of N.A.V.H.

A CLANDESTINE OPERATIONS NOVEL

# CURTAIN OF DEATH

# W.E.B. GRIFFIN
# AND WILLIAM E.
# BUTTERWORTH, IV

**THORNDIKE PRESS**
*A part of Gale, Cengage Learning*

Farmington Hills, Mich • San Francisco • New York • Waterville, Maine
Meriden, Conn • Mason, Ohio • Chicago

**LIBRARY OF CONGRESS CATALOGING-IN-PUBLICATION DATA**

Names: Griffin, W. E. B., author. | Butterworth, William E. (William Edmund), author.
Title: Curtain of death / W.E.B. Griffin and William E. Butterworth IV.
Description: Large print edition. | Waterville, Maine : Thorndike Press Large Print, 2017. | Series: A clandestine operations novel| Series: Thorndike Press large print core
Identifiers: LCCN 2016045909| ISBN 9781410493293 (hardback) | ISBN 1410493296 (hardcover)
Subjects: LCSH: United States. Central Intelligence Agency—Fiction. | Intelligence officers—United States—Fiction. | Espionage—Fiction. | Cold War—Fiction. | Large type books. | BISAC: FICTION / Action & Adventure. | GSAFD: Spy stories. | Suspense fiction.
Classification: LCC PS3557.R489137 C87 2017 | DDC 813/.54—dc23
LC record available at https://lccn.loc.gov/2016045909

Published in 2017 by arrangement with G. P. Putnam's Sons, an imprint of Penguin Publishing Group, a division of Penguin Random House LLC

26 July 1777

"The necessity of procuring good intelligence is apparent and need not be further urged."

George Washington
General and Commander in Chief
The Continental Army

# FOR THE LATE

WILLIAM E. COLBY
An OSS Jedburgh First Lieutenant
who became director of the Central
Intelligence Agency.

AARON BANK
An OSS Jedburgh First Lieutenant
who became a colonel and
the father of Special Forces.

WILLIAM R. CORSON
A legendary Marine intelligence officer
whom the KGB hated more than any
other U.S. intelligence officer —
and not only because he wrote the
definitive work on them.

RENÉ J. DÉFOURNEAUX
A U.S. Army OSS Second Lieutenant

attached to the British SOE
who jumped into Occupied France alone
and later became a legendary
U.S. Army intelligence officer.

## FOR THE LIVING

### BILLY WAUGH
A legendary Special Forces
Command Sergeant Major
who retired and then went on to hunt
down the infamous Carlos the Jackal.
Billy could have terminated Osama bin
Laden in the early 1990s
but could not get permission to do so.
After fifty years in the business, Billy is
still going after the bad guys.

### JOHNNY REITZEL
An Army Special Operations officer
who could have terminated
the head terrorist of the seized cruise
ship *Achille Lauro* but could not
get permission to do so.

### RALPH PETERS
An Army intelligence officer
who has written the best analysis of our
war against terrorists and of our enemy
that I have ever seen.

## AND FOR THE NEW BREED

MARC L
A senior intelligence officer,
despite his youth, who reminds me of
Bill Colby more and more each day.

FRANK L
A legendary Defense Intelligence Agency
officer who retired and now follows in Billy
Waugh's footsteps.

### AND

In Loving Memory Of
Colonel José Manuel Menéndez
Cavalry, Argentine Army, Retired
He spent his life fighting Communism and
Juan Domingo Perón

OUR NATION OWES THESE PATRIOTS
A DEBT BEYOND REPAYMENT.

# I

## [ONE]

*The WAC Non-Commissioned Officers' Club*

*Munich Military Post*

*Munich, American Zone of Occupied
  Germany*

*0005 24 January 1946*

Two women, both wearing the olive drab
uniform of an "Ike" jacket and skirt, came
out of the club and started to walk through
the parking lot. They had come to the club
late and had had to park at just about the
far end of the lot.

One of the women, a somewhat stocky
dark-haired thirty-five-year-old, had the
chevrons of a technical sergeant on her
sleeves. The other, who was a trim, twenty-
nine-year-old blonde, had small embroidered triangles with the letters "U.S." in
them sewn to her lapels. That insignia

11

identified her as a civilian employee of the U.S. Army.

At the extreme end of the parking lot were two ambulances parked nose out. One had large red crosses on its sides, rear doors, and roof of the body. On its bumpers the white stenciled letters "98GH" and "102" identified it as the 102nd vehicle assigned to the motor pool of the 98th General Hospital, which served the Munich area.

The red crosses on the second ambulance had been painted over, and on its bumpers had been stenciled "711 MKRC" and "17," which identified it as the seventeenth vehicle assigned to the 711th Mobile Kitchen Renovation Company.

When they reached the 711th vehicle, the WAC tech sergeant started to get in the passenger seat beside the driver, and the woman with the civilian triangles insignia started to climb in behind the wheel.

Three men, all wearing dark clothing, erupted from the 98th General Hospital ambulance. One of them came out the passenger side, ran around to the front of the other ambulance, where he pulled the woman with the triangles out of her ambulance, and after giving her a good look at the knife he held, placed it across her throat.

The other two men came out the rear of

the ambulance. As one opened the second of its doors, the other ran to the 711th ambulance, pulled the technical sergeant from it, and, as the other had, showed her a knife and then placed it across her throat.

He then marched her to the rear of the hospital ambulance. By then, both doors were open, and the man who had opened both doors was inside.

"Get in!" the man holding the knife against the sergeant's neck ordered.

When she was halfway in, the man inside the ambulance, now wielding the same kind of knife as the others, ordered her: "Get on the forward stretcher. On your stomach. And don't move."

The sergeant complied, crawling on her hands and knees to the stretcher, which was on the left side of the body, and then onto it.

The man who had brought her to the rear of the ambulance then ran to the passenger seat and got in.

The man who had pulled the woman from behind the wheel of her ambulance now marched her up to the open ambulance doors. His knife was still against her throat.

"Get in!" he ordered. "On your belly on the lower stretcher in the back."

She complied.

The man then shut the left door, climbed into the ambulance, and, kneeling on the floor, pulled the right door closed.

"Go!" he shouted to the driver.

Then, still on his knees, he made his way forward to the front. There he stopped, turned his head, and called out, "If you make a sound when we pass through the gate, he will slit your friend's throat." Then he turned his head forward and again shouted, "Go!"

The driver ground the gears as he revved the engine.

The man in the aisle pushed aside the curtain separating the stretcher portion of the body from the driver and passenger seats.

The blond woman with the civilian triangles began to slowly move her right hand from her side to the neck of her Ike jacket.

The ambulance began to move.

The blond woman unbuttoned her second and third khaki shirt buttons, and then put her hand in the opening. Then she pushed aside the top of her slip. Finally, she put her hand inside her brassiere.

And then she slowly removed it.

It now held a small, five-shot, snub-nosed Smith & Wesson .38 Special caliber revolver.

She pushed herself off the stretcher onto

14

the floor and, supporting herself on her elbows and holding the pistol in both hands, took aim.

The man holding the knife against the tech sergeant's neck was trying to look though the small opening the other man had made. He heard, or sensed, her movement and started to turn for a look.

Her first shot hit him just below the ear, and the bullet exploded his brain before making a large exit wound in the upper portion of his skull.

The technical sergeant began to scream.

The woman wearing triangles fired a second shot. It hit the man who had opened the curtain just below the left eye, exploded his brain, and then created a large exit wound in his cranium.

She fired two more shots, first one to the left, where she hoped the bullet might find the driver, and then one to the right, where she hoped it might find the man in the passenger seat.

Her third shot apparently missed, for the ambulance kept moving. The fourth, to judge by someone screaming in pain, had hit, but was not immediately fatal.

The driver, perhaps not wisely, pushed the dividing curtain aside to see what was going on in the back. She fired her fifth shot, the last she had, and it hit the driver just about in the center of his forehead.

Moments later the ambulance crashed into something and stopped.

The technical sergeant was still screaming hysterically.

"Florence!" the woman wearing triangles called. "It's over! Shut the fuck up!"

Then she crawled back onto the stretcher.

*Get your little ass out of the line of fire.*

*The sonofabitch in the passenger seat may be alive, and he probably has a gun.*

She realized her ears were ringing painfully from the sounds of five shots going off in the confines of the ambulance.

And then she felt dizzy.

And then she threw up.

## [Two]

*Hotel Vier Jahreszeiten*

*Maximilianstrasse 178*

*Munich, American Zone of Occupation, Germany*

*0215 24 January 1946*

Chief Warrant Officer August Ziegler, who was thirty-one but looked younger, walked down the nicely carpeted third-floor corridor and stopped before the double doors

16

of Suite 507. Above the door a neatly lettered sign announced XXVIITH CIC.

There was a brass door knocker on each of the double doors, so Ziegler lifted the one on the right and let it fall, and then did the same with the knocker on the left.

After he lifted the first knocker, he thought he heard a faint ringing of a bell, not inside 507 but somewhere close, and when he lifted the second knocker he knew he heard it again.

There was no response to Ziegler's rings from inside 507, so he lifted and dropped both knockers again.

This time he heard both bell rings and then the sound of an opening door. Then he saw someone coming down the corridor. It was a plump young man in his twenties. He was wearing a rather luxurious red silk dressing gown, very cheap cotton shower shoes, and he had around his waist a leather belt supporting a Colt Model 1911A1 pistol in a holster Ziegler instantly recognized to be a "Secret Service High Rise Cross Draw" holster.

He knew it because few people anywhere — except of course the Secret Service — had such holsters. Augie Ziegler was one of the few people who did. He was wearing one right now under his Ike jacket, the

17

lapels of which bore triangles, the idea being that people would think he was a civilian employee of the Army, and that he was not armed.

He was in fact not only a chief warrant officer but also a supervisory special agent of the Criminal Investigation Division — called the CID — of the Provost Marshal General's Department.

Aware that on general principles he and others in the CID did not think much of the CIC — and that the reverse was true — Augie smiled, and turned on cordiality.

"Sorry, sir, to disturb you at this hour," he said. "I wouldn't do it, sir, if it wasn't important."

When he spoke, sort of a German accent was apparent. It was not a German accent precisely, but a Pennsylvania Dutch accent. Augie was from Reading, Pennsylvania.

"No problem," the chubby man said. "What can I do for you at this obscene hour of the morning?"

When the chubby man spoke, a German accent also was apparent. Staff Sergeant Friedrich Hessinger had been born in Germany. A Jew, he and his family had gotten out of the Thousand-Year Reich just in time to miss getting sent to the gas chambers.

18

Hearing the accent, Augie wondered, *Is this CIC sonofabitch mocking me?*

He said: "Does the name Claudette Colbert mean anything to you?"

"I've always thought she is better-looking than Betty Grable. Why do you ask?"

*There's that Kraut accent again!*

*The sonofabitch is mocking me!*

Augie took his credentials — a leather folder holding a badge and a plastic-sealed photo identification card — and held them before the chubby man's face.

Hessinger examined them and nodded his understanding of what they were.

"I am investigating a shooting," Augie announced.

"Somebody shot Claudette?" Hessinger asked. "Somebody" came out *Zumbody.*

*You sonofabitch!*

"I asked if you knew her," Augie snapped.

"Is she all right?"

"So you do know her?"

"I asked if she's all right."

"I'm asking the questions," Augie snapped.

Hessinger shrugged in resignation, and then leaned toward the door to Suite 507 and unlocked it with a key he had hanging around his neck with his dog tags. He then went through it, and turned on the lights.

"Shit!" Augie said, and followed him inside.

He found himself in a luxuriously furnished office. He saw Hessinger sit behind a large, ornately carved desk and pick up the telephone.

"Sorry, sir, to wake you," Hessinger said. "But you better come to the office right now."

The German accent was still there, so Augie put that together:

*He doesn't look like a Jew — but what does a Jew look like?*

*He's a German Jew. The CIC is full of them.*

*Why didn't I think of that before? So is the CID full of ex–German Jews?*

"My boss is coming," Hessinger announced.

He then rose from the desk and walked across the office and opened a door.

"Where do you think you're going?" Augie demanded.

"To the coffee machine," Hessinger replied. "I don't think well when somebody gets me up in the middle of the night until I have my coffee."

Augie saw Hessinger switch on an electric coffeemaker.

Hessinger turned from it and said, *"Sie haben einen Akzent."*

20

*I have an accent?*

*What's that, Chubby, the pot calling the kettle black?*

Hessinger went on: *"Sind Sie ein Deutscher? Ein deutscher Jude?"*

Augie, without consciously deciding to do so, angrily replied in German: *"Nein, ich bin kein Deutscher. Und kein Jude. Ich bin ein gottverdammter Amerikaner! Meine Familie ist amerikanisch seit der gottverdammten Revolution gewesen!"*

Hessinger nodded, then replied in English: "If you've been American since the revolution, that makes you a Pennsylvania Dutchman. I know a great deal about you people."

" 'You people'?" Augie repeated incredulously.

"Gilbert du Motier, Marquis de Lafayette, went to General Washington and told him that the peasants conscripted to serve in the Landgrave de Hesse-Kassel's Regiment of Infantry, commonly called 'the Red Coats,' were unhappy with their lot and could probably be induced to desert if they were offered six hundred and forty acres of land and a mule. Washington thought it was a good idea, and told the Marquis to give it a try. It succeeded. About thirty percent of the regiment went, as we say, 'over the hill.' Where do you live in the States? Bucks

County, Pennsylvania?"

Augie replied, without thinking: "Berks County. Outside Reading."

"When I heard your Hessian accent, I should have put it all together."

The conversation was interrupted when the door opened and a tall, blond, muscular young man in his early twenties came into the room. He was wearing a bathrobe with the logotype of Texas A&M University on its breast and battered Western boots.

"What's up?"

"He's from the CID," Hessinger replied. "He says somebody shot Claudette."

"Jesus H. Christ! Is she all right?"

"Who are you, sir?" Augie asked.

"I asked if Claudette is all right. What the hell happened?"

"The woman —"

"Her name is Claudette Colbert," the young man said.

"Sir, who are you?" Augie asked.

"Freddy, show him your DCI credentials. Mine's in my room."

"Yes, sir," Hessinger said.

He walked to the wall, moved an oil painting out of the way, and began to work a combination lock.

"My name is Cronley," the young man said to Augie. "I'm the big cheese around

22

here and I asked about Claudette. You would be ill-advised to fuck with me."

Augie decided not to do so.

He said: "A woman carrying the identification card of Technical Sergeant Claudette Colbert is being detained for interrogation in connection with a shooting in the WAC NCO club parking lot just after midnight."

"For the last fucking time, is she all right?"

"She is uninjured, sir."

Hessinger held out an open leather folder before Augie's eyes.

Office of the President
of the United States
Central Intelligence Directorate
Washington, D.C.

The Bearer Of This
Identity Document

Friedrich Hessinger

Is an officer of the Central
Intelligence Directorate acting
with the authority of the
President of the United States.
Any questions regarding him or
his activities should be

addressed to the undersigned only.

*Sidney W. Souers*
Sidney W. Souers,
Rear Admiral, USN
Director, DCI

"You understand what that is?" the young man asked.

"I've never seen one before, but yes, sir, I think I understand what it is."

*Jesus Christ, what's going on around here?*

"There's one just like it with my name on it in my room, okay?"

"Yes, sir."

"Okay, now what's happened?"

"About 0015 hours, sir, an MP patrol responded to a call of shots fired, ambulance required, at the parking lot of the WAC NCO club. MP protocol requires that the CID be notified whenever there's shots fired. I was working late at the office and took the call.

"When I got there, there were three bodies, white males, in a 98th General Hospital ambulance, all with bullet wounds to the head. A fourth man had taken a bullet in the shoulder and was being loaded into an ambulance —"

24

"They sent MPs with him, I hope?" the young man interrupted.

"Sir, I don't know if they did, or not."

"Okay, priority one, get on that phone and make sure there are at least two — four would be better — MPs sitting on this guy and that no one but doctors gets near him."

Augie looked at him and thought: *I don't know if this guy has the authority to order me to do that, but it's a good idea.*

"Yes, sir," Augie said.

"Freddy, didn't you tell me Colonel Whatsisname, the provost marshal, lives in the hotel?"

"Kellogg, sir," Hessinger furnished. "He does."

"Try to get Colonel *Kellogg* on the phone. Ask him to come here right away. Tell him it's important. If he's not in the hotel, find out where he is."

"Yes, sir."

Cronley turned to Augie: "You heard me, get on the goddamned phone, whatever your name is, and make sure MPs are sitting on the guy in the hospital."

"Yes, sir. My name is Ziegler, sir."

#### THREE

Colonel Arthur B. Kellogg, a portly forty-six-year-old in uniform, came through the door of Suite 507 five minutes later.

"Your man caught me as I was going through the lobby, Cronley. There's been a . . . an incident I suspect you've already heard about. Hello, Mr. Ziegler."

"Good evening, sir. I guess I mean 'good morning.' "

"What the hell went down at the WAC club? Three dead?" Kellogg said.

"And one wounded, sir. Not counting the hysterical WAC they had to sedate before they could get her in the ambulance."

"What hysterical WAC?" Cronley asked.

"Miller, Florence J., Tech Sergeant," Ziegler reported. "One of yours?"

Cronley nodded.

"We need MPs sitting on her, too," he said.

"Won't that wait until Ziegler brings me up to speed?"

"Sir, I'd be really grateful if you'd indulge me," Cronley said.

Kellogg considered that a moment, then pointed to the telephone.

As Ziegler was walking to it, Cronley said, "Freddy, while he's doing that, call Max at the Compound. Tell him to put a dozen of his guys in ambulances and get them headed this way."

"Can I tell him why?"

"No. And when you've done that, how's the coffee machine working?"

"I'm way ahead of you on that," Hessinger said.

"Okay, Mr. Ziegler," Colonel Kellogg ordered perhaps three minutes later. "Start at the beginning."

"Yes, sir. About 0015 hours, sir, an MP patrol responded to a call of shots fired, ambulance required . . ." Ziegler began. A minute later, he finished: ". . . A fourth man had taken a bullet in the shoulder and was being loaded into an ambulance. And the medics were sedating a WAC tech sergeant so they could take her to the 98th."

"What was her problem?" Kellogg asked.

"She was hysterical, sir."

"Because of the shooting?"

"The shooter, who we believe to be another WAC by the name of Claudette Colbert, knew what she was doing. She shot the three dead guys with a .38, which I'm guessing had hollow-points in it. To judge from what I saw of the shoulder of the fourth guy. They expand on contact —"

"I know," Kellogg interrupted impatiently.

"So when she popped these guys in their heads," Ziegler went on, "first we got their brains sort of exploding, and then making a large exit wound in the skull, through which a couple of handfuls of brain and a lot of blood then erupted. Two of the three men were in the back of the ambulance. Both then fell on the sergeant, still spouting blood and brains all over her."

"My God!" Kellogg said. "Why did she shoot them? Fun and games in the back of the ambulance go wrong?"

"Sir," Cronley said, "the woman Mr. Ziegler believes to be WAC Technical Sergeant Colbert . . ."

"That's what her ID says," Ziegler challenged.

". . . is actually the administrative officer of DCI-Europe. I would be very surprised if she and Technical Sergeant Miller, who is one of our cryptographers, were involved in fun and games in the back of an ambulance in the parking lot at the WAC NCO club."

"Then what were they doing there?"

"Okay," Cronley said, "I should have done this before. What are you, Ziegler, a master sergeant?"

"I'm a chief warrant officer, sir."

"Okay, Mr. Ziegler, you — and you, too,

Colonel Kellogg, sir — are hereby advised that any and all information relating to the incident which took place at the WAC NCO club tonight is classified Top Secret–Presidential, and further that the Central Intelligence Directorate–Europe is taking over the investigation thereof. Do you both understand that?"

Ziegler's eyes darted to Kellogg.

"Colonel, can he do that?" Ziegler asked, on the edge of outrage.

"Yes, I'm afraid he can," Kellogg said. "And he doesn't even have to tell us why."

Cronley went on: "Because I think the most likely scenario is the shooting came when an attempt to kidnap Miss Colbert and Tech Sergeant Miller went wrong. Miss Colbert took her pistol from where she usually carries it — concealed in her brassiere — and started shooting."

"My God!" Colonel Kellogg said.

"Jesus Fucking Christ!" Augie Ziegler said.

"Colonel Kellogg, I need a favor," Cronley said. "Badly. I want you to put Mr. Ziegler on temporary duty with . . . What do we call it, Freddy?"

"Military Detachment, Central Intelligence Directorate, Europe, APO 907," Hessinger furnished.

"Certainly," Kellogg said. "I'll have orders cut in the morning."

"Am I allowed to ask why?" Ziegler said.

"Because there's something about you that smells smart cop," Cronley said. "And I want everything that happened tonight (a) to be investigated thoroughly and (b) the results of that investigation to be neatly summarized and typed up neatly with no strikeovers so that I can give them to General Bull, and (c) to help us with another investigation we're running that probably has something to do with this. You have any problems working with us?"

"No, sir."

"Okay, now fully aware that when I finish saying this to you, you will seriously consider putting my photo in your urinal so that you can piss on it, I want to warn you, Mr. Ziegler, that if I catch you running at the mouth, even running a little at the mouth, about what you see, hear, or intuit about what's going on around here, if I don't have you killed, or court-martialed, which will be the first things that will occur to me, you will spend the rest of your MP career handing out jaywalking tickets in the parking lot of the PX at Fort Abercrombie, which is on Kodiak Island, in Alaska. Do I make myself clear?"

"Yes, sir," Augie replied. He could not suppress a smile.

He thought: *This guy, who looks like he made second lieutenant last week, is a real hard-ass.*

*A genuine hard-ass.*

*I think that whatever I'm going to be doing here is going to be a lot more fun than investigating dependent domestic disputes and catching people importing coffee and cigarettes from the States to sell on the black market.*

"Okay," Cronley said, "now before I send you and Freddy over to get Claudette out of wherever you have her, I'll give you my take on what's happened here."

"Please do. That's presuming I can be told?" Colonel Kellogg said.

"I think you should hear this, sir," Cronley said. "Before Mr. Hessinger recruited Claudette for us, she was in the Army Security Agency, as an intercept operator and cryptographer and debugger. That means she knows how to find hidden microphones. And that means she knows how to install them, too. She was a tech sergeant.

"Now she carries one of these . . . Freddy, show Colonel Kellogg your credentials."

"Yes, sir," Hessinger said, and did so.

"She needs one of those, Colonel, because

31

she is privy to everything that goes on around here. Everything."

"I understand," Kellogg said.

"DCI agents have assimilated field grade officer rank. They're treated as at least majors when they need a hotel room, et cetera. Claudette lives here in the Vier Jahreszeiten — down the corridor. We have the entire wing on this floor. She's on per diem, and takes her meals in the restaurant downstairs.

"Shortly after she came here, she suggested to Hessinger that he recruit Tech Sergeant Miller, a pal of hers in the ASA, and also a cryptographer and debugger. So we had her transferred to us."

"Question?" Augie asked.

"Shoot."

" 'Pal of hers'? How close a pal?"

"If you're suggesting what I think you are, no, not that kind of pal."

"You understand why I had to ask."

"That's why I recruited you, Ziegler. Because I thought you would ask the indelicate questions that have to be asked.

"Tech Sergeant Miller lives in the Pullach compound with other WACs. The ASA has an intercept station in the Pullach compound.

"But Claudette and Miller were still buddies even after Claudette moved into the Vier Jahreszeiten. So with one a tech sergeant and one an assimilated officer, what could they do together? Go to the PX and the movies, and that's about it. Except the WAC NCO club. Claudette still had her sergeant's ID card. So I think they went there to have a steak and some drinks. I think maybe Claudette left her DCI credentials in the safe. Freddy?"

"I'll check."

"She customarily went around armed?" Ziegler asked.

"We all do," Cronley said. He chuckled and pointed at Hessinger. "Freddy even wears his with his bathrobe."

"Hessinger's carrying a .45," Ziegler said. "Colbert had a non-issue S&W .38 with the thumb part of the hammer filed off. It could only be fired double-action. One of your fancy weapons?"

"No. But I'm going to say it is, so we — *she* — gets it back. Is there going to be a problem with that?"

"Far be it from me to deny a good-looking blonde her right to file three notches in the grip of her trusty .38," Ziegler said.

"Here it is!" Hessinger called, waving a credentials folder in the air. "She left it in the safe."

"One more point for my yet-to-be-proven, or disproven, theory," Cronley said.

"Which is, Mr. Cronley?" Kellogg asked.

"Sir, I think the NKGB may have attempted to kidnap Miss Colbert and Sergeant Miller."

"The NKGB?" Kellogg asked incredulously. "Why?"

"To see what they know about certain subjects."

"What certain subjects? Isn't that germane to this investigation?"

Ziegler thought: *Dumb question, Colonel.*

"Colonel, with all respect, answering that would cross a line I'm not willing to cross."

"I understand," Kellogg said, his face and tone making it clear that while he understood, he didn't like being told it was none of his business.

Then he stood up.

"I'd better get over to the scene," Kellogg said. "The post commander by now has heard of the shooting and is liable to be there. What do I tell him?"

"That DCI-Europe has taken over the investigation, and you have been told the less said about it, the better."

Kellogg nodded at Cronley, and then walked out of the room without saying another word.

"I think he's pissed," Ziegler observed.

"Can't be helped," Cronley said, and added: "I'm used to people being pissed at me."

He looked at Hessinger.

"Get dressed, Freddy, and go with Ziegler and bring our Claudette home."

"What about Sergeant Miller?" Hessinger asked.

"If she's been sedated, she's better off in the hospital. When Max gets here, I'll have him send people to sit on her."

"You ever hear of the 711th MKRC?" Ziegler asked.

"Why do you ask?"

"Right next to the ambulance with the bodies was another one, red crosses painted over, with those bumper markings."

"And what did Miss Colbert tell you about that?" Cronley asked.

"All Miss Colbert said to me — again and again — was that she wasn't going to say a thing — actually she said 'a fucking thing' — until you were either in the room or on the telephone."

"It stands for 711 Mess Kit Repair Company," Cronley said. "Or did, until Freddy, who has no sense of humor, changed that to Mobile Kitchen Renovation Company. It's our version of a police unmarked car.

I'd say Claudette drove it over there."

"And I would say," Hessinger put in, "that either the NKGB or maybe the Odessa Nazis have seen through your clever subterfuge. It looks to me like they followed Claudette over there from the garage in the basement here."

"Take notes, Ziegler. Freddy is much smarter than he looks."

"One final off-the-wall question," Ziegler said. "How did you know she carried a .38 in her bra?"

"She told me. Boy Scout's honor and cross my heart and hope to die, I have never seen Miss Colbert in her underwear."

*I've said, and think, that he's a smart cop.*

*Will a smart cop sense that is exactly the opposite of the truth, the whole truth, and nothing but the truth?*

# [FOUR]

*Interrogation Room Three*

*Military Police Station*

*Heinrich-Heine-Strasse 43*

*Munich, American Zone of Occupation, Germany*

*0335 24 January 1946*

The MP captain sitting across a small desk from Claudette Colbert looked up in annoyance when he heard the door behind him opening. When he turned to see who was coming in, his expression changed to one of mingled annoyance and curiosity.

Hessinger, now wearing officer's "pinks and greens" with triangles on the lapels, walked into the room, followed by Augie Ziegler.

"Ziegler," the captain snapped. "When that light over the door is on, it means that no one is to go through it. You should know that."

"Captain, this is Mr. Hessinger of Central Intelligence," Ziegler said.

"What the hell is Central Intelligence?" the captain asked.

Hessinger held out his credentials folder to the captain, who examined it carefully.

"DCI is taking over the investigation of this incident," Hessinger announced. "How are you doing, Miss Colbert?"

"Not too well," she said.

Hessinger nodded. He could see evidence on her uniform that her attempt to clean up after the shooting had not been entirely successful.

" 'Taking over the investigation'?" the captain parroted. "Two questions. What exactly does that mean? And what's the provost marshal got to say about you taking over our investigation?"

"What it means is that you will conduct the same kind of investigation of this incident you normally do. With the following exceptions: You will not give information to, or request information from, any other agency regarding this incident unless, in every instance, DCI tells you that you can.

"Further, any information you gather, any evidence, will be classified Secret, and held — separate from anything else — until DCI decides what should be done with it.

"As far as Colonel Kellogg is concerned, Captain, he is not only fully aware of our involvement in this incident but has loaned us Mr. Ziegler to assist in our investigation and, of course, to serve as liaison between us and the provost marshal."

"Interesting," the captain said.

"You are advised, Captain, that what I just told you is classified Top Secret–Presidential and is not to be shared with anyone without the express permission in each instance of the DCI. Do you understand what I have just told you?"

After staring at Hessinger for a long moment, the captain turned to Ziegler.

"You're sure Colonel Kellogg knows about this?"

"Yes, sir, he does," Ziegler said. "We just left him."

"Did you understand what I just told you, Captain?" Hessinger pursued.

The captain nodded, and belatedly added, "Yes, sir."

"Thank you," Hessinger said.

"I guess I'm dismissed, right?" the captain said.

"It would be helpful, Captain, if you assisted Mr. Ziegler in gathering up all the paperwork, the photographs, et cetera, everything the Military Police has generated so far with regard to this incident so that I can take it with me. More than likely it will be returned, but tonight — this morning — the chief wants a look at everything."

"Does that include the shooter's weapon, sir?" Ziegler said.

"Including the shooter's weapon," Hessinger said. "All weapons. I understand that knives were involved?"

"Yes, sir. There were knives," Ziegler said.

"Additionally, Captain, please advise your men at the 98th that our security people are en route to the hospital, where they will take responsibility for security. I would be grateful if you would leave your MPs there to assist them."

"Certainly."

"They and everybody else involved has to be told that the investigation has been assigned to another agency — please don't mention the DCI — and that all details are classified Secret — just Secret, not Top Secret–Presidential, as that would arouse their curiosity."

"I understand, sir."

"Two more things," Hessinger went on. "Presuming you still have men at the scene of the incident?"

"Yes, sir."

"Please advise them that I will be taking the ambulance parked next to the ambulance where the shooting took place."

"Yes, sir. Sir, on the subject of ambulances, the one in which the shooting took place was stolen from the 98th General Hospital's motor pool sometime today — I mean, yesterday."

"Mr. Ziegler, you will look into that?" Hessinger asked.

"Yes, sir."

"The other ambulance, sir, the one with the red crosses painted over, is a questionable item."

"How so?"

"The bumper markings say it's from a unit, the 711 MKRC, that's not on the USFET list of organizations."

"Don't worry about it. It's ours. That's why I'm going to go pick it up," Hessinger said.

"Can I ask what MKRC stands for?"

"It's not important."

*And as soon as I get it in the Vier Jahreszeiten garage, that will be changed to something else.*

*My God, I can't do that! Cronley's Nazi cousin swallowed that Mobile Kitchen Renovation Company story whole!*

"The second thing I want you to do, Captain," Hessinger said, "in case the men looking through that one-way mirror . . ."

He pointed to a large mirror mounted flush on the wall.

". . . didn't hear what I said in here, is make sure you tell them. Before you get them out of there."

41

"Yes, sir," the captain said, then saw that Ziegler was smiling and gave him a dirty look.

Hessinger went on: "And hurry it up, please, Mr. Ziegler. I want to take Claudette home as soon as possible."

"Yes, sir," Ziegler said.

The captain's face told Ziegler that the captain had picked up on Hessinger's "take Claudette home" remark and was puzzled by it. Ziegler smiled.

The captain saw the smile and glowered at him.

Ziegler thought: *I'll pay for those smiles when my TDY with these DCI people is over.*

*So what? It was worth it to see Hessinger cut Captain Chickenshit off at the knees.*

*And maybe I can arrange to stick around this DCI for a long time.*

As soon as the door to Interrogation Room Three closed, Claudette started to get out of her chair.

Hessinger shook his head and held up his hand, signaling her to stay put.

Thirty seconds later, he walked to the wall and put his back to the one-way mirror, completely covering it. Confident that he could not be seen if anyone was still on the other side of the mirror, he signaled Claudette to come to him.

She went to him. He opened his arms and embraced her.

"Oh, Freddy!" she said, and then began to sob.

He patted her back comfortingly.

"There's a reason you're upset," Hessinger said. "It's to be expected. Killing someone isn't easy."

She pushed herself away from him far enough so that she could look up into his face.

"What I'm upset about is that I'm upset. If I hadn't shot those bastards, they'd have killed me. And Florence. What's happened to her?"

"She's been taken to the 98th. She had to be sedated. MPs are sitting on her, and as soon as Max can get his people over there, they'll sit on the MPs."

"And Jim Cronley?"

"I think right now he's on the telephone to Wallace, telling him what we know."

"What I need right now is a bath and clean clothes," she said. "I didn't know that heads really explode when you put a bullet in them."

She pushed herself farther away from him and looked at his body.

"And some of what landed on me is now

on you. Sorry, Freddy."

"Don't worry about it."

"And after . . . *before* I get out of my clothes and into the shower, I need a drink."

He reached into one of the pockets of his tunic and came out with a leather-covered flask.

"Cognac," he said, as he handed it to her.

"Freddy, you're amazing," Claudette said, as she unscrewed the top.

"I know."

She giggled, then took a heavy pull on the flask.

## [FIVE]

*The WAC Non-Commissioned Officers' Club*

*Munich Military Post*

*Munich, American Zone of Occupied Germany*

*0415 24 January 1946*

Claudette sat in the front seat of Ziegler's car, a 1941 black Ford sedan, and watched as Ziegler watched Hessinger drive the ambulance past the MPs and Polish security guards at the gate.

Then he trotted to the car, got quickly behind the wheel, and started out after the ambulance.

"Miss Colbert," Ziegler said, "Mr. Hessinger introduced me to you as 'Mr. Ziegler.' My name is August. My friends call me Augie."

He put his hand out to her, and she shook it.

"My name is Claudette, and my friends call me Dette."

"Hello, Dette."

"Hello, Augie."

He smiled, then reached inside his Ike jacket, came out with a short-barreled Colt "Detective Special" .38 Special caliber revolver, and handed it to her.

She looked at it, saw lead bullets in its cylinders, and then opened the action to see how many of its five cylinders contained cartridges, and then closed it.

"What am I supposed to do with this?" Claudette asked.

"You can borrow it," he said. "Mr. Cronley told me to get your snub-nosed back to you, but I don't want to do that until the lab in Heidelberg establishes that the bullets in the dead people — and the bad guy still alive — came from your gun."

"Dotting the *i*'s?"

"And crossing the *t*'s."

"Thank you," she said. "I've got a .45 in the safe in the office, but . . ."

"That .45 will be easier to carry?"

"You're right. Thank you for this. I'll take good care of it."

She put it in her purse.

"I used to be a cop in Reading, Pennsylvania," he said.

*Why am I telling her this?*

*For that matter, why am I loaning her my gun?*

"My father, who is also a cop in Reading, gave me that .38 when I passed the detective exam."

"Really?"

"I never got to be a detective. When I missed the cut for detective, I got pissed and told the draft board they could have me."

"Missed the cut?"

"Four detective vacancies. I scored fifth on the test."

"Oh."

"So here I am, a CID agent in Munich, loaning my .38 to a good-looking blonde."

"And if she knew, what would your wife think about that?"

"No wife. And no girlfriend, either."

Neither said another word until they were in the basement garage of the Vier Jahreszeiten, when she said, "The elevator's over there," and he said, "I know."

When they got to the elevator, Augie remembered his manners.

"After you, Dette."

She smiled at him and got on the elevator. As he got on after her, Hessinger trotted up, got on, and after examining the bloodstains and brain tissue on his tunic in the light provided by the elevator, said, *"Scheiss!"*

# II

## [ONE]

*Suite 507*

*Hotel Vier Jahreszeiten*

*Maximilianstrasse 178*

*Munich, American Zone of Occupation, Germany*

*0415 24 January 1946*

Augie Ziegler saw that Cronley had dressed, more or less, while he and Hessinger had been bringing Claudette home. His bathrobe had been replaced with a sweatshirt — also bearing the logo-type of Texas A&M — and olive drab (OD) trousers. He was still wearing the battered Western boots.

With him were two other men, one a

47

muscular blond whom Augie judged to be in his late twenties. He was wearing ODs with triangles. His Ike jacket was unbuttoned, and Augie saw that he had a Secret Service High Rise Cross Draw holster supporting a .45 on his left hip.

The other was an enormous, very black captain, whose OD uniform lapels carried the crossed sabers of cavalry. Augie decided he was probably in his late twenties or early thirties.

Augie decided the captain was not the sort of person one wished to meet in a dark alley, and not only because he, too, had a .45 in a Secret Service holster.

"You all right, Dette?" the black captain greeted her. He had a very deep, melodious voice.

"I need a shower and a change of clothes," she said.

"What the hell is that mess on your tunic, Freddy?" the black captain asked.

"You don't want to know," Hessinger said.

"Can you hold off on your shower and give us a quick after-action report?" Cronley asked.

"Yes, sir," Claudette said.

She then delivered a concise report of what had happened.

"What language were these guys speaking?" Cronley then asked.

"English. Foreign accent. Could have been German or Russian. Or something else."

"Was their ambulance there when you got there?" Cronley asked.

"No," Claudette said. "I remember seeing an empty space beside us when we parked. The lot was just about full."

"That suggests they followed you there."

"Could be."

"Go have your shower, and then go to bed," Cronley ordered. "Wallace said he'll take off as soon as he can in the morning, which should get him and the general here about half past nine. Be prepared to be grilled then."

She smiled and said, "Yes, sir."

Augie wondered: *Who is Wallace? Take off from where he's been? Where's that? And what general?*

"What about Florence?" Claudette asked.

"My people tell me," the big man in the uniform with triangles said, "that her sedation will have mostly worn off by morning —"

"Your people are sitting on her?" Claudette interrupted.

Augie thought: *Who is this guy? He sounds like he's an Englishman.*

"Eight of them," the man said. "On her and the chap you popped. At the moment, he's out of surgery, in stable condition. Would you be distressed to hear that you tore up his shoulder joint to the point where he's in great pain and can look forward to having a somewhat immobile right arm for the rest of his life?"

"Not at all," she said matter-of-factly.

"Unfortunately, the palliatives they have given him for his discomfort will keep us from talking to him until sometime this afternoon."

"I don't suppose we could talk the hospital into not giving him any more palliatives for his pain?" she asked.

Cronley laughed.

"Go to bed, Dette."

"Yes, sir."

"Freddy, when you're cleaned up, you come back. We're going to go over what the MPs have turned up before Wallace gets back."

"Yes, sir."

Claudette and Hessinger left the office.

"A formidable female, in more ways than one," Augie said.

"Methinks our Claudette has caught this gentleman's eye," the large civilian said.

"Meaning she hasn't caught yours?" the

black captain challenged.

"Meaning I've learned the Ice Princess has not yet been taken in by my soulful Polish eyes."

"She's probably waiting for Mr. Right to come along, and found us all wanting," Cronley said.

The black man laughed and put out his hand to Ziegler.

"Since the boss has once again forgotten his manners, I'll introduce myself. C. L. Dunwiddie. People call me 'Tiny.' "

*Jesus, he's six-foot-six, or more, and weighs three hundred pounds!*

"I can't imagine why," Augie replied. "My name is Augie Ziegler."

"I'm Max Ostrowski, Ziegler," the blond man said. "I understand you've been temporarily banished to us?"

"It looks that way," Augie replied, and then asked, "You're Polish?"

"Guilty."

Augie nodded.

"Let's have a look at what the MPs have come up with," Cronley said.

"I'll have to tell you what the inside of the ambulance looked like," Augie said. "The photo lab isn't finished. I told them to send prints as soon as they're done."

# [Two]

*U.S. Constabulary School*

*Sonthofen, Bavaria*

*American Zone of Occupied Germany*

*0655 24 January 1946*

There were twelve officers seated around the heavy table in the senior officers' dining room of what had once been the Adolf Hitler Schule, where the sons of the Nazi aristocracy had been trained to assume leadership roles in the Thousand-Year Reich. The dozen officers at the table were dressed in woolen ODs. Their shoulder insignia was that of the U.S. Constabulary, a three-inch yellow circle outlined in black, with a "C" in the center. A red lightning bolt pierced the "C."

Major General I. D. White — a stocky forty-six-year-old who had led the 2nd "Hell on Wheels" Armored Division to the banks of the Elbe River, and then, after the Russians had been allowed to take Berlin, into the German capital — sat at the head of the table, where Der Führer had once reigned over his dinner guests.

Sitting at the table were a full colonel of cavalry, a full colonel of infantry, a lieutenant colonel wearing the insignia of an aide-de-camp to a major general, a captain wearing the same insignia, a lieutenant colonel and a lieutenant of artillery (both wearing liaison pilot wings), a colonel and a lieutenant colonel whose lapel insignia identified them respectively as chaplains of the Jewish and Christian faiths, a colonel and a lieutenant colonel of the Medical Corps, and a lieutenant colonel of the Judge Advocate General's Corps.

General White believed that command problems could be discussed and possibly resolved over a meal at least as well as, and possibly better than, gathering everyone around a table in a conference room. Thus, once a week, on Thursdays, he scheduled a breakfast — "So everyone will be bright-eyed and bushy-tailed" — to which were invited those officers concerned with a problem who might have a solution for it. Their invitations provided the subject to be discussed.

General White waited until everyone invited had entered the dining room and was standing behind the ornate chairs at the table. Then he walked — marched would be more accurate — into the room.

His senior aide-de-camp called, "Ah-ten-hut!" and everyone came to attention.

"Be seated, gentlemen," General White

said, and sat down.

"For obvious reasons it would be inappropriate to discuss the subject of the day while we're eating our breakfast," he went on. "So we'll hold off until we're having our coffee."

Thirty minutes later, after two young men wearing starched white jackets over their uniforms cleared the table of dishes and placed coffee cups in front of the diners, the moment to discuss the subject of the luncheon conference had come.

General White did so without rising from his chair.

"The problem we have, gentlemen," he said, "is social disease, which is a polite way of saying venereal disease. How does this affect the Constabulary? And what do we do about it? Your thoughts, please, Lieutenant."

He pointed to the lieutenant wearing the liaison pilot's wings.

The lieutenant, visibly surprised to be called on, rose to his feet. And appeared to be struck dumb.

"Didn't they teach you at West Point, Lieutenant Winters, that the junior is called upon first, so we get his honest opinion, rather than what he thinks his superiors want to hear?"

The lieutenant flashed White what could have been a dirty look. The general did not seem to notice.

"Yes, sir. I was taught that," he said. "Sir, venereal disease is a problem . . ."

"That's why we're having this conference," White agreed.

". . . not only in that men are sick in hospital rather than available for duty, but that it poses a problem, sometimes a fatal problem, for them for the rest of their lives."

"I couldn't have summed it up better myself," White said. "And how would you suggest we deal with the problem?"

The lieutenant visibly thought his reply over before making it.

"If it were up to me, sir, I would open first aid stations for any German girl who wanted to come in, get examined, and then if she had the clap, syphilis, or scabies, treat her. And I would examine all the prostitutes in the brothels and walking the streets, whether or not they liked it, and offer them the choice of getting treated or going to jail."

"Nonsense!" the Christian chaplain said, for which he was rewarded with a withering glance from General White.

"And what about our Constabulary troopers?" White asked.

The lieutenant again debated replying, but

finally said, "Sir, you're probably not going to like this."

"Nevertheless?"

"Sir, I'd see to it they had a chance to do what the officers do."

"Which is?"

"Sir, they find some friendly doctor to give them penicillin so they don't have to go to the hospital and wear a bathrobe with VD stenciled on the back. And get it in their service record."

"General," the Medical Corps lieutenant colonel said, "I have to protest!"

"Duly noted," General White said. "Lieutenant, are you saying you have personal knowledge of officers who" — he paused, and then repeated verbatim what the lieutenant had said — "who 'find some friendly doctor to give them penicillin so they don't have to go to the hospital and wear a bathrobe with VD stenciled on the back'? 'And get it in their service record,' or do you just think that's what's going on?"

"I have personal knowledge of that happening, sir."

"And what would you do with our enlisted troopers, Lieutenant?"

The lieutenant's mouth ran away with him. Or perhaps he consciously decided that since he had just flushed his military career down the toilet anyway, *What the hell? Why not?*

"Sir, I'd get the doctors to determine who had the clap and scabies and nothing worse, and teach the first sergeants how to give them the six shots of penicillin to kill the clap and stuff to kill the scabies. I'd have the doctors send the people with syphilis to the hospital, but I'd diagnose it as something besides syphilis so that it wouldn't fuck up their careers."

He heard what he had said, and added, "Sorry, sir. That 'fuck' just slipped out."

The Medical Corps colonel said, "General, if I may —"

"You may not. I decide who speaks here and when," General White replied, not at all pleasantly. He paused, obviously in thought, and then went on. "I've just decided that's me."

He gestured for the lieutenant to sit down.

"While I am sorely tempted to do so," he began, "I am not going to quote the late General George Smith Patton's insightful comment on officers and enlisted men and the carnal union of the sexes . . ."

All the officers in the room knew that Patton had famously said, *"A soldier who won't fuck won't fight."*

More than half of the officers at the table

57

laughed or chuckled. The rest showed shock or disapproval or both.

"... but I don't think anyone can honestly argue with the fact that the ideal solution to our venereal disease problem, abstinence or chastity, is simply not going to be available.

"I have also believed since I first heard this at Norwich that if something valuable is going to be issued by the Army, the officer corps gets theirs after the enlisted men do. I can see no reason that this shouldn't apply to the curing of social diseases. Finally, when I first learned that patients in hospital suffering from venereal disease were forced to wear bathrobes with VD stenciled on them, I thought — I *knew* — that this was going to keep soldiers from seeking the treatment they needed.

"So, what we are going to discuss now —"

The door to the dining room opened and a second major general practically burst into the room.

He was wearing, like the others, a woolen olive drab Ike jacket but, unlike the others, instead of OD trousers he was wearing riding breeches and highly polished riding boots. He carried a leather riding crop. His shoulder insignia was that of the Constabulary. The opposite shoulder carried the insignia of the 2nd Armored Division, indicating that the general had served in wartime with the division.

Major General Ernest Harmon had in fact commanded Hell on Wheels until, on assuming command of the VI Corps, he had turned it over to I. D. White. He was scheduled to turn over command of the Constabulary to General White on February 1.

General White was the first to see General Harmon. He rose to his feet. So, quickly, did everyone at the table.

"Gentlemen, I'm really sorry to bust in this way, but I have to have a few minutes with General White."

Harmon had a harsh, grating voice, which had caused his subordinates to call him, behind his back, "Old Gravel Voice."

"General," White said, "we're discussing VD. Your knowledge of that subject would be welcome."

Harmon glared at him.

"Well, in that case," White said, and raised his voice, "meeting adjourned. To reconvene at eleven hundred in my conference room. Think about what Lieutenant Winters said."

He then pointed at the lieutenant colonel with wings and at Lieutenant Winters.

"You two stay."

When everyone else had filed out of the room, Harmon offered his hand to the

59

lieutenant colonel.

"Billy, what is General White going to tell me you did wrong now?"

"Sir, I am as pure as the driven snow," Lieutenant Colonel William W. Wilson said.

"Ernie, this is Lieutenant Tom Winters," General White said.

"It's been a long time since I've seen you, son. How's your dad?"

"Mom sent me a picture of her and Dad in kimonos. He's got the First Cav."

"I heard. Please give them my best when you write."

"Yes, sir, I will. Thank you."

"What's I.D. got you doing in the Constab, Tom?" Harmon asked.

"Just before you came, I was testing him to see how well he thinks on his feet," White said.

"And?"

"He's a chip off the old blockhead," White said. "Even under pressure he said only one dirty word." He paused and then asked, "Tom, you sure you want this transfer?"

"Yes, sir. I've thought about it carefully."

"Okay. Billy, Cronley can have him. And the A&M lieutenant, too."

"Thank you, sir," Lieutenant Colonel Wilson said. "Permission to withdraw, sir?"

White nodded.

The lieutenant colonel and then Lieutenant Winters shook hands with the generals, and then the lieutenant colonel came to attention and saluted. General Harmon returned it, and then the two younger officers marched out of the dining room.

When the door had closed, Harmon asked, "I.D., what the hell is going on?"

Before White could finish framing his reply, Harmon went on: "Harry Bull called me in last night, told me I was not going home, and would have to put my retirement on hold. When I asked him what the hell was that all about, he said it had come from McNarney and was not open for debate. He said you knew what it was all about, but might not be able to tell me unless the CID gave you permission."

"Did Harry say 'CID'? Or 'DCI'?"

"I don't remember. What the hell is the DCI?"

"The Central Intelligence Directorate. They can't use the same acronym — CID — as the MP's Criminal Investigation Division, so they say 'DCI.' "

"Okay, then what the hell is the DCI? More important, what's it got to do with you and me?"

"That brings us back to what Harry said about me needing the permission of the

DCI to tell you," White said.

"What's so classified about this? How highly classified is it?"

"It doesn't get any higher: Top Secret–Presidential."

"I.D., how the hell long am I going to have to stand around with my thumb in my ass waiting for you to tell me what the hell's going on?"

"Captain Cronley called me last night and gave me permission to tell you anything you want to know."

"Cronley? As in, *'You can tell Cronley'*?"

"Yes. He's the chief, DCI-Europe."

"And he's a captain?"

"A twenty-two-year-old captain. He didn't make captain as soon as Billy Wilson made captain — Billy wasn't out of West Point six months before he made captain — but he's cast from the same mold."

"You know I like, and respect, Billy Wilson. But I have a lot of trouble with him being a twenty-five-year-old lieutenant colonel. I was older than that when I made first lieutenant."

"And so was I. Different Army, Ernie."

"I sort of liked the one we had. Okay, start telling me what this twenty-two-year-old captain told you you can."

"The question is where to begin."

"Try the beginning."

"All right then: How come I never told you anything about it? Because I was ordered not to."

"By who? Harry Bull? McNarney?"

"By Admiral Souers."

"And who the hell is Admiral Souers?"

"Souers — Sidney W., Rear Admiral, Reservist. He came to Fort Riley, where I was making plans for the Constabulary —"

"A Navy admiral — a *reserve* Navy admiral — went out to the plains of Kansas to see an armored general? What the hell, I.D?"

"There I was, sitting on the porch of Quarters 24 — you know, what they call 'Custer's House'?"

"I've been to Fort Riley," Harmon said. "Jesus Christ!"

"Then I guess you already know it isn't really Custer's house. The house from which Lieutenant Colonel Custer actually rode forth to immortality by getting his entire command wiped out at the Little Big Horn burned down."

"Goddammit, I.D.!"

"As I was saying, they put me in Quarters 24, Tom Davis having decided that it was appropriate accommodation for a distinguished general officer such as myself, who outranked him, and was at Riley for an unspecified purpose, but which Tom thought might have something to do with me being sent there to spy on him."

"I didn't think about that," Harmon said, smiling.

"Or that I had been sent there because it was suspected I agreed with Georgie Patton that we should rearm the Wehrmacht and march on Moscow and had been sent to Riley while they decided what to do with me."

"That was the rumor going around."

"So, there I was sitting on the porch of Quarters 24, innocently going over proposed Tables of Organization and Equipment for the Constab, when a staff car with a two-star plate pulled up at the curb. I presumed, of course, it was Tom.

"It wasn't. I suspected Tom was in — or his aide was in — a staff car that seemed to be following the one that stopped at my curb.

"A Navy lieutenant got out of the car and opened the rear door, and then a civilian and an admiral got out. They marched up onto the porch, and the admiral said, 'General White, I'm Sid Souers,' and handed me an envelope.

"Inside the envelope was a note on White House stationery. The note — handwritten, not typed — read 'Dear General White. I have sent Admiral Souers to see you. He will explain. Best wishes, Harry S Truman.' "

"Jesus!"

"Which the admiral promptly did. He told me that Truman had realized he had made a mistake when he disestablished the OSS. Everybody who had been saying the OSS was useless, a threat to democracy, et cetera, and had to be abolished — by everybody I mean Army G-2, Navy Intelligence, the FBI, and the State Department — was now angling to take it over.

"The admiral told me that Truman had decided, when he ordered the dissolution of the OSS, to turn over to him certain operations which had to be kept running."

"Him? Why? The Navy? Who is this admiral, anyway?"

"I later found out he's a longtime crony of the President, going back to Missouri, where Truman was a weekend warrior in the National Guard and Souers a weekend sailor in the Naval Reserve."

"I'd heard Truman was a National Guard colonel," Harmon said.

"He was an Artillery captain in France in the First World War. Anyway, when I said the admiral was the President's crony, I meant just that. When Souers went on active duty when the war started, he was assigned to Naval Intelligence in Washington. Where he moved into Senator Harry Truman's apartment, and they were bachelors together."

White paused in thought, then went on: "Where was I? Oh, yeah. The admiral told me that when Truman signed the order disbanding the OSS, Truman had decided where he would put the OSS operations that couldn't be shut down. He promoted Souers to rear admiral, had him named deputy chief of ONI. Then he gave responsibility for these clandestine operations to the deputy chief of ONI.

"Next, when the President decided he really needed a clandestine espionage, et cetera, organization answering only to him, he signed an Executive Order establishing the Directorate of Central Intelligence as of January first and named Admiral Souers as director."

"That's three weeks ago," Harmon observed.

"Just before I came back here," White said. "Somewhere during our conversation on the porch, Souers introduced the civilian. His name is Schultz. Souers said that Schultz had been Number Two in the OSS operation in the Southern Cone — Uruguay, Argentina, and Chile — during the war. He had just retired as a commander and was now Souers's Number Two. The 'executive assistant to the director.'

"Souers then told me 'it had been decided' that the Constabulary was going to provide whatever support was requested by DCI-Europe . . ."

"Decided by who?"

"He didn't say. I got the feeling that Souers has the authority to do whatever he thinks has to be done. Anyway, he said that Harry Bull was in the loop, as is a brigadier general named Greene."

Harmon shook his head, signaling he didn't know who Greene was.

"He runs the CIC for USFET," White said. "I had met him once, but didn't know him. And the head of the Army Security Agency in USFET, a major named Mc-Clung, and a Major Wallace, who used to run OSS Forward and is now ostensibly working for Greene."

"Didn't . . . What's his name? *Mattingly* . . . Didn't Colonel Bob Mattingly, who used to be in Hell on Wheels before he went to the OSS, command OSS Forward?"

"When I asked the same question, Schultz — who is known as 'El Jefe,' which means 'the Chief' in Spanish, because he was once a chief petty officer —"

"An ex-CPO is now Number Two in this DCI?" Harmon interrupted, his tone incredulous.

White nodded. "He is. Schultz told me that Colonel David Bruce, who ran the OSS in Europe, decided that OSS Forward could function more efficiently if 'the Army' thought it was commanded by Bob Mattingly, when it was in fact commanded by Major Harold Wallace, who was — is — in fact *Colonel* Harold Wallace. Schultz also told me that Bob Mattingly, who is now Greene's deputy, would not, repeat *not,* be in the loop."

"What's that all about?"

"G-2 wants to take over DCI-Europe. Quote, Since Colonel Mattingly has applied for integration into the Regular Army . . ."

"I always thought he was a fine officer," Harmon said.

"He was. Is. Let me finish the quote . . . he might consider his primary loyalty was to the Army, rather than to DCI. End quote. So Mattingly is not in the loop. Lieutenant Colonel Billy Wilson is."

"Billy's part of this?" Harmon asked, shaking his head in disbelief.

"You remember that during the war he was always doing things for the OSS?"

Harmon nodded.

"Among those things he did for the OSS was fly Major Wallace to the rendezvous point where Generalmajor Gehlen surrendered. Among the things he's done recently for the OSS — now the DCI — was arrange for the pickup across the border in Thuringia of the wife and two kids, boys, of an NKGB colonel the DCI had bagged and sent to Argentina."

"How do you know all this?"

"Because Billy — not knowing that I was already in the loop — came to me and asked for permission to participate. Knowing Billy, if I had said, 'Hell, no!' he probably would have done what he did anyway, but I thought it was nice of him to ask. You'll recall Billy doesn't always ask permission."

Harmon laughed. "Billy once told me, with a straight face, that if you think you're going to get your ass chewed anyway, it makes more sense to get it chewed after you've done what you want to do instead of getting it chewed just for asking."

"Maybe that's the way you get to be a twenty-five-year-old lieutenant colonel. Why didn't we think of that?"

Harmon laughed. It came out as a grunt.

"I've been trying to figure out what you think of all this," Harmon said.

White understood he had been asked a question, and he answered it: "I don't think we should rearm the Wehrmacht and head for Moscow, but I believe the Soviet Union is a real threat. And it looks to me like few people outside of the loop realize how serious a threat. And I'm a soldier, Ernie. When someone gives me an order I know is lawful, I salute and say, 'Yes, sir.' "

When Harmon didn't immediately reply, White went on: "To answer your original question, *Why am I not going home?* Apparently Ike decided that the role originally envisioned for the Constabulary is not going to happen. The Germans are behaving. The Russians are not. The Constabulary is going to have to be more border police than anything else, at least for the time being. And Ike also probably realized that the support the Constabulary has been ordered to provide DCI-Europe is going to go far beyond sending a platoon of M8 armored cars somewhere.

"I think Bull decided — and I don't know this, Ernie — that I had too much on my plate to handle, and that the solution to that was to keep you in command for a little longer, until things sort themselves out."

For a long moment Harmon was silent.

Then he said: "I knew the minute I laid

eyes on the dependent housing officer at Fort Knox that if I took him under my wing, sooner or later he was going to royally fuck me up."

"That's why you got me out of that damned job and gave me that battalion of Armored Infantry, right?"

"But, me too, I.D."

"Excuse me?"

"I'm a soldier, too. When I get a lawful order, I salute and say, 'Yes, sir.' "

## [THREE]

*Office of the Chief, Counter Intelligence*
*Corps*

*Headquarters, U.S. Forces European Theater*

*The I.G. Farben Building*

*Frankfurt am Main*

*American Zone of Occupation, Germany*

*0715 24 January 1946*

A tall, hawkish-featured man in his early thirties in ODs with triangles pushed open the door to the outer office of the chief, CIC USFET, and smiled at the WAC chief warrant officer, an attractive woman in her late twenties sitting behind the desk. She was

71

wearing the female version of pinks and greens.

"What got you up so early?" he asked.

"The Greene monster," she replied. "Someone had to cut your orders."

"What orders?"

"He'll tell you all about it," she said, and pointed at an interior door. On it was a neatly lettered sign: BRIG. GEN. H. P. GREENE.

The man went to the door and knocked.

"Come."

The man pushed the door open. A stocky, forty-three-year-old officer with a crew cut waved him in. His olive drab uniform had the single star of a brigadier general on its epaulets.

"Come on in, Jack," he said. "And close the door."

The man did so.

"Good morning, General."

Greene waved him onto a couch before a coffee table, and then rose from his desk and joined him.

The door opened and the WAC came in with a thermos and two coffee mugs.

"I've been reading your mind," she said.

"Good for you. Don't let anybody in but Major Wallace and/or General Gehlen," General Greene ordered.

The WAC nodded, poured coffee into the mugs, and then left.

"General *Gehlen*?" Jack asked.

Greene nodded.

"What Helen has been doing is cutting orders putting you on indefinite temporary duty with Military Detachment, Central Intelligence Directorate, Europe, APO 907," he said.

"Jesus! What —"

"And if that didn't get your attention, Jack, maybe this will: You play your cards right, you just might get your commission back."

"I'm all ears."

Brigadier General Homer P. Greene and CIC Supervisory Special Agent John D. "Jack" Hammersmith were old friends.

Hammersmith had been an enlisted man before the war, quickly promoted to technical sergeant when he had become a CIC special agent. When war came, he had been directly commissioned into the Military Intelligence Service as a first lieutenant.

His first assignment had been to the 1st Army Counter Intelligence Detachment, Major H. P. Greene, commanding. They had later served together in Morocco, England, and then France and Germany.

Greene had come out of the war with a brigadier general's star and Hammersmith a major's gold leaf.

As soon as the war was over, the Army began a Reduction in Force. Fearing that he was likely to be among the first majors to be "RIFed" as he had only a high school education, Hammersmith had accepted relief from active duty as a reserve major to reenlist as a regular Army master sergeant. That way, he would not only have a job, but when he retired he would do so at the highest rank held in wartime.

It had seemed to be the smart thing to do, although when he heard about it, General Greene told him he had been a damned fool, and Hammersmith had come to agree with him. A great many officers had been RIFed, but only a very few from Intelligence.

"Major Harold Wallace?" Greene began, and continued after Hammersmith's nod told him he knew who Wallace was: "He got me out of bed at quarter to four this morning to tell me —"

Greene interrupted himself.

"Jack, this is all classified Top Secret–Presidential. Got it?"

"Yes, sir."

". . . To tell me there had been a shooting in Munich. One of his WACs had killed three men and wounded another. Wallace's initial take on the incident was that the NKGB and/or Odessa had tried to kidnap the WAC . . . actually two WACs . . . whereupon one of the WACs had popped all of them."

"Jesus Christ! What the hell was that all about?"

"Wallace said what he wanted from me was my best agent, and he wanted him yesterday. I said 'sure' and called Marburg and told you to shag your ass down here bringing a change of clothes.

"The reason I said 'sure' so quickly was because General Harry Bull told me that I was to give Wallace — this Directorate of Central Intelligence–Europe he runs — anything at all he wants, emphasis on anything."

"It's not under Seidel?"

Major General Bruce T. Seidel was US-FET's G-2, in charge of Intelligence.

"It's under a rear admiral, Sidney Souers, and he reports to President Truman."

"What does it do?"

"You've heard the rumors that we struck a deal with General Gehlen?"

"He gave us everything he had, including

agents in place, and we kept him and his people out of the hands of the Russians?"

"His people and their families. We sent the Nazis among them to Argentina."

"I didn't believe that rumor."

"It's called Operation Ost, Jack. And it includes setting up Gehlen — what was Abwehr Ost — in a compound outside Munich, where he now works for us."

"And Wallace runs this whole thing? He's only a major."

"The chief of DCI-Europe is Captain James D. Cronley, Junior."

"You just said Wallace runs it."

"Wallace looks over Cronley's shoulder while Cronley runs it."

"What's that all about? My take on the Gehlen deal is that it's important."

"Very important."

"And if it gets out that we're slipping Nazis out of Germany . . ."

Greene nodded. "The political implications are frightening."

"So why isn't somebody senior running it? Mattingly comes to mind. At the end of the war Wallace was his Number Two at OSS Forward."

"At the end of the war it was decided that OSS Forward could function more effectively if people thought that Colonel Bob

Mattingly was running it, leaving Major Harold Wallace — actually Colonel Wallace — free of Army interference to do what he thought had to be done."

"Everybody was smoking funny cigarettes?"

"It worked, Jack, and it works now."

"Something wrong with Mattingly?"

"G-2 wants to take over DCI. Admiral Souers decided that Mattingly, who has applied for integration into the regular Army, wouldn't want to get in a scrap with G-2."

"How do you know all this?"

"Admiral Souers told me."

"You're part of this 'Alice in Wonderland Through the Looking Glass' business?"

"I am. Iron Lung McClung is. I.D. White is. And so is Harry Bull."

Hammersmith ran that all through his mind: Major James B. "Iron Lung" McClung was chief, Army Security Agency, Europe. Major General I. D. White was scheduled to assume command of the U.S. Constabulary, charged with patrolling the American Zone of Germany, on the first of February. Major General Harold R. Bull was chief of staff to General Joseph McNarney, commander of U.S. Forces European Theater (USFET).

"And General McNarney?" Hammersmith asked.

Greene didn't reply.

"Sorry. Stupid of me to ask."

Greene agreed with that by saying nothing.

"So I'm to go to Munich to work for who?" Hammersmith asked.

"For DCI-Europe. Whose chief is Captain Cronley."

"Jesus!"

"You've got something against Cronley?"

"I don't like the idea of working for a twenty-one-, twenty-two-year-old captain."

"Twenty-two."

"Who may not even be a captain. Is he?"

"He is."

"He was a second lieutenant in Marburg a couple of months ago. Or was he really a twenty-nine-year-old captain, who looks young, pretending to be a second lieutenant?"

"Jack, do you want to get your commission back?"

They locked eyes for a moment.

"You know I do, Homer. So I will go to Munich, smile, and salute the boy captain and do what I'm told."

"He got his railroad tracks from President Truman. The bars and the Distinguished Service Medal."

"For what?"

"That's classified Top Secret–Presidential, and you don't have the Need to Know."

"Jesus!"

"What did Cronley do in Marburg to piss you off?"

Hammersmith didn't reply for a moment, and then he said, "Nothing. I thought he was a nice kid. Smart. Not your typical second lieutenant. He speaks fluent German. And then he pissed off Connell, which I enjoyed."

Major John Connell was the executive officer of the XXIInd CIC Detachment.

"How did he do that?" Greene asked, smiling and shaking his head.

"Connell put Cronley in a jeep to watch the MPs at a refugee checkpoint. I went out there one day with him. Connell chewed his ass because the kid was wearing a .45 in a holster slung cowboy style, and not the prescribed snub-nosed .38. So the next time Connell went out there, the kid —"

"Think 'Captain Cronley,' Jack," General Greene interrupted.

"— is wearing triangles and cowboy boots and has the .45 hanging from the jeep windshield. Connell was so pissed that he just turned around and headed back to town. He said, 'I'm going to burn him a new asshole.' "

"And did he?"

"Later that day, Cronley found the Kraut woman —"

"Think Frau von Wachtstein, Jack. Hitler hung her father and her father-in-law from butcher's hooks. And she has friends in high places."

"— *Frau von Whateveryousaid.* And the next thing we know he's transferred to OSS Forward. The next time I saw him was when Mattingly caught him smuggling coffee and canned hams —"

"As I remember that incident," Greene interrupted, "the CID intercepted packages of coffee and ham, and told us. Whereupon Bob Mattingly made sure everybody knew Cronley had been caught black-marketing."

"You sound as if you don't like Mattingly much."

"When you get to Munich, and start making reports to me, keep in mind that Colonel Mattingly is not in the loop."

"That bad, huh?"

"I am presuming you are telling me that you will have no problems in Munich working for Captain Cronley?"

"I will try very hard to be a very good boy in Munich."

"Think Major Hammersmith, Jack."

"It will be foremost in my mind, sir. How do I get to Munich? That's a long haul in a jeep."

"Leave your jeep here. I'll see that it gets back to Marburg. What happens now is that after Major Wallace tells General Bull about this shooting, which is probably happening right now, he and General Gehlen will come here and have a look at you.

"Presuming you remember to think *Colonel* Wallace, don't break wind, and you pass their muster, the three of you will go out to Eschborn. There, Gehlen and Wallace will get in their Storch."

"They have a Storch?"

"DCI-Europe has two of them. The one they'll be in will be piloted by a guy who used to fly Gehlen around the steppes of Russia in one."

"A German?"

Greene nodded.

"Now a special agent of DCI. *Major* Wallace and *Mr.* Gehlen of the Süd-Deutsche Industrielle Entwicklungsorganisation."

"The South German Industrial Development Organization?" Hammersmith made the translation. "Which is what?"

"What we are now calling what used to be Abwehr Ost. They will be flown to a village about twenty miles from Munich, Pullach,

81

which is now the organization's headquarters. You will follow in an L-4 that the U.S. Constabulary has generously provided. Have a good time in Munich, Jack."

"I appreciate this, Homer. Thank you."

"No thanks required. I was asked to provide my best CIC agent. I have done so."

"Nevertheless, thanks, Homer."

"You're welcome, Jack. Now don't embarrass me."

# [FOUR]

*Suite 507*

*Hotel Vier Jahreszeiten*

*Maximilianstrasse 178*

*Munich, American Zone of Occupation, Germany*

*0815 24 January 1946*

Cronley came out of the corridor into the office. He was wearing ODs with triangles.

"I thought you'd still be in bed," he said to Claudette, who was sitting, in triangled pinks and greens, at her desk. "You all right?"

"Under the circumstances."

"Wallace and the general won't be here until nine-thirty or later."

"Later. The major called just now. They're about to take off from Eschborn."

"That'll get them here about eleven-thirty. Dette, you sure you don't want to go back to bed?"

"Duty calls," she said. "Besides, when I lie down, I start to feel that sonofabitch's knife at my throat. And I hear Florence losing it."

"Jesus. I'm sorry. I should . . ."

"Jim, if you're thinking you should have tried to comfort me last night . . ."

"I should have."

"Jim, you coming to my room last night would have been ill-advised. I thought that through . . ."

"I didn't know what to do. I guess I decided to take the coward's way out."

"Give yourself the benefit of the doubt. You were right."

"Thank you. Which brings us back to why don't you go back to bed?"

Lieutenant Thomas Winters walked into the office.

"That's why," Claudette said softly. "Duty calls."

She raised her voice: "Good morning, Lieutenant. How can I help you?"

Winters saluted Cronley.

"Lieutenant Winters reporting for duty, sir."

"We don't do much saluting around here," Cronley said, as he returned it. "And never when somebody's wearing triangles."

"Sorry, sir."

Winters handed Cronley a thin stack of mimeographed orders.

Cronley read them, and handed them to Claudette.

"Take over, Administrative Officer," he ordered. "Get our bureaucracy rolling."

Claudette read the orders:


SECRET


HEADQUARTERS


U.S. Constabulary
APO 701, N.Y.

*23 January 1946*

E*X*T*R*A*C*T

SPECIAL ORDERS 21:

PARA 4:

Following Off Hq & Hq Company
11th Constabulary Regt APO 723
NY trans PCS this date WP Mil

Detachment, Central Intelligence Directorate-Europe, APO 907. Mvmt Dep auth.

Winters, Thomas H. 1LT Arty 0638383

Moriarty, Bruce T. 2LT Cav 0558281

Auth: VOCG U.S. Constabulary 23 Jan 1946

E*X*T*R*A*C*T

By Command of Maj Gen Harmon:

*Bruce T. Nettles*
Bruce T. Nettles
Colonel, AGC
Adjutant General

**SECRET**

Claudette looked up from the orders. "Welcome, welcome, Lieutenant Winters!"

He smiled. "Thank you . . ."

"This is Miss Colbert, Lieutenant Winters," Cronley said, "who, as I mentioned, is our administrative officer. If she decides to like you, she may allow you to call her Dette. If she decides not to like you, you'll be in the deep doo-doo."

"Duly noted," Winters said, smiling, and put out his hand to Claudette. "You can — and I hope you will — call me Tom."

"Welcome, Tom," Claudette said. "Where's the other one? And does that 'Dep Auth' apply to both of you, and if not, to which one of you?"

"You will notice, Winters, that our Dette is already asking the piercing questions for which she is famous. And where is Bonehead?"

" 'Bonehead'?" Claudette parroted.

"When Lieutenant Moriarty and I were Fish at our beloved Texas A&M," Cronley explained, "he was chastised for his hair being too long. So he got another haircut, which also failed to meet the high standards imposed on us by upperclassmen, who were kindly introducing us to *la vie militaire,* so he shaved his skull."

"You were at A&M with this Lieutenant Moriarty?" Claudette asked.

Cronley nodded. "For four long years. Which brings us back to, where is he?"

"He's in Fritzlar, waiting for the wrath of Colonel Fishburn to fall on his head."

"He still shaves his head?" Claudette asked.

"Ginger, Mrs. Bonehead, cured him of that," Cronley said. "To answer your original question, both of these officers are married men."

"Children?" she asked.

"That will occur shortly in both cases," Cronley said.

" 'Wrath of Colonel Fishburn'?" Claudette parroted again.

"The commanding officer of the 11th Constabulary Regiment is not going to like losing these two officers, which he will learn of as soon as a copy of these orders come to his attention. Which will be when, Tom?"

"We fly — Constab Headquarters flies — a daily round-robin messenger service to all the regiments. I'd guess Colonel Fishburn will get a copy of these orders before noon."

"Whereupon his anger will likely fall on Bonehead," Cronley said.

The door opened again and Hessinger walked in.

"You're a little late, Freddy," Cronley greeted him. "Had a little trouble getting the fräulein to go back to her village, did you?"

*"Ach, du lieber Gott,"* Hessinger said resignedly.

"Lieutenant Winters, this is my executive assistant, Mr. Hessinger," Cronley said.

The two shook hands.

"I'm sure Mr. Hessinger will have some

87

clever ideas about how we're going to get Mrs. Winters, Lieutenant and Mrs. Moriarty, and their household goods down here from Fritzlar," Cronley said.

Claudette handed Hessinger the orders.

"Fact bearing on the problem," Cronley said, "both ladies are in the family way. Conspicuously so."

"How much household goods are involved?" Hessinger asked. "Specifically, could we get it all in the back of an ambulance?"

Winters thought that over before replying, "Unless Bruce and Ginger have more than I think they do, yeah."

"POVs?" Hessinger asked.

"I have a Plymouth, Bruce has a Buick, a great big one, a Roadmaster. I was thinking that my Barbara could ride with Ginger in that and Bruce could drive my Plymouth —"

"It's not that simple, Tom," Cronley interrupted.

"I suggest we send two ambulances, four Poles, and four of Tiny's Troopers," Hessinger said. "The Poles could drive the POVs. On the road, it would be one ambulance with the household goods, then the POVs and then the second ambulance with Tiny's guys."

"That'd work," Cronley said, after thinking it over. "Set it up, Freddy. Get them on the road as soon as you can."

"Sir, I'm a little confused," Winters said.

"That's par for the course around here. What are you confused about?"

" 'Poles' and 'Tiny Troopers'?"

"For security," Cronley said. "We had a little problem last night."

"What kind of a problem?"

Cronley visibly considered what he should say. Then he shrugged and said, "Four guys — probably NKGB agents — tried to kidnap Dette and one of our WAC ASA cryptographers just after midnight."

"Holy Christ!" Winters exclaimed. And then, "What happened?"

"Dette shot three of them and wounded the fourth guy in the shoulder," Cronley said.

"By shot, you mean killed, right?" Winters asked, looking at Claudette in disbelief.

She shrugged.

*My God, she did kill three people! And wounded a fourth man!*

"And to answer the question in your mind," Cronley said, "your wife, and Bonehead's Ginger, are going to be perfectly safe in the Pullach compound. Well, as safe as three barbed wire fences and a battalion of guards can make them."

"I didn't know about this when you were in Fritzlar," Winters said.

"It hadn't happened when we were in Fritzlar," Cronley said, a bit impatiently. "So, what you do now is get on the phone to Bonehead. We've got encrypted lines, but if we used one now, Colonel Fishburn would hear about it, and I'd rather have him learn of the transfers from the orders when he gets them. Talk in tongues, in case anybody is listening . . ."

"Anybody meaning the NKGB?"

"And the FBI and maybe the CIC and the CID. So whenever you have to get on an unsecure line here — and always make every effort not to get on an unsecured line — talk in tongues."

"I'm not sure I know how to do that, sir."

"Without saying it in so many words, tell Bonehead to have your wives pack everything up and have it ready to load in the ambulances either late tonight or first thing in the morning. Got it?"

"I'll try, sir."

"I think maybe I should go with the ambulances," Hessinger said.

*He wants to play an active role.*

"You're needed here."

"I could be back tomorrow night."

"Somebody with DCI credentials should go," Claudette said. "I could."

Cronley looked at her, then said, "Okay, Freddy. I need Dette here. You go. How about this? We fly you up there. When you're on the Air Corps side of the base, call Mrs. Moriarty and have her meet you in the PX or someplace. Tell her what's going on, get her and Mrs. Winters to pack their stuff. Then, either tonight — or in the morning, when they've left Fritzlar — you fly back."

"That'd work," Hessinger said.

"Or I could go, sir," Winters said. "And do the same thing. I came here in an L-4, and . . ."

"You'd like to be with your wife?"

"Yes, sir."

"That's understandable," Cronley said.

*But unless I make it clear right now that this is DCI, and not a Constabulary regiment, where you can ask for — and get — time off to deal with family problems, this will quickly get out of hand.*

*Was getting him and Bonehead and their very pregnant wives transferred here yet more proof that I'm a loose cannon fucking things up because I don't think things through?*

"I need you here, Winters. Sorry. What did you say about coming here in an L-4?"

"Colonel Wilson arranged that, sir. It's

91

the one we get."

*On the other hand, he didn't remind me his wife is pregnant, and couldn't I please reconsider his request? And he said "we."*

*Doesn't that confirm my snap character judgment that he's a good, duty-first officer?*

"Where is it?"

"Schleissheim."

Schleissheim was the Munich Military Post airfield.

"Well, we can't leave it there," Cronley said. "So what's going to happen now is we'll get in the Kapitän, and Freddy will take us to Schleissheim and then drive to the Compound. We'll get in the Piper Cub and fly it to the Compound. While that's going on, Dette, you will call the Compound and tell Max —"

"Max is taking your guest to the monastery," Claudette interrupted.

"I stand corrected. You will tell the Pole duty officer and the trooper NCOIC to load up the ambulances and head for the Air Corps, repeat Air Corps, side of the base at Fritzlar, where Freddy will meet them and tell them what to do.

"Freddy, on his arrival at the Compound, will send the Kapitän back here with two or three Poles in it. The Poles, who will have by then been instructed never to get more than ten feet from you, Miss Colbert, will then drive you to the Compound."

"That's not necessary," Claudette protested. "I can take care of myself."

"That was not a suggestion," Cronley said. "Meanwhile, at the Compound, Lieutenant Winters and I will shoot touch and goes until he feels confident in his ability to do it by himself. We will then park the Piper, and taking Major Bischoff with us in a Storch, fly to the monastery so that Konrad can have a nice long chat with our guest.

"Once that's been set up, we'll go back to the Compound. By then, it is to be hoped, Winters will have absorbed enough of my expert instruction to be able to land the Storch at the Compound. If we live through that, we will tell General Gehlen and Colonel Mannberg what we have learned about our guest at the monastery, and what Bischoff thinks we might learn in the future. Got it?"

"One more fact bearing on the problem," Claudette said. "Major Wallace said to reserve a room here, long term, for a CIC agent named Hammersmith. What's that all about?"

"You said Hammersmith?"

"CIC Supervisory Special Agent John D. 'Jack' Hammersmith."

"If that's who I think it is, he's a heavy-duty CIC agent I knew when I was in Marburg. He used to be a major, now that I think about it. I have no idea what it's about. Probably something to do with what happened to you last night. Ready, Freddy?"

"Yes, sir."

# III

## [ONE]

*Kloster Grünau*

*Schollbrunn, Bavaria*

*American Zone of Occupation, Germany*

*1005 24 January 1946*

"Follow me through, Tom," Cronley ordered.

"Yes, sir," Winters replied, and put his hand very lightly on the stick of the Fieseler Fi-156 Storch, and then put his feet very lightly on the rudder pedals.

"First we put the flaps down," Cronley said, as he pointed the nose of the aircraft at a dirt road just outside a small compound in the foothills of the Bavarian Alps.

Flaps came out of the trailing edge of the aircraft's wing.

The Storch — a high-wing three-seater

with long-legged landing gear, hence *Storch,* which is German for "stork" — was painted a dull black. Visible on the wings and fuselage from, say, fifty feet, but no farther than that, were the insignias identifying it as a military aircraft in the service of the U.S. Army.

"Which of course slows us down," Cronley said conversationally, "which, in turn, causes the leading edge of the wing, previously held in place by air pressure, to drop."

Winters looked up at the wing in time to see the leading edge drop.

"I'll be damned," he said.

"No man is without sin," Cronley said. "Which in turn slows us down even more, at the same time giving us a little more lift."

Ten seconds later he said, "Which permits us to land at about forty kilometers an hour. I presume you've noticed the airspeed and altimeter give readings in klicks?"

"Yes, sir."

The wheels chirped as they touched down.

"Which in turn permits us to stop in about two hundred, two hundred fifty feet."

The Storch slowed and stopped.

"That's amazing," Winters said. "It stalls at forty kilometers?"

"A little under that," Cronley said, and then added, "You have the aircraft. Taxi to the end of the runway and turn it around."

When Winters reached the end of the runway — which was actually a dirt road — he saw that two jeeps were waiting for them. One, with a pedestal-mounted .50 caliber Browning machine gun, held two Poles. The other held a first sergeant, a black man, and a man in triangle ODs.

"You want me to go through that again," Cronley asked, "or do you think you can take off and land safely at your present skill level?" He paused, but before Winters could reply, he added, "If you make me go through it again, I will be annoyed. If you bend my bird trying to get it back onto the ground, I will really be annoyed. Your call."

"He's going to take off again?" a third voice, belonging to the man in the third seat, came over their headsets.

"I'm waiting for him to tell me, Konrad," Cronley said.

"May I get out now, Herr Cronley?" Major Konrad Bischoff said.

"No. I want him to try this in a maximum weight — or nearly maximum weight — condition. Think of yourself as a sandbag, Konrad."

*"Gott im Himmel!"*

"Major Bischoff apparently doesn't have much faith in your flying skill, Lieutenant

Winters. How about you?"

Winters replied by advancing the throttle. Ten seconds and two hundred fifty feet later, the Storch was airborne.

"Congratulations, Lieutenant," Cronley said eight minutes later. "By the power vested in me, I declare that you have passed your Storch check-ride. You are also herewith designated Aviation Officer, Military Detachment, DCI-Europe."

"This is one hell of an airplane," Winters said.

"It is," Cronley agreed. "It is also irreplaceable, so keep that in mind while you're flying it."

"Yes, sir."

"Shut it down, and then we will have a look at our guest."

"You keep saying that," Winters said. "Who's your guest?"

"One of the guys who tried to kidnap Dette and Florence. Max brought him here from the 98th General Hospital so that he and Konrad can have a little chat."

"What is this place?" Winters said. "Am I allowed to ask?"

"Yeah. You're now in DCI. As soon as I can get Dette to make them up, you'll get DCI special agent credentials. You're supposed to know everything — well, almost everything — that's going on. If you don't know, ask. Consider that an order."

"Bonehead, too?"

"Yeah, Bonehead, too."

"Sir, what is this place?"

"When this whole Operation Ost thing started, and we needed someplace to hide General Gehlen and Abwehr Ost, Wallace got this place from the Vatican."

"From the Vatican?" Winters blurted.

"That's what they mean by strange bedfellows. They had — have — a number of unsavory people they wanted to get out of Europe. We had one means of doing that. They are scratching our back, and we are scratching theirs. I don't like that much, but it's necessary and has proved very useful.

"Anyway, after we moved Abwehr Ost, now known as the Süd-Deutsche Industrielle Entwicklungsorganisatio — South German Industrial Development Organization — to the Compound, I decided we should keep this place, known as the monastery, as someplace we could do things we really didn't want anybody to know about.

"The signs on the fences identify it as the home of the 711TH QM MOBILE KITCHEN RENOVATION COMPANY, and that — 711 MKRC — is painted on vehicle bumpers. It allows us, I think, to be anywhere in Germany or Austria without raising suspicion."

"What sort of things you . . . *we* . . . don't want anybody to know about?"

"You're about to find out," Cronley said, and gestured for him to get out of the Storch.

By the time they had, the jeep with the first sergeant and the blond man in triangled ODs had driven up to it. Cronley made the introductions.

"Lieutenant Winters," he said, "this is First Sergeant Abraham Lincoln Tedworth of Company 'C,' 203rd Tank Destroyer Battalion, which provides our security. When Lieutenant Moriarty assumes command of Charley Company, I hope he remembers what we were taught at A&M — that first sergeants are really in charge and that company commanders are just window dressing. And you know DCI Special Agent Max Ostrowski, who, in addition to his many other duties, controls our Poles."

The men shook hands.

"Where's our guest?" Cronley asked. "And what shape is he in?"

"I put him where we had Colonel Likharev," Ostrowski said. "I did so because he's in rather bad shape. His shoulder joint was shattered. They showed me the X-rays, and I felt sorry for him. In other words, I thought it better to put him there right away than have to move him later."

"I would have put him there right away," Bischoff said.

"But you would have done that, Konrad, to make him uncomfortable," Cronley said. "We are going to start to conduct our interrogation of our guest with kindness. You did the right thing, Max. Let's go see the sonofabitch."

The men climbed into the jeep.

"You need fuel for the Storch?" Ostrowski asked.

"Normally," Cronley said, "I top off whenever possible. Since we're only going back to the Compound, I think we're all right. But thanks."

The jeep lurched into motion.

They stopped before an ancient, cross-topped building, and everyone got out and went inside. There were no pews or other religious trappings, but Winters could see what had obviously been the altar, and high above it was a small leaded multicolored glass window centered with a cross.

Tedworth led the way through the area where worshippers had once prayed and listened to homilies, then through a door.

Inside was an area Winters, who had once been an altarboy, strongly suspected had been where priests and altarboys had once changed into — and out of — their vestments.

It was now occupied by four men, two American sergeants and two men in black-dyed ODs. All were armed with .45 pistols. Four Thompson submachine guns with fifty-round drum magazines hung from wooden pegs on the wall.

The four men popped to attention when they saw Cronley.

"Rest," Cronley ordered, gesturing with his hand. He then said, "He's not alone, is he? He's one of the guys who tried to kidnap Colbert and Sergeant Miller last night."

"Sergeant Tedworth told us, sir," a very tall, very thin, coffee-skinned staff sergeant said. "We got one of each downstairs and one of each in with him. Tedworth said she popped three others. She all right, Captain?"

Cronley nodded.

"That is one tough lady," he said, and then gestured for Tedworth to proceed through a door.

It opened on a stairway. They went down it and found themselves in a small room. In it were a Pole and an American, this one an ebony-skinned sergeant. Both had Thompsons slung from their shoulders and .45 pistols in holsters. Pegs on the wall held two more Thompsons and web belts with holstered .45s.

The men came to attention. Wordlessly, Cronley signaled for them to relax.

"You heard what this guy did?" Cronley asked.

"Abe Lincoln told us," the sergeant said.

"I don't want anybody to hurt him, or even be mean to him," Cronley said. "Anybody. You understand that?"

"Yes, sir," the sergeant and the Pole said on top of each other.

"Max, when we get in there, say 'Good morning' in Russian. Maybe he'll slip and reply or start to."

Ostrowski nodded.

"Open the door, Honest Abe," Cronley ordered.

Tedworth pulled a heavy wooden door outward. The hiss of Coleman gas lanterns could be heard.

Cronley went through the door. There was another American sergeant and another Pole, unarmed, in a small windowless chamber. They were in straight-backed chairs.

There was a hospital bed, cranked up so that the man in it was half sitting up. He looked to be Slavic and in his mid-thirties. He was wearing hospital pajamas and a bathrobe. Beside the bed was a white hospital table, and under it a hospital bedpan.

"Good morning," Max said in Russian.

The man in the bed didn't respond.

"Where," Cronley asked in German, "did you get the hospital bed and stuff?"

Max replied in German: "The hospital loaned it to us."

"And what," Cronley asked in English, "was his prognosis?"

Max, still in German, replied: "He'll probably have limited use of his right arm from here on, but aside from that, he's all right. In pain, but all right. The hospital gave us some morphine."

"Enough?"

"I think so," Max replied in English and then switched to Russian. "Are you in pain? Would you like some morphine?"

The man in the bed showed no signs of understanding.

"This is Major Bischoff," Cronley said in English. "Formerly of Abwehr Ost. Which I think you already know. I also think you speak English, Russian, and German. Your eyes gave you away. So when Major Bischoff comes back in here to talk to you, you can't get away with pretending you don't understand him."

He gestured for the others to leave the room and then followed them out.

Tedworth closed the heavy door.

"Konrad," Cronley said, "inasmuch as I don't trust you — based on what you were doing to Colonel Likharev before I stopped you — to do nothing but try to talk to this guy, I'm ordering Sergeant Tedworth to break all the toes on your right foot *before* he calls to tell me you don't know how to obey orders."

"You really don't have to be so melodramatic, Herr Cronley."

"I think of it as being careful," Cronley said. "I really want to turn this guy. And I really don't want to put him in —"

"I will of course obey your orders, Herr Cronley."

"As First Sergeant Tedworth will scrupulously obey mine. And now that's been said, what are you thinking?"

"My intuition is that this man — he was in the passenger seat of their ambulance, not in the back or driving — is the officer in charge. And I think you are right that he speaks Russian, which is to be expected, and also German and English. All of that — plus the importance of the mission to kidnap Fräulein Colbert and her sergeant friend — makes me think he's probably a senior NKGB captain, perhaps a major."

"Not a lieutenant colonel or a colonel?" Tedworth asked.

"They've already lost one colonel. I doubt if they'd risk a colonel to kidnap a female sergeant."

"They save the colonels to kidnap me?"

"Yes. I believe they would."

"Do you think he can be turned?"

"Possibly. He knows what the alternative would be. It would be better for us if he knew Colonel Likharev is safe with his family in Argentina."

"How could we do that?"

"A photograph of the Likharevs standing in front of a Buenos Aires landmark with one of them holding a recent copy of the *Buenos Aires Herald* showing readable recent headlines would probably do it."

Cronley thought that over and grunted.

"As soon as I get back to the Compound, I'll get that started," he said. Then he turned to Tedworth. "Honest Abe, as I've told you before, Major Bischoff is very good at what he does. Watch him carefully and learn from him. And at the same time make sure —"

"That he obeys your orders. Yes, sir."

"You about ready to go back to the Compound, Max?"

"Yes, sir."

"Off we go."

Cronley punched Tedworth affectionately on the arm and started up the stairs.

# [Two]

*The South German Industrial Development*

*Organization Compound*

*Pullach, Bavaria*

*1125 24 January 1946*

The sun had come out, which was unusual for late January, and Hammersmith got a good look at the village as the single-engine L-4 aircraft circled it, losing altitude to land.

It was a typical small Bavarian village, one nestled in the foothills of the Bavarian Alps. There were perhaps a hundred fifty or so houses, most of them small cottages, plus some barns. On the village square was a church. There were also three large three-story buildings — *kasernen* — which had been built in the 1930s to house the reserve 117th Bavarian Infantry Regiment.

An outer fence ten feet high circled the village. On it every twenty yards or so were signs Hammersmith tried and failed to read.

One hundred meters inside that fence, and probably not visible from the road passing

Pullach, was a second fence, this one topped by barbed concertina wire. On it every twenty meters were more signs that Hammersmith also could not read.

There was a gate through the second fence guarded by both Poles and Americans, two of each. Hammersmith could see that the Americans, both sergeants, were very large black men, armed with Thompson submachine guns. Their shoulder insignia was a triangular insignia that Hammersmith decided was most likely that of the 2nd "Hell on Wheels" Armored Division. One of them, and one of the Poles, manned the barrier.

One hundred yards inside the second fence was a third.

This one, also ten feet high, had concertina barbed wire on top and laid on the ground, the latter to make getting close to the fence difficult. At one-hundred-meter intervals along this fence line were guard towers equipped with floodlights and machine guns.

On the third fence were signs every twenty meters. He couldn't read these, either, although he could make out skulls and crossbones that signaled danger.

The L-4 aircraft, which was the Army designation for the Piper Cub, dropped its nose and landed on what Hammersmith decided was a recently built crushed stone runway between the second and the inner fence.

The pilot taxied to the end of the runway, stopping at a sort of a hangar there — tarpaulins held up by poles. Workmen were laying bricks on what was going to be a permanent hangar. Under the tarpaulin were two Fieseler Storch aircraft, the Wehrmacht's version of the L-4, which Hammersmith had heard were far superior to the Army's Piper Cubs.

Two jeeps were waiting for them. One held two black soldiers, both three-stripe "buck" sergeants, in a jeep with a .50 caliber Browning machine gun on a pedestal mount. It wasn't for show. Hammersmith saw a belt of ammunition was in place. And he saw that he'd been right — the triangular shoulder patch was that of "Hell on Wheels."

The second jeep, which did not have a pedestal-mounted Browning, held an American technical sergeant, a large black man, and a large white man in a dyed black U.S. Army uniform.

*The white guy's a PSO guard,* Hammersmith decided.

He knew all about the PSO, which stood for Provisional Security Organization. It had been formed from former members of either the Free Polish Army or the Free Polish Air Force. After escaping captivity by the Germans or the Russians when Poland had been overrun in the early days of the war, they had made their way to England. There, they had spent the rest of World War II serving with the Free Polish Armed Forces.

When those organizations had been disbanded almost immediately after VE Day, the discharged officers and soldiers had refused to be repatriated. They knew the Russians had murdered in cold blood more than eight thousand Polish officers, and had good reason to believe the Russians would do the same to them.

Although the Soviets had angrily demanded their forced return, General McNarney flatly refused to do so.

And then someone in the Farben Building in Frankfurt am Main, now the headquarters of U.S. Forces in the European Theater (USFET), decided that the former Polish soldiers and officers, who were languishing in displaced persons camps, were the answer to a serious problem USFET faced.

Guards were needed to protect Army Quartermaster Corps supply depots from the German population, which was on the cusp of starvation. The U.S. Army was short of soldiers to perform the guarding. And since the Polish "DPs" had military training, and hated the Germans nearly as much as they hated the Russians, they seemed to be ideally suited to guard Quartermaster depots.

McNarney agreed, and the Provisional Security Organization was formed. A school had been hastily set up in Griesheim, outside Frankfurt. There the Poles had been issued fatigue uniforms that had been dyed black, taught how to fire the carbine and the .45 pistol, and been quickly put to work as guards at Quartermaster — and other — supply depots.

Hammersmith had thought the idea made as much sense as putting foxes in chicken houses, and predicted there would be mass thefts of Army property.

As the PSO Pole in the jeep got out and walked toward the L-4, Hammersmith thought about this, and admitted he had been wrong. No mass plundering of depots had occurred.

Then he had other thoughts.

The Pole walking toward him had a Thompson submachine gun slung over his shoulder.

*Jesus, when did they start issuing Tommy Guns to the Poles?*

And then he saw that the Pole's dyed-black uniform wasn't baggy cotton twill fatigue jacket and pants.

*That's a dyed-black woolen OD Ike jacket, trousers, khaki shirt, and necktie.*

*When did they start issuing the PSO regular uniforms?*

*And those aren't combat boots, either. What they look like is German Fallschirmjager boots.*

*When did they start issuing the PSO German paratrooper boots?*

Hammersmith crawled out of the L-4, took his small bag out, thanked the pilot for the ride, and turned to face the PSO Pole.

"Mr. Hammersmith?" the Pole inquired politely.

Hammersmith nodded.

"May I see your ID, sir? It's the protocol."

*He sounds like a fucking Limey.*

Hammersmith produced his CIC credentials. The Pole examined them carefully and then handed them back.

"Thank you, sir. If you'll come with us, we'll take you over to the office. They're waiting for you."

"Who's 'they'?" Hammersmith said, as they began walking to the jeep.

"Why don't you get in front, sir? I'll hop in the back."

111

Hammersmith got in the jeep beside the driver, who smiled broadly at him and said, "Welcome to the Compound. How was the flight in the puddle jumper?"

"Long, noisy, and a little bumpy," Hammersmith said. "Who's the guy in the back?"

"That's Senior Watch Chief Wieczorek. He's a Pole in the PSO. That's like a first lieutenant, a senior watch chief is."

"He said they're waiting for me. Who's 'they'?"

"Well, I guess that would be General Gehlen, and Major Wallace, plus of course the chief."

"And the chief is?"

"Mr. Cronley. Nice guy. You'll like him."

"Whoopee!" Hammersmith said. "Drive on, Sergeant!"

And then he remembered what General Greene had advised him to do, and did it.

*Think Major Hammersmith! Think Major Hammersmith! Think Major Hammersmith! Think major! Think major!*

# [THREE]

*The South German Industrial Development*

*Organization Compound*

*Pullach, Bavaria*

*American Zone of Occupation, Germany*

*1205 24 January 1946*

Neat, and obviously new, signs, one nailed above the door of the small, freshly painted cottage and another stuck into its snow-covered lawn, read OFFICE OF THE OMGUS LIAISON OFFICER.

OMGUS was the acronym for Office of Military Government, U.S.

It was, de facto, the headquarters of DCI-Europe.

The chief, DCI-Europe, one James D. Cronley Jr., sat near the head of a conference table in the main downstairs room. At the head of the table, wearing a shabby suit, shirt, and necktie, was a slight, pale-faced forty-three-year-old with a prominent thin nose, piercing eyes, and a receding hairline. He was former Generalmajor Reinhard Gehlen.

Across from Cronley was the only woman in the room. Claudette Colbert was wearing a WAC officer's pinks-and-greens uniform with triangles. Her first role in the meeting had been that of witness to the attack on her and Technical Sergeant Miller. Following that, for the past hour and a half, she had been performing her duties as administrative officer of DCI-Europe, which translated to mean she was taking notes in case it was decided — as Cronley or Major Wallace almost certainly would — that a record of the meeting be kept. Augie Ziegler was sitting next to her.

Wallace was sitting on the other side of the table beside Cronley. Jack Hammersmith was sitting next to Wallace. Scattered elsewhere around the table were former Oberst Ludwig Mannberg, a tall, aristocratic-looking man who had been Gehlen's deputy in Abwehr Ost and now held the same position in the Süd-Deutsche Industrielle Entwicklungsorganisation, who was wearing a well-cut single-breasted glen plaid suit; Max Ostrowski; and Captain "Tiny" Dunwiddie.

The table was just about covered with documents of all kinds, photographs, ashtrays, and coffee mugs.

"My stomach just told me for the third time that it needs to be fed," Cronley announced. "And my watch just told me it's the noon hour. And all we're doing here is

114

kicking the same thoughts around."

"I think Jim is suggesting we adjourn for lunch," Mannberg said, lightly sarcastic.

Mannberg had a pronounced upper-class British accent. It was the result of his having spent four years in London, the first two (1933–1935) as a junior military attaché of the German embassy, and the last two, ending in 1939, as the military attaché. He had spent most of 1936 and 1937 in Russia, with the result being that his Russian was nearly as fluent as his English.

"We didn't get to discuss two things," General Gehlen said, his English also fluent, sounding almost American, but with a pronounced accent. "What was the motive for the attempted kidnapping and who did it? Depending on who did it, the NKGB or Odessa, the motive, I suggest, may be different."

"I've been holding off on that, General," Wallace said. "The admiral has some thoughts on Odessa he wants me to share with you during our deliberations."

"In that case, may I vote with Jim?" Gehlen asked, and got to his feet.

The others followed, then started to walk out of the room. Wallace made a discreet gesture to Hammersmith not to rush.

When they were the last in the room,

Wallace gestured again, signaling Hammersmith to slow down.

Outside the cottage, as the others walked ahead of them toward the nearest of the three *kasernen,* Wallace put his hand on Hammersmith's arm.

"We need a quick word," he said. "Which I would rather have had before that meeting got started. But you weren't here, then."

"Yes, sir?"

"But, since you were there, give me a quick take on what you thought."

"About what, sir?"

"Start with Cronley."

"He acts like he's in charge," Hammersmith said.

"He is."

"I should have said, he acts like he's Gehlen's chief of staff. Gehlen was running that meeting."

"No. Cronley was running it. He was just being polite to General Gehlen. Mannberg is Gehlen's chief of staff."

"General Greene told me you're really the man in charge."

"Officially, I'm the CIC representative at the table. I make *suggestions* to Captain Cronley only when I think it's necessary."

"Yes, sir."

"What about the CID guy? Ziegler?"

"He struck me as a good deal smarter than most of them."

"What about Captain Dunwiddie?"

"Interesting guy. Real regular Army, if you know what I mean."

"I'll tell you about that when there's time. What I'm asking now, Jack, is whether you would be comfortable working for Cronley, who is both only twenty-two years old and can be damned difficult, and Gehlen, who has not forgotten he was a generalmajor, and Ziegler, who knows he's smart and doesn't think much of CIC special agents. You know what I'm asking?"

"I really don't have much choice, do I?"

"Yeah, you do. Which brings me to the real point of this little chat. General Greene told me he told you if you played your cards right, you could probably get recalled to active duty as Major Hammersmith."

Hammersmith nodded.

"He was wrong to tell you that. He should have known better."

"That's not in the cards?"

"The only general officer — or colonel — in the Army intelligence establishment in Europe who doesn't seriously think that DCI is a dangerous bastard organization that should be gotten rid of — 'for the good of the service' — as soon as possible by any

117

means required is Greene."

"It's that bad, huh?"

"And they are encouraged by G-2 in the Pentagon. Homer Greene should have known, and told you, that the better job you do here, the more it will piss off the G-2 establishment. Especially if you refuse to be their mole in DCI — and, trust me, you will be asked — they will see you as a traitor, and they are not going to see somebody they perceive as a traitor to the establishment rewarded by pinning his gold leaf back on him.

"And I've got one more thing to say that will probably piss you off. Right now, we really don't need you here."

"General Greene told me you asked for a good agent."

"I did. I asked for his best agent and hoped he'd send me you. That was before I knew that Cronley had found and drafted Ziegler. My take on Ziegler — based on what we saw just now of his investigation of the shooting — is that he's a first-class investigator. You agree?"

Hammersmith nodded. "He's very good."

"We don't need two investigators right now."

"So I'm fired before I get started?"

"Your call. If you want, I'll send you back

to the CIC, where Greene can probably figure out some other way to get you your commission back, and nobody ever has to know you were ever even in Pullach.

"Or you can stay here, where, because Cronley likes him and doesn't know you, you'll probably be working for Ziegler until Cronley, or I, come up with something appropriate to your talents. And where you can forget your commission, unless you do something spectacular that comes to the attention of the admiral, or better yet, El Jefe, which would cause them to lean on the Pentagon to get you your commission back. Frankly, I wouldn't hold my breath waiting for that to happen. And, if you stay here, and the intelligence establishment does manage to flush us down the toilet, which is a real possibility, you go down the hole with the rest of us."

"How much time do I have to think this over?"

"Ten seconds."

"How come so long?"

"Because when we get to the senior officers' mess" — Wallace pointed to the nearest *kaserne* — "there will be two officers there, Lieutenant Colonel George H. Parsons and Major Warren W. Ashley, having their lunch. They are the liaison officers between DCI-Europe and the Pentagon G-2. Once they see you, it will take them probably at least thirty minutes to let their superiors know there's a new pariah."

Hammersmith considered his options for perhaps five seconds, and verbalized his conclusion by saying "Shit!" and then asking: "How am I going to get my things down here from Marburg?"

## [FOUR]

*The South German Industrial Development*

*Organization Compound*

*Pullach, Bavaria*

*American Zone of Occupation, Germany*

*1310 24 January 1946*

When Cronley, Gehlen, and the others walked back to the cottage from the *kaserne,* they found an MP jeep among the others. In it, looking annoyed, were two MPs, a sergeant and a master sergeant in full MP regalia.

They were annoyed because they had been told by a large Negro staff sergeant sitting in a jeep with a pedestal-mounted Browning .50 to "stay in the jeep until they come back from lunch."

120

Augie Ziegler walked up to the jeep and extended his hand to the master sergeant.

"Hey, Phil," he said.

"I've got your pictures, Augie," he said. "What the hell is this place?"

"Read the sign," Ziegler said, pointing to the OFFICE OF THE OMGUS LIAISON OFFICER sign, and then put his hand out for the large manila envelope on the sergeant's lap.

The sergeant handed him the envelope.

"I guess you're not going to tell me," the sergeant said.

"I just did. Come with me."

The sergeant followed him into the building, where Augie laid the envelope before Cronley.

"Master Sergeant Phillips has brought us the pictures, sir."

"Thanks," Cronley said to the sergeant. "Stick around a minute, please."

He took an inch-and-a-half-thick stack of 8×10-inch black-and-white photographs from it and then quickly flipped through them.

"I'm glad you brought these after I had my lunch," Cronley said.

"They are pretty grim, sir," the MP said.

"Negatives?"

"Sorry," the MP said, and took several 4×5-inch envelopes from his breast pocket and handed them over.

"And the fingerprints?" Cronley asked.

"The hospital won't hand them over until they finish the autopsies," the MP said. "Then they'll give us both the autopsies and the prints."

"Damn!"

"How important are the fingerprints right now?" Ziegler asked.

"Excuse me?" Cronley asked.

"They won't be much use to us until we identify those people, Jim," Mannberg answered for him. "And then all we'll have is confirmation that 'Body A' is really so-and-so."

"I see that my monumental ignorance has once again surfaced," Cronley said. "But then, Ziegler, why did you ask for them 'as soon as we can have them'?"

"I think they call that 'dotting the *i*'s and crossing the *t*'s,'" Claudette said.

Ziegler looked at her and they smiled.

"The thing to do, I suggest," Mannberg said, "is to see if General Gehlen or I can identify these people — which is unlikely — and then send them over to *Kaserne* Two and see if anyone there can. Unlikely, but possible."

"You obviously think identifying these people is very important," Cronley said, as he shoved the stack of photographs and the negatives to the center of the table. He then added, "I don't think you want to see those, Dette."

"I don't want to, but . . ."

"As the victim you think you should?"

"As both the victim and the administrative officer, I think I should," she said, and pulled the stack of photographs to her.

"I thought Freddy was the administrative officer," Mannberg said.

"Freddy is now the 'executive assistant to the chief, DCI-Europe,' " Cronley said.

"What's that all about?" Wallace asked.

"You were there when Freddy let us know he thought he was unappreciated," Cronley said.

"Yes, I was," Wallace said, smiling.

"I thought giving him that title might please him," Cronley said. "And it did. He now thinks of himself as the DCI-Europe version of El Jefe."

"Good thinking," Wallace said, chuckling.

"This is the guy who had the knife at my throat," Claudette said, sliding one 8×10 over to Mannberg, who studied it and shook his head, and then slid it over to Gehlen, who also shook his head.

"You asked a moment ago why I think identifying these people is important,"

Mannberg said.

"I'm betting they're NKGB. Both Ostrowski and I are convinced the guy at the monastery speaks Russian."

Mannberg said something in Russian.

"I don't speak Russian," Cronley said. "But I'll bet I can translate that: *So do a number of Germans who used to be in the SS and just might be involved with Odessa.* How close did I come?"

"You obviously have a flair for the language," Mannberg said.

"I don't think that's true," Cronley said. "What I do have a real flair for is overlooking the obvious." He paused, then said: "Tiny, where's Sergeant Finney?"

"Probably in the sergeants' mess."

"Just as soon as Dette, the general, and Colonel Mannberg finish going through those pictures, why don't you take them over to *Kaserne* Two. Who should he give them to, Colonel?"

"Oberstleutnant Schulberg," Mannberg said. "I'll call and tell him what to do."

He reached for the telephone.

"And give them to Oberstleutnant Schulberg, telling him that identifying these people is really important. And then run down Finney and send him here. On the way to the sergeants' mess — where you will see they are well fed, it's after the noon meal and the mess sergeant may have to be encouraged — make sure the sergeants understand why regaling anyone with tales of what they saw here would be ill-advised."

"Yes, sir," Dunwiddie said with a smile. "I will encourage the mess sergeant to do his best despite the hour."

Cronley turned to the MP master sergeant.

"Sergeant, you didn't hear anything that was said in here just now. You understand that? It's important."

"I'm getting the message, sir," the MP said.

### [FIVE]

Staff Sergeant Albert Finney, a very large, very black twenty-four-year-old, came into the room ten minutes later. He marched up to Cronley and saluted.

"Come on in, Al," Cronley said, casually returning his salute. "Have a seat. We're about to talk about Odessa."

"Yes, sir," Finney said, and then, *"Guten Tag, Herr General, Herr Oberst."*

"And good afternoon to you, too, Finney," Wallace said, smiling.

"No offense meant, sir."

"I took none, Al, but Dette thinks you don't like her."

"She knows better than that, Major. How you doing, Dette?"

"A lot better than Florence. She's still in the 98th."

"But just shook up, right? Not cut or shot?"

"Shook up is bad enough," Dette said.

"Before we get into the subject of Odessa," Wallace said, "when I called El Jefe to tell him what happened to Dette and Florence, he said that he had been thinking — which I believe means that the admiral had been thinking — that those scurrilous rumors saying we've been sending people the CIC has been looking for to Argentina could be put to rest if we had proof that Odessa is the villain."

"Hmm," General Gehlen said. "Interesting point."

"Schultz said, 'If there was proof that three or four former senior SS officers the CIC is already looking for turned out to be the culprits.' "

"Yeah," Cronley agreed thoughtfully.

"Which suggests to me, Jim, that your previously made decision to put those sleeping dogs — your cousin Luther and Commandant Jean-Paul Fortin of the Strasbourg

office of the Direction de la Surveillance du
Territoire — on the back burner has been
overridden by El Jefe."

"Looks that way, doesn't it?"

"And with that in mind, and seeing you
have two new members of your staff who
have no idea what we're talking about, may
I suggest that you do a recap, starting at the
beginning, of what has gone before?"

"Let Finney do it," Cronley said. "I'm
personally involved."

"Sergeant Finney, you have the podium,"
Wallace said.

Finney stood up, looking a bit uncomfortable.

Understanding why, Cronley said, "I've
done it again. Sergeant Finney, that's CID
Supervisory Special Agent Ziegler and that's
CIC Supervisory Special Agent Hammersmith, both of whom saw the error of their
ways and begged to be taken in by us. In
other words, Al, they're in the loop."

Hammersmith thought: *Wiseass!*

The men nodded at each other.

"From the beginning, Al," Cronley ordered. "Whoops, one more thing. I should
have introduced you as DCI Special Agent
Finney. Which raises the question, why are
you wearing stripes?"

"Fat Freddy said I should ask you if you

127

wanted me in stripes or triangles."

"Your call, Al. Whichever is right at the time. Please proceed."

"I guess it goes back to when the CIC guy brought the black market packages that the CID grabbed" — Finney looked at Hammersmith and Ziegler — "that was you guys, right?"

"That was me," Hammersmith said.

Ziegler shook his head and said, "This is all new to me."

"The captain's mother," Finney went on, "had sent him several packages of black market goodies — canned hams, coffee, cigarettes — which somebody in the CID grabbed in the APO. Because they had the captain's CIC address on them, the CID turned them over to the CIC . . ."

*Where,* Wallace thought, *good ol' Bob Mattingly, seeing his chance to stick it to Cronley, grabbed it.*

". . . who sent a CIC agent to deliver the packages to Captain Cronley with a letter saying 'please let us know in advance if you are going to require such materials in connection with your DCI activities.' "

Wallace thought: *And made damned sure Greene and everybody else in USFET G-2 and provost marshal's office got a copy.*

"When . . ." Finley went on, and looked

128

at Hammersmith. "What would you like me to call you?"

*In a just and fair world, Sergeant, I would be able to tell you to call me "Major Hammer-smith, sir."*

"Jack will work," Hammersmith said.

"When *Jack* walked in here . . . this room . . . with the packages, he had another letter —"

"One from my father to me," Cronley interrupted. "It explained the packages. My father reminded me that when he married my mother, who's from Strasbourg, right after World War One, there had been some trouble with her family and that after they went to the States, she'd had little, practically no, contact with then.

"Then, Dad said, one of them, her nephew — which makes him my cousin — Herr Luther Stauffer, apparently decided his aunt might be a warmhearted sucker who would take pity on him and his poor family, and send them stuff, so he wrote her a letter. She sent me four boxes of black market goodies, which I was supposed to give to him.

"My father, who didn't like Cousin Luther playing my mother for a sucker, said it was my call. What I should do was decide what was best for my mother. So I put the boxes away while I thought that over.

"Then we had to go to Vienna to meet Seven-K —"

"Who is?" Ziegler asked.

"Shorthand, an NKGB agent," Wallace furnished. "Leave it at that for now. Go on, Jim."

"By which time I had decided, what the hell, I'll give Cousin Luther the goodies and then tell Mom to stop sending packages because it's against the law. Problem solved. So I told Freddy to get me an ambulance and I would drive to Strasbourg, drop the goodies off, and then go to Vienna. Pick it up, Al."

"Freddy said 'no.' He believed that the captain alone in an ambulance would make the Frogs curious — Strasbourg is in France — and what we should do is have a little Mess Kit Repair Company convoy, a staff car, and an ambulance —"

"Mess Kit Repair Company?" Augie Ziegler asked. "What the fuck . . . sorry, Dette . . . is that?"

Claudette looked at Cronley for permission, and when he nodded, she answered the question.

"Since we didn't want to put DCI, or even CIC, on our bumpers, and had to put something, Captain Cronley had 711th

MKRC painted on the bumpers. He said it meant the 711th Mess Kit Repair Company . . ."

"Which Fat Freddy said was sophomoric," Cronley said.

Hammersmith thought: *And it was. Just the sort of thing you'd expect from a twenty-two-year-old captain.*

"So," Cronley went on, "Freddy changed it to Mobile Kitchen Renovation Company. Same letters. Go on, Al."

"Then Freddy put on stripes and QM lapel insignia, and a second john's bar and QM insignia on the captain, and off we went to Strasbourg with me driving the Ford staff car and six of Tiny's Troopers in the ambulance."

" 'Tiny's Troopers'?" Hammersmith parroted.

"As our security force is fondly known," Cronley explained. "Making reference to their former first sergeant, Captain Dunwiddie, who for some unknown reason is known as Tiny."

Wallace smiled.

Hammersmith thought bitterly: *That figures. The big black guy was a first sergeant and now he's a captain. And Major Hammersmith is now a master sergeant.*

Then he had a second thought: *Maybe*

*Greene knew that, and that's what he was thinking when he said if I played my cards right, I could get my commission back. If this DCI can pin railroad tracks on a first sergeant, they can probably pin my gold leaf back on me.*

*But that's not what Wallace said.*

"So we go to the address that the captain had," Finney went on, "and asked the woman who opened the door — we later found out she was Frau Stauffer — for Cousin Luther. She never heard of him until Freddy told her the captain was Luther's cousin. Then he appeared.

"He seemed very happy to meet his long-lost relative who had the black market goodies for him, and he seemed fascinated with the detachment of the Mobile Kitchen Renovation Company on its way to Salzburg to renovate kitchens.

"We left him two boxes of goodies, and the captain told Cousin Luther that he would try to come back to see him, which also seemed to please him.

"Something wasn't right, and we all smelled it, so Freddy suggested we go see if the DST had anything on Cousin Luther . . ."

"DST?" Ziegler interrupted.

"Direction de la Surveillance du Territoire," Finney said. "Sort of a Frog version of the CIC and the CID combined. Where we met Commandant Jean-Paul Fortin of the Strasbourg office of the DST. Who is one smart sonofabitch."

"Why do you say that?" Wallace asked.

"Well, before we went to see him, we dropped the QM disguise. The captain and Hessinger put on triangles and the captain showed Fortin his CIC credentials."

"Cut to the chase, Al," Cronley ordered.

"It came out, after Fortin had played cute with us for a while, that he'd had people sitting on Cousin Luther's house. And those people had told him about the 711th staff car and ambulance, so he'd called USFET and asked what it was. So Fortin asked if the captain could explain what he was doing in a vehicle with the markings of a non-existent QM outfit."

"Meaning your clever idea is now known to USFET?" Hammersmith asked.

"I asked him what USFET had told him," Cronley said. "He told me that my secret was safe. So I showed him my DCI credentials, and he let me know he knew about the DCI, even when it had been formed. That told me Fortin was far more important than he wanted people to think. I think he's a colonel, not a major."

"I understand that happens from time to time," Wallace said.

"So then he gets me Cousin Luther's dossier," Cronley said. "Which showed that shortly after the Germans came to Strasbourg, Luther joined the LVF — Légion des Volontaires Français. He was sent to Russia, won the Iron Cross, and got himself promoted to lieutenant. Later on, he was taken into the SS as a *sturmführer* — a captain.

"There was a photo of Cousin Luther in his *sturmführer*'s uniform" — Cronley pointed to the top of his head — "skull-and-crossbones insignia and all. He didn't mention that in his letter to my mother.

"Anyway, Fortin said that Cousin Luther had next gone, near the end of the war, to the Waffen-Grenadier-Brigade der SS Charlemagne. Fortin said he thought it was likely Luther knew the war was lost, deserted the SS, made his way home to Strasbourg, and went into hiding."

"Did this officer tell you why he gave you access to Herr Stauffer's dossier?" Mannberg asked. "That seems a bit odd."

"I thought so, so I asked, and Fortin said he was hoping the DCI was working on the Odessa Organization. He said he was almost as interested in Odessa as he was in dealing with collaborators."

"Is Odessa for real?" Ziegler asked. "The story I've been getting is that it's like those SS werewolves who were supposed to be around Obersalzberg prepared to die to the last man defending Hitler. Which was pure bullshit."

"Unfortunately, Herr Ziegler," Gehlen said, "Die Organisation der Ehemaligen SS-Angehörigen — the Organization of former German SS officers — is real, is efficient, and, in my opinion, is very dangerous."

"That's quite true," Mannberg said. "But I wasn't aware that the French were actively involved in doing anything about it. Did Commandant Fortin —"

"I don't know about the French being interested, Colonel," Cronley interrupted, "but I believe Fortin is, and he explained why. And his explanation explains why I think he's a lot more important than he wants people to think he is."

"And you're going to explain to us that explanation, right?" Wallace said.

"I would be crushed to think you were making fun of me, Major, sir."

"Perish the thought. Just get on with explaining the explanation, please, Captain Cronley."

"Certainly, sir. I am always happy to

explain things to people who have trouble understanding things."

Hammersmith thought: *The word is "sophomoric."*

*But everybody, including Gehlen, is smiling. My God!*

"You will be rewarded in heaven, Captain, if you do so," Wallace said.

"Okay. Fortin is an armored officer, which of course sets him above officers in lesser services . . ."

"Okay, Jim. Enough," Wallace said.

". . . who was a captain at Saumur, the French cavalry school, when the war started. Then he was at Montcornet with de Gaulle. Freddy told us that was the only battle the Germans lost in France in 1940 —"

"General Rommel," Gehlen offered, "once told me, with admiration, that de Gaulle attacked with two hundred tanks and recaptured Caumont. And was stopped only when his tanks were taken out by Stukas."

Cronley nodded thoughtfully, then went on: "Fortin said that when de Gaulle got on a plane to England, de Gaulle took him along. That's what they call having a friend in high places. During the war, Fortin said he served with Leclerc's 2nd Armored Division. He said he returned to Strasbourg with

Leclerc, who left him there in charge of the DST.

"Now, if I were a cynical man, which Major Wallace here has been urging me to be, I would wonder why a guy who was with de Gaulle at Montcornet, and fought with the 2nd Armored Division in Africa and then across Europe, was only a major."

"And what do you think is the case?" Mannberg asked.

"Well, I think he's probably a colonel, and that he's doing something in Strasbourg for de Gaulle besides being the local CIC or CID guy."

"He also knows a lot more than you would expect," Finney said.

"For example?" Wallace asked.

"He knew all about the DCI . . . that it was like three weeks old," Finney said. "And he knew who General Greene is."

"So, what do you think Fortin is doing for de Gaulle, besides being the local CIC or CID guy?" Wallace asked.

"I don't have a clue. But I think I know why he's personally interested in Odessa."

"Why?"

"His family was in Strasbourg . . ." Cronley said.

"And he picked up right away on the captain's Strasbourg accent," Finney said.

"Which may have had something to do with the way he opened up to us."

"May I ask a question?" Hammersmith asked.

"Shoot," Cronley said.

"I'm getting the feeling that you were all talking with this man in German."

Cronley nodded.

Hammersmith said: "Hessinger is a German Jew. And you got your German from your mother."

"So how come I speak German?" Finney asked.

Hammersmith nodded.

"Tell him, Al," Cronley said.

"I grew up in Yorkville," Finney said. "Upper East Side of Manhattan. Lots of Germans. My pals were Germans. I went — kindergarten up — to a German school. We went to a Lutheran church, services conducted in German. So when I turned eighteen and promptly got drafted and I told the Army I spoke German, they tested me, and then the SNAFU began —"

"As another linguist, General," Cronley put in, "let me translate. SNAFU means Situation Normal, All Fucked Up."

Gehlen gave one of his small smiles.

"I was told that was FUBAR," he said.

"No, sir. That means Fucked Up Beyond

All Repair."

"Thank you," Gehlen said.

"Go on, Al," Cronley ordered.

"So some guy comes to see me in basic training, flashes his CIC credentials — which having never seen them before, impressed hell out of me — and then asks, in German, how come I speak German, and says, 'Answer in German.'

"So I did. Then he tells me the CIC is looking for people who speak German to chase Nazis, and was I interested? I knew my other option was being sent overseas to work as a stevedore, or fix roads, et cetera, which is where the Army was assigning people with my complexion, so I told him I was really interested. So I'm off to Camp Holabird —"

"You're CIC?" Hammersmith blurted in surprise.

"I was for a while, Jack," Finney said.

"What the hell do you mean, you were for a while?" Hammersmith asked.

"Let him finish, Hammersmith," Cronley ordered curtly.

"And I'm about halfway through the course, they decided they needed people in Europe right away, so they gave me credentials and put me on a plane."

"Much the same happened to me, Hammersmith," Cronley said. "I like to think the Holabird authorities recognized that Al and I were already so smart that further education would be a terrible waste of the CIC's time and money."

"Jesus Christ!" Wallace exclaimed, smiling.

"So I'm in a repple depple — the Tenth Replacement Depot — in Le Havre, and a CIC officer shows up and tells me he's really glad to see me, they're having a problem. They got word that the Communists are trying to cause trouble in the Negro units. And because the white officers aren't too close to the black troops, they can't get a handle on it.

"So he says instead of looking for Nazis because I speak German, I am going to be sent to a Negro unit, undercover, which means as a private, to root out the Communists. I have visions of myself in the . . . I don't know, the 711th Stevedore Battalion. I'm not that lucky. I get sent to Charley Company, 203rd Tank Destroyer Battalion, of 'Hell on Wheels.' The first sergeant there turns me over to a great big buck sergeant . . ."

"By the name of Chauncey Dunwiddie," Cronley furnished.

Hammersmith wondered: *Dunwiddie?*

*Some relation to this black captain?*

". . . who asks me what I know about destroying tanks — which is nothing — and then starts teaching me how to destroy tanks. I was into *that* school about five days when the Germans started to come through the Ardennes Forest.

"And guess what outfit was ordered to hold in place while we tried to destroy German tanks?

"Cutting to the chase, when the Battle of the Bulge was over, Charley Company was down to no officers and sixty-seven troopers, including Sergeant Dunwiddie, who was now first sergeant."

"And wearing the Silver Star and two Purple Hearts," Cronley said. "And Finney, who in his undercover role as Private Finney, had been promoted to sergeant and awarded one each Bronze Star and Purple Heart."

Finney went on: "While the Bulge was going on, the CIC tried to contact me. When they couldn't, they decided I'd been captured, and they sent my folks a telegram saying I was missing in action.

"When they finally pulled Charley Company off the line, I went to Tiny and fessed up that I was CIC, and told him I was going to take off and go back to the CIC."

Dunwiddie picked up the story: "So I told Al . . ."

Hammersmith wondered, incredulously: *You were this sergeant, now first sergeant?*

". . . by then we were pretty close, that I had learned Charley Company was about to be assigned to provide security for OSS Forward, and that I thought the smart thing to do was stick around until that happened. It would be smarter than wandering around France with nothing to prove he was CIC, that he'd probably get grabbed by the MPs as a deserter. He asked how I *knew* Charley Company was going to go guard the OSS, and I told him."

"And how the hell did you know?" Hammersmith blurted.

Dunwiddie looked at Hammersmith for a moment before saying, "General White told me."

"The commanding general of the 2nd Armored Division personally told you, a first sergeant, where your unit was to be assigned?" Hammersmith challenged.

"Yes, he did," Dunwiddie said.

"What happened, Hammersmith," Wallace said, "was that when SHAEF ordered White to come up with a company to be put on indefinite temporary duty with the OSS, he looked at the morning reports to see which company he could best spare. He came on Charley Company, which was down to zero officers and sixty-seven EM, and was being temporarily commanded by its first sergeant.

"And then he noticed the first sergeant's name — Chauncey L. Dunwiddie is not a common name — so he got on the horn and called First Sergeant Dunwiddie and learned he was indeed his godson. General White and Tiny's father, Colonel Dunwiddie, are Norwich classmates — class of '20. First Sergeant Dunwiddie was supposed to be '45, but he resigned from Norwich and enlisted because he was afraid the war would be over before he got in it.

"General White then got on the horn again and tried to call Bob Mattingly at OSS Forward, to tell him who was commanding the company he was sending him. Mattingly was off somewhere, protecting the OSS from the Army, so I took the call.

"Tiny reported to me at OSS Forward, and as soon as I'd told him what was going to be expected of Charley Company, he told me one of his sergeants had 'an unusual personnel problem.' Enter Al.

"I got on the horn to General Greene, and asked him about CIC Special Agent Finney. Greene said he thought he was MIA, either dead or a POW. I told him he was alive and well and had gotten himself promoted to sergeant and had picked up a Purple Heart and a Bronze Star while looking for Communist agitators during the Battle of the Bulge . . ."

"Which resulted," Finney put in, smiling, "in my dad and mother getting three more telegrams, one saying I had been 'recovered,' a second saying I had the Bronze Star, and a third saying I had been wounded in action but was expected to recover. They were going crazy."

". . . and how I had found this out," Wallace continued. "Then I asked Greene what he wanted me to do with Al. After thinking it over for maybe ten seconds, he said something to the effect that if he was such a lousy CIC agent that he couldn't find Communist agitators in a unit commanded by the son of an old pal, he probably couldn't find them anywhere, so why didn't I just keep him. 'And tell Tiny to say hello to his dad.'

"A couple of days later, orders came down transferring Al to the OSS, and we've been stuck with him since."

"Why don't we get back to why Jim thinks Commandant Fortin is interested in Odessa?" General Gehlen asked.

"Fortin told us, sir," Finney said, "that when the Germans — the SS — learned that he was in England with de Gaulle — they and the Milice, their French assistants — arrested Fortin's mother, wife, and two young children for interrogation. When that was over, they threw their bodies in the Rhine.

"Fortin told us the only reason he hadn't arrested Luther Stauffer and had him tried as a collaborator was that he had become convinced that Stauffer was involved with Odessa, and that breaking that up and catching the people involved was more important to him than putting Stauffer in jail."

"And then he asked," Cronley said, "how I would feel about using Al to get inside Odessa. What he proposed was that Al return, alone, with more PX goody packages, and tell Cousin Luther he was en route to Salzburg. Cousin Luther would then ask a favor, a small favor — something like giving the packages to someone in Salzburg, or someplace else over the border. Maybe he'd offer to pay him. Anything that would put Al on the slippery slope."

"And what did you say?" General Gehlen asked.

"I told him I'd think about it, and also

that I would ask General Greene for what he had on Odessa and pass it on to him. I was also planning on asking you, General, but I didn't tell Fortin that."

"And did you contact General Greene?" Gehlen asked.

"No, sir. When we came back from Vienna, Major Wallace said, 'Let the CIC deal with that. It's none of our business.' And then we got involved getting the Likharevs across the border and I didn't do anything."

"You'd say Commandant Fortin's idea is still active?" Mannberg asked.

Cronley nodded.

"Al, are you willing to get involved in something like this?" Wallace asked.

"Yes, sir."

"Knowing that if you find something interesting, and Odessa learns you have found — or are even looking for — something interesting, you're liable to find yourself tossed into the Rhine?"

"Yes, sir."

"Jim, I would like to report to El Jefe that you have decided this Odessa business is DCI-Europe's Number One covert project," Wallace said.

Cronley raised his hand in the manner of a Roman emperor.

"I so decree," he pronounced solemnly.

"You may so inform El Jefe."

"El Jefe will be *so* pleased," Wallace said, shaking his head and smiling.

# IV

## [ONE]

*Main Dining Room*

*Hotel Vier Jahreszeiten*

*Maximilianstrasse 178*

*Munich, American Zone of Occupation, Germany*

*0815 25 January 1946*

When Captain Jim Cronley walked up to the table where Lieutenants Tom Winters and Bruce Moriarty were sitting with their wives and Claudette Colbert and Freddy Hessinger, the men rose.

"Sit," Cronley ordered. "Good morning. Sorry to be late. Major Wallace asked if I could spare him a minute, which turned out to be fifteen."

His statement earned polite chuckles.

He pulled the chair away from the head of the table, placed a very full leather briefcase on the floor, and sat down.

A waiter appeared almost immediately

and took Cronley's order for ham and eggs, rye toast, orange juice, milk, and a coffee. Without consciously deciding to do so, he had spoken in German.

"I'm impressed," Ginger said. "I wish I could speak German like that."

"How was the trip from Fritzlar?" he asked.

"Just dandy. I felt like a movie star. That was my first time being driven anywhere by a chauffeur armed with a submachine gun."

"Has Bone . . . *Bruce* . . . told you why that was necessary?"

"Mr. Hessinger," she said, "told me part of it in Fritzlar, and then he and Bruce filled in the details when we got here."

"And has Freddy assured you there's nothing to be worried about? That we were just being careful?"

"He and Claudette told us that," Barbara Winters said. "And she also told us why."

"What happens next," Cronley said, "is that whenever you're ready — today or tomorrow, whenever — Claudette will take you out to the Compound and you can pick your quarters. They're actually very nice."

"And inside three barbed wire fences," Ginger said, somewhat sarcastic, "or so Claudette told us."

"Enough, honey," Moriarty said, on the

edge of unpleasantly. "We're here. Adjust to it."

"Sorry," she said, sounding genuinely contrite, which surprised Cronley.

"You said Tom and I can go out to this place whenever we're ready," Barbara Winters said. "How about right after breakfast?"

"That's not an option," Cronley said. "Right after breakfast, Tom and I are going flying. Sorry."

"Flying where?" Claudette asked.

"That's what Wallace wanted to talk to me about. Greene sent a briefcase full of material about a certain subject he thought I should pass to the Frenchman as soon as possible."

"What we could do, Barbara," Claudette said, "is go out to the Compound with them. And then I could show you around the Compound, look at quarters, and then bring you back here."

"You don't need me to pick quarters, sweetheart," Winters said.

"I like to pretend your opinion matters," she said, smiling.

"Can we all fit in the Kapitän?" Cronley asked, and then answered his own question. "Yeah. Six'll fit."

"Does that mean Bruce and I get to go?" Ginger said.

"I would never leave you out of anything, Ginger," Cronley said. "You know that."

She snorted.

Cronley's breakfast was delivered.

"You're going to leave what Major Wallace gave you with the Frenchman?" Hessinger asked, and then when Cronley nodded, asked, "Do Dette and I get a look before you do that?"

"You'd have to take it to the office," Cronley said.

"I think we should have a look, Captain," Claudette said.

"I will finish my breakfast slowly," he said. "But don't dally."

Cronley handed the briefcase to Hessinger and then Claudette followed Hessinger out of the dining room.

Ten minutes later, Augie Ziegler walked up to the table. As soon as Cronley had introduced him, he asked, "Dette not here yet?"

"Dette has been here, and is now in the office," Cronley replied. "Looking at something you should see."

"Before or after I have my breakfast?"

"Now."

"I hear and obey," Ziegler said, and quickly left.

"Claudette's gentleman friend?" Ginger asked.

"I don't know," Cronley said.

"He acted like it."

"I don't know about that, either. But come to think of it, you're kindred souls."

"How so?"

"He's a CID agent. Always asking questions."

"It sounded as if he was working for you," Ginger said.

"Ginger said," Bonehead said, "proving Jim's point."

"Score one for Bonehead," Cronley said.

Claudette, Ziegler, and Hessinger walked up to the table. Hessinger handed Cronley the briefcase.

"Colonel Bristol called when we were in the office," Claudette said. "He's at the Compound and would like a word with you. Something about having to lay more 110-volt lines to the houses. The refrigerators came, but they won't run on 220."

"Would that be Lieutenant Colonel Jack Bristol? Engineer type?" Winters asked.

"You know him?" Cronley asked.

"He's Barbara's cousin," Winters said.

"That should prove very useful," Cronley said.

"We really should have a copy of what's in that briefcase in our files," Claudette interrupted. "Augie says if you can give him two hours, he can Leica them."

"I don't have two hours," Cronley said, and stood up. "But you're right. We need that stuff copied. I'll have to think of something. Let's go, people."

## [Two]

*The South German Industrial Development*

*Organization Compound*

*Pullach, Bavaria*

*American Zone of Occupation, Germany*

*0905 25 January 1946*

While they were in the car — Cronley driving, Winters and Moriarty in the front seat beside him, and the women in the back — en route to the Compound, Winters had asked, in almost a whisper, "What the hell does 'Leica them' mean?"

"What?"

"Miss Colbert said something about Ziegler being able to 'Leica.' "

"You can say 'Leica' out loud," Cronley explained, chuckling. "It's no big secret. If you have a Leica Model Ic or better camera,

152

and a holder for it, and the right film, you can take pictures of documents. And then if you have a Leica whatchamacallit — Leica Projector — to *project* the negative, you can make prints that are a hell of a lot easier to read than blueprints — they're in black and white and color — and you can do that a hell of a lot faster than you can make blueprint copies."

"I thought everybody knew that," Bonehead said.

"Fuck you," Lieutenant Winters said.

"Watch your mouth!" Mrs. Winters snapped from the backseat.

Lieutenant Colonel John J. Bristol, CE, was sitting in his jeep at the inner checkpoint waiting for Cronley to arrive at the Compound.

When he did, Bristol got out of the jeep and walked up to the Kapitän. Cronley rolled down the window of the driver's door.

"I guess Claudette's already told you," Bristol greeted Cronley, "about the refrigerators?"

"Yes, she did."

"We have a tractor trailer full of them from the Giessen Quartermaster Depot, none of which run on 220 volts DC."

"So she said," Cronley said.

"If you need a few of them right away . . ."

"I need two right away."

"Okay. I can run temporary 110 lines from the power station this morning. Where do you want them?"

"Off the top of my head, one of them probably goes to wherever your cousin Barbara picks for her quarters."

"My cousin Barbara?" Bristol said, and then looked into the backseat, where Claudette, Ginger, and Barbara were sitting.

"Jesus, Barb! I didn't see you back there. Sorry. What the hell are you doing here?"

"First, I'm going to select quarters, and then I'm going to sit around waiting to be a mother."

"You're going to be in the Compound?" he asked, surprised.

"Hello, Jack," Tom Winters said, leaning across Cronley to offer his hand.

"And this is Bruce Moriarty," Cronley said. "He's taking over Compound security. And Mrs. Moriarty."

The men shook hands. Bristol said, "Lieutenant," and Moriarty said, "Colonel."

Mrs. Moriarty said, "I'm Ginger, who's also going to need a refrigerator while I'm locked up behind barbed wire waiting to be a mother."

"Speaking of barbed wire, Jim," Bristol

said, "now that we don't really need it, we got a tractor-trailer load of that last night. Should I send it back?"

"If you've got somewhere to store it," Cronley replied, "I suggest keeping it."

"There's a rumor going around that Dette —"

"Unfortunately, it's not a rumor," Cronley said. "She can tell you all about it while you're showing the ladies the quarters. But right now, and I mean right now, Tom and I have to go flying. How about you follow us to the airstrip?"

### [THREE]

*Entzheim Airport*

*Strasbourg, France*

*1120 25 January 1946*

When Winters parked the L-4 in front of Base Operations at the airfield, Commandant Jean-Paul Fortin, a natty man in his early thirties with a trim mustache, was waiting for them. Fortin was wearing U.S. Army ODs with his French rank insignia — shoulder boards with four gold stripes — on the epaulets and a French officer's "kepi."

Cronley saluted and Fortin returned it.

"Your man Hessinger telephoned to tell me you were coming," Fortin said in German.

"Thank you for meeting us," Cronley replied in German. "Commandant, this is Lieutenant Winters."

Winters saluted and said, "Mon Commandant."

"You speak French," Fortin said in French. It was impossible to determine if it was an observation, a question, or a challenge.

"Sir, let's say I was exposed to French for four years at school," Winters said in English.

"So was I," Cronley said. "With little or no effect."

Fortin switched to German: "So you are now Captain Cronley's French-speaking pilot, Lieutenant?"

"Why do I suspect you're really asking, 'How much can I say before this officer?'" Cronley said.

"Because you have a naturally suspicious nature?"

"That's supposed to be an asset in our line of work," Cronley said. "I wouldn't want this to get around, Commandant, but Lieutenant Winters is a special agent of the DCI. You can tell him all your secrets."

"People in our line of work should never tell anyone all their secrets."

"Write that down, Tom," Cronley said. "And remind me when I forget."

"Hessinger said you have something for me," Fortin said.

Cronley handed him the briefcase.

"This is?"

"What General Greene has on Odessa."

"It all fits in one briefcase?"

"I haven't had a chance to look at it, but I suspect it's what he thought you don't already have."

"You don't know what's in here?"

"Which brings us to that. Have you the facilities to copy what's in there?"

"You didn't make copies?"

"I'm sure General Greene did. What I would like to do is see that you have copies. Then, when I get back to Germany, I will give General Greene his originals back, and he will give me his copies."

"Was there some reason you didn't have copies made before you came here?"

Cronley raised his eyebrows. "Which brings us to that. My superiors have told me that if we can slow down, or at least seriously impede, Odessa, at the same time bagging three or four former senior officers of the SS — even better, of the SS-

Sicherheitsdienst — who are running it, it would tend to squash those terrible rumors going around that there's something called Operation Ost which has been slipping Nazis out of Germany to Argentina. With that in mind, I wanted to get the briefcase to you as soon as possible."

"May I infer that DCI is now going to work with the DST to deal with Odessa?"

"You may infer that DCI is now going to work with Commandant Jean-Paul Fortin. I don't know anyone else in the DST and I don't trust anyone I don't know."

"You seem to be trusting me."

"You have such an innocent face, Mon Commandant, how could anyone not trust you?"

"So that's why it took you so long to get back here: You were waiting for permission from your superiors."

Cronley nodded.

*I didn't say, "That's it."*

*But I nodded. And he thinks I said, "Yes."*

*The reason I didn't get back here before this is because Wallace told me to let Odessa lie.*

*Which makes my nod a lie.*

*And I didn't think it through before I lied. My mouth went on automatic.*

*As it tends to do.*

"Sergent Deladier's over there with my

car," Fortin said, pointing. "I suggest we get in it, go to the DST photo lab, tell them to Leica everything in here, and while they're doing that, go have our lunch. I am so pleased that DCI's going to work on Odessa with me that I will even pay for the lunch."

## [FOUR]

*Gurtlerhoft*

*13 Place de la Cathédrale*

*Strasbourg, France*

*1215 25 January 1946*

"The cellar is about the only part of the building that wasn't torn up in the war," Commandant Jean-Paul Fortin said as he led them through the basement of the building. He pointed to the high arched ceiling. "Those held up is why. I requisitioned it for DST. I'm still wondering why."

"Excuse me?" Cronley asked.

"Perhaps it was because my mother used to bring me here as a child, and later, I used to bring my wife here. Or maybe because it was the favorite place for SS officers when les Boches were here. Anyway, I requisitioned it for DST, and it's proved quite useful."

As they entered a small alcove, Fortin

pointed again to the arched ceiling and to the walls.

"It's impossible to hide a microphone in the masonry, and when Sergent Deladier puts the heavy felt drape in place — which he is about to do . . ."

*"Oui, Mon Commandant,"* the sergeant, who looked to be in his fifties, said.

". . . one could set off a bomb in here, and it wouldn't be heard on the other side. So no one — save Sergent Deladier, who is one of the DST people I hope you will learn to trust as I do — will overhear our conversation."

There was one table, set for six, in the alcove. A waiter immediately appeared.

Fortin turned to Winters and said, "I don't know if Captain Cronley has told you this, Lieutenant —"

"I thought we were now pals," Cronley interrupted, "on a first-name basis."

"And so we are," Fortin said. "I will call the lieutenant by his Christian name. Which is?"

"Thomas, sir," Winters said. "Or Tom. Whichever you prefer."

"Thomas. And the both of you may call me either 'sir' or 'commandant,' whichever you prefer."

Winters wondered, *Is he kidding, or does*

160

*he mean that?*

"Don't hold your breath, Jean-Paul, waiting for me to call you 'sir,' " Cronley said. "Our relationship is that of partners, equal partners."

"The reason Jim is so suspicious of me, Thomas, is that he's half Alsatian, and is aware that we Alsatians are infamous for our ability to charm people out of their shoes. Or into the pants of the gentle sex."

*It looks like you Alsatians share a sense of sarcastic humor, too, Mon Commandant.*

*You sound just like Cronley.*

"Jim even knows what Choucroute Garnie à l'Alsacienne, which is what — before I knew you were coming — I told the kitchen to prepare for our lunch. It's sauerkraut garnished with smoked pork. If that doesn't please you, I'm sure the kitchen can fix a hamburger or something else from your barbaric American cuisine."

"What you said sounds fine, sir," Winters said, smiling.

"Why are you not in your usual sour mood?" Cronley asked.

Fortin didn't reply for a moment, and when he did, the tone of his voice made it clear he was now being absolutely serious.

"Because we are, as you put it, going to be partners. When you didn't come back, I

161

began to think that you, too, had gotten a message from on high to leave Odessa alone."

"Quite the opposite," Cronley said. "But have people on high told you to leave Odessa alone?"

"Not in so many words. But subtly. So subtly that I suspect the Vatican is involved. I was actually about to go to Le General de Gaulle. I didn't want to do that, and now I don't think I will have to. I think I can get from you the logistical and other support that has been denied me."

"Whatever you need."

"Thank you. Starting with photographic paper and chemicals, I hope. Leica-ing the contents of that briefcase is going to just about exhaust what's in my lab."

"Get me a list of what you need and get me on a secure line, and I'll have it on its way here this afternoon."

"Deladier, make up a list of what the lab needs. Captain Cronley can take it back with him to Munich."

*"Oui, Mon Commandant,"* the sergeant said, and went to a sideboard and took out a telephone.

A white-jacketed waiter appeared.

"Getting back to the more pleasant subject of our lunch," Fortin said, "I suggest we

162

begin with a bottle of Crémant d'Alsace. It's a sparkling wine, champagne in everything but name."

"We'll have to pass, thanks," Cronley said.

"Because you think I am going to ply you with champagne to loosen your tongues?"

"That, too, but Tom and I are flying, and I like to do that sober."

"I'd forgotten," Fortin replied. "I often think it was probably much more pleasant a century ago when officers could take a little wine and then get on a horse which knew the way home."

"I would hate to have to ride a horse back to Munich," Cronley said.

Fortin ordered their meal, and the waiter left.

"Are you going to tell us what you know about Odessa now?" Cronley asked. "Or hold us in suspense until after we have our lunch?"

Fortin shrugged.

"It actually started here," he said, "or *Die Spinne* — the Spider — did. In August 1944. In the Maison Rouge Hotel, right around the corner from here, on Rue Des Francs-Bourgeois —"

"Excuse me, Mon Commandant," Winters interrupted. "I never heard any of this before. I'd like to take notes."

"I have full confidence that any notes you make will not become general knowledge," Fortin said. His tone suggested that his confidence was anything but full.

"No, sir, they won't get out. They're just for me."

"Good idea, Tom," Cronley said. "This is all new to me, too. But on the subject of notes, make one to tell Barbara that anything that goes on in the Compound is not to be shared with the OLIN. And if you see him before I do, make sure Bonehead gets the same message to Ginger. No offense, Tom, but I have very painfully learned the hazards of pillow talk."

"None taken, sir. Barbara — my wife, Commandant — is an Army brat. She knows the rules. And I tell her as little as possible. I'll talk to Moriarty."

"What's OLIN?" Fortin asked. "Who's Bonehead?"

"It's short for the Officers' Ladies Intelligence Network," Cronley explained.

Fortin laughed, and then asked, "And Moriarty is Bonehead? Meaning not too bright?"

"Quite the opposite," Cronley said. "He got that name in our first year in college."

"That would be Texas A&M, correct?" Fortin said. "The military school?"

*How the hell did he find that out?*

"That's right. Anyway, after his haircut was found unsatisfactory, Private Moriarty shaved his head."

"And, if I may ask, where did you go to university, Lieutenant?"

"The U.S. Military Academy, sir," Winters said. "West Point?"

"I'm sure Captain Cronley has told you how important it is that it not get out that we're — how should I phrase this? — *intensifying* our interest in Odessa."

"Yes, sir, he has."

"But on that subject, Jean-Paul," Cronley said, "the night before last an attempt was made to kidnap two of my people."

"And?"

"It failed. My administrative officer killed three of them with head shots from a pistol she carries in her brassiere. And she wounded a fourth man. We are now interrogating him. Odds are they're NKGB but we don't know that."

"This woman . . ."

"Claudette Colbert, like the movie star. You'll be dealing with her."

". . . killed three of these people? With a pistol she carries in her brassiere? Did I understand you to say that?"

Cronley nodded.

"Formidable!" Fortin said admiringly.

"Yes, she is."

"Let me know what you find out about an NKGB connection."

"Absolutely," Cronley said, and then went on: "You were telling us how Odessa was started here in Strasbourg."

"It wasn't called Odessa then," Fortin said. "What was formed here was called 'the Spider.' Odessa — Organisation der Ehemaligen SS-Angehörigen — former members of the SS — wasn't formed until after the German capitulation.

"What happened was that after Operation Overlord — the Normandy landing — was successful, and the Soviet advance from the East couldn't be stopped, it became obvious to just about everybody but Hitler himself that the war was lost.

"The upper level of German industrialists and bankers, who were the opposite of stupid, had heard of SS plans to escape the wrath of the Russians by going to South America. And they had figured out that senior SS officers were interested only in getting themselves out and didn't care about German businessmen. So they set up a secret meeting here. At the Maison Rouge."

"Who were 'they'?" Cronley asked.

"There were about thirty participants. I

can give you a complete list, but I would be surprised if there's not already one in General Greene's material. The important ones were Kurt von Schröder, the banker; Emil Kirdorf, who either owned outright or controlled Germany's coal mines; Georg von Schnitzler of IG Farben; Gustav Krupp von Bohlen und Halbach — Herr Krupp himself; and Fritz Thyssen, who owned just about all of the steel mills.

"There were also a number of Roman Catholic clergy at the meeting. The Vatican has always been good at keeping secrets, and we don't know much about them. They are identified in the minutes of the meeting, which we think we have intact, as Father G. and Bishop M., and the like. The tentative identifications I have made of the Vatican contingent I will give you, although I suspect General Greene already has them."

"It might be interesting to compare your list with Greene's," Cronley said.

"Yes, it would," Fortin said. "What I was going to say is that there is a common thread in my tentative identifications. Many of the priests and two of the bishops were Franciscans."

"May I ask a question? Questions?" Winters asked.

"You're supposed to," Cronley said.

"Why was the Church involved in this?"

"You said 'the Church,' " Fortin said. "That suggests you're a Roman Catholic."

"I am."

"Others would have said 'the Roman Catholic Church.' "

"I suppose that's true," Winters said.

"What about you, Jim?"

"I'm Episcopalian. Church of England."

"And your mother?"

"She left the Catholic Church — maybe was kicked out — when she married my father. Now she's head of the Altar Guild at Saint Thomas's Episcopal Church in Midland."

The waiter returned, carrying an enormous tray with one hand.

He laid plates of Choucroute Garnie à l'Alsacienne before them. Winters saw that it was mounds of browned sauerkraut heavily laced with chunks of roasted pork. The smell made him salivate.

"My father was Roman," Fortin said, after he'd finished his first mouthful and then washed it down with healthy swallows of the sparkling Crémant d'Alsace. "When he married my mother — an *Evangalische,* a Lutheran — she had to sign a document stating any children of the union would be raised as Romans. I was. My mother was in the habit of saying unkind things about the Roman Church. This invariably distressed my father, who was rather devout. Are you distressed, or outraged, Thomas, when someone questions the motives of Holy Mother Church?"

"Annoyed, usually, depending on what is said, and by whom."

"My mother used to say that the primary responsibility of Roman Catholic Church clergy is the preservation of the Roman Catholic Church. Does that offend you, Thomas?"

Winters visibly considered the question before replying, "I'm not sure I agree with it, but it doesn't offend me."

"I began to be disillusioned about the Roman Church at Saint-Cyr," Fortin said. "My fellow cadets began to say terrible things about it . . ."

"What sort of terrible things?" Winters asked.

". . . yet seemed to get away with it. There was no lightning bolt from heaven to incinerate them where they stood."

"What sort of terrible things?" Winters repeated.

"Well, for example, that the Pope — *Popes,* Pius the Eleventh, and Pius the Twelfth, who succeeded him, were, if not actually Fascists, then the next thing to Fascists."

"Did they say why?" Winters asked softly.

"They pointed to the Vatican Concordat of 1929," Fortin said.

"I have no idea what that is," Cronley said.

"It was the deal struck between the Roman Church — Pius the Eleventh — and Italy — Mussolini — which made the Vatican — all forty-four hectares of it — a sovereign state."

"A hectare is two and a half acres, right?" Winters asked.

Both Fortin and Cronley nodded, and Fortin went on.

"With a population of about eight hundred people. Now, my irreverent classmates pointed out to me, while this was certainly a good thing for the Roman Church, it also silenced criticism by the Church of Mussolini and his Fascists.

"They also pointed out to me that Hitler freely admitted that Mussolini was his inspiration for the Nazi Party. Which brings us to the Reichskonkordat of 1933."

"I have to confess I don't know what that is," Winters said. "Which probably makes me look more stupid than I like to think I am."

"I don't know what that is, either," Cronley confessed.

"There is a difference between ignorance and stupidity," Fortin said. "I know Jim isn't stupid, and I don't think you are. But ignorant, yes. The both of you are ignorant of things you really should know in our line of business."

Cronley thought: *I have just been called ignorant. Why am I not pissed off?*

*Because ol' Jean-Paul is right on the fucking money.*

*I've never heard of the Vatican Concordat or — what the hell did he say? — the Reichskonkordat — until just now.*

"What's the Reichskonkordat?"

"A treaty signed between what was by then the sovereign state of the Vatican and Germany in July of 1933, just as Hitler was coming to power. It did the same thing, basically, as the Vatican Concordat. The Germans agreed to recognize most of what the Vatican wanted recognized, and the Vatican shut off criticism of the Nazis by the clergy of the Roman Church in Germany.

"It was signed on behalf of the Vatican, or Pius the Eleventh, if you prefer, by Vatican Secretary of State Eugenio Cardinal Pacelli. He was later Papal Nuncio — ambassador — to the Thousand-Year Reich, and later, when Pius the Eleventh died in 1939, Cardinal Pacelli became Pope Pius the Twelfth."

"Frankly, I never heard any of this before," Winters said. "Either I was asleep during that history class at West Point . . ."

Cronley thought: *Me, too. I did a lot of sleeping through classes at College Station.*

". . . or that wasn't presented," Winters went on. "The only time I thought about the Church and the Nazis was when I heard that Count von . . . Whatsisname? The blind-in-one-eye guy who put the bomb under Hitler's table . . ."

"Von Stauffenberg," Cronley furnished. "Colonel Count Claus von Stauffenberg."

". . . and just missed blowing the sonofabitch up was a devout Catholic. I wondered how he handled the 'Thou Shalt Not Kill' commandment."

"I was probably asleep, too, during that class," Cronley said. "I heard about von Stauffenberg from a friend of mine. Hitler hung — strangled — my friend's father from a butcher's hook for his involvement in the bomb plot."

"Your friend?" Fortin asked.

"Hans-Peter von Wachtstein. Now the Graf von Wachtstein. He was a Luftwaffe fighter pilot. Now he's a pilot for SAA."

"For what?"

"South American Airways. Argentine. It's a DCI asset."

"You . . . we . . . have an airline?" Winters asked, visibly surprised.

"At the moment. Juan Domingo Perón, the Argentine strongman, is threatening to seize it."

"So that's how you've been getting people to Argentina. You own the Argentine airline," Fortin said.

"Operative phrase 'at the moment.' "

"I'd like to hear more about that, but right now" — he paused and then continued — "the argument advanced to justify the Vatican Concordat and the Reichskonkordat was that the Italian Fascists and the German Nazis would have been even nastier to the Italians and the Germans — and of course the Church — had there been no concords.

"I accepted that all through the war, until I came back to Strasbourg and learned what the Church had done, or had not done, with regard to my family."

"I don't understand," Winters said.

"You didn't tell him, Jim?" Fortin asked.

Cronley shook his head. "Not in detail. Just what happened to them."

"When France fell," Fortin said, "I went to England and served with the Free

French. The Germans — actually their lapdogs, the Milice — here in Strasbourg —"

"The Milice?" Winters parroted. "Doesn't that mean 'militia'?"

"The word does. *The* Milice was a paramilitary organization set up by the Vichy government, primarily to fight the Underground. Some of them — like Jim's cousin Luther — were Nazis, or at least Nazi sympathizers. Others believed they were doing God's work fighting the Underground, which after Hitler invaded Russia had become substantially — or even predominantly — Communist. And other men joined the Milice to keep from getting sent to Germany as slave laborers.

"Anyway, the Milice here in Strasbourg somehow got the idea that I had returned to work with the Underground and arrested my family — my mother, my wife, and my children — for interrogation. When the interrogation was over, the Milice threw their bodies into the Rhine."

"Captain Cronley told me that," Winters said, adding, "Jesus Christ!"

"I was never in the Underground. I served at General de Gaulle's headquarters and returned to Strasbourg only with General Leclerc's 2nd Armored Division. My wife and my mother knew where I was, and — through my mother — our priest knew that I was not, and never had been, in Strasbourg since the war began.

"When I asked Father Kramer why he had not gone to SS-Brigadeführer Kollmer, to whom he was serving Mass every Sunday in the Cathedral of Our Lady of Strasbourg and with whom he was dining — in this very restaurant — on a weekly basis and told him that he knew my mother and my wife and my children had no information of any kind of any possible interest to the Sicherheitsdienst, he said that as much as he would have liked to have done so, I would understand he couldn't, as doing so would endanger the relationship he — the Church — had built with the Sicherheitsdienst."

"Nice guy," Cronley said bitterly.

"You have to understand, Jim, that he believed in what he told me. His most important duty was to protect the Church."

"Fuck him!" Cronley said.

"Is this priest still here in Strasbourg?" Winters asked.

"No. They found Father Kramer's body floating in the Rhine. Person or persons unknown had apparently shot him four times with a .22 caliber weapon. In his elbows and knees. If he tried to swim, when he was thrown off the wharf, it must have been excruciatingly painful."

Fortin paused long enough for this to sink in, and then went on:

"I thought it should be understood between us that if, as we try to shut down Odessa and find the people running it, we find that members of the Catholic clergy are involved, I am going to find it hard — virtually impossible — to look away, to accept the rationale that all they are doing is their duty to the Church."

For a long moment there was silence. Cronley finally broke it.

"I think it should be understood between us, Jean-Paul, that if — when — we find such people, what happens to them will be mutually agreed between us. If you can't live with that, it's what in Texas we call a deal breaker. Are we agreed?"

Fortin shrugged, then nodded.

"As I was saying," Fortin went on, "what the German industrialists and the representatives of the Vatican did was set up a system — the Spider — to get the industrialists and — how do I put this? — *friends* of the Vatican out of what was to become Occupied Germany through Switzerland and then into Italy. From Italy, they made their way to South America. This involved arranging for false identity documents, passports, contacts, and safe houses. It came to be known as the Monastery Route because most of the safe houses were in monasteries."

"Mon Commandant," Winters said, "I'm willing to take your word that the Church was involved in this, but I don't understand why they would be."

"A variety of reasons, starting with, I suggest, what my mother was always saying about the first responsibility of the Church being its self-preservation. The most dangerous enemy of the Church was — is — the Soviet Union. The Nazis had fought the Communists. What's that line in the Bible about enemies?"

"It's in Exodus," Cronley said, and then quoted: " 'I will be an enemy to your enemies, and I will oppose those who oppose you.' "

"Again, you surprise me, Jim," Fortin said. "I would never have guessed you were a biblical scholar."

"When I was a choir boy at Saint Thomas, I used to read the Bible during the sermons to keep me awake. That line stuck in my mind."

"Philosophy aside," Fortin went on, "there was — is — a great deal of money involved.

I probably should say 'treasure.' The Church wanted to get its money — and to be fair, its holy relics, including those few not encased in solid gold — out of the areas it knew the Soviets would now control, especially in Hungary and elsewhere in Eastern Europe, before the Reds got their hands on any of it.

"Anyway, that's how it got started. When Germany surrendered, the worst of the Nazis — those who went into hiding to avoid being hung — took the Spider over from what few businessmen were still left in Germany. It became Odessa."

"But the Church is still involved?" Winters asked.

"There is absolutely no question that it is involved. What is not clear is how deeply. That is one of the things I intend to find out."

"Can I ask how?" Winters said. "I mean, isn't the CIC already doing that?"

"I am told that they are, but with little success that I'm aware of," Fortin replied, then looked at Cronley. "Jim?"

"According to General Greene, they haven't been at all successful," Cronley said. "We know some names — that's another list you should compare with yours — but we can't find them. Which Greene attributes to their having lots of dollars."

"Dollars are still even more valuable in the current economy than Nescafé, cigarettes, and canned hams," Fortin said. "Which brings us back to that. The last time Jim was here, Thomas, we were agreed that since infiltrating Odessa at the top was just about impossible — they don't trust anyone they don't know — the only way to do that is from the bottom."

"I don't understand," Winters said.

"Luther Stauffer, we believe, thinks his cousin Jim is a pleasant, none-too-bright second lieutenant of the Quartermaster Corps, one who unknowingly controls a means to transport things — and things would include people — all over Occupied Germany, Austria, and this part of France without raising suspicion as he and his team renovate mess hall equipment."

"Clever," Winters said.

"I'm tempted to say 'thank you,'" Cronley said, "but the truth is that it wasn't planned. It just happened. Dumb luck. We were wearing that Quartermaster disguise to get us into Vienna without attracting the attention of the NKGB, not to fool my cousin Luther."

"Nevertheless, the situation exists," Fortin said, "offering us a chance to, at the very least, track somebody being moved through Odessa, to see where he goes, and maybe even where he came from."

"What we talked about doing, Tom," Cronley said, "is sending Sergeant Finney and some of Tiny's Troopers back here to drop off more PX goodies from my mother, while he's en route to Salzburg and then Vienna . . ."

He paused, smiled, chuckled, and added: "We could put a couple of those refrigerators that won't run on 220 volts in the ambulance. Who but the Quartermaster Corps would have new refrigerators that don't work?"

Winters chuckled.

Fortin said, "I have no idea what you're talking about."

"Jean-Paul, I just happen to have a trailer-load of brand-new 110-volt refrigerators," Cronley said, and told him why. "Would you like one?"

"Oh, yes! Actually, I could use two. One to replace the one in my house, which is ancient, and another for Sergent Deladier."

Winters thought: *He has to be kidding!*

"Then two you shall have," Cronley said. "Any preference in color? How about pastel yellow?"

"But," Fortin said, "I would have to send

for them . . ."

*I'll be a sonofabitch, he's not kidding! He wants the refrigerators!*

". . . and questions would be asked if you unloaded them from your ambulance at the home of the chief of DST. I know Odessa is watching me, and I suspect so is the NKGB. Would two of them fit in a jeep trailer?"

"I think so," Cronley said.

"We could have Jack take a couple of them to the Engineer Depot," Winters said. "And the commandant's people could pick them up there instead of from the Compound."

"Perhaps we could get the photographic supplies the same way," Fortin said. "That way there would be only one supply mission."

"Lieutenant Winters will set it up, Mon Commandant," Cronley said.

"And Jack probably has 220-to-110 transformers," Winters said.

"Who is this Jack?" Fortin said. "Is he going to ask questions?"

"Lieutenant Colonel Jack Bristol, who happens to be Lieutenant Winters's wife's cousin, is the Corps of Engineers officer charged with setting up and maintaining the Pullach Compound," Cronley said. "He's both in the loop and knows how to keep his mouth shut."

"Sergent Deladier," Fortin said. "Two things."

*"Oui, Mon Commandant?"*

"First, arrange a jeep with a trailer attached for Capitaine DuPres to drive first thing in the morning to Munich — where in Munich, Jim?"

"The Engineer Depot."

"The Engineer Depot, to pick up our refrigerators and photographic supplies."

*"Oui, Mon Commandant."*

"And now, before DuPres shows up here with the Leica-ed Odessa material, load two cases of the Crémant d'Alsace into our car, so that our friends here can take them, as a gesture of our appreciation, with them in their airplane."

*"Oui, Mon Commandant."*

"There's no way we can get two cases of champagne into an L-4," Cronley said.

"One case?"

"One case'll fit," Winters said.

"Then we'll put one case in your airplane, and the second in Capitaine DuPres's jeep," Fortin said.

As if on cue, the heavy curtain separating the alcove from the rest of the basement restaurant was suddenly pushed aside by a man so strange-looking that Cronley started to reach for his pistol.

182

He was very tall, had a very dark complexion, large dark eyes, and was wearing a turban and what looked like a bathrobe. A Thompson submachine gun hung from his shoulder. Two stick magazines for the Thompson and a knife almost large enough to be called a sword were jammed behind his wide leather belt.

Cronley relaxed when a second man came into the alcove.

This one was a very short, very thin French Army officer, who, like Fortin, wore U.S. Army ODs with the insignia of his rank — in this case, the triple stripes of a *capitaine* — on shoulder boards.

The *capitaine* marched up to Fortin, saluted crisply, and when it was returned, laid Cronley's briefcase on the table.

"Gentlemen, may I present Capitaine DuPres?" Fortin said.

Captain DuPres exchanged salutes with Cronley and Winters separately before shaking their hands.

"Capitaine DuPres is another of us who I think you should trust," Fortin said. "In support of that argument, he ran off from Strasbourg in 1941 at age seventeen to join first the Underground, and then the Free French in Morocco. During the war, the Milice rounded up the Jews in Strasbourg,

183

DuPres's entire family among them, and shipped them off to the ovens in Germany."

Without thinking about it, Cronley did the math.

*I'll be damned.*

*I am not the only twenty-two-year-old captain in the world!*

"May I ask who this fellow is?" Winters asked, nodding at the turbaned man.

"When DuPres managed to get himself out of France," Fortin went on, "he was given a commission as a *sous-lieutenant* and assigned to the 2nd Moroccan Tabors — these are mostly, as is Sergent-chef Ibn Tufail, Berbers from the Atlas Mountains. As the Goumiers were approaching Strasbourg —"

"Tabors? Goumiers?" Winters interrupted.

"Tabors are regiments, essentially, of Moroccan native troops, who are known as Goumiers. If I may continue?"

"Sorry, sir. You told me I might ask questions."

"If you're going to be in this business, Thomas, you're going to have to learn not to take anything anyone tells you at face value."

*Jesus, there he goes again with that Cronley-like sarcasm.*

"I'll make a note of that, Mon Com-

184

mandant," Winters said.

"To resume," Fortin said, "as the Goumiers were working their way toward Alsace, DuPres came to my attention."

"How?" Cronley asked.

"I was about to explain that before you interrupted me."

"Pray continue, Mon Commandant."

"DuPres — by then Capitaine DuPres — was having remarkable success in the interrogation of German officers. This came to my attention —"

Cronley broke in: "As you were rolling across France with Leclerc's 2nd Armored Division in the turret of your Sherman tank, right? Shouting, *'Allons, mes enfants, allons au Rhin'*?"

Winters made the translation without thinking about it.

*Cronley just stuck it to him.*

*There's no way a major riding in a tank in Northern France shouting, "Come on, my children, on to the Rhine!" would know anything about a Goumier captain in southern France saying anything, much less about his skill at interrogation.*

*Unless of course the major was something other than an armored major — say, a colonel in intelligence.*

"I thought you didn't speak French," Fortin said.

"If you're going to be in this business, Jean-Paul, you're going to have to learn not to take anything anyone tells you at face value."

It was too much for Winters to contain. He laughed. And then DuPres did.

"Actually, at the time I had been given certain other duties by General de Gaulle," Fortin confessed.

"I wouldn't think of asking what those might have been," Cronley said.

"When I met Capitaine DuPres, he explained to me his interrogation technique," Fortin said. "When he had captured, for example, an *oberst,* he would put him in a cell, where he would announce that he was a Jew and then order Herr Oberst to strip himself naked. He would then leave him alone for an hour or so to consider his plight. Then he would send Sergent-chef Ibn Tufail, whom he had taught to speak passable German, into the cell. Tufail would then smile at Herr Oberst in an intimate way and ask if the Herr Oberst was familiar with how friendly Lawrence of Arabia had become with his Turkish captors when he was in their custody."

*Am I supposed to believe this?* Winters wondered, and then realized, *God, it's prob-*

*ably true!*

"Whereupon Herr Oberst would do one of two things. He would either turn onto his stomach and spread his cheeks, or he would ask Sergent-chef Ibn Tufail if there was anything, anything at all, he'd like to know."

"Except for the Lawrence of Arabia business, that was clever," Cronley said. "Once someone told me that there are almost no Negroes in Russia, I've been using my deputy to help in the interrogation of the NKGB people we've bagged. Captain Chauncey Dunwiddie is six feet five or six, weighs nearly three hundred pounds, is built like a Sherman tank, and is, literally, as black as coal."

*And Cronley's not kidding, either!*

*Either about Dunwiddie's size or using black people to intimidate the Russians.*

*The NKGB officer I saw at the monastery was visibly afraid that Tiny's Troopers were planning to boil him in a pot and have him for supper.*

"I shall look forward to meeting the captain," Fortin said. "If I may continue?"

"Pardon the interruption, Mon Colonel . . . excuse me . . . Mon Commandant."

"Shortly after I met Capitaine DuPres, higher authorities decided he would be of more value attached to General de Gaulle's headquarters than he would be serving with the Goumiers. And so would Sergent-chef Ibn Tufail."

"You mean working for you," Cronley said.

"Refuting the common belief that higher headquarters are usually wrong, both Capitaine DuPres and Sergent-chef Ibn Tufail have proved themselves quite valuable to the DST."

"I was thinking," Winters said, "that it would probably be very useful for Capitaine DuPres and Sergent-chef Tufail to meet Captain Dunwiddie and Sergeant Tedworth."

"Great minds walk similar paths," Cronley said. "That can happen tomorrow. But right now, we have to get going. There's no runway lighting at the Compound, and as you may have noticed, it gets dark early this time of year. Did you say something, Mon Colonel, about a case of champagne?"

"That was before you started calling me 'colonel,'" Fortin said. "But we Alsatians are well known for our compassion toward foolish Americans who say foolish things, so you may have the Crémant d'Alsace."

# [FIVE]

*The South German Industrial Development*

*Organization Compound*

*Pullach, Bavaria*

*American Zone of Occupation, Germany*

*1705 25 January 1946*

"That was cutting it pretty close," Tom Winters said to Cronley, when Cronley had shut down the L-4's engine.

"I've always found it exciting to land in the dark," Cronley said, then turning serious, went on: "I was tempted to play it safe and go into Schleissheim, but I hate to land there." He paused, and added in a mock thick German accent, "I think the NKGB is watching."

"What would they have seen?"

"You and me and the tail number of this aircraft. If they were watching Strasbourg, they saw us take off. But where did we go? Since they can't get close enough — especially when it's getting dark — to the Compound strip to read the tail number, they don't *know* we landed here. They can guess, but they don't know, and the less they know about anything the better."

"It's that bad?"

189

"Write it on your forehead."

"Yes, sir."

"To coin a phrase, 'All's well that ends well.' We got in here all right, Tom — and with a case of champagne."

Claudette Colbert pulled up in a Ford staff car just as they had finished taking the case of Crémant d'Alsace from the plane.

"Welcome home," she said. "How'd everything go?"

"Very well. Where's Freddy?"

"He went into the office. You need him?"

"I can tell him what and why when we get there."

Winters said: "Did my wife find quarters to her satisfaction?"

"She did and she's already moved into them. She and Mrs. Moriarty. They're right next to each other."

At the refurbished cottage that was now the quarters of Lieutenant and Mrs. Thomas Winters, the case of Crémant d'Alsace was divided. The Winterses got two bottles, both of which were promptly chilled and then consumed by Lieutenant Colonel and Mrs. Jack Bristol, the Moriartys, the Winterses, Miss Colbert, and Captain Cronley to "wet down" the Winterses' new quarters.

Two bottles went to Lieutenant and Mrs. Moriarty, who promised to save them for the wet-down supper she would have for her new quarters just as soon as she could, and to which she hoped her new friend Claudette would come. "With anyone Dette wishes to bring with her," she said.

When Cronley and Claudette left, he took the remaining two bottles with him.

Cronley walked toward the driver's door of the staff car.

Dette said, "It would look better if I drove."

Cronley went and got in the front passenger seat.

"Look better to whom?" he then asked.

"Think about it," she said as she started to drive off.

Three minutes later, as they waited in line to be passed through the checkpoint in the center fence, she said, "Them," and nodded toward the Pole and soldiers who were examining the identity cards of the people in the car ahead of them.

Cronley didn't reply.

"What do you think they see?" she asked.

"I don't know," he said sarcastically, "maybe the commanding officer being driven somewhere by his administrative officer?"

"Right. And if you were driving?"

He didn't reply immediately as it became their turn to have their identities checked.

As they began rolling toward the next checkpoint, he said: " 'There goes the CO again. He likes to drive himself.' "

"Or maybe," Dette said, " 'There goes the CO again with that blond, quote, administrative officer, unquote, he's probably screwing.' "

Cronley couldn't reply as they were now at the final checkpoint.

As they moved away from the outer checkpoint, Cronley asked, "Why would they think that?"

"That's what Freddy thinks."

"What makes you think Freddy suspects anything?"

"From the look on his face when I told him I was going to stick around to see if you were going to make it back from Strasbourg."

"He say anything?"

"Just, 'Of course.' "

"Oh."

"I was actually sticking around because I thought the commanding officer would need a ride. But while I was doing that, I wondered how long it was going to be before others — Tiny, Major Wallace, Max

Ostrowski, that CIC agent Wallace brought down here, Sergeant Tedworth, Augie Ziegler — started wondering what the real nature of our relationship is."

"Why do I think this is leading up to some sort of announcement?"

"We have to quit, Jim. Neither of us can afford to get caught."

"This wouldn't have anything to do with Augie Ziegler, would it?"

"It does. He's coming on to me pretty strong. He wants to take me to dinner tonight, for example."

"And you want to go?"

"Well, there it is — what I was afraid of, the Green-Eyed Monster."

"Don't be silly."

"If I keep pushing Augie away, he's going to wonder who his competition is. Eventually, he'll get to you. Bingo!"

"Yeah," Cronley said.

"Well?"

"Why don't you get Augie to take you to the Engineer Officers' Club for dinner? According to Major Wallace, they have a nice kitchen. And Colonel Bristol and his wife are likely to be there and will see you."

"You are pissed, aren't you?"

He thought for a moment, then said, "What I am, really, is grateful that one of us was smart enough to see a major disaster looming."

Claudette reached for his hand and brought it to her mouth and kissed it.

"You're a good guy, Captain, sir. You go in the Great Memories file."

# V

## [ONE]

*Suite 507*

*Hotel Vier Jahreszeiten*

*Maximilianstrasse 178*

*Munich, American Zone of Occupation,
   Germany*

*1920 25 January 1946*

When Captain James D. Cronley Jr. and Miss Claudette Colbert walked into the office — the former holding the foil-wrapped necks of two bottles of Crémant d'Alsace, the latter carrying the heavy leather briefcase stuffed with the Odessa material — they found several people waiting for them.

"The man at the Compound airstrip told me you landed at seventeen hundred," Lieutenant Colonel George H. Parsons — the assistant chief of staff, G-2, the War

194

Department's senior liaison officer to the Directorate of Central Intelligence–Europe — greeted Cronley.

It came out as an accusation, and Cronley's temper flared and his mouth went on automatic.

"Mr. Hessinger," he said, "find out who told Colonel Parsons that, and tell him the next time he tells anyone but you or Miss Colbert when and where I land anywhere, I will be very distressed and will deal with him accordingly."

Hessinger said, "Yes, sir."

He thought, *Scheiss! He's about to get into it with Parsons!*

Major Warren W. Ashley, who was Colonel Parsons's deputy, said, not very pleasantly, "The colonel needs to talk to you concerning an important matter, Captain!"

Cronley turned to Claudette and extended the bottles to her.

"Miss Colbert, will you put these in the refrigerator, please, while I see what's on Colonel Parsons's mind?"

Claudette said, "Yes, sir."

She thought, *Oh, Jimmy, watch your mouth!*

"We have been waiting for you since seventeen-thirty," Colonel Parsons said. "No one seemed to know where you were."

"Colonel, with all due respect," Cronley

said, his tone short, "I don't see how you can fault me for not being where and when you expect me to be if I don't know where and when you expect me to be."

CIC Supervisory Special Agent John D. Hammersmith thought: *You arrogant little sonofabitch! That's a lieutenant colonel you're talking to!*

CID Supervisory Special Agent August Ziegler thought: *Five to one this light bird is going to stand him tall and eat his ass out!*

*Then what's Cronley going to do?*

*And what the hell has he been up to for two hours with Claudette and that champagne?*

"I think it might be a good idea to set up a protocol, Captain Cronley," Colonel Parsons said, "so that I can contact you in an emergency."

"Hessinger," Cronley snapped, "did Colonel Parsons tell you he wanted to see me about an emergency?"

Before Hessinger could reply, Parsons said, "Actually, this isn't an emergency."

"Oh," Cronley said. "Colonel, about an emergency protocol to contact me: There is one. If you had told Mr. Hessinger you wanted to see me on an emergency basis, he would have put it into play."

"And what would have happened had he

done so?" Major Ashley demanded sarcastically.

Cronley looked as if he was about to say something and then changed his mind.

"Four people know where I am at all times, and where I am expected to go from there," Cronley said finally. "They are Mr. Hessinger, Miss Colbert, Mr. Ostrowski, and Lieutenant Moriarty. If you had declared this to be an emergency — or even a very important situation — and Mr. Hessinger didn't know himself where I was, and Miss Colbert was not available, he'd have gone next to Mr. Ostrowski, and finally to Lieutenant Moriarty. Had it gone that far, the lieutenant would have told Mr. Hessinger, and he would have told you, that I was — and Miss Colbert was — in Lieutenant Moriarty's quarters at the Compound, having a little champagne to celebrate the Moriartys having just moved into their quarters."

Augie Ziegler thought: *Well, Major, that should answer your question.*

*But what was Claudette doing drinking champagne with everybody?*

Hammersmith thought: *And with that answer he's succeeded in pissing both Colonel Parsons and Major Ashley off.*

*Doesn't he know that, or doesn't he care?*

*Or, Christ, is he pissing them off on purpose?*

Hessinger thought: *Well, that's what would have happened, but it's not a standard in-place protocol.*

*He just made that up.*

"What's on your mind, Colonel?" Cronley asked.

"Odessa," Colonel Parsons said.

"Odessa?"

"You have heard of Odessa?" Major Ashley asked sarcastically.

"You mean that place on the Black Sea?" Cronley asked. "Where Roosevelt, Stalin, and Churchill held that conference?"

"Major Ashley is asking about the organization," Parsons said, "called Odessa, which is allegedly getting Nazi war criminals out of Germany to Argentina."

Hammersmith thought: *And you know that, you smart-ass!*

"I thought that Odessa was — excuse the expression — bullshit, like the werewolves," Cronley said.

"I can assure you, Captain Cronley, that it is not," Colonel Parsons said.

"What's Odessa got to do with me?" Cronley asked. "Or the DCI?"

"This afternoon we received a Priority message from the War Department," Parsons said, "asking that we furnish, ASAP, whatever information we have, or can collect from any source, about Odessa."

"They think it's real?"

Ziegler thought: *You know it is. You've got a briefcase stuffed with Odessa material.*

Claudette thought: *Jimmy, please be careful!*

Hessinger thought: *What are you up to now? You know very well Odessa is real!*

"I would say that's rather obvious, wouldn't you, Captain Cronley?" Major Ashley said.

"Did they say why they're interested?" Cronley asked.

"Is that any of your business?" Major Ashley asked.

"Yes, I think it is."

"You don't use the term 'sir' very much, do you, Captain?" Ashley snapped.

"No disrespect intended, Major, sir," Cronley said.

His tone suggested that might not be true.

Claudette thought: *Oh, Jimmy!*

"Back-channel, Cronley, for what it's worth," Colonel Parsons said, "I've heard that our military attaché in Buenos Aires . . ."

Cronley thought: *That would be the guy*

*Cletus — or was it Ashley? — described as a horse's ass who can't find his ass with both hands.*

". . . has been working with the FBI on the Odessa question."

"Colonel, may I make a suggestion?" Cronley asked.

"Certainly."

"Why don't you get in touch with General Greene? I know the CIC has been investigating this Odessa thing. Maybe he'd be able to help."

"You can't?" Major Ashley said.

"So far as I know, Odessa is bullshit," Cronley said. "I don't know anything about it."

"Actually, I have been in touch with General Greene," Colonel Parsons said. "He apparently got essentially the same message I did from the Pentagon. He said he sent them what very little he had, and suggested that you might be able to help."

"I don't know a damned thing about Odessa, but . . ."

Cronley did not finish his sentence.

Hammersmith thought: *The Uniform Code of Military Justice 1928 Article 107. False official statements. Any person subject to this chapter who, with intent to deceive, makes any false official statement knowing it to be*

200

*false, shall be punished as a court-martial may direct.*

*And you know what you just told him is blatantly false, Cronley!*

*What the hell are you up to?*

"But what?" Major Ashley challenged. "You either know something, or you don't. Or do you have knowledge of Odessa and don't want to share it with us?"

Hammersmith thought: *Ashley just nailed you, Cronley.*

*If you tell him you don't have any information on Odessa, then you're making another false statement, and Article 107 comes into play.*

*If you now come up with something, that means you lied to Colonel Parsons a moment ago, making it a violation of Article 107.*

*This just may get you court-martialed, you smart-ass sonofabitch!*

*Colonel Parsons, who is no fool, is probably looking for a chance to hang you out to dry!*

*You're not half as smart as you think you are! Not a quarter!*

"I was about to suggest that Mr. Hammersmith may be able to help, Colonel," Cronley said. "General Greene told me that not only was Hammersmith one of his best agents, but that he often worked on investigations that no one else knew about. Maybe

201

some of that involved Odessa."

"Really?" Colonel Parsons said. "Well, Mr. Hammersmith, can you help G-2 out? Did you ever do any work with regard to Odessa for General Greene?"

Hammersmith felt a cramp in his stomach. He thought: *Cronley, you sonofabitch!*

*You just blindsided me, and I really didn't see it coming!*

*Just about everything Homer Greene knows about Odessa he got from me.*

*But Parsons just said Homer told him he had "very little"!*

*Why the hell did he do that?*

*If Homer didn't give Parsons everything he had . . .*

*If he told him he had very little . . .*

*Homer had to have a reason.*

*Well, the one thing I'm not going to do is tell this Pentagon sonofabitch that Homer Greene lied to him.*

"Sorry, Colonel," Hammersmith said. "I'm afraid I can't be of any help."

"That's a pity," Colonel Parsons said, and then went on: "You realize, of course, Cronley, that I'm going to have to tell G-2 that DCI has absolutely nothing of importance on Odessa. Is that going to embarrass you?"

"I don't see why it should, sir. I can't give them anything I don't have. May I suggest you tell them that if we turn up anything, I'll immediately give it to you?"

"Of course," Parsons said. "Let's hope that happens. G-2 obviously thinks this is important."

He gestured to Major Ashley that they should leave.

"We'll be in touch, Cronley," Parsons said. "Good evening, gentlemen. Miss Colbert."

When the door had closed behind them, Cronley said, "Thanks, Hammersmith."

"What for?" Hammersmith replied.

Cronley chuckled.

"I wondered why the admiral suddenly decided we should start looking into Odessa," Cronley said. "And now we know."

"I don't understand," Hammersmith said.

"G-2 was told to stay away from Operation Ost. That cut the military attaché in Buenos Aires, who is under G-2, out of the picture. But that doesn't mean the attaché doesn't have a pretty good idea what's been going on. But the 'leave it alone' order has meant he can't officially report what he's found out since he's been told to leave it alone. But because the FBI is asking about it, what choice does he have but to cooperate with the FBI?

"And the joint FBI–G-2 investigation will

come up with what we've been doing. In other words, there are Nazis in Argentina, sent there by mysterious, certainly illegal, organizations called Odessa and Operation Ost, which are probably the same thing. When Hoover lays this on President Truman's desk, as he will, the President will have no choice but to be terribly surprised, shocked, and outraged.

"Which means we get — DCI gets — flushed down Sir Thomas Crapper's marvelous invention, taking with us a bunch of good people."

Hammersmith thought: *Damn. He's right.*

*And among the good people getting flushed down the crapper will be Homer Greene.*

*And his old friend Jack Hammersmith.*

"Unless, of course, we can catch some senior people in Odessa," Cronley went on, "and damned soon, before the FBI and G-2 finds out too much. Then, when Hoover lays their report on Truman's desk, Truman can say, 'Edgar, old buddy, the reason I told you to lay off this was because I knew those brilliant people in my DCI-Europe were about to lower the boom on Odessa. Which they did last week.' "

Hammersmith thought: *There's damned little chance of that happening.*

"And how are we going to do that?"

Hessinger asked.

"I don't have a fucking clue," Cronley said. "Sorry, Dette."

She made a disparaging wave of her hand.

"But in the last few minutes, I've had a couple of wild ideas," Cronley said. "Based on my vast experience as an intelligence officer."

"Let's hear them," Hammersmith said, and was surprised when he heard himself.

"Okay. I had lunch today with Commandant Jean-Paul Fortin, of the DST —"

"The Direction de la Surveillance du Territoire?" Hammersmith interrupted.

"Uh-huh. You know about it?"

"I even know about Commandant Fortin," Hammersmith said.

"I think he's more than a major," Cronley said. "I think he's a colonel."

Hammersmith thought: *So do I.*

"Whatever his rank, he's one smart sonofabitch," Cronley went on. "And he has a personal interest in taking down Odessa. In his professional judgment, the only way to get inside Odessa is from the bottom."

"I tend to agree," Hammersmith said thoughtfully.

"To which end, we are about to send Sergeant Finney to Strasbourg with a load of cigarettes, canned hams, and coffee from my mother for my cousin Luther. Cousin Luther, we hope, will then skillfully put Al Finney on the slippery slope to corruption so that eventually he can — or the ambulances of the 711th Mobile Kitchen Renovation Company can — be pressured into moving people across borders as he and his men move around Germany, Austria, and Italy repairing mess hall stoves and electric potato peeling machines."

"And get into Odessa from the bottom," Hammersmith said. "That just might work."

"It probably will," Cronley said. "But we (a) don't *know* if it will work, and (b) I don't think we have the time to wait and see if it does."

"What other choice do you have?" Hessinger asked.

"Can I go off on a tangent here?" Hammersmith asked.

"Why not?" Cronley replied.

"I have a theory how Odessa is moving their people," Hammersmith said. "I've been asking General Greene for the assets to check it out. They haven't been available. Maybe this new situation will change that."

'What's your theory?" Cronley said.

"That they're moving them on *Stars and Stripes* distribution trucks," Hammersmith said.

"On what?" Ziegler asked incredulously.

Hammersmith didn't reply directly, instead saying, "*Stars and Stripes* prints more than a half-million newspapers a day . . ."

"Jesus! That many?" Ziegler said.

"Shut up, Ziegler," Cronley snapped. "Let him finish."

". . . which are distributed all over the U.S. Forces European Theater, from Berlin to Italy. The printing plant is in a little *dorf* — Pfungstadt — twenty-five miles south of Frankfurt. Trucks set out seven days a week down the autobahns and major highways into Czechoslovakia, and down through the Brenner Pass through the Alps on the Italian-Austrian border. And into France.

"The longest hauls — the ones to Trieste, Rome, Naples, and Vienna — run as high as three hundred and eighty miles. Which means that since they can't make a round-trip that long in a day's time, that at any time there are maybe eight or ten trucks heading south loaded with newspapers, and that many headed back to Pfungstadt empty.

"The Constabulary's got roadblocks all over their routes, but, human nature being human nature, I don't think they look as closely as they should at what the *Stars and Stripes* trucks have in the back. They're there every day."

"Yeah," Cronley said thoughtfully.

"Clever," Hessinger said.

"And you say Greene told you . . ."

Hammersmith thought: *That's General Greene, Captain.*

". . . you couldn't have what you needed to really check this out?"

"Checking it out would be more difficult than it looks like," Hammersmith said.

"Why?" Ziegler asked.

"Think about it, Augie," Cronley said before Hammersmith could reply. "You'd have only one shot at it."

"I don't understand," Ziegler confessed.

"Neither do I," Hessinger said.

"Because you'd have to stop and search every truck — and Hammersmith just said there are at least sixteen trucks — at the same time. These Odessa people are not putting one or more bastards in every truck every time they go onto the autobahn. I'd guess only one truck at a time is carrying one of these sonsofbitches, and that maybe a day or two goes by when they're not carrying anybody . . ."

"And the chances of one of these Odessa people being on the one truck the CIC stopped are very slight," Hessinger said, picking up Cronley's chain of thought.

". . . and once the CIC stopped and

searched one newspaper truck, the game is up," Cronley went on. "They'd stop using the *Stripes* trucks. The only way to do this would be to have credible intel — or at least a damn good suspicion — that Odessa was on that day going to move somebody. And then stop and search every truck at the same time. And be lucky."

"Doing that would require," Hessinger said, "sixteen trucks times four CIC people — and six or eight would be better — per truck. That's at least sixty-four CIC people. Probably more. And we all know the CIC is short of competent people."

"Especially since you, Finney, and I have left the CIC," Cronley said, laughing, and then asked rhetorically: "And if you bagged one of the bastards, what would you have? Probably some SS sonofabitch whose sense of honor would prohibit him from implicating anybody."

"Or who didn't know anything beyond, 'Get on the truck, Karl,' " Hessinger picked up. "I would think that a substantial percentage of people Odessa is trying to get out don't know anything about how Odessa is organized. They're being gotten out for what they know about SS operations before the surrender."

"I'll bet Greene told you something like

this when you asked him about those assets he didn't have, right?" Cronley asked. "That you'd be pissing in the wind, even if he came up with — what did you say, Freddy? — 'at least sixty-four CIC agents'?"

Hammersmith thought: *What these two have just done — obviously off the top of their heads — is come up with the story I was going to give them why we haven't stopped Odessa from using the* Stars and Stripes *trucks.*

*They're the reasons General Greene gave me for not coming up with fifty or sixty agents to search the trucks.*

*And he actually used the same words — told me I'd be pissing in the wind.*

*And then he told me the real reason I was to stop working on the* Stripes *trucks.*

*Are these two a lot smarter than I'm giving them credit for?*

"Actually, that's pretty much what he did say," Hammersmith said.

"Which brings us back to my wild idea," Cronley said.

"Which is?"

"The Russians are looking for the people behind Odessa, too. So let's turn to them for a little assistance."

Hammersmith thought: *Now where the hell is he going?*

"Jean-Paul Fortin told me thirty-odd people set up the Spider — not counting the Vatican contingent." Cronley pointed at the briefcase. "And Greene told me the same thing and said it was in the stuff he was giving me." He paused, then added: "Going off at a tangent, Augie, get started on Leica-ing everything in there just as soon as we finish here."

"Yes, sir."

Cronley looked back at Hammersmith and said, "Fortin gave me his list to compare with Greene's. As soon as we stop talking here, Dette will make up a combined list of names. We give this list to the general, who will mark off anybody we know has already escaped from Germany, and then we send the list via SIGABA to Polo — Colonel Ashton — in Argentina and ask him if any of them are there. And get him to start looking for any of them. Also, we get General Gehlen to come up with a list of these guys who may have gone the other way, into what Major Wallace calls 'the Soviet sphere of influence.' And we give Seven-K the list and see if she's got any of them."

"Good idea," Hessinger said.

"Who is Seven-K?" Hammersmith asked.

Cronley looked at him for a long moment, and then turned to Hessinger.

"Do I tell him?"

"The possibility has to be considered that Mr. Hammersmith will feel he has to tell General Greene what we're doing," Hessinger said.

"Dette?" Cronley asked.

"Freddy's right," Claudette said. "You'll have to weigh (a) how much damage that might cause, (b) how Major Wallace will react when he hears you have told him, and (c) if Mr. Hammersmith is a member of the team, or just a visitor."

Cronley snorted, then asked, "What about our Pennsylvania Dutchman? Should Augie be in this loop?"

"Dette raised the significant question," Hessinger said. "Are Augie and Mr. Hammersmith to be members of the team . . ."

"Augie has my vote," Claudette said.

". . . or just visitors?" Hessinger finished.

Hammersmith thought: *Ziegler gets her vote and I don't? Does that mean she doesn't know enough about me to give me a recommendation, or that she thinks she knows me well enough to think I'm not trustworthy?*

*And Hessinger calls Ziegler by his first name. But I'm "Mr. Hammersmith"?*

*How much weight does Cronley give to the opinion of either of them?*

Cronley looked between Ziegler and Hammersmith.

"You two want in DCI all the way?" he asked. "Before you answer, this caveat. If you say you want in — and I admit we need you — if you say 'yes,' do so with that line from the oath of office we all took: *Without any mental reservations whatsoever.* If I find out later you wanted in because you wanted to learn something you can pass on to someone else, and I learn that you have passed something on, I'll kill you."

Ziegler thought: *I think he means that.*

*Dette voted for me.*

*Do I want in?*

*Oh boy, do I!*

Hammersmith thought: *He doesn't really think anyone is going to believe that melodramatic "I'll kill you" threat, does he?*

*Or is he serious?*

*There are rumors of unmarked graves at that monastery.*

*Could they possibly be true?*

"I'm in, Captain," Ziegler said, and turned to Claudette. "Thanks for the vote of confidence."

"Hammersmith, if you're having trouble making up your mind with my conditions," Cronley said, "you get a pass with regard to General Greene. He's one of the good guys . . ."

Hammersmith thought: *You approve of General Greene, do you?*

*How nice of you, Captain Cronley!*

". . . and he's in the loop. The only reason I don't keep him up to speed on everything is so he can look G-2 and the FBI in the eye and truthfully say, 'I don't know anything about that.' "

Hammersmith thought: *Christ, he's right.*

*He is smarter than I've been giving him credit for.*

"Well, are you in or out?" Cronley asked.

Hammersmith thought: *I owe it to Homer Greene to stay here.*

"In, Captain Cronley," Hammersmith said.

"Okay, I'll take you at your word. When Major Wallace told me about you, he said you and Greene are pals. That's good enough for me. If Greene trusts you, I will."

"Captain, can you give me a minute in private?"

"To tell me something you don't think Freddy and Dette — and now Augie — should know? No. It would be a waste of time, because as soon as you told me I'd have to tell them. What were you going to tell me?"

Hammersmith thought: *If I tell him, am I betraying Homer Greene?*

*What's that line? "In for a penny, in for a pound . . ."*

"What do you know about Operation Paperclip?" Hammersmith asked.

"Never heard of it. Dette? Freddy?"

"It has something to do with German scientists," Claudette said.

"German rocket people," Hessinger clarified.

"What about it, Jack?" Cronley asked.

Hammersmith thought: *Now I'm Jack?*

*Is he trying to be nice?*

*Should I be pissed off or pleased?*

"When I started looking into Odessa, I suspected the *Stars and Stripes* trucks were being used. I figured out — much as you did just now — how difficult it would be to catch them in the act. And that even if I got lucky and did, that I wouldn't have much, if anything.

"So I went to General Greene and explained where I was. He said not to worry about it, and specifically told me to leave it alone."

"Why?" Cronley asked.

"He . . . I have to tell you this is classified Top Secret–Paperclip," Hammersmith said. "I'm reluctant to —"

"Tell us anything classified Top Secret–Paperclip?" Cronley asked softly.

"Yes, sir," Hammersmith said simply.

"Well, Jack, none of us have a Top Secret–Paperclip clearance. But not to worry, we've got something just as good. Actually, a lot better. Miss Colbert, will you go in the safe and get the Twenty Commandments?"

Hammersmith thought: *Twenty Commandments?*

*Now what the hell?*

Claudette went to the safe, worked the combination, and then took from the safe a business-sized envelope.

When she started to hand it to Cronley, he shook his head and pointed to Hammersmith.

"Jack," he said, "the first couple of pages deal with not making graven images, honoring your parents, not committing adultery, and such, so why don't you just read the last page? When you're finished, hand it to the Dutchman."

Hammersmith opened the envelope, turned to the last page, and read the document:

**TOP SECRET–PRESIDENTIAL Page 3 of 3**

17. The director is, and subordinate directors are, authorized to investigate anything he believes, or subordinate directors believe,

would be of interest to the President. In this connection, the director and subordinate directors, and any DCI personnel they designate, are authorized access to any and all classified files, without exception, generated by any agency of the United States government.

18. If the director initiates any investigation on his own authority he will notify the President by the most expedient means, classified Top Secret–Presidential, that he has initiated such an investigation, and his reason for so doing.

19. If a subordinate director initiates any investigation on his own authority he will notify the director by the most expedient means, classified Top Secret–Presidential, that he has initiated such an investigation, and his reason for so doing.

20. The President reserves to himself the authority to disseminate any intelligence acquired by the director, or subordinate directors, of the Central Intelligence Directorate.

*Harry S Truman*

**TOP SECRET — PRESIDENTIAL**

Hammersmith thought: *My God! It's signed*

*by Truman himself!*

*I wonder if Homer has seen this.*

*Of course he has. For one thing, that explains his turning over his — my — intel on Odessa to Cronley.*

When both Hammersmith and Ziegler had read it, Cronley said, "Anyway, that's what we live by. So tell us about Operation Tie Clip."

"That's *Paperclip,* sir," Hammersmith said.

Hammersmith heard himself, and thought: *I just called him "sir." Not to be polite, but because I subconsciously just accepted that he's not only in charge, but entitled to be. He's operating with the authority of the President.*

"Okay, Operation Paperclip," Cronley said.

"G-2's hands aren't clean about getting Nazis out of Germany," Hammersmith said.

"That's interesting. Bearing in mind the Twenty Commandments I just showed you, tell us all about that."

"Were you aware the Germans had their own atomic weapons program?"

"Oh, yeah. I even know they tried to ship some of their experts and half a ton of uranium oxide to Japan just as the war ended."

Hammersmith thought: *There's more proof. He's not kidding. He knows about that, and he shouldn't* know *anything about it!*

*But let's make sure.*

"You mean *there was a rumor* they tried to do that?" he asked.

"No. I mean that General Gehlen and a very young intelligence officer whom modesty prohibits me from naming put their heads together and decided where U-234, which had the scientists and the uranium oxide aboard, was probably hiding in Patagonia, at the southern tip of South America.

"Said very young intelligence officer then climbed into a Storch and found U-234. He then took down SS-Oberführer Horst Lang, who was in the process of trying to sell said scientists and uranium oxide to the Soviets, with a blast from his trusty Thompson, thereby securing both the scientists and the uranium oxide for our side."

Hammersmith thought: *He's talking about himself? Am I supposed to believe that?*

"And that, Jack, is how I became a twenty-two-year-old captain," Cronley said. "I think you've been wondering, so I reluctantly pushed modesty aside and told you because I think you should know. I hope it makes taking orders from me a little easier. But don't pass that story around. My promotion orders and the citation for my Distinguished Service Medal — which I can't wear because people would ask questions — are classified Top Secret–Presidential."

*Jesus Christ, it's true!*

Ziegler looked at Claudette, who smiled and nodded.

Hammersmith thought: *I'll be a sonofabitch. It's true. All of it is true!*

"I honestly don't know what to say, Captain Cronley."

"Try telling us about G-2's unclean hands."

After a moment to gather his thoughts, Hammersmith began to do so: "The technical services — the Signal Corps primarily, but also the Ordnance Corps, which is where the rocket scientists come in, and even the Medical Corps, and others — wanted early on to get their hands on German technology.

"They set up special teams to accompany the lead elements of the Army as it entered Germany, to capture German equipment. The Signal Corps, for example, wanted to get their hands on German radar, and, for one other example, a machine the Germans had developed that records speech and data on wire, wire recorders. Do you understand what I'm saying?"

"I'm a little slow, but Freddy, Dette, and Augie are pretty swift, so keep going," Cronley said.

"Two things soon became apparent to the Signal Corps, and then, importantly, to the Ordnance Corps. First, that just having the equipment to study wasn't enough. They needed the people who had invented, for example, the wire recorder and the V-1 and V-2 rockets, to explain these devices. And second, that the Germans could do a much better job doing this at Fort Monmouth and Fort Bliss than they could in Germany. Still with me?"

Cronley nodded.

"So they got special permission from President Truman to bring German scientists to the United States. Truman wanted to make sure that no Nazis got to go to the States, so when the War Department's Joint Intelligence Objectives Agency was formed it specifically prohibited bringing to the States any German who had been a member of the Nazi Party who had been more than a 'nominal participant' in Nazi activities."

"And the scientists they wanted had all been Nazis?" Cronley asked.

"Not all of them, but many. And the problem was compounded when we found out that the Russians were grabbing all German scientists they could lay their hands on and shipping them to Mother Russia, together with their laboratories. And further compounded when we learned how far ahead of us the Germans were in certain areas, particularly rockets and rocket-propelled missiles like the V-1 and V-2.

"The 82nd Airborne Division was ordered to send a task force to the main German rocket establishment, Peenemünde, which is on a small island, Usedom, in Mecklenburg. They were ordered to grab the rockets and the rocket scientists before the Red Army grabbed them and sent them to Russia.

"They did so. The 82nd grabbed all the rockets at Peenemünde, plus several hundred scientists, including the head man, a fellow named Wernher von Braun. The rockets were flown to Fort Bliss and the scientists locked up in what was to become the American Zone of Occupied Germany."

"Where they found out that all the scientists were Nazis," Hessinger asked, "and could not be sent to the States?"

"Not all of them were Nazis," Hammersmith said. "But many were. Including von Braun."

"Which made all the rockets at Fort Bliss

so much scrap metal," Hessinger finished. "From which, without the scientists, we could learn nothing."

"So this Joint Intelligence Objectives Agency shipped the Nazi scientists anyway, and let's hope Truman — or J. Edgar Hoover — doesn't find out?" Cronley asked.

"Major Wallace had the same problem with Abwehr Ost," Hessinger said.

"I was afraid, Freddy, that you were going to introduce that into the equation," Cronley said.

"It's pertinent," Hessinger said.

"You did the same thing?" Hammersmith asked.

"Jack asking that question is why I was afraid you'd mention this, Freddy," Cronley said.

"It's pertinent," Hessinger said again.

"The scenarios are not the same," Cronley said. "Allen Dulles made a deal with Gehlen. Almost certainly with Eisenhower's approval, and probably the President's. In exchange for everything Gehlen had, we would protect him and his people from the Russians."

"So you faked the denazification trials?" Hammersmith asked.

Instead of answering, Cronley asked, "Is that what this Joint Intelligence Objectives

Agency did?"

Hammersmith nodded and said, "So I understand."

"What I understand happened," Cronley said, "is that after we shipped the known Abwehr Ost Nazis and their families to Cletus Frade in Argentina, Wallace and Colonel Robert Mattingly ran the others through the Denazification Court process and got them cleared."

"Gehlen, too?" Hammersmith said.

Cronley nodded.

"The chief of Abwehr Ost wasn't a Nazi?" Hammersmith said.

"He was. And so were all of his senior officers. But they got a pass, because Gehlen — and Obersts Ludwig Mannberg and Otto Niedermeyer . . ."

"Niedermeyer?" Ziegler said.

". . . were up to their ears in most of the plots to take out Hitler. Not just the von Stauffenberg bomb plot."

"But didn't get caught?" Hammersmith asked incredulously.

"Just before the war ended, the SS was looking for them so they could hang them from butcher's hooks like the others."

"Who's Oberst Niedermeyer?" Ziegler pursued.

"He's the guy Gehlen sent to Cletus Frade

in Argentina to keep an eye on the Nazis we sent there. He's even more anti-Nazi than the others. Devout Catholic and a pal of von Stauffenberg."

"So you didn't pass any Nazis through the courts by faking their records?" Hammersmith asked.

"One we did. Major Konrad Bischoff. You met him. He was Himmler's mole in Abwehr Ost, a dedicated Nazi who deserved to be hung from a butcher's hook by his nuts."

"I don't understand."

"When Gehlen caught him, early on, he realized that if Bischoff had some sort of fatal accident in the East, somebody would replace him. So he turned him. Instead of being Himmler's mole in Abwehr Ost, Bischoff became Gehlen's mole in the Sicherheitsdienst.

"And Gehlen trusts him?"

"Put it this way: Bischoff has been around Gehlen long enough to fully appreciate what happens to people who betray Gehlen."

"Off the top of my head," Hammersmith said, "the Joint Intelligence Objectives Agency denazified hundreds, maybe thousands, of Nazis in questionable circumstances. Since they did, they probably assume you did the same thing. I mean, denazified a bunch of people. If they can prove that, and if — when — they get caught, they can say, 'The DCI did the same thing.' Therefore, they really want to catch you. And will do anything they have to in order to do so."

"Off the top of my head, Comrade Hammersmith, I would judge that to be a splendid analysis of the plans of our enemy. Enemies."

"Thank you, Comrade Cronley."

"We're getting off the subject," Hessinger said. "I think you were about to tell Comrade Hammersmith about our friend in Russia."

"So I was," Cronley said. "Where did I get sidetracked?"

"You were about to tell Jack and Augie about Seven-K," Claudette said.

"Right. Caveat, Jack and Augie: talking about Seven-K is right at the head of the list of things that you talking about will get you killed."

"I took your point, Captain Cronley, the first time you made it," Hammersmith said, his annoyance showing.

"Better safe than sorry, Mr. Hammersmith," Cronley said. "Is your ego so sorely outraged that we can't go back to 'Jim' and 'Jack'?"

"That would be nice, Jim, if we could do that."

"Well, Jack, Seven-K is an NKGB colonel with whom Gehlen has been doing business since the Wehrmacht was at the gates of Moscow. And probably before that. She's also a Mossad agent . . ."

"She?" Ziegler said.

". . . who during the war, and now, gets Russian Jews — Zionists — out of Russia so that they can go to Palestine. To do this, she needs money. Lots of money. Gehlen used to give it to her. Now we do. In exchange, she answers questions and does things for us."

"What sort of things?" Ziegler asked.

"The last thing she did for us was get an NKGB colonel's wife and two kids from their apartment in Leningrad to a field in Thuringia, where they could be picked up and then sent to join Daddy in Argentina."

"Holy Christ!" Augie said. "What was that all about?"

"What the hell did that cost?" Hammersmith asked.

"Two hundred thousand dollars," Cronley said matter-of-factly.

"That's a hell of a lot of money!" Augie exclaimed.

"Not to put an NKGB colonel on the path

of righteousness, it's not," Cronley said. "Anyway, I think we should ask Seven-K what she can tell us about Odessa. At the very least, I'm sure she can — more importantly, will — tell us which guys on the list Gehlen's going to give us have gone to, as I have learned from the general to say, the East."

"Yeah," Hammersmith said thoughtfully, and then asked, "Who picked up this woman and her children in East Germany?"

"Max Ostrowski, Kurt Schröder, and me. We used our Storches."

"Who's Schröder?" Ziegler asked.

"He used to fly the general around those steppes in Russia. He taught Max to fly Storches. Max used to fly Spitfires in the Free Polish Air Force."

"And they're now working for the DCI?" Hammersmith asked. "You have the authority to recruit people like that?"

"They're in the DCI and have DCI credentials to prove it," Cronley said. "Which reminds me. Dette, would you get Comrade Hammersmith and the Dutchman credentials?"

"Yes, sir."

"I think what we have to do now is go see the general," Cronley said, and stood up. "And after that we'll see to getting two

228

refrigerators to the Engineer Depot for our French friends."

# [Two]

*Ward 17 (Secure Psychiatric)*

*98th General Hospital*

*Munich, American Zone of Occupation, Germany*

*2050 25 January 1946*

"Colonel, I told these people that they had to have permission from you, sir, to even be in this ward, much less to visit the patient in 303," Major Bethany Cramer, ANC, an intense woman who stood five feet three inches tall and weighed 105 pounds, announced, righteously indignant. "They refused to leave, and I called you."

Colonel Oscar J. Davis, MC, who was serving as Medical Officer of the Day for the 98th General Hospital, looked coldly between Augie Ziegler and the woman with him.

"Who the hell are you?" he demanded.

"My name is Ziegler, Colonel. I'm with the CID."

Ziegler showed the colonel his credentials. Colonel Davis examined them and then said, "These don't give you the right to be here."

"No, they don't, Colonel," Claudette Colbert said. "But these give me the right to be here, and Mr. Ziegler works for me."

She held out her DCI credentials.

"Well, Miss Colbert," Colonel Davis said after he had examined them, "I was told you DCI people — frankly, no offense intended, I didn't expect a woman — would be involved and to cooperate fully with you. If you had checked in with me before you came here, we wouldn't have had this misunderstanding."

"Since I knew the hospital had been made aware of DCI's interest in Sergeant Miller, I didn't think that would be necessary."

"Well, what can we do for you, Miss Colbert?"

"We have been informed that the sergeant has fully recovered from the effects of sedation she was given. True?"

Colonel Davis looked at Major Cramer, who nodded.

"That being the case, all DCI is here to do is take the sergeant off your hands," Claudette said. "I suspect the presence of the MPs and our security people has disrupted the major's running of her ward . . ."

She nodded toward the two MPs and two

PSO guards in the hall.

". . . and that she'll be glad to see the sergeant go."

"Is there any reason the patient can't be discharged, Major?" Colonel Davis asked.

"No, sir."

"Then how about unlocking that door so I can get in to see the sergeant?" Claudette asked.

"Unlock the door, Major, please," Colonel Davis said.

"Thank you for your cooperation, Colonel," Claudette said.

"My pleasure, ma'am," Colonel Davis said.

"Wait here, Mr. Ziegler," Claudette said as Major Cramer unlocked the door. "The PSO people will come with us. Your call what to do with the MPs."

"Yes, ma'am," Ziegler said.

Technical Sergeant Florence J. Miller was in the bed, the top of which had been cranked up, when Claudette walked in and closed the door after her.

"Smile," Claudette said, "Princess Charming is here to rescue you."

"It's about fucking time," Florence said. And then quickly demanded, "Give me a cigarette."

"Cigarettes are bad for your health, as I'm sure Major Cramer told you. But I'll give you one if you say please."

"Fuck you."

"Okay, no cigarette. Put your clothes on and we'll get out of here."

"Everything but my goddamn bra and panties was covered with blood and brains, and I had to beg that bitch to give me them back so I could wash them."

"I'm delighted to see that you're in such good spirits. Come on, let's go."

"Wearing what?"

"That bathrobe," Claudette said, pointing. "I didn't think about your clothes. So what I'll do is call the Compound and have one of the girls send a fresh uniform to the Vier Jahreszeiten."

She picked up the bedside telephone and did so.

When she had finished, Florence said, "Please," and Claudette handed her a package of Parliaments and a Zippo lighter.

"Okay," Claudette said, "your uniform will probably be at the Vier Jahreszeiten before we get there. Outside is a guy named Augie Ziegler. CID agent. Now works for us. We're in his car. We go to the Vier Jahreszeiten, you put your uniform on, and we'll call room service and get you something to eat."

"And a double Jack Daniel's," Florence said.

"And a double Jack Daniel's," Claudette said.

"I forgot," Florence said.

"Forgot what?"

"To say thank you for saving my life. I owe you a big one, Dette."

"I don't need a goddamn wheelchair," Florence said thirty seconds later.

"Hospital regulation, Sergeant," Major Cramer said. "All patients being discharged —"

"Shut up and get in it, Flo," Claudette interrupted.

Florence got into the wheelchair, and Major Cramer pushed it down the corridor and into an elevator. Augie and Claudette then got on, and then two PSO men who had Thompson submachine guns slung from their shoulders got on.

Claudette reached for the elevator control panel.

"Hold it!" Florence ordered.

"What?" Claudette asked.

"What about my fu . . . *upgefukt* uniform?"

"It's in the CID forensic lab in Heidelberg," Augie said. "They're matching the . . .

stuff . . . on it with the guys Dette took out."

"Great! And when am I going to get it back?"

"Probably never," Augie said. "It has become what we call evidence."

"And what's with these guys?" Florence asked, pointing at the PSO men.

"Get used to them, Flo," Claudette said.

"We're your security detail, miss," one of them said. He had a pronounced British accent. "Wherever you go, we do."

"What if I have to go to the ladies' room?" Florence challenged, and then without waiting for a reply, made another challenge: "You sound like an Englishman."

"Any more questions, Flo? Or can I push the down button?" Claudette asked.

"Push away," Florence said.

"I've spent some time in England, Miss Miller," the PSO man said.

"I never would have guessed," Florence said.

# [THREE]

*Suite 507*

*Hotel Vier Jahreszeiten*

*Maximilianstrasse 178*

*Munich, American Zone of Occupation, Germany*

*2130 25 January 1946*

When Florence walked through the doorway that Augie Ziegler had just opened for her, she saw that her uniform had indeed reached the hotel before they had. Her uniform skirt was draped over the edge of Hessinger's desk, with a pair of shoes, a shirt, a necktie, and a pair of stockings sitting on it. And she saw Hessinger was cutting at her chevrons with a razor blade.

"Freddy, you sonofabitch, what the fuck are you doing to my fucking stripes?"

Captain James D. Cronley Jr. answered for him.

"Cutting them off. You can't wear triangles and stripes."

She looked at him in utter confusion.

"We have a new rule around here," Cronley went on. "That whenever the bad guys try to kidnap one of our enlisted people and said enlisted person behaves well during such attempted kidnapping, they get promoted. Welcome to the DCI, Special Agent Miller."

"Shit!" Florence said.

And then started to sob.

Claudette rushed to her and somewhat awkwardly put her arms around her.

"That isn't quite the reaction I expected," Cronley said.

"Captain," Augie Ziegler said, "she's still pretty shook up."

Florence freed herself from Claudette's embrace and faced Cronley. Tears ran down her cheeks.

"Captain, with respect. I goddamned sure didn't behave well when those bastards grabbed us. I fucking lost it. I really want to wear triangles, but because I'm doing what Dette's doing, not because you feel sorry for me. So thanks, but no fucking thanks."

Cronley didn't reply for a long moment.

"Miller," he said finally, "now that you're a DCI special agent, you're going to have to stop cussing like a bull dyke WAC sergeant. Clear?"

After another long moment, Florence asked, "Is that what I sound like?"

"That's what you sounded like just now."

"Sir, with respect, you know that I'm no —"

Cronley held up his hand to silence her.

"And you're going to have to learn not to question my judgment. I decide who has behaved well, and who hasn't. Is that clear?"

"Yes, sir."

"Now that Hessinger has finished removing your chevrons, I think you should take your uniform to the room Hessinger arranged for you, sew triangles on the lapels, and then hang it up. Then go to bed. In the morning, put your uniform with triangles on and report to Dette for duty. Clear?"

"Yes, sir. Sir, permission to speak?"

"Speak."

"Sir, in Mr. Ziegler's car, on the way here, Dette said that she and Mr. Ziegler had a briefcase full of stuff that had to be Leica-ed. I'm good at that."

"Dette?" Cronley asked.

"It would free Augie and me to get the refrigerators to the Engineer Depot."

"Freddy, as soon as Florence can sew triangles on her uniform, take her and the Odessa material to the photo lab."

"Yes, sir," Hessinger said.

# [FOUR]

*The Cocktail Lounge*

*Hotel Vier Jahreszeiten*

*Maximilianstrasse 178*

*Munich, American Zone of Occupation,
  Germany*

*2215 25 January 1946*

Alphonse Bittermann, the senior bartender of the cocktail lounge, who was sixty-two and had the reddish plump cheeks of a postcard Bavarian, had worked continuously at the Vier Jahreszeiten for forty-six years.

He had never been called to serve in uniform because of an unusual heartbeat pattern, until the very last days of the war, when he had been mustered into the Volkssturm. Heinrich Himmler had drafted, at Hitler's orders, every male from age sixteen to sixty-five who was not already in uniform into the militia.

Alphonse was captured by the U.S. 20th Armored Division, which (together with the 3rd, 44th, and 45th Infantry Divisions) took Munich against light resistance on April 29–30, 1945. He was then serving as an interpreter. He had become fluent in French, Italian, Spanish, Hungarian, Polish, and

English while working his way up from dishwasher to senior bartender in the Vier Jahreszeiten, and was conversant in several other tongues, including Russian.

He had been a POW for two weeks when the POW camp commander, for whom Alphonse had been serving as an interpreter/bartender, decided Alphonse was just the man to take over the bar in the Vier Jahreszeiten, which had just been requisitioned by the U.S. Army for service as a senior officers' hotel.

Six weeks after he had been mustered into the Volkssturm, Alphonse was again wearing his white jacket and mixing drinks in what he thought of as his bar.

Alphonse quickly became friendly with the American officers, majors and up, who patronized the bar off the Vier Jahreszeiten's lobby. While Alphonse was, perhaps understandably, something of a snob, he could tolerate most of the Americans, even though he quickly decided that only a very few of them genuinely could be called gentlemen.

Conversely, he didn't *dislike* many of his American customers, although there were a few that he really disliked.

When the Army had taken over the Vier Jahreszeiten, among the first people to move in were officers of the Office of Strategic Services. They took over the entire fifth floor of one of the wings.

Their commanding officer met Alphonse's criteria as a gentleman. His name was Robert Mattingly and he was a colonel of cavalry. His uniforms were impeccable, he was never in need of a haircut or a shave, and he spoke German fluently with a Hessian accent.

His deputy, Major Harold Wallace, not only also spoke German fluently, with a Berliner accent, but decent French and Italian as well. But that was about all that could be said in his favor. While he rarely needed a shave, he often needed a haircut, and he was seldom seen in pinks and greens, but rather in a brown woolen uniform indistinguishable from that worn by common enlisted men. And his shoes often needed a shining. And he had the disconcerting habit of opening his jacket, revealing a large pistol in a shoulder holster.

Their administrative officer wasn't really an officer at all, but a sergeant who wore the insignia of a civilian employee on the lapels of an officer's pinks-and-greens uniform. Friedrich Hessinger spoke German with a Bavarian accent fluently. He was a Bavarian, a Jew who had gone to America

and was now back as a member of the oc-
cupying army.

Hessinger frequently brought to the bar
statuesque blond German women, sometimes two of them at once. Alphonse didn't
hold the women against him — to the victor
go the spoils — or blame the women. But a
German Jew who was really a sergeant
bringing women of dubious morality into a
senior officers' bar was obviously inappropriate.

When Colonel Mattingly left Munich for
duty at a higher headquarters, Major Wallace and Sergeant Hessinger remained, now
as members of something called the
XXVIIth CIC, which had replaced the OSS,
and which Alphonse understood to be
something like the Sicherheitsdienst in the
former regime.

And then the one American whom Alphonse really didn't like appeared in the
XXVIIth CIC. He was a captain, although
he didn't look to be old enough to hold that
rank. He often appeared in a uniform with
triangles, suggesting he was a civilian employee. When wearing the latter — and
sometimes when wearing ODs and pinks
and greens with his captain's insignia — he
wore cowboy boots. Sometimes they were
highly polished, and sometimes they looked

as if he had walked from Moscow to Munich in them.

Alphonse didn't think the young captain was a Jew. He was blond and didn't have Semitic facial features. Alphonse strongly suspected the young captain was a German, because he spoke German fluently with a strong Alsatian accent. He was invariably armed, carrying a huge pistol either in a holster, or sometimes simply jammed in his waistband.

Once, when this "officer and gentleman" had appeared in the bar wearing a gray woolen upper garment on which was printed in red a map of Texas and the lettering "A&M" — plus of course his battered cowboy boots — and was accompanied by two German men, whom he addressed in German as "Herr General" and "Herr Oberst," Alphonse knew he had to do something about it.

Alphonse tried to hear what they were talking about, but every time he sidled close as he polished glasses, they stopped talking. He would have liked to hear them talking about what he thought they were talking about — specifically, black market prices — so he could take that information with him when he went to Lieutenant Colonel Matthews, who was the club officer.

He went to Colonel Matthews anyway, where he suggested that since it was not his position to say anything, perhaps the colonel might see fit to have a word with the young captain about his presence in a senior officers' bar wearing a garment more suited to a gymnasium and with a pistol jammed in his waistband, and bringing with him two Germans whom regulations forbade being in the Vier Jahreszeiten at all.

"Between you and me, Alphonse," Colonel Matthews had replied, "yours is not the first complaint I've heard about Cronley. A number of the officers' ladies have complained. But the thing is, he's the chief of something called the DCI and so far as his being quartered in the Vier Jahreszeiten, this DCI thing gives him the assimilated rank of lieutenant colonel. And this DCI, whatever the hell it is, is not under Munich Military Post. And so far as those two Germans are concerned, they have documents identifying them as members of this DCI, and they can come in here, too. We just have to live with this situation. Sorry."

When Captain James D. Cronley Jr. walked into the Vier Jahreszeiten bar and took a stool, Alphonse Bittermann saw that again his dress did not meet the standards of the house. The wearing of pinks and greens was "strongly recommended" after 1930 hours. And not only was the young captain wearing OD, he was wearing it with civilian triangles and a turtleneck sweater instead of a shirt and tie. And of course cowboy boots, the ones that looked as if he had walked in them all the way from Moscow.

Alphonse draped his barman's napkin over his left arm, walked quickly to him, smiled, and greeted him in English.

"Good evening, Captain Cronley, sir. What can I fix for you this evening?"

Cronley replied in German: "What's new, Fritz? How about pouring me a double Jack Daniel's? Water on the side. I'm entitled. I've had a long day."

"Yes, sir. Double Jack Daniel's. Water on the side," Alphonse parroted in English, and then added, "My name is Alphonse, sir."

"I don't know why I can't remember that. One of my favorite gangsters is named Alphonse. Alphonse Capone."

Alphonse smiled although he had heard Cronley's little joke before. He suspected the *gottverdammt Amerikaner* called him Fritz just so he could make his little joke. He had vowed he wouldn't give him the chance again but had forgotten.

As Alphonse took the bottle of Jack Daniel's from the row of bottles behind the bar, he saw in the mirror that the *gottverdammt Amerikaner* was looking with interest at a woman sitting far down the bar.

This pleased him. The woman, who was in her late twenties or early thirties, had been in the bar for about an hour. She had attracted the attention of three different officers, all of whose advances she had bluntly rejected. The woman was wearing a pink-and-green uniform with a gold-thread-embroidered patch sewn to her sleeves at the shoulder. It read US WAR CORRESPON-DENT.

With just a little bit of luck, Captain Cronley would make a play for the woman, and she would reject him at least as humiliatingly as she had the other officers, all of whom, Alphonse recalled, were not only in the proper uniform but senior — one major and two lieutenant colonels — to him.

And then, after he had placed the bottle of Jack Daniel's, two glasses, a water decanter, and a silver ice cube bucket with tongs on his tray and turned to carry it to Cronley, Alphonse saw something that really pleased him.

Colonel Robert Mattingly, as usual splendidly turned out, had entered the bar together with another officer, a major, whom Alphonse did not recognize, and was headed for Cronley. Mattingly certainly would be offended by the turtleneck sweater and he would correct him. Cronley could not ignore Mattingly.

"Colonel Mattingly," Alphonse called out. "How nice to see you again, sir!"

"Hello, Alphonse," Mattingly said, and offered his hand. Then he turned to Cronley.

"Cronley," he said.

"Good evening, Colonel," Cronley said.

"Steve, this is Captain Cronley. Cronley, Major Davis."

"How do you do, sir?"

"Captain."

"We were upstairs," Mattingly said. "The office is locked."

"Yes, sir," Cronley said. "It is."

"What may I get you, Colonel?" Alphonse asked.

Colonel Mattingly ordered Dewar's on the rocks, and Major Davis said, "The same, please."

"I was afraid I wouldn't find you. Or anyone," Mattingly said. "We have to make the Blue Danube at 2330."

"I left word with the switchboard that I'd be in here," Cronley said. "They didn't tell you?"

"I didn't ask, actually," Mattingly said.

"What brings you to Munich?"

"We had some business with Colonel Parsons at the Compound," Mattingly said. "And while we were there, he told us that Sergeant Colbert got involved in something pretty nasty."

"That's Miss Colbert now. I made her a DCI special agent."

"*You* made her a DCI special agent?"

"Uh-huh."

"The correct answer to that question would have been, 'Yes, sir.' "

"No disrespect intended, sir. But the colonel did notice that I'm not wearing any insignia of rank?"

"Before we get into it yet again, Cronley, when I get back to Frankfurt, I'd like to tell General Greene about this incident Sergeant Colbert was involved in. So, what can you tell me about it?"

"Sir, Major Wallace has already brought General Greene up to speed on the incident."

"In other words you're not going to tell me what you know?" Mattingly snapped.

"Sir, with respect, I don't believe you have the Need to Know."

"And you think you have the authority to make that decision?"

"I know I do, Colonel."

"Captain," Major Davis said, "I'd like to know where the hell you think you got the authority to refuse to tell Colonel Mattingly anything he wishes to know."

Cronley reached in his pocket and took out his DCI credentials. He held them open for them to read.

"With all respect, this is where I get the authority."

"What's that?" Major Davis asked.

Mattingly did not reply to the question, instead saying, "Well, it didn't take long for this to go to your head, did it, Cronley?"

Cronley didn't reply.

"Keep in mind, you arrogant pup," Mattingly said, "that you're still a serving officer, and that what goes around comes around, and is going to bite you hard on the ass just as soon as someone comes to his senses and takes those goddamn credentials away from you."

"I'll keep that in mind, sir."

"Let's go, Davis," Mattingly said, and marched out of the bar.

Alphonse didn't understand much of what he overheard, but it was clear that Colonel Mattingly was quite angry with Cronley about something, something much more important than Cronley's turtleneck sweater.

He started to remove Mattingly's and Davis's untouched drinks.

"Leave them, Alphonse," Cronley ordered in German. "Didn't your mother teach you 'Waste not, want not'?"

Ninety seconds later, just after Cronley had tossed down what was left of his Jack Daniel's and taken the first sip of what had been Mattingly's scotch, the woman at the bar moved down and took the stool beside Cronley.

"You're just the man I'm looking for," she said. "Can I buy you a drink?"

"I don't know what you have in mind, but you better understand from the get-go that I am a practicing Episcopalian who doesn't let himself get picked up by strange women in bars."

"Maybe you ought to try it sometime," she said, and put out her hand. "Janice Johansen, AP."

He shook her hand, but said nothing.

"And you are?"

"I never give my name to strange women. If I do, then they want my telephone number, and the next thing I know, there are lewd phone calls at three a.m."

"Your name is Cronley and I already have your phone number," she said, and proceeded to recite it. "There was no answer when I called, so I thought I would hang around the bar and see if the mysterious chief of the Central Intelligence Directorate came in for a nightcap. I was looking for somebody twenty years older with a paunch."

"Sorry to disappoint you."

"Don't be. I would much rather wield my feminine charms on someone your age."

"You're a cradle robber?"

"Why not? I'd like to ask you a couple of simple questions."

"I don't answer questions from strange women, so I'll tell you what: Why don't you help yourself to that Dewar's and then go back down the bar?"

"We can start with that," she said, and picked up the glass.

She took an appreciative sip, and then asked, "Can I try a couple of questions on for size?"

"Can I stop you?"

"You're pretty good at pissing people off, aren't you? I thought that colonel was about to throw a punch."

"He wouldn't do that. He's an officer and a gentleman."

"What was it that you showed him that so pissed him off? Can I see it?"

"None of your business, and no."

"I'll show you mine if you show me yours."

"Presumably you're speaking of identification documents."

"Not exclusively. What did you have in mind?"

"Next question?"

"I heard this Sergeant Colbert killed three guys . . ."

"Is that so?"

". . . with a snub-nosed .38 she carries in her brassiere. True?"

"Who the hell told you that?"

"I have friends in the MPs."

"Interview over."

"Consider this. A woman blowing away three guys trying to rape her and her girl-friend is a real man-bites-dog yarn. It's not going to go away. I'm going to write it with what I have. If for some reason there's some aspects of the story you don't want me to write, you're going to have to tell me what they are, and why I shouldn't write them."

"Jesus H. Christ!"

"Your call."

"I can't talk about this in here."

"Are you trying to get me into your room?"

"My office. To talk about this. Yeah."

"And for that purpose only?"

"Boy Scout's honor, cross my heart and

251

hope to die."

"Pity," she said. "Okay, let's go."

"I'm a little disappointed," Janice Johansen said, when they were in 507. "This is really an office."

"Take a look at this, please, Miss Johansen," Cronley said, and handed her his credentials.

She read them.

"I'll be damned! If you wanted to dazzle a girl who has evil intentions, you succeeded. And you can call me Janice."

"I frankly don't know what to do with you, Miss Johansen. So, what I'm going to do is tell you the truth and then appeal to . . . Jesus . . . your patriotism."

"The last refuge of a scoundrel, they say."

"If after I tell you this story and what I don't want to see in the papers appears in the papers, and any of my people get hurt, I'll kill you."

"This just stopped being fun. Still exciting, but not fun."

"I'm not trying to be clever."

"You've succeeded. What you are is menacing. So let's have the story."

Five minutes later, she said, "If you had your druthers, Cronley, what would my story not contain?"

"Any reference to DCI. Any reference to Claudette or Florence being DCI agents. Any reference to the guys Claudette took down being either NKGB or Nazis. Any reference to one of them still being alive."

"The sign outside says Twenty-seventh CIC. What's that?"

"Off the record it's the cover for DCI. On the record, it's what it says."

"And would the Twenty-seventh CIC have WAC cryptographers?"

"Yes."

"And they go around with pistols?"

"Usually in their purses. Sometimes in holsters."

"Can I use this one carrying her gun in her bra?"

"She'd probably be embarrassed. But maybe not. She's a hell of a woman."

"He says with admiration."

"Yeah. A lot of admiration."

"Anything happen to be going on between you two?"

"No."

"Good. I wouldn't want to fool around with the boyfriend of a woman who just killed three guys with a gun she took out of her brassiere."

"Don't you ever get in trouble making

those wise-ass sexual remarks? Aren't you afraid someone's going to get the wrong idea?"

"Are you telling me you're not interested?"

After a long moment Cronley said, "No. I'm not saying that."

"So I'll tell you what happens next. First thing, you tell me what you want me to call you."

"Jim."

"Then I tell you the truth."

"What truth is that?"

"Two things. First, when you came in the bar, I thought what a goddamn pity that blond Adonis is not this Cronley guy. I'd love to put the make on him. Second, when you said you would kill me, I believed you and found that very exciting."

"Jesus Christ!"

"So now that you know my sexual secrets, why don't we go to a room with a bed, and you can tell me yours?"

When he didn't reply, she said, "And whenever we finish that, we can come back in here, and I'll write the story and show it to you. Just so long as I can get the story on the wire to *Stars and Stripes* before they go to bed at midnight. How's that strike you?"

"I'm so innocent I don't know what the hell you're talking about."

"I'm going to send my story to *Stripes*. They'll put it on the AP wire. After they go to bed — start printing — at midnight."

"So that's what 'go to bed' means."

"That's one meaning. When we get to your room, I'll show you another."

"It's right down the hall," Cronley said, and waved Janice out of his office.

# VI

## [ONE]

*The Main Dining Room*

*Hotel Vier Jahreszeiten*

*Maximilianstrasse 178*

*Munich, American Zone of Occupation, Germany*

*0945 26 January 1946*

Major Harold Wallace looked into the dining room and found what he had failed to find the last four times he had looked in the past half hour.

James D. Cronley Jr. was sitting alone at a table. He was neatly attired in pinks and greens with triangles, watching a waiter fill his coffee cup.

Now that he had found him, Wallace

wasn't happy. He didn't want to do what he realized he had to. But he had reached the conclusion as he had flown to Munich from the Eschborn airstrip that Mattingly was right.

Cronley, the poster child for loose cannons, had to go.

This time he had gone too far.

Colonel Robert Mattingly had come to Wallace's room in the Schlosshotel Kronberg at 0500, as Wallace was shaving and preparing to go to the airstrip for his flight to Munich.

He had begun the conversation by telling Wallace how unhappy Lieutenant Colonel Parsons, the War Department G-2 officer stationed at the Compound, was with the young chief, DCI-Europe.

Some of Parsons's complaints were bullshit — that Cronley did not treat him with the crisp military courtesy to which Parsons felt entitled headed that list — but some of them, when Parsons, as he threatened to do, took them to General Seidel, the USFET G-2, Seidel was going to think perfectly valid.

Mattingly had told him that suspecting what Cronley was up to, Parsons had stood a young ASA sergeant tall and got him to admit that ASA intercept operators, at

Cronley's orders, were intercepting all of Parsons's communications with the Pentagon — incoming and outgoing — and giving copies to Cronley.

It had also somehow come to Parsons's attention that Cronley had been in contact with Commandant Jean-Paul Fortin of the Direction de la Surveillance du Territoire in Strasbourg. When asked about this, even after Parsons had told him that the Pentagon was especially interested in Fortin's role in investigating Odessa, Cronley had told Parsons he knew nothing about Fortin, the DST, or Odessa.

Mattingly had suggested — and Wallace was forced to conclude he was right — that the proper way to deal with a situation in which Cronley didn't want to share intelligence with Parsons was to tell him he couldn't share the intelligence without the approval of Admiral Souers in Washington, and then ask the admiral for that permission.

To boldly lie to the War Department G-2's man in Germany, since he knew Cronley was lying, was tantamount to telling Parsons and the War Department G-2 to go piss up a rope.

Mattingly had then proceeded to report what had happened when he had gone to

Cronley for two reasons. First to see if he couldn't reason with him and possibly make him see the wisdom of pouring oil on the troubled waters between him and Colonel Parsons.

Wallace thought this was bullshit. Mattingly, who devoutly believed he should be chief, DCI-Europe, was almost certain to have been delighted to see Jim Cronley's ass in a crack, which might see him getting canned, and leaving the chief, DCI-Europe, slot open for someone highly qualified, such as Colonel Robert Mattingly.

The second reason Mattingly said he had gone to Cronley was to ask him about what he had heard from Colonel Parsons about Sergeant Colbert shooting three people in the NCO club parking lot.

Cronley had no reason not to tell Mattingly everything about that. Mattingly might be a prick, but he was also deputy commander of CIC-Europe and not a Russian spy.

Instead, he had told Mattingly he didn't have the Need to Know, and when Major Davis, who was Seidel's man in CIC-Europe, asked him where he thought he had the authority not to tell Colonel Mattingly anything he wanted to know, Cronley had whipped out his DCI credentials.

Despite all this, Wallace had not firmly decided to relieve Cronley until he walked into the lobby of the Vier Jahreszeiten.

There were reasons not to fire him, starting of course with the fact that President Truman had personally named Cronley as chief, DCI-Europe. And then there was the question of what to do with him. He couldn't be sent to some tank company in the Constabulary. Argentina was a possibility, but Cletus Frade was there, and he was not going to take kindly to his little brother getting fired because he had pissed off some Pentagon chairwarmer. And Cletus Frade had the ear of El Jefe Schultz, executive assistant to the director of Central Intelligence.

And then Major Wallace had walked into the lobby of the Vier Jahreszeiten and absentmindedly helped himself to a copy of *Stars and Stripes* from a stack on a small table.

He had glanced at it casually, and then a story on the first page caught his attention. He read it quickly and then again very carefully.

# ATTEMPTED RAPE OF WACS FAILS
## Would-be Rapists Pick Wrong Victims

By Janice Johansen
Associated Press Foreign Correspondent

**Munich Jan 25 —**

Three would-be rapists died on the spot and a fourth died later in the 98th General Hospital when their attempted assault of WAC Technical Sergeants Claudette Colbert and Florence Miller went very wrong for them early in the morning of January 24.

The men, so far unidentified but believed to be Polish DPs who escaped from the Oberhaching Displaced Persons Camp, forced the two WAC non-coms into an ambulance the would-be rapists had stolen earlier from the 98th General Hospital and driven to the parking lot of the Munich Military Post Non-Commissioned Officers' Club.

With knives at their throats, neither Colbert nor Miller offered resistance until they were inside the stolen ambulance. Then, as soon as the ambulance began to move and she saw her opportunity, Sergeant Colbert took her .38 caliber revolver from where she had it concealed in her brassiere and opened fire. Three of the would-be rapists died instantly in the ambulance and a fourth was declared dead on arrival at the 98th General Hospital.

Sergeants Colbert and Miller are cryptographers assigned to the Army Security Agency's Munich station. They are required to be armed because of the classified material they deal with daily.

"Normally, I leave my pistol in the office," Sergeant Colbert said. "But last night, thank God, I had it with me."

Asked why she had concealed the weapon in her brassiere, the sergeant said that since she didn't want to walk into the NCO club with a holstered weapon, and couldn't leave the pistol in the vehicle in which she and Sergeant Miller had driven to the NCO club, "I didn't have any other option."

Colonel Arthur B. Kellogg, the Munich provost marshal who investigated the shooting incident, offered high praise to the WAC noncom: "Sergeant Colbert's courage and professional cool-mindedness when dealing with a life-threatening situation like this reflects great credit not only upon her personally, but on all the members of the WAC. I am going to recommend to her commanding officer that she be recommended for at least the award of the Army Commendation Medal."

"Jesus H. Christ!" Wallace said.

261

*The question of whether Cronley gets re-
lieved is out of my hands.*

*As soon as El Jefe — or the admiral —
hears about this, we'll both get relieved.*

*DCI is supposed to be a secret organiza-
tion, not written about on the front page of a
goddamn newspaper.*

*If I can't shut up one lousy goddamn reporter
— and they'll come after me on this, not Cronley — I don't belong in the goddamn Girl
Scouts, much less the DCI.*

*What did Truman say? "The buck stops
here!"*

*And when both Cronley and I are sent . . .
Where was it they sent Napoleon?*

*Elba!*

*And when Cronley and I are counting snow-
balls on some Aleutian island version of Elba,
who's going to take my place?*

*That fucking Mattingly, that's who!*

*And that'll see DCI taken over by G-2 in no
more than two hours!*

Major Wallace then began his search for
Captain Cronley, whom he intended to
politely ask if he had any conception whatever of the damage he had caused by failing
to take into consideration the enormous
damage one lousy fucking journalist can do,
and therefore doing nothing whatever to
silence said one fucking journalist and as a

result of which he and I will be counting snowballs in fucking Alaska through all eternity. Amen.

Major Wallace marched across the dining room to where a waiter was pouring coffee from a silver urn into Captain Cronley's coffee cup.

*What I would like to do is shove that god-damn coffeepot up his ass.*

*But I will not do that because I am an officer and a gentleman.*

*And if I did, there would be a story in tomorrow's* Stars and Stripes.

*By Janice Whatever the fuck her name is.*

*"Army Colonel Goes Berserk. In Munich Hotel.*

*"Strangles Young Captain.*

*"Then Shoves Silver Coffeepot Up His Ass."*

"I've been looking all over for you, Jim," Major Wallace greeted him. "Where the hell have you been?"

"Why, good morning, Major Wallace, sir. Are you free to join me, sir?"

"Free's not the word," Wallace said, and sat down.

"Give the Herr Major some coffee, please," Cronley ordered the waiter in German.

"You seem to be in a very cheerful mood.

Any particular reason?" Wallace asked, and then before Cronley could reply, got to the point. "Did you really tell Colonel Mattingly that he didn't have the Need to Know about what happened to Claudette and . . . the other one?"

"You mean, Technical Sergeant Miller, sir?"

"Yes or no, goddammit, Jim!"

"Yes, sir, I did."

"Why, for Christ's sake?"

"For one thing, he *didn't* have the Need to Know. And I confess to being annoyed with him at the time."

*"You* were annoyed with *him?"*

"He told me that he and a major named Davis he had with him had just come from the Compound, where they had business with Colonel Parsons."

"So?"

"He was supposed to tell us when he wanted to visit the Compound, and he didn't. And he took Davis inside with him."

*Sonofabitch! He's right.*

*I told Mattingly that he could go to the Compound, but only after he told us when, and that he was not authorized to take anybody with him.*

"You know Davis works for General Seidel," Wallace said. "He's sort of Seidel's

264

liaison officer with General Greene."

"I didn't know that being a liaison officer — read 'spy' — for the USFET G-2 gets you a pass into the Compound. Or have you changed the rules?"

"No, I haven't changed the rules. You realize you have really pissed Mattingly off?"

"I suspected he was pissed when he stormed out of the bar, but not as pissed, I suggest, as he would have been if I had told him in front of that Major Davis that he had no right to go into the Compound without telling us first and absolutely no right to take some USFET G-2 officer with him. And don't do it again."

Wallace exhaled.

*Well, he's right about that, too.*

"The first thing Colonel Mattingly did when he got to the Schlosshotel Kronberg at five this morning — just as I was leaving for the airstrip — was tell me (a) what you had done, (b) that your DCI credentials have obviously gone to your immature head, and (c) ask me how long it was going to be before I came to my senses and put somebody in charge of DCI who knows what he's doing."

"Well — and I'm not trying to be flip — at least we now know he doesn't know who made me chief of DCI and why, does he?

Or did you tell him?"

"Of course I didn't tell him."

"How long do you think it's going to take for him to figure that out?"

"We can only hope, Captain Cronley, that the colonel is not nearly as smart as he thinks he is."

"I did what I thought I should. If that puts you on a spot, I'm really sorry."

*That didn't put me on a spot, my young loose cannon.*

*The goddamn story in the goddamn* Stars and Stripes *is what put both of us on the fucking spot.*

Wallace made a deprecating gesture and said, "He's really going to be pissed when he reads *Stars and Stripes* and sees that what you wouldn't tell him is all over the front page."

"Really? On the first page?"

"Have a look," Wallace said, and handed him a copy of the tabloid-sized newspaper. "Somebody's been talking to this goddamn reporter. Even if she did, predictably, get most of the facts wrong, this is a fu . . . disaster."

"I think I can plead guilty even before I read it. But let me have a look."

"What do you mean, 'plead guilty'? Don't tell me you have been talking to this goddamned reporter!"

Cronley looked at Wallace, then past him.

"Speak of the devil — is there a feminine term for that? 'Deviless,' maybe?"

Cronley stood up as Janice Johansen approached the table.

"Good morning, Janice," Cronley said. "You look bright and chipper. Sleep well?"

"You know I did."

Wallace got to his feet.

*Nice-looking. A little old for my tastes, but well preserved.*

*What did she do to get him to run at the mouth?*

*What women always do when they want something from a man?*

*That's why the sonofabitch is so cheerful!*

*So what does that do to my suspicions that Loose Cannon and Sergeant Colbert have a closer relationship than is considered appropriate for a commanding officer and a female non-com?*

"Major Wallace, may I introduce Miss Janice Johansen of the Associated Press?"

"Well, you're not as good-looking as Jim said you were, Major, but I'm pleased to meet you anyhow."

Janice pulled up a chair, then saw the *Stars and Stripes* and reached for it.

"Let's see where those bastards buried my

267

yarn," she said. To which she immediately added, "I'll be damned! Front page, above the fold! They do recognize a good story when they see one."

"I don't think Major Wallace thinks that's such a good story," Cronley said.

*That's the understatement of the fucking century!*

"And you do?" Wallace challenged.

"Yes, I do," Cronley said. "Thank you, Janice."

"Anything I can do, within reason, of course, to help you Good Guys in your valiant battle with the Red Menace."

"What don't you like in Janice's story, Major Wallace?" Cronley asked.

*Christ, do I have to spell it out for you?*

*That it's in the fucking newspaper at all, is what's wrong with it.*

*And shit, she's an Associated Press correspondent. That story went out on the AP wire.*

*The admiral and El Jefe will read it in the* Washington Star *over their morning coffee in Washington!*

"For one thing, it's got Colbert's and Miller's names on the front page of the *Stars and Stripes,*" Wallace said, a little awkwardly.

"Describing her as an ASA cryptographer," Janice said. "Not a mention of the

268

DCI, which Jim says is something patriotic Americans such as myself should not say out loud. What's wrong with that?"

Wallace visibly could not come up with an instant reply.

A waiter appeared.

"Thank God!" Janice said. "I'm ravenous! That always happens when I exercise before going to bed. Correction, before going to sleep."

*Not only has she been fucking Cronley, she wants me to know she has.*

"Orange juice, ham and eggs, easy over, rye toast, and fried potatoes, please," Janice ordered.

"Same for me, please," Cronley said. "Major Wallace?"

"Make it three orders, please," Wallace ordered. Then he asked, "I gather you're also ravenous, Jim?"

"If you're asking why, I've been up since oh-dark-hundred trying to stuff two very large refrigerators into a very small jeep trailer. It was pretty exhausting."

"How'd that go?" Janice asked.

"As we speak, the refrigerators are on their way to cement Franco-American relations in Strasbourg."

*Jesus Christ, did he tell her about Strasbourg?*

"Jesus Christ, what did you tell her about Strasbourg?" Wallace demanded.

"I suspect what you meant to ask is what has Jim told me about your problem with Odessa," Janice said.

*Right on the fucking money, sweetheart!*

"I'm afraid of what I'm about to hear," Wallace said.

"Jim said when you heard about this, you were going to be highly pissed," Janice said. "So let's clear the decks."

*Well, at least he got one thing right. Highly pissed is a gross understatement.*

"That sounds like a good idea," Wallace said.

"Whether you like it or not, Major — what's your first name, by the way?"

"If you consider it germane, it's Harold."

"Okay. Well, Harry, whether or not you like it . . ."

*She's doing that to piss me off!*

"I said Harold."

"So you did. As I was saying, Harry, a WAC blowing away three guys with a snub-nosed .38 she carries in her brassiere is a story that's going to get out whether or not it's convenient for you."

"Who told you about that?"

"It's what we call 'unidentified military police officials speaking off the record.' "

"By the name of Ziegler, maybe?"

"When I asked Augie, he told me that if I didn't back off this story, a hard-ass guy named Cronley of the DCI was going to bury me. I'd already heard his name connected with this DCI, about which I was also very curious. So I went looking for DCI Chief Cronley. I expected an old fart with a paunch, and instead I got this blond Adonis. So, batting my eyes at him, I told him I had the story, and was going to write it and the only choice he had in the matter was to tell me what DCI didn't want in the story and why."

"He could have had you arrested."

"Killed, sure. He threatened that. Convincingly . . ."

*What the hell does she mean by that?*

*Did my loose cannon actually threaten seriously to take her out?*

*Why not? He may look like an aging choir boy, but . . .*

". . . Arrested, no. People don't seem to give a damn when they hear of some journalist getting blown away. But people go ballistic when they hear that somebody is trying to lock reporters up to shut them up."

*Well, she's right about that.*

"Interesting point," Wallace said.

"So, Harry, he told me what he'd rather

271

not see in my story and why. And, since what he told me made sense, I wrote it that way."

"Am I supposed to say, 'Thank you'?"

"That would be nice. You're welcome. Anyway, Harry, at some point in our conversation, Odessa came up. I told Jim that was a story I'd really like to write and was going to write whether he liked it or not, but maybe we could scratch each other's back. Or rub each other's back, whichever he might prefer. So we made a deal."

"As I understand that, what he contributes is telling you things you have no right to know. So what are you contributing to this mutual back rubbing?"

"For openers," Cronley answered, "she's going to arrange for us to get a guy into the *Stars and Stripes* plant in Pfungstadt."

"How?"

"She's got a jeep. From USFET Public Relations —"

"The USFET Press Office," she corrected him.

"No driver," Cronley said. "So we give her a driver, one of Tiny's guys, and they drive this jeep to Pfungstadt. She leaves Tiny's guy there to see what he can find out about Odessa using the *Stripes* trucks —"

"She's not going to stay there?"

"No. Just the driver. I'll go pick her up in an L-4, or send Winters, and bring her back here. If our guy is going to find anything out, he should be able to do it in three or four days. Then she calls Pfungstadt and tells them to send her driver down here with the jeep."

*That just might work. I'll be damned.*

"Miss Johansen . . ."

"You can call me Janice, Harry."

"Only if you call me Harold, Janice."

"Does that mean you've accepted me as a fellow warrior in the holy war against the Red Menace?"

*Yeah, I guess it does.*

"I don't have much choice, do I?"

"Well, in that case, Harold, I'll call you Harold."

"I was about to say I hope you really understand my uneasiness about —"

"Me hearing things I shouldn't be hearing?"

"Yeah."

"Not to worry, Harold. As there are very few Army officers who can actually find their own rear ends with one hand, there are a very few journalists who can be trusted. I'm one of them. I'm not going to blow what you guys are doing for the sake of a byline. Okay? Do we understand each

273

other, Harold?"

"I really hope so," Wallace said. "So when are you going to drive to Pfungstadt?"

"Just as soon as Jim and I get back from the monastery."

*My God, he's not going to take her out there!*

"What's your interest in Kloster Grünau?"

"I want to have a look at the guy Colbert popped — the one who was dead on arrival at the 98th Hospital. Resurrection is always a good story."

"Jesus Christ!"

"Even if I can't write it right now. What are the Brits always saying, Harold? 'In for a penny, in for a pound'?"

After a perceptible pause, Wallace said, "That's what they're always saying."

Two waiters appeared carrying their breakfasts.

# [Two]

*Suite 507*

*Hotel Vier Jahreszeiten*

*Maximilianstrasse 178*

*Munich, American Zone of Occupation,
Germany*

*1025 26 January 1946*

Captain Chauncey L. Dunwiddie, Miss Claudette Colbert, Mr. Friedrich Hessinger, Mr. August Ziegler, and Mr. John D. Hammersmith were in the office when Major Harold Wallace, Captain James D. Cronley, and Miss Janice Johansen walked in.

"Surprise, surprise," Wallace greeted them. "The enemy is at the gates."

"You can close your mouth now, Captain Dunwiddie," Cronley said.

"Good morning," Janice said.

"Change in the Order of Battle," Wallace said. "Johansen, Janice, from Enemy to Ally."

"Thank you, Harold," Janice said.

"Don't make me regret it," Wallace said.

"Perish the thought," she said.

"I have jumped to the conclusion that everyone has read this morning's *Stars and Stripes,*" Wallace said, making it a question.

275

Everyone nodded.

"Janice has told us (a) that her splendid story will already have made its way on the AP wire to all the world's newspapers, including the *Washington Star,* which both the admiral and El Jefe read over their morning coffee, and (b) that the *Washington Star* will almost certainly run a story of great international significance, such as a WAC non-com blowing away four evil men intent on stealing her virtue with a .38 she carries around in her underwear.

"To that end, Freddy, get on the horn to the ASA in Fulda to make sure I have an encrypted voice line to El Jefe at noon. That will be 0700 in Washington, and with a little bit of luck, I'll be able to talk to El Jefe before he or the admiral reads Miss Johansen's article. I suspect both the admiral and his executive assistant will wish to chat with me about it. I would prefer to have that chat before they are enraged by it."

"Yes, sir," Hessinger said. "I'll arrange the line."

"I am now going to my room, where I will try to figure out what to say. Captain Cronley will bring you up to speed on this disaster. If Colonel Mattingly calls, tell him I'm skiing in the Alps."

"Is Colonel Mattingly somehow involved

276

in this?" Claudette asked.

Wallace hesitated before replying.

Finally he said, "Dette, would you be surprised to hear that once again Captain Cronley has grossly annoyed Colonel Mattingly and that as we speak the colonel is probably telling General Seidel why he is displeased?"

"No, sir."

"That's something else I fear I will have to discuss with our naval superiors. How am I going to talk them out of keelhauling our chief?"

"I see the problem," Hessinger said.

"Good," Wallace said, and walked out of the office.

Everybody looked at Cronley.

"While Freddy is talking to Fulda," he said, "what I need from you, Tiny, is one of your troopers, a German speaker, to drive Miss Johansen to Pfungstadt, where he will spend several days becoming chummy with the *Stars and Stripes* delivery truck drivers."

"Good idea!" Hammersmith said.

"I want him ready to go the minute Miss Johansen and I get back from Kloster Grünau."

"What's that about?" Hessinger asked.

"Miss Johansen is interested to see the man we reported as dead."

"Resurrection always makes a good story," Janice furnished.

"I won't even get into that," Claudette said. "But before you go out there, I think you'd better have a look at this."

Cronley read the SIGABA printout she handed him:

```
Priority

Top Secret Lindbergh

Duplication Forbidden

From Polo
via Vint Hill Tango Net
2210 Greenwich 25 January 1946

To Altarboy

Pilot of SAA flight 777 eta Rhine
main 1700 local 26 Jan has
photos you requested of daddy
showing wife and kiddies buenos
aires cultural attractions.

Polo

End

Top Secret Lindbergh
```

Cronley handed it to Janice.

"What am I looking at?" she asked.

"This changes our schedule," he said. "I think we should have these pictures before we go see Lazarus."

"Who the hell is Lazarus?" Augie asked.

"You should have paid attention in Bible class, Augie," Cronley replied. "If you had, you would know that Lazarus is the guy Christ raised from the dead. Religiously speaking . . ."

"Or blasphemously," Tiny said.

". . . the guy Dette popped and we reported as dead has probably decided he's in purgatory, which, Augie, my heathen pal, is the place between heaven and hell. He expects that he will soon be on his way to hell, with his mortal remains buried in an unmarked grave in Kloster Grünau. I will show him his other option by showing him photographs of former NKGB Polkóvnik Sergei Likharev and his wife and children in heaven. In other words, Buenos Aires. I wouldn't be at all surprised if ol' Sergei and his family are shown saying 'cheese' before the Colón Opera House. Which Lazarus, the Russians being big on opera, will recognize. He then has the choice between going to heaven or to the unmarked grave I mentioned."

Both Ziegler and Hammersmith wondered: *Is he actually thinking of shooting this guy?*

"So the first thing we have to do is get Janice and her driver to Pfungstadt."

"That driver is going to be a problem," Tiny said. "You said you want a German speaker. Unless *schlafzimmer* Deutsche counts, my guys don't."

"We need somebody who speaks German and knows what to listen for," Cronley said.

"I got a guy," Ziegler said.

Cronley motioned for him to continue.

"He speaks Pennsylvania Dutch, which is really Hessian German."

"Another Pennsylvania Dutchman?" Hessinger asked.

Ziegler nodded. "He's an MP PFC. Seventeen years old."

"Wonderful!" Cronley said.

"I was in the PX snack bar when I heard someone cussing in Dutch. He had spilled his Coke and hot dog in his lap. So I talked to him. He's from Kunsterville in Bucks County. He finished high school in June, joined the Army to get the GI Bill. They ran him through six weeks of basic training and sent him over here. The 403rd MPs had him working as a translator."

"You said *you* had a guy," Cronley said.

"I decided I needed a translator more than the 403rd did."

"And he was a fellow Dutchman," Cronley said. "You're not seriously proposing we send this kid to snoop around Odessa?"

"His ambition in life is to be a CID agent. And he's smart."

Cronley sighed audibly.

"Jim," Hammersmith said, "I can't believe I'm saying this, but why not? Ziegler says he's smart, he speaks the language, and who's going to suspect a seventeen-year-old PFC of being anything but a seventeen-year-old PFC? All he's going to have to do is hang around the *Stars and Stripes* motor pool and keep his eyes and ears open."

"Oh, shit," Cronley said. "Well, let's get him over here and have a look at him."

PFC Karl-Christoph Wagner appeared fifteen minutes later, in full MP regalia. He was not what Cronley expected. Wagner had the innocent face of a seventeen-year-old, but he was six feet two and obviously weighed more than two hundred pounds.

"Karl, this is Captain Cronley," Augie said.

Wagner saluted crisply.

Speaking in German, Cronley said, "Mr. Ziegler has been telling us you want to be a

CID agent. Why?"

"I want to better myself, sir."

*Well, he speaks German.*

"Just for the sake of conversation, Wagner, would you be interested in taking on an assignment under Mr. Ziegler that would involve a certain element of risk to yourself? To your life?"

"Yes, sir."

Cronley had a mental image of PFC Wagner in a Boy Scout uniform solemnly reciting the Boy Scout oath — *On my honor, I will do my best to do my duty to God and my country . . .* — on the occasion of his promotion from Tenderfoot to Second Class rank while his mother and father watched proudly.

*What this kid is doing is thinking, "I am now going to have the opportunity to go out and slay dragons!"*

"Karl," Augie said, "we have reason to believe that the drivers, the German drivers, of the trucks who distribute the *Stars and Stripes* every day, are carrying contraband."

"You mean black market stuff, sir?"

"That, too, probably, but what we're looking for is people."

"Nazis, you mean, sir?"

"Yes, Nazis," Augie said. "Here's the deal,

Karl. Miss Johansen here . . ."

"I thought that might be who you are. I saw your story in the *Stripes* this morning about Miss Colbert, Miss Johansen."

"What we're thinking of having you do, Karl," Augie said, "is drive Miss Johansen in her jeep to the *Stars and Stripes* printing plant in Pfungstadt, which is twenty miles south of Frankfurt. She will then leave for a couple of days, leaving you there to just hang around the motor pool and see what you can learn. For example, does one of the drivers seem to be the guy running things? Or look like he's into moving PX goodies? Just get his name. Don't even think of arresting anybody even if you catch him with fifty cartons of Chesterfields and fifty pounds of coffee he stole from the PX. You understand?"

"Got it, sir."

"You think you could handle that, Karl?" Augie asked.

"Yes, sir. I'm a dumb PFC just hanging around."

"Is there a PX in Pfungstadt?" Hammersmith asked.

"Yes. And a QM clothing store," Janice said.

"What I'm thinking is that Wagner could go to the PX and stock up on cigarettes,

Hershey bars, et cetera. And maybe to the QM store. I understand jockey shorts and T-shirts are a hot item on the black market. Maybe one of the drivers might make him an offer."

Cronley had an epiphany.

"Time out," he said. "Are we really seriously considering sending this kid — no offense, Wagner, but you're seventeen — to do something like this? These are not nice people. We don't even know for sure that it was the NKGB that tried to grab Dette and Florence. Lazarus might be Odessa. Or connected with it."

"I can do this, sir," Wagner said.

"On the other hand," Hammersmith said, "he is seventeen, and we agreed that the NKGB or Odessa is unlikely to think a seventeen-year-old is a DCI agent."

"Tiny?" Cronley asked.

"I'm glad, frankly, that I don't have to make the call," Dunwiddie said.

Cronley looked at Wagner.

"You sure you want to do this, son? That you know what you're volunteering for?"

"Yes, sir. I understand."

*"Yes, sir, I really want to help the old lady cross the street. To do my duty to God and my country!*

*"And slay dragons!"*

"How long's it going to take you to go to your *kaserne* and pack an overnight bag?" Cronley asked.

*Why do I think I'm going to regret this decision?*

"I won't have to do that, sir. If there's a PX and a clothing store at Pfungstadt, I can get whatever I need there."

Cronley considered that for a moment.

"Okay, here's the schedule: Wagner drives Miss Johansen to Pfungstadt. If they leave now — it's about a hundred and sixty miles, all autobahn, so that's about four hours — they'll get there about 1500. That'll give Miss Johansen time to tell the *Stripes* people that she's going to leave Wagner there for a couple of days. And for them to go to the PX and the clothing store. And while that's happening, I'll go to the PX here and get the goodies Sergeant Finney is going to take to Strasbourg. Then I'll get in a Storch and fly to Eschborn, pick up one of the Ford staff cars we've got stashed there, and go to Rhine-Main to meet the SAA flight arriving at 1700 and get the tourist pictures of the Likharevs seeing the sights in Buenos Aires. It's a short haul from Rhine-Main to Pfungstadt, so I should get there by 1800. That makes it too late to get back here today, but we can take off at first light and be at Kloster Grünau by, say, ten tomorrow morning."

"Where will you spend the night?" Claudette asked.

"I hadn't thought about that," Cronley admitted.

"I'm surprised," Claudette said.

Cronley sensed something in her tone of voice and looked at her.

*What is that, the Green-Eyed Monster?*

He saw in her eyes that it was.

"Eschborn is right down the road from the senior officers' hotel, Schlosshotel Kronberg," Janice said. "What about that?"

"That'd work," Cronley said.

"I'm sure it will," Claudette said, with a knowing smile.

*Is Augie picking up on this? Or anybody else?*

"Well, let's get the show on the road. Get out of that MP gear, Wagner," Cronley ordered.

"Yes, sir," Wagner said, and began to divest himself of the white MP Sam Browne belt and holster, the MP brassard on his arm, and the white leggings.

"I'll hang on to that stuff for you, Wagner," Ziegler said.

"Thank you, sir."

"Dette, give him fifty — no, a hundred —

dollars from the safe," Cronley ordered.

"Yes, sir," she said.

Ziegler saw Wagner take the .45 Colt semiautomatic pistol from his holster.

"Karl, you can leave the .45 in its holster," Ziegler said. "I'll take care of it."

Wagner ejected the magazine, racked the action, checked to see that it was unloaded, and then reinserted the magazine.

"I thought I'd take it with me," Wagner said, holding the pistol in his large hand.

"I'm not sure that would be a good idea, Wagner," Cronley said. "People would wonder what a Press Office jeep driver was doing with a pistol."

"I'm not going to wave it around, sir," Wagner replied. "No one would know I have it."

He pulled up the hem of his Ike jacket, jammed the pistol inside the waistband of his trousers, and then pulled the Ike jacket down over it. There was no indication that the jacket now concealed a weapon.

"See, sir? Who would know I had it?"

When Cronley didn't immediately reply, Wagner pressed his case.

"After what happened to Miss Colbert and the other lady, sir, I really would like to have it with me."

"Captain?" Ziegler asked.

After a moment Cronley said, "I think that is what is known as irrefutable logic. Okay, Wagner, but be careful with it."

"Yes, sir. Thank you, sir."

# [THREE]

*Suite 522*

*Hotel Vier Jahreszeiten*

*Maximilianstrasse 178*

*Munich, American Zone of Occupation, Germany*

*1201 26 January 1946*

When the telephone rang on the bedside table, Major Harold Wallace grabbed it.

"Wallace."

"ASA Fulda, Major. The line is secure. Ready to connect with Commander Schultz."

"Thank you."

"Vint Hill, Fulda. Major Wallace on a secure line for Commander Schultz."

"Acknowledge. Hold one."

"Schultz."

"Commander, Major Wallace for you on a secure line."

"Put him through."

"Go ahead, Major."

"I hope I'm not getting you out of bed, Chief."

"The admiral got me out of bed five minutes ago. He's been reading the newspaper. What the hell is going on? Sergeant Colbert killed four guys? Who the hell were they?"

"Three. One of them is still alive."

"Tell me everything about everything, Harry."

Five minutes later, Wallace had finished.

"First," Schultz said after a moment's thought, "tell Cronley, 'Well done.' That could have been a lot worse. You said you trust this dame from the AP, too?"

"Not that I have much choice. But, yeah, I do."

"I'll tell the admiral. Thanks for the call."

"Unfortunately, there's more."

"Oh, shit!"

"Parsons found out that we've had the ASA intercepting his messages between him and G-2. He went to Mattingly with it, and they're going to Seidel with it. Probably first thing this morning."

"How long has the interception been going on?"

"I'd guess from the time Parsons got to the Compound."

"You'd *guess*?"

"Cronley ordered the interception. I just heard about it."

"So a lot of people are going to be embarrassed."

"Obviously."

"Cronley for getting caught. And you, me, and the admiral for not thinking about reading their mail before Cronley did."

"Excuse me?"

"The admiral trusts G-2 about as far as he can throw it. He's going to be embarrassed — as I am, and you should be — for not thinking about intercepting their traffic and telling Greene we wanted it done. Does Greene know that Cronley ordered it?"

"I don't know, but I'd bet he doesn't. Cronley usually just does what he thinks should be done without asking anybody."

"As chief, DCI-Europe, he doesn't have to ask anyone. It would have been nice if he told you what he was doing, but the fact is, he did not have to. Or maybe he didn't tell you because he wanted to cover your ass in case he got caught."

"Or because he was afraid I'd tell him not to."

"Is that what you would have done?"

"I don't think getting into a war with G-2 is smart."

"Write this down, Harry. We are already

in a war with G-2."

"And all's fair in love and war?"

"Write that down, too. Okay, here's what I'm going to do. I'll tell the admiral about Mattingly and Parsons going to Seidel. He will then call Seidel and tell him we knew about the Parsons intercepts. Or tell me to call. That'll solve that problem. Temporarily."

"Why temporarily?"

"Harry, the problem here is Mattingly. You told me he went to the Compound without telling you and taking with him this Major Davis, even though you had told him (a) to tell you where and when he was going there before he went, and (b) that he was not authorized to take anybody with him. Now, one of two things is true. Seidel asked Mattingly if he could get Davis into the Compound, and Mattingly said, 'Yes, sir, General Seidel, sir.' Or, worse, Mattingly went to Seidel and said he was going to the Compound to see Parsons, and he thought he could get Davis in with him, 'If you think that would be a good idea, General Seidel, sir.' "

"If I didn't know better, I'd start to think you're not a Colonel Bob Mattingly fan."

"He's got to go, Harry. I know he's an old buddy from the OSS, and I'm sorry. But

291

the sonofabitch has proved what I — and, more importantly, the admiral — suspected from the start. Mattingly would flush DCI down the crapper, twice, if he thought he was buying a regular Army commission and a seat on the board of directors of the intelligence community."

"How are you going to get rid of him?"

"I'd like to cut his balls off and watch him bleed to death, but now that I'm a very senior civilian, I can't do that. But I'll think of something."

When Wallace didn't reply, Schultz said, "I'll be in touch. Vint Hill, break it down."

Almost instantly there was a hiss on the line, telling Wallace that the executive assistant to the director of the Central Intelligence Directorate had said all he was going to say.

## [FOUR]

*The* Stars and Stripes *Facility*

*Pfungstadt, American Zone of Occupation,*

*Germany*

*1815 26 January 1946*

Cronley, wearing pinks and greens with triangles, drove the 1942 Ford staff car — its bumper markings identified it as Vehicle

11 of the 711th MKRC — up to the unimposing white building and found an empty parking space right next to the main door. It was labeled: OFFICIAL VISITORS.

"God favors the virtuous," he said to himself as he pulled into the parking spot.

He entered the building under a sign that was a blown-up facsimile of the *Stars and Stripes* logotype. In the lobby a large sign with an arrow pointing right read PRESS CLUB.

He followed it and when he went through the next open door he saw Janice Johansen and PFC Karl Wagner sitting at a table with an infantry captain and a man whose pinks and greens had a war correspondent's patch sewn to its sleeve.

Cronley walked up to the table. Both the captain and the war correspondent did not seem pleased. Neither Janice nor Wagner seemed to recognize him.

"Miss Johansen?" Cronley said.

She nodded.

"My name is Fulmar," Cronley said.

"The man from Quartermaster?" Janice asked.

"Yes, ma'am."

"You're late."

"Yes, ma'am. There were two Constabulary checkpoints on the autobahn from

Frankfurt."

Janice stood up.

"Duty calls," she said. "I am forced to leave this charming company."

"What's the story, Janice?" the war correspondent asked.

"You'll have to wait to read it in *Stars and Stripes*," Janice said. "Karl, I'll be back either tomorrow or the day after. I'll call and let you know when."

"Yes, ma'am," Wagner said.

Janice waved her hand as an indication Cronley should precede her out of the Press Club. He did so.


"How'd things go at Rhine-Main?" Janice asked as they turned north on the autobahn.

"There's an envelope in the glove compartment. Have a look."

The envelope contained a dozen 8×10-inch photographs of the Likharev family being shown the sights in Buenos Aires.

"Very nice. And obviously legitimate."

"Meaning what?"

"Meaning someone like me can spot — as you should be able to, Mr. Spymaster — a staged photo. These people, especially the kids, clearly are having a good time."

She held up one of the photographs for him to see.

Cronley saw one of the faces he recognized more than the others. It was of the older boy, Sergei. He was eating — devouring — an empanada, an Argentine meat pie, with a huge smile on his face.

The last time Cronley had looked closely at Sergei's face, they had been in the Storch in which Cronley had picked him up across the East German border in Thuringia. He had just been torn, almost literally, from the hands of his mother and little brother, then thrown, again almost literally, into Cronley's airplane.

Sergei's face had then been distorted with abject terror.

Cronley had never seen anything like that before and that memory flooded his mind now as he looked at the photograph.

"Nice-looking boy," he said.

"Yeah. Like Wagner," Janice said as she stuffed the photographs back in the envelope.

"I'm worried about him."

"I gave him a long big-sister talk on what he should . . . and, more important, should not . . . do on that long ride from Munich. He'll be all right."

"Christ, I hope so."

"So, what happens now?"

"We make an early evening of it at Schlosshotel Kronberg, rise with the chickens, get in my airplane, and go show Lazarus proof of the good life in Argentina that's one of his options."

"Going to bed early seems to be a good idea, but I'm not so sure about getting up with the chickens."

"You said it, Janice. Duty calls."

"So does yours, Adonis."

Janice placed her hand so that there was no question in her mind what she meant.

## [FIVE]

*Schlosshotel Kronberg*

*Hainstrasse 25, Kronberg im Taunus*

*Hesse, American Zone of Occupation, Germany*

*1910 26 January 1946*

"Either they heard we're coming, or the MPs are having a convention," Cronley said as they drove up to the castle converted to a "senior officers' recreation facility."

There were maybe a dozen Military Police vehicles crowding the entrance to the castle's lobby — jeeps, former ambulances, a half-dozen staff cars, even an M-8 armored car.

When he parked the Ford, an MP lieutenant came to the car and politely announced: "Sir, you should have been stopped before you got here. This is a crime scene and you'll have to move, sir."

"What kind of a crime scene?" Janice asked.

The MP lieutenant ignored her.

Cronley showed him his CIC credentials.

"Tell the lady what kind of a crime scene, Lieutenant," he ordered.

The lieutenant examined the credentials.

"Sir, General Greene is in the lobby. He's in charge. I suggest you ask him."

"Do I still have to move the car?" Cronley asked.

"No, sir. If you're CIC, you're fine. We're just saving these parking spaces for people involved in the investigation."

Brigadier General Homer P. Greene, chief of USFET Counter Intelligence, saw Cronley and Janice as soon as they walked into the lobby. Greene was standing with a major general in MP regalia — the first time Cronley had ever seen a general officer so uniformed — and two full colonels.

"Good evening, sir," Cronley said.

"Major Wallace said he thought you would be coming here, Mr. Cronley," Greene said. "But he didn't suggest you would have Miss

Johansen with you."

"Is that a polite way of telling me to get lost, General?" Janice asked.

"No."

"What the hell is going on?" Janice asked.

"Do you know General Schwarzkopf, Miss Johansen?" Greene asked.

"I have that privilege," General H. Norman Schwarzkopf said. "But not this gentleman."

"General, this is Mr. James D. Cronley, the chief, DCI-Europe. Jim, this is General Schwarzkopf, the USFET provost marshal."

They shook hands. The two colonels were not introduced, but their curiosity about Cronley was visible on their faces.

"Just before you walked in, Miss Johansen," Greene said, "General Schwarzkopf and I agreed that what happened here should be released to the press. We made that recommendation to General Bull and he agreed."

"And what happened here?" Janice said.

"Colonel Robert Mattingly, my deputy, had an 0900 appointment with General Seidel. When he did not make that appointment, General Seidel's aide called my office to inquire. I tried to telephone Colonel Mattingly here — he is quartered here — and there was no answer. His car — that enormous Horch he drives — was not in the Farben Building parking lot, or in the parking lot here at the Schlosshotel. I called General Schwarzkopf and requested him to ask the MPs to look for it. I came out here and had the manager let me into Colonel Mattingly's room. There was nothing out of the ordinary, and we confirmed he had spent the night here.

"A little after two o'clock, a Constabulary road patrol was directed by a German forest master to a wooded area about two miles from Eschborn Army Airfield. There they found Colonel Mattingly's Horch. There were three bullet punctures in the interior of the driver's door, and two fired bullets — later confirmed to be nine-millimeter Parabellum — were later recovered. As were three fired .45 ACP cases, suggesting Colonel Mattingly resisted whatever happened to him. There was blood, which has been determined to be of the same blood type as Colonel Mattingly's, on the car upholstery."

"Jesus Christ!" Cronley said.

"Can I write this?" Janice asked.

"General Greene told you that you could, Miss Johansen," General Schwarzkopf said.

"I was asking Mr. Cronley," she said.

"Why do you want the story out?" Cronley asked General Greene.

"Maybe somebody — German, American, anybody — saw something. We're going to put out a press release asking the public to come forward. It will be in *Stars and Stripes* and broadcast over AFN. And of course in the German press and radio. We're determined to find out what has happened."

"The NKGB got him," Cronley said matter-of-factly. "For some reason, probably to make a prisoner swap, they grabbed Mattingly. The silver lining is he's probably still alive. If they killed him, they'd have just left the body."

"About Mr. Cronley's mention of the NKGB, Miss Johansen," General Schwarzkopf began. "It might not be a good idea —"

"I already figured that out, General," Janice interrupted him.

"Or maybe he is dead and they want us to think he's alive," Cronley said. "The more I think about it, what those NKGB bastards are after is a prisoner swap."

"What prisoners are we talking about, Mr. Cronley?" one of the colonels asked.

Cronley ignored him.

"General Schwarzkopf, can we offer a reward for information?" Cronley asked.

"I don't know where we'd get it, Mr. Cronley."

"Give me a figure."

"A thousand dollars. Perhaps a little more."

"How about five?"

"The more the better, of course."

"You've got it," Cronley said, and then went on: "For her story, the MPs are offering the award, not the CIC. And certainly not DCI. Okay?"

"Fine."

"Tell her how much of a reward."

"How about twenty-five hundred dollars?" Schwarzkopf suggested.

"You got that, Janice?"

"Got it."

"And no mention of the NKGB. Okay?"

"None. And after I do this, will you buy me dinner?"

"It will be my pleasure."

"Ten minutes," she said, and walked farther into the hotel.

"Jim, when I spoke with Major Wallace, I asked him to send Jack Hammersmith up here. I hope that's all right."

"Fine with me."

"One of your people will fly him up at first light."

"If that's the case, I'll get on the horn and tell Winters to use a Storch and bring Augie Ziegler with him. And twenty-five hundred in greenbacks, not script."

"Augie Ziegler is?" Greene said.

"He used to be a CID agent. Now he's DCI. One smart cop."

"You mentioned something about a prisoner swap," General Schwarzkopf said.

"You don't want to know about that, General," Cronley said.

"There's two things I'd like to say to you, Mr. Cronley," General Schwarzkopf said. "First, that you are everything General Greene said you would be, and more, and that I am very impressed with you."

"Why is that, sir?"

"The last time I tried to tell Miss Johansen something to do, she told me to go fu— attempt self-impregnation. What's your secret?"

"I don't think you want to know about that, either, General," Cronley said.

# VII

## [ONE]

*Kloster Grünau*

*Schollbrunn, Bavaria*

*American Zone of Occupation, Germany*

*0920 27 January 1946*

"How's the shoulder this morning, Comrade?" Max Ostrowski asked in Russian.

There was no response from the man sitting up in a hospital bed in the cell under what had been the chapel of Kloster Grünau.

"And how was your breakfast?" Max went on in Russian, indicating the remnants of a breakfast sitting on a tray. "Get everything you want?"

The man didn't respond.

"You really should build up your strength," Max said. "After what you've been through."

The man continued to look without expression at him.

"Mr. Smith and Miss Mata Hari here have brought some photographs to show you of an old comrade of yours who also fell into our hands," Ostrowski said.

He held out a manila envelope to him.

The man made no move to take it.

"Some of them are pretty grim," Max went on. "Especially the ones showing us poisoning former Polkóvnik Likharev's sons. Here, have a look."

He took one of the photographs from the envelope and laid it on the man's lap.

"What Pavel is eating is an empanada, a meat sandwich," Max said. "And that's the Colón, in Buenos Aires, in the background. The world's largest opera house. Next week they'll be doing Borodin's *Prince Igor.*"

Cronley saw the man's eyes drop to the photograph.

Ostrowski laid the other photographs, one at a time, on the man's lap.

When he had finished, Ostrowski gathered them up and put them back in the envelope.

"The reason we're showing these to you, Comrade, is to show that you have an alternative to what you might be thinking is your future. Mr. Smith and I are thinking you're thinking you have two alternatives. The best of these is that you can somehow be returned to the NKGB. We don't think that would be a happy reunion. I mean, how are you going to explain to Comrade Serov your failure not only to kidnap two U.S. Army enlisted women, but to lose three of your men in the process and get yourself captured?

"From what I know of Polkóvnik Serov, your failure has made him quite unhappy. If you're lucky, he might send you to Siberia after your interrogation. Or he might not. And I'm sure, Comrade, that you've been thinking of what might happen to you here when our patience with you is exhausted."

The man showed no expression.

"Well, Comrade, we'll leave you to think things over," Ostrowski said, and gestured for Cronley and Johansen to precede him from the cell.

"Since I don't speak Russian, I don't know what you said to him, but it looked to me that that worked well," Cronley said when they were climbing the stairs up to the chapel.

"He took in the pictures," Janice said. "I saw that."

"I think we're getting to him," Max said. "Let him think about it a little."

As they were walking through what had been the chapel itself, First Sergeant Abraham Lincoln Tedworth walked up to them.

"Major Wallace is holding on a secure line for you, Captain."

"He say what he wants?"

"He sounded pissed."

"Major Wallace, Fulda. I have Mr. Cronley on the line. The line is secure."

"Put him through."

"You're connected with Major Wallace, Mr. Cronley. The line is secure."

"Let me guess," Cronley said, without any preliminaries. "You need a ride to Frankfurt to see if you can help find Mattingly."

"I had Kurt Schröder fly me up here at first light," Wallace said, "expecting to see you. What the hell are you doing at the monastery?"

"Max just showed Lazarus the Buenos Aires pictures. Janice thinks they got to him."

"General Seidel was going to hold a conference at 0900."

"Past tense?"

"He's postponed it until you can get here."

"Please express my regrets to General Seidel and tell him I am not available."

"I tried that. He wants you there."

"Did he say why?"

"No."

"I don't want to go. I really have other things to do."

"Get back in your airplane and get your ass up here."

"That sounds like an order, Major, sir."

"Thirteen-thirty, Seidel's office in the Far-ben Building. Be there. Break it down, Fulda."

## [Two]

*Office of the Deputy Chief of Staff,*
  *Intelligence*

*Headquarters, European Command*

*The I.G. Farben Building*

*Frankfurt am Main*

*American Zone of Occupation,*

*Germany*

*1335 27 January 1946*

Cronley considered, and decided against, walking into Major General Bruce T. Seidel's office, popping to attention, saluting, and announcing, "Reporting as ordered. Sir."

Not that it would make Seidel forget that he was a captain, but rather in the hope that it would make the European Command G-2 remember that he was chief, DCI-Europe, and DCI-Europe was not a subordinate command of the European Command.

Cronley saw the others in the room:

307

Generals Greene and Schwarzkopf; one of the colonels who had been at Schlosshotel Kronberg; the major — he remembered his name, Davis — who had been with Mattingly when they'd had their last confrontation; Major Wallace; and a man in a business suit he had never seen before.

"Good afternoon, gentlemen," Cronley said politely.

"Thank you for finding time in your busy schedule for us, Mr. Cronley," Seidel said, his tone clearly sarcastic.

"There were headwinds all the way from Munich, General," Cronley said. "I regret being late. I did my best to get here on time."

"I'm sure you did," Seidel said. "I don't believe you know Mr. Preston." He indicated the man in the business suit.

"No, sir, I don't."

"Mr. Preston is the SAC — senior agent in charge — of the FBI office attached to USFET."

The two wordlessly shook hands.

"And Colonel Nesbitt of my staff," Seidel said, indicating the colonel who had been at Schlosshotel Kronberg.

The two shook hands wordlessly.

"The problem we are all facing, obviously, is learning what has happened to Colonel

Mattingly. The reason I have called this meeting is that certain things have come to light that bear on that. I thought we should try to clear these things up as quickly as possible.

"This morning as I was waiting for Colonel Mattingly, I had a telephone call from Mr. Oscar Schultz, who, as you all know, is the executive assistant to Admiral Souers, the director of the Central Intelligence Directorate. He told me that it had come to his attention that Colonel Mattingly was coming to see me to report that at your direction, Mr. Cronley, the ASA has been intercepting communications between the G-2 liaison office and the Pentagon — and others — and turning such communications over to you. He also asked me to remind Colonel Mattingly that his looking into the activities of the DCI was outside his area of responsibility and suggested I tell him this."

Cronley did not reply.

"Did you go to the ASA and direct them to intercept G-2 liaison office communications, Mr. Cronley?"

"Yes, I did," Cronley said.

"And did you know that Colonel Mattingly, having discovered this, intended to report it to me?"

"What I know was that while Colonel

Mattingly was in the Compound —"

"The what?" SAC Preston interrupted.

". . . he grabbed an ASA sergeant, stood him tall, and browbeat him into admitting we were — I was — reading Colonel Parsons's mail. I didn't know he was going to report this to you, but it doesn't surprise me."

"You apparently feel that — your words — 'reading Colonel Parsons's mail' is perfectly all right?"

"General, the Presidential Finding which established the DCI gives DCI access to — and this is just about verbatim — 'any and all classified files, without exception, generated by any agency of the United States government.' I was led to believe you were given a copy of the Finding."

"I'm not going to debate this with you now, Mr. Cronley. But this issue remains alive."

"General, with respect, why did you ask me to come here today?"

"I thought that would be obvious to you: to learn what has happened to Colonel Mattingly. Which brings us to Special Agent Preston. Mr. Preston came to me and told me he had received a communication from unknown parties alleging that the death of Lieutenant Colonel and Mrs. Anthony

Schumann was not an accident but, in fact, an assassination, and that former General-major Reinhard Gehlen and what is now known as the Süd-Deutsche Industrielle Entwicklungsorganisation were almost certainly involved."

*Shit! I thought that was water under the bridge.*

"General, that's nonsense," General Schwarzkopf said. "I personally investigated the explosion at Schumann's quarters and so did the Frankfurt Military Post engineer. Then it was investigated again by the CIC with General Greene looking over their shoulders. He had a personal interest in Schumann's death. They were friends. Their goddamn water heater blew up. Period."

*The NKGB, Cronley thought, the "unknown party" that sent the FBI that letter, knows better. And so do I.*

*Schumann was an NKGB operative. And so was his wife.*

*Rachel played me like a violin.*

*I ran at the mouth to her, which damned near got Likharev killed.*

*And when I confessed my stupidity — my unbelievable fucking stupidity — to General Gehlen, and told him I was going to fly to Frankfurt and confess my stupidity to Mattingly, and then shoot both Schumann and his loving wife, he told me that wouldn't be wise, and reminded me that Cletus Frade had told me — had ordered me — to get out of Gehlen's way.*

*So I got out of the way.*

*And shortly thereafter, the Schumanns' water heater developed a gas leak and blew them both up.*

*Problem solved.*

*I don't know that Gehlen did it — or had it done — which is on the order of me not knowing the sun will rise tomorrow, either.*

Cronley heard Major General Seidel respond: "If that's your professional opinion, General."

"And the professional opinion of the best CIC special agent I have ever known, Jack Hammersmith, who I told to investigate the explosion," General Greene said.

*Which proves that Gehlen's people are very clever in making an explosion look innocent.*

*And smarter than the MPs, the CID, and the CIC combined.*

*Not to mention me.*

"As I say, if that is your professional opinion, we'll leave it at that for the moment. Which brings us to Major Derwin, who replaced Lieutenant Colonel Schumann as the CIC inspector general."

"What about him?" General Greene asked.

"Major Derwin had a fatal, quote, accident, unquote, in the Munich railway station."

"Oh, for Christ's sake!" Schwarzkopf said. "Derwin fell under a freight train passing through the station. The Munich provost marshal personally investigated the incident and declared it an accident."

"Really?"

"And," Schwarzkopf said, "this is out of school, okay?"

"Very well," General Seidel said. "Out of school."

"His report said that Derwin had stumbled and fallen under the train. Left out of that was the fact that there was a perceptible smell of alcohol on the corpse, and that there was a paper cup of coffee from the PX coffee shop in the station found with the body which contained whisky, most probably from the fifth of Jack Daniel's in Derwin's suitcase."

"You're saying the Munich provost marshal filed a dishonest report?" SAC Preston challenged.

"I don't know how much you know about what happens in the Army when there is a death, Mr. Preston," Schwarzkopf said. "But one of the things that has to be determined is if the death occurred in the line of the deceased's duty. In this case, it was determined that Major Derwin was in the Munich station because he was either on his way to, or coming from, General Gehlen's compound."

"It is not General Gehlen's compound, General," Cronley said. "It is the DCI's compound."

"I stand corrected, Mr. Cronley," Schwarzkopf said.

"Where Derwin had no right to be," Cronley added. "The Compound is not subject to investigation by the CIC's IG."

"Please let me continue, Mr. Cronley," Schwarzkopf said.

"Sorry."

"General Greene told me there was some question about what Major Derwin was doing at the *DCI* compound — whether he had gone there on duty or not, or whether he had been there, or was intending to go there — in addition to the questions raised by the alcohol. So we decided to give him the benefit of the doubt, so to speak. The report of his death did not raise the question of whether or not he was on duty, or sober, when he fell under the freight train. His death was adjudged to be accidental, while he was on duty. This gave his family all the benefits which accrue to someone who dies while on duty."

"That was very generous of you and General Greene," General Seidel said sarcastically.

"May I have the floor a minute?" SAC Preston asked.

"Certainly," General Seidel said.

"Mr. Cronley, there is a story going around that you shot at Colonel Schumann on one occasion, specifically when he was seeking entrance to your Kloster Grünau compound. Is there any truth to it?"

"No. I didn't shoot at him. However, one of my men acting on my orders put a .50 caliber round — one round — in his engine block. This was after he announced his intention to gain entrance to Kloster Grünau after I told him he couldn't come in."

"Why wouldn't you let him in?"

"Because he had no right to go in."

"You denied the USFET CIC inspector general, who, one would presume, has all the necessary security clearances, entrance to your compound?"

"He was not authorized to enter Kloster Grünau. On the other hand, I had the authority to keep unauthorized people out of the Compound by whatever means necessary, including the use of lethal force. What does this have to do with Colonel Mattingly going missing?"

Preston ignored the question, instead asking, "Were you aware of this incident, General Greene?"

"Colonel Schumann reported it to me," Greene said. "And I told him that he was not authorized to inspect — or even visit — any DCI installation."

"What has this got to do with Colonel Mattingly?" Cronley asked again.

"All right," Preston said, "I'll tell you. When I heard that Colonel Mattingly had gone missing, I saw what I thought was a pattern."

"What kind of a pattern?"

"First, you — how do I say this? — *vigorously* deny Colonel Schumann access to the Kloster Grünau compound. Shortly thereafter, Colonel Schumann and his wife die in an 'accident.' Next, Major Derwin goes to the other, the 'Gehlen,' compound, and shortly thereafter, Major Derwin falls 'accidentally' under a freight train. And now this."

"This being what?" Cronley said.

"Colonel Mattingly visits the Gehlen compound, apparently without your permission, taking with him Major Davis, which apparently was against some sort of agreement he had made with you. And we know he told you what he had done, because Major Davis was with you in the bar of the Vier Jahreszeiten hotel when he told you."

"And now Mattingly's gone missing?" Wallace asked.

"Colonel Mattingly *is* missing," Preston said.

"That's a crock of shit," Wallace exploded. "No apologies for the language. You're as much as accusing Cronley of being responsible for Mattingly having gone missing."

"I've made no such accusation, even though I have learned there was bad blood between the two of them. What I am suggesting is possible is that Mr. Cronley has not been keeping as close an eye as he should on a former Nazi major general who is quite capable of murder."

"So then you're suggesting Gehlen is responsible for the Schumann water heater and the freight train that Derwin fell under?" Wallace asked.

"I think it behooves us, Major, under the circumstances, to consider all possibilities," Preston said.

"There are those, Major Wallace," General Seidel said, "as I am sure you know, who wonder if Mr. Cronley has the experience to cope adequately with the responsibilities he has been given."

"And I'm aware that Colonel Mattingly felt that way," Wallace agreed. "On the other hand, I don't think any of us are willing to question the judgment of the man — I'm referring to our commander in chief, President Truman — who gave him his present responsibilities, are we?"

Seidel didn't reply for a moment, and then he said, "I have a suggestion that would probably answer all these questions to everyone's satisfaction."

"Which is?" Schwarzkopf asked.

"That we ask Mr. Preston and his people to help us with the disappearance of Colonel Mattingly."

"I got the impression, General, that you'd already done that," Schwarzkopf said.

"With the permission of Mr. Cronley," Seidel went on, "for Mr. Preston's expert FBI investigators to have a look at both the Gehlen compound and the monastery."

"No," Cronley said. "I'm not going to agree to that. For that to happen, I would have to have the okay of Admiral Souers."

"May I ask why, Captain . . . excuse me . . . Mr. Cronley?" Seidel said.

"What have you got against the FBI,

Cronley?" Preston said. "More to the point, what is there in these places that you don't want the FBI to see?"

"Is there something else you'd like to ask me, General Seidel?" Cronley asked.

"Excuse me?"

"If not, I have things to do."

"I have nothing further for you, Mr. Cronley. But may I suggest that you keep yourself available in case General Bull might wish a word with you?"

"Good afternoon, gentlemen," Cronley said, and got up and walked out of the room.

## [THREE]

*Visiting Senior Officers' Parking Area*

*The I.G. Farben Building*

*Frankfurt am Main*

*American Zone of Occupation, Germany*

*1435 27 January 1946*

When Cronley saw Major Wallace walk into the parking area, Cronley tapped the horn of the Ford staff car he had driven to the Farben Building from the Eschborn airfield.

Wallace saw him and walked to the car and got in the front passenger seat.

For a moment Wallace said nothing. Then he said, "Jesus, what smells in here?"

"That's me. Sorry. It must have been something I ate. As I started down here, I tossed my cookies before I could make it to a men's room. Most of it went into a wastebasket, but some of it, a lot of it, got on my trousers and shoes."

Wallace rolled down his window.

"Or it could be," Wallace said, "that you were just a little worried about what was going to happen to you now after you had, in effect, told the USFET G-2 to go fuck himself."

"What was I supposed to do?"

Wallace exhaled audibly.

"Don't let this go to your head, Loose Cannon, but I was proud of you in there. You did exactly what was called for in the circumstances."

"So what do I tell General Bull?"

"Bringing him into the conversation was an idle threat and, I think, directed more to me and Greene than to you. Seidel's not going to go to Harry Bull. Not now. Bull's not part of the Let's Kill the DCI Conspiracy. What happened in there, Jim, was that Seidel took his best shot and missed. That doesn't mean the war is over, just this one battle. What he was hoping was that the FBI would find unmarked graves."

"And they would have."

"Which would have lent credence to their theory that Gehlen was responsible for them, and that further would lend credence to their theory that he was also responsible for Schumann's water heater and Derwin getting shoved under the freight train."

*Which theories are right on the fucking money.*

*Doesn't Wallace know this?*

*Is this where I tell him?*

*Which brings us to the new question: Does Gehlen have anything to do with Mattingly going missing?*

"And finally to their theory," Wallace went on, "that Gehlen is responsible for Mattingly going missing."

*Christ, he's reading my mind!*

"Seidel doesn't give a damn about Mattingly, but if he can prove — even credibly allege — to Bull and ultimately McNarney that Gehlen is responsible for his disappearance — better yet, from his standpoint, his murder —"

"McNarney gets on the phone to the admiral and very politely suggests that since the very young and very junior officer who is chief, DCI-Europe, obviously can't keep the murderous Nazi General Gehlen under

321

control, perhaps it would be the time to — at least temporarily — replace him with someone wiser, older, and senior?"

"Or, more likely," Wallace said, "to put DCI-Europe temporarily under the guidance of someone wiser, older, and more senior, like Major General Bruce T. Seidel. Just until the present situation is rectified. I think that's what they call getting the camel's nose under the tent flap."

"So, what do we do?" Cronley said.

"The obvious solution is to find out who grabbed — or assassinated — Bob Mattingly, said villain having nothing to do with Generalmajor Reinhard Gehlen."

*But what if Gehlen is responsible?*

*Has Gehlen been playing me as Rachel Schumann played me?*

*And why am I unwilling to tell Wallace that I think — am sure — Gehlen was responsible for whacking the Schumanns and that it's entirely possible that he had Derwin pushed under the freight train?*

*Several reasons. Maybe the most important one is that if I do, he will quite reasonably decide I should have told him long before this and be really pissed. More important than his being pissed is that he could reasonably decide that Seidel is right.*

*Why do I trust Gehlen?*

*Because I'm arrogantly sure — despite my youth, inexperience, and all-around proven stupidity — that I can tell whether or not the German general who successfully matches wits with the entire fucking NKGB — and was smart enough to stay out of the hands of the SS when he was up to his ears in the plans to whack Adolf Hitler — is playing me at least as skillfully as Rachel played me?*

*Or because he saved my ass?*

*If he hadn't talked me out of going to Frankfurt and shooting Rachel and her husband, and then going to Mattingly and telling him why I had, I would now be under suicide watch in the USFET stockade awaiting my general court-martial for a double murder.*

*Seidel and the FBI are looking for the wrong suspect in who whacked the Schumanns. They should be looking at me. Getting out of Gehlen's way was just about the same thing as me shooting them. I knew what was going to happen to them, and since I got out of Gehlen's way, I'm just as responsible for what happened as Gehlen is.*

"That glazed look in your eyes suggests you're thinking," Wallace said. "What about?"

*Okay, here's where I confess all.*

"Well?" Wallace pursued.

"I've been wondering whether I can get

back to Kloster Grünau before it'll be too dark to land. I'd really like to get there today."

"Why?"

"Just before you called me, I gave the NKGB guy who's supposed to be dead the photos of Likharev and family in Buenos Aires. He's had time to think that over. Unless you've got a better idea, that seems to me the best place to start."

Wallace grunted.

"And then I'll see if my cousin Luther has tried to corrupt Sergeant Finney and see where that may lead us. Or maybe PFC Wagner will have infiltrated Odessa at the *Stars and Stripes* plant, and that will solve all our problems."

Wallace didn't reply.

"It's not much, is it?" Cronley said.

"No."

"But I don't see any point in hanging around here. Augie Ziegler and Hammersmith can find out what they can about Mattingly without my expert help."

"You go with what you have," Wallace said.

He put out his hand.

"Maybe, Jim, if you leave the side window in your airplane open, it will help with the smell."

He punched Cronley affectionately on his

shoulder and got out of the staff car.

Cronley drove out of the Visiting Senior Officers' Parking Area before Wallace reached his car.

## [FOUR]

*Kloster Grünau*

*Schollbrunn, Bavaria*

*American Zone of Occupation, Germany*

*1740 27 January 1946*

It was dark when Cronley got to the monastery. Not only dark, but snowing. The snow made the headlights on the jeeps and trucks and ambulances — which had come on to illuminate the strip when he'd flown over the former monastery — into fuzzy orbs of white, when what he needed was clear light.

That the lights had come on told him both that Major Wallace had gotten on the horn to give them a heads-up and that Max Ostrowski had set up the vehicles immediately in case Cronley was really crazy enough to attempt to land at Kloster Grünau at night in a snowstorm.

He got the Storch onto the ground all right, which was not the same thing as saying safely. He realized this was a tribute to the flight characteristics of the airplane, which permitted him to make his approach at a speed not much faster than a walk, rather than to his flying skills.

Cronley was fully aware that he should have gone into Schleissheim, the Munich Military Post airfield, whose runways were fully lighted. He had not done so for three reasons. He didn't want to have the Storch seen at Schleissheim; he didn't want the airfield officer of the day running up to the airplane when he parked it, asking, *Are you out of your mind, flying in this weather?* and he didn't want to go through the hassle of getting a car, either at the airfield or from the Vier Jahreszeiten, to drive to Kloster Grünau.

He knew he was taking a chance. He'd become used to taking chances, so far successfully.

But as he was landing the airplane, he had another thought, this one sobering: *One of these days, sooner or later, and probably sooner than later, one of the chances I'm taking is going to bite me in the ass.*

Max Ostrowski met him with a jeep.

"You were pushing it, old chap, flying in this weather," he greeted him in his heavy British accent. "I'm presuming there is a reason you felt you had to get back today?"

"I really needed a shower, Your Majesty," Cronley replied.

"Why do I have the feeling that's the truth? Or at least part of the truth."

"Because you are a PP, Max."

"What's a PP?"

"A Perceptive Pole," Cronley said. "How's Lazarus?"

"As in the chap Christ brought back from the dead?"

"See, you are perceptive. Maybe even a VPP."

"Let me guess: Very Perceptive Pole."

"Correct. Take me to the palace, please, driver. I need a hot shower and a cold Jack Daniel's."


"Colonel Mattingly gone missing is problem enough," Max said, after Cronley had finished telling him of his encounter with General Seidel. "If he's killed . . ."

"I'm taking what comfort I can from thinking they may want to swap him for Likharev," Cronley said.

"Or Lazarus."

"They don't know he's alive."

"We don't know that. For that matter, we don't know who 'they' is. Are."

"Any further reaction from Lazarus to the pictures?"

Ostrowski shook his head.

"But there's something about him that bothers me, Jim."

"What?"

"I've been trying to put my finger on it, but the best I can come up with is that he is remarkably calm for someone in his situation. I started thinking he was resigned to . . . his fate."

"Which he thinks is?"

"Being disposed of. He knows we're not going to turn him loose. But as I say, that thought gave way to thinking he's confident he won't be . . . disposed of. He's confident that we're not going to shoot him, that somehow he's going to get out of the mess he's in."

"Prisoner swap? Mattingly for Lazarus?"

"Now that we know they have Mattingly, it's certainly a possibility, isn't it?"

"But they — whoever they are — don't know we have Lazarus."

"We don't know that for sure, do we? What I was thinking before I heard that Mattingly had gone missing was that maybe he thinks somebody is going to break him out of here."

"With your guys and Tiny's Troopers guarding the place?" Cronley challenged.

"He becomes ill. Concerned for his safety,

and unwilling to bring medical personnel here . . . and they know that."

"How do they know that?"

"That brings me to that theory," Ostrowski said. "The person — possibly, even probably, persons — they, whoever they are, have in Kloster Grünau told them."

"Have in here, or in the Compound. Or the 98th General Hospital."

Ostrowski looked at him questioningly.

"There are more people in the Compound than here," Cronley explained. "Yours, Gehlen's, mine. People gossip. Everybody knows what happened with Claudette and Florence, both from Janice's story in *Stars and Stripes* and what they saw — two ambulances full of your guys rushing to the hospital. The story said Dette killed three in the parking lot, and the fourth died in the hospital."

"So?"

"The bodies of the three she killed were taken to the hospital for autopsy. They were photographed before they were turned over to whoever buries people. Graves Registration? The city of Munich? But what happened to the fourth body? For the sake of argument, let's say the bodies were photographed again before they were buried."

"I see where you're going," Max said.

329

"They, whoever they are, managed to get photos of the bodies. They would know who they were. One face is missing . . ."

"Lazarus," Cronley picked up. "If he's not dead, where is he?"

"And they're in the hospital. I don't think that it's a coincidence that ambulance at the NCO club came from the 98th General."

"And since they're in the hospital, one might logically presume they saw Lazarus being taken from the hospital in one of our ambulances . . ."

"Together with the hospital bed, et cetera, in another of our ambulances . . ."

"Yes."

"And they would assume we brought him here. Which brings us back to my theory that since they have someone in here, they know Lazarus is here. And that they can't assault the place . . ."

"But can intercept an ambulance, even one accompanied by two or more of Tiny's jeeps . . ."

"As we take Poor Sick Lazarus to the 98th on a little-used country road in the middle of the night," Max finished the thought.

Cronley grunted and then asked, "Are we just making all this up?"

"As a product of our fevered imaginations? I don't think so, Jim."

"For them to go to all this trouble would seem to make Lazarus very important to them," Cronley said thoughtfully.

"All this trouble including the kidnapping of Colonel Mattingly. Just in case rescuing Lazarus doesn't work."

"Yeah."

"So, what are you going to do?"

"Seek the counsel of someone far wiser than James D. Cronley Junior."

"Major Wallace?"

"Former Generalmajor Gehlen. I'll take the Storch to the Compound at first light."

"Not Wallace?"

"I don't know how this is going to turn out, Max. But the real priority is to keep DCI from getting taken over by Seidel and Company. If whatever I do here goes wrong, and frankly it looks like it will, and I go down, I don't want to take Wallace with me. I want him here to take over DCI. And I don't want to take you down with me, either, so we never had this conversation. All you know is that I flew in here, asked you about Lazarus, then flew out at first light."

"That presumes we'll be able to get the snow off what passes for our runway. You could drive in tonight . . ."

331

"There will not be too much snow on the runway for me to take off at first light."

". . . and have a late dinner with Janice. She said she'd be at the Vier Jahreszeiten until she heard from you."

"I can't handle Janice tonight."

"That, if I may be permitted a personal observation, strikes me as a wise decision."

"I'm not really as stupid as I look, Max. And so far as snow on the runway is concerned, that will not be a problem. There will be no snow. God takes care of fools and drunks, and I qualify on both counts."

"You're not a fool, Jim, and as far as being a drunk is concerned, you took one sip of your drink and put it down."

Cronley picked up the glass and drained it.

"Okay, VPP? Now let's have something to eat."

# [FIVE]

*The South German Industrial Development*

*Organization Compound*

*Pullach, Bavaria*

*American Zone of Occupation, Germany*

*0750 28 January 1946*

When Cronley walked into the Senior Officers' Mess, he was afraid that more people would be there than he wanted to see. His fears were realized. The table was full. Seated at it were former Generalmajor Reinhard Gehlen, former Oberst Ludwig Mannberg, Lieutenant Colonel John J. Bristol, former Major Konrad Bischoff, Captain C. L. Dunwiddie, and Lieutenants Tom Winters and Bruce T. Moriarty.

The only people he wanted to see — had business with — were Gehlen and Dunwiddie.

As he walked toward the table, he thought, *Fuck it. This is no time to worry about hurt feelings.*

*I'll tell Gehlen and Tiny I want to see them, alone, right now, in my office.*

And then he had an epiphany, or several epiphanies, one after the other.

*The last thing I can afford to do right now is*

*make anybody feel that they are second-class members of DCI, not trusted enough to be told everything that's going on.*

*I either trust them, or I don't.*

*But Jack Bristol's not in DCI, he's the engineer in charge of building and maintaining the Compound. And related to Bonehead Moriarty.*

*And they both went to Norwich.*

*As did Tiny.*

*And General White.*

*Do I have the right to try to involve him in this?*

*Bottom Line: I need all the help I can get.*

*I don't know if, or how, Bristol can help, but I know I don't want to run him off.*

"I thought you'd be snowed in at Kloster Grünau," Tiny greeted him.

"When was the last time they swept this room?" Cronley said.

The question obviously puzzled Dunwiddie.

"I don't know. Last night. Maybe this morning. Why?"

"Get somebody over here right now and sweep it. And then put a couple of your guys outside to make sure nobody can hear what's said in here."

It was an order, and Dunwiddie recognized it as such.

"Yes, sir," he said, and got up from the table.

"Colonel," Cronley said to Bristol, "we're about to discuss some things in here that are not only none of your business but also, I suspect, things you'd rather not hear."

"I understand," Bristol said, and got up out of his chair.

"Having said that, I wish you would stay," Cronley said.

Bristol didn't reply.

"I'm not being polite," Cronley said. "And I don't want you to stay to be polite. Staying may be costly."

Bristol's eyebrows rose in question, but he said nothing.

"I'm in a jam," Cronley went on, "and need all the help I can get. So I'm going to tell you that General White, if he doesn't already know what's happened, is about to learn. And he's with us, not with those who want to either take over DCI or flush it down the crapper."

"Do 'those' have a name?" Bristol asked.

"Major General Bruce T. Seidel, the US-FET G-2, heads the list. And it's a long list."

Bristol looked intensely at Cronley for a moment, then shrugged and sat down.

*What do I do now, say "Thank you"?*

"Thank you," Cronley said.

A WAC staff sergeant — a formidable, stocky woman — came in the room.

"Sir, I swept this room at 0700. You want me to sweep it again?"

"No. But I want it, and my office, swept every six hours until I tell you different."

"Yes, sir. Is there something I don't know?"

"Just being cautious. I don't *know* anything."

"Yes, sir," the sergeant said, and left.

Tiny came back in the room and took his seat.

Everybody looked expectantly at Cronley.

*Well, here's where the chief explains the problem, and tells his subordinates how he wants them to deal with it.*

*It would be a lot easier if I wasn't just about convinced I'm wholly unqualified to be the chief and had any idea how to deal with the problem.*

He walked to the head of the table, and saw all eyes were on him.

Primarily because he didn't have any idea how to begin, he paused to take a cigar from his tunic, clip the end, and carefully light it.

"Yesterday," he began, letting out a cloud of smoke, "I was summoned to a meeting presided over by General Seidel. Generals Greene and Schwarzkopf, Colonel

Thomas B. Nesbitt, who works for Seidel, and the senior agent in charge of the FBI office attached to USFET, a Mr. Preston — I don't know his first name — and Major Wallace were present . . ."

"Preston's first name is Douglas," former Major Konrad Bischoff furnished.

*Rather than being helpful, Konrad, ol' buddy, that was intended, I think, to show everybody how smart you are.*

*The only reason I don't allow myself to think you are the mole/traitor around here is because I really can't stand you, and I don't want that to color my thinking.*

"After some preliminaries, during which General Seidel suggested I'm not up to meeting the responsibilities of chief, DCI, he explained Mr. Preston's presence. Mr. Preston has developed the theory that the death of Colonel and Mrs. Schumann was not accidental."

Cronley met Gehlen's eyes. Gehlen's face showed nothing.

"Both General Greene and General Schwarzkopf challenged this theory, saying that they had both personally investigated that tragedy and found nothing suspicious about it. Neither General Seidel nor Mr. Preston seemed to accept what Greene and Schwarzkopf thought.

"Next, Mr. Preston said that he not only suspected that Major Derwin did not really fall under the freight train in the Munich *bahnhof,* but had been pushed, but also saw a pattern in the two deaths. Both Colonel Schumann and Major Derwin had shown great interest in both Kloster Grünau and the Compound, and Major Derwin had met his end shortly after visiting the Compound. The third suspicious coincidence was that Colonel Mattingly had gone missing shortly after he had made a visit to the Compound, which to his mind suggested that General Gehlen was responsible for all three incidents."

"He actually made that accusation?" Colonel Bristol asked incredulously.

"Seidel said he thought it was 'a possibility we could not ignore.' And that he had a solution which would clear everything up. That was that 'we' seek the assistance of the FBI's excellent investigators, which would include granting them access to both the Compound and Kloster Grünau."

"What was Major Wallace doing during all this?" Tiny asked.

"Not much while it was going on, but afterward when we were alone in the parking lot, he said he hoped I realized I had as much as told the USFET G-2 to go fuck himself when I told him that I was not going to let the FBI anywhere near the Compound or Kloster Grünau."

No one said a word.

"He also said that the war is by no means over. Seidel and the Pentagon G-2 are determined to either swallow DCI or flush it down the toilet."

"And what do you propose we do to stop that?" Tiny said.

"The only thing I can think of is somehow to get Colonel Mattingly back alive and catch somebody important in Odessa. And I don't have a clue how we can do that."

"If I may, Jim," Gehlen said, "I have some thoughts on the subject."

"Please."

"Colonel Parsons came to see me right after you flew the journalist . . ."

"Miss Johansen," Bischoff furnished.

Gehlen very slowly turned his head to Bischoff. His left eyebrow rose.

Bischoff's face first flushed and then went pale.

*"Vergeben Sie mir, Herr Generalmajor,"* he muttered.

Gehlen turned his head back to Cronley and went on: ". . . to Pfungstadt."

Cronley thought: *So that's how a German general shuts off someone who has spoken out of turn. A raised eyebrow and a glance icy enough to freeze the blood in the offender's veins.*

He looked at Bristol, and saw from the faint smile on his lips that he shared Cronley's admiration.

"The timing here is important," Gehlen went on. "This occurred before Major Wallace, and then you, called to tell me that Colonel Mattingly had gone missing."

"He told you about that?" Cronley asked.

"Not at first. At first, he said he had come to ask clarification of the report on the significance of the recent movement of Soviet armored units in Hungary we'd given him the day before. When I answered his questions, he said that he wanted me to know that G-2, both here in Europe and in the Pentagon, was very impressed with the quality of the intelligence he was getting from me.

"Then he said he had come into intelligence himself that he felt he should share with me, but that doing so raised the delicate question of doing so because of you. He hoped I would consider what he was about to tell me as a confidence.

"Colonel Parsons then said he had been informed by General Seidel that Colonel Mattingly had gone missing, and that he presumed Major Wallace, and ultimately you, would be told of this by General Seidel very shortly, and that one or the other or both would probably be calling to tell me about Colonel Mattingly.

"He then went on to say that he knew I was aware of the friction between you and Colonel Mattingly and was sure that I knew it was nothing personal, that Mattingly's only interest, and his, was that we — the Süd-Deutsche Industrielle Entwicklungsorganisation — continue to furnish the high-quality intelligence we have been furnishing.

"Colonel Parsons then said, 'between soldiers' — don't quote me — that he saw the root of the problem was that DCI was under a couple of sailors. He said something to the effect that I probably agreed that the Army and the Navy think differently. That he could not imagine, if Admiral Souers was a general, that he would have given such heavy responsibility to a young and inexperienced officer as he had to you."

"The sonofabitch!" Cronley said, which earned him a raised eyebrow and a look nearly as icy as the one General Gehlen had given Bischoff.

When he looked at Colonel Bristol, he saw both admiration and amusement in his eyes and his smile.

Gehlen continued: "Colonel Parsons then said he had reason to believe that certain changes in the command structure were about to be made, and that . . . I forget exactly how he phrased it, but I took it to mean that he felt if I didn't raise any objections to the change, or question it, I — the Süd-Deutsche Industrielle Entwicklungsorganisation — had nothing to worry about."

Gehlen looked at Cronley as if waiting for his reaction.

When Cronley, not without effort, kept his automatic mouth in the off position, Gehlen went on: "Admiral Canaris once told me that it was a given that people would tell you untruths. The trick was to not only recognize this when this happened, but to ask oneself the liars' motives."

He paused, and — now with a faint smile on his lips — added: "In this case, I would suggest that even a young and inexperienced intelligence officer would have much difficulty in guessing the motives of this liar."

"No," Cronley said, "I think they're pretty clear."

"If I may, Jim," Gehlen said. "I'm not quite finished."

*"Vergib mir, Herr Generalmajor,"* Cronley said.

Bischoff flashed Cronley an angry glance.

Cronley saw that Gehlen, former Oberst Ludwig Mannberg, and Colonel Bristol were smiling.

"My old friend Rahil has been heard from," Gehlen said. "The essence of her message is that we have something Nikolayevich Merkulov wants back, and he has something we want back. She suggests that not only should you, Jim, and I meet with Ivan Serov to discuss an exchange, but where we should do so and when."

"I don't understand any of that," Bristol blurted, and then when he heard what he had said, added, *"Vergib mir, Herr Generalmajor."*

Bischoff glared at Bristol. Gehlen and Mannberg smiled.

"And I can't tell you, Colonel, without Jim's permission," Gehlen said.

"Please tell everybody," Cronley said. "This young and inexperienced intelligence officer doesn't understand, either."

Now there were chuckles from everybody — including Lieutenants Winters and Moriarty.

"Rahil, Colonel, gentlemen, is an NKGB officer with whom I've had dealings over the years. She was instrumental in getting Polkóvnik Likharev's wife and sons out of

Russia. Nikolayevich Merkulov is the commissar of State Security. His deputy, whom Rahil suggests we meet at the Drei Husaren restaurant in Vienna at our earliest convenience, is Ivan Serov."

"She?" Bristol asked.

Gehlen nodded.

"She," he confirmed, and went on: "And since this slightly older and marginally more experienced intelligence officer intuits that Comrade Merkulov is interested in exchanging Colonel Mattingly for Colonel Likharev, I think we should go to Vienna and hear what Serov has to say."

There were more smiles.

Cronley's mouth went on automatic: "Not only no, but hell no!"

The look on Bristol's face was now one of surprise.

Gehlen's eyebrow rose but Cronley saw there was no ice in his eyes.

*He knew I wouldn't go along with that.*

*He's curious to hear my objections, but he's not outraged that I would dare question him.*

"When I am relieved as chief, DCI-Europe," Cronley said, "I don't want Seidel and Company to be able to crow that my most spectacular fuck-up was being responsible for getting you, General, grabbed by the NKGB. I'm expendable. You're not."

Gehlen nodded. "I admit that possibility — Merkulov wanting to get his hands on both of us — crossed my mind. But I thought we could take the necessary precautions — the Drei Husaren is in Vienna's Inner City, which the Russians do not control absolutely — to see that didn't happen."

"And I have no intention of swapping Colonel Likharev for Colonel Mattingly," Cronley said. "What I intuit here is that Likharev's defection burned the NKGB badly. If we swapped Likharev for Mattingly, Merkulov could parade him in chains before the rest of the NKGB and announce, 'This is what happens to NKGB officers who try to defect. Even if they make it as far as Argentina.' "

"Point taken," Gehlen said.

"But having said that, it might be useful to hear what Serov has to say. But since I don't speak Russian . . ."

"When do you think you and I should go to Vienna, Jim?" Oberst Mannberg asked.

"The problem there, Ludwig, is that you're not expendable."

"Neither, I suggest, are you. And *that* suggests we should make the precautions the generalmajor mentioned we take with great care."

"You're willing to go?"

"Of course," Mannberg said.

*So I guess Mannberg and I are going to Vienna.*

They both looked at Gehlen.

"What precautions did you have in mind?" Cronley asked.

"Where is this restaurant?"

"Within walking distance of the Hotel Bristol," Mannberg answered.

"I wonder how much we can lean on the CIC in Vienna," Cronley said.

"I think all you would have to do is ask General Greene," Tiny Dunwiddie said. "He runs the CIC all over Europe."

"I don't think I want to ask him."

"You think he'd tell General Seidel about this?"

"He wouldn't tell Seidel, but he'd probably tell Wallace, and Wallace would tell me not to go."

"Because of the risk to you?"

"Because of the risk to Mannberg," Cronley said. "If the Russians grabbed me, a lot of Wallace's problems would be solved."

"You don't mean that," Tiny challenged.

"I think Wallace, personally, would be unhappy if I got bagged by the NKGB. But I think a small, still voice in the back of his mind —"

"I don't believe that," Tiny said.

"Neither do I," Cronley said, chuckling. "So here's what we're going to do. Have the switchboard set up a secure call to the CIC agent-in-charge in Vienna. I don't remember his name, but we met him when we were in Vienna the first time. Ludwig will ask him to meet us —"

"Colonel Mannberg will ask?" Tiny asked.

"One of the CIC Vienna guys, Spurgeon, remembers me from Camp Holabird. If I told him I'm chief, DCI-Europe, I don't think he'd believe it. On the other hand, Ludwig not only dazzled everybody with his DCI credentials, he looks much more like a senior, experienced intelligence officer than I do."

He paused and looked at his watch.

"It's about two hundred twenty miles as the bird flies. Make that three hundred, as I'm going to have to fly through the Alps, rather than over them. That means I'll have to stop for fuel. And as I don't know of an airfield where I can do that without raising a lot of questions, I'll have to land on a road or in a field somewhere. Not a problem. We'll take four jerry cans of gas with us. If we leave in an hour, say, ten o'clock, that'll put us into Schwechat about fourteen hundred hours."

"Why do I think this is not the first time

you've thought about flying to Vienna?" Gehlen asked.

"Because you are, General, an older and far wiser intelligence officer than I am. The last time we were there I did think about flying a Storch there without asking official permission of the Russians to overfly their zone. It can be done."

"And what if you have to land in the Russian Zone?" Tiny challenged.

"I don't plan to, but worst scenario, if I have to, I tell the people pointing their PPSh-41 submachine guns at Ludwig and me to call Comrade Serov, who will tell them we're on our way to see him."

"If you have to land in the Russian Zone, they'll have you and Colonel Mannberg as well as Colonel Mattingly to swap for Likharev," Dunwiddie argued, in exasperation.

For a moment Cronley didn't reply.

"Tiny," he said finally and very softly, "neither Oberst Mannberg nor I are going to allow ourselves to be taken alive by the NKGB, either in the Russian Zone of Austria or in the Drei Husaren restaurant in Vienna."

There was an awkward silence for a moment, and then Tiny asked, very softy, "Is meeting this Serov man so important?"

"I've decided it is," Cronley said. "So Ludwig will ask the head of CIC in Vienna to meet him at the Hotel Bristol at, say, sixteen hundred. And ask him to provide people to make sure that neither Ludwig nor I are kidnapped on our way to or from having our dinner at the Drei Husaren."

"That would work," Mannberg said.

"Now, what, besides putting four jerry cans of gas in my Storch, has to be done? I'll start with you, Bonehead. Make sure absolutely nobody gets into either the Compound or Kloster Grünau who Colonel Bristol or Captain Dunwiddie doesn't know about. And get that word to Ostrowski."

"Yes, sir," Lieutenant Moriarty said.

*He hasn't said "Yes, sir" to me since we were at College Station.*

"By now, Sergeant Finney is on his way to Garmisch-Partenkirchen from Strasbourg. With a little bit of luck, my cousin Luther will have tried to enlist him in Odessa. I have a hunch that's going to work. I want to know if it did, or not. So you, Tom, get in the other Storch and go get him."

"Yes, sir," Lieutenant Winters said. "When should I go?"

"It would be better if you were in Garmisch-Partenkirchen when he gets there, so pretty soon."

"Yes, sir."

"Which brings us to PFC Wagner," Cronley said. "Who I never should have sent to Pfungstadt in the first place. Tom, as soon as you get Sergeant Finney back here, get in the Piper Cub and go get him. As soon as you find him, call Tiny. As soon as you get that call, Tiny, tell Janice Johansen that we're going to let her use one of our Ford staff cars as long as she needs it, and that she should call the USFET Press Office and tell them she's through with the jeep they gave her and that it's at Pfungstadt."

"Yes, sir," Winters said.

"Do I tell her we went to get Wagner?" Tiny asked.

"Yeah. Why not? Tell her I'll explain everything when I come back."

"She's going to want to know where you went."

"I'll explain that to her when I get back."

"With all possible respect, sir," Tiny said, "wouldn't it be easier to explain all that to her before you go?"

"As surprising as you may find this, Captain Dunwiddie, I don't think I can handle Miss Johansen right now. On the other hand, you're expendable."

Dunwiddie gave Cronley the finger.

Cronley stood up.

"Ready, Ludwig, for some of that Viennese *Gemütlichkeit* we hear so much about?"

"Frankly, no," Mannberg replied. But he stood up.

*"Mit ihrer Erlaubnis, Herr Generalmajor?"*

"Go with God, Ludwig," Gehlen said, then added, "The both of you. And remember, as outnumbered as we are, neither of you is expendable."

# VIII

## [ONE]

*Suite 304*

*The Hotel Bristol*

*Kaerntner Ring 1*

*Vienna, Austria*

*1605 29 January 1946*

There came a melodious chime indicating someone at the door of the suite, and Cronley went to the door and opened it.

Two men were standing there, both wearing ODs with triangles. One was in his late thirties, and the other in his twenties.

"Please come in," Cronley said.

"How are you, Jim?" the younger man said, offering his hand.

Cronley thought: *What the hell is his first name?*

"Good to see you, Spurgeon," Cronley said.

Mannberg rose from the couch on which he was sitting.

The older man offered him his hand, but neither spoke.

Mannberg gestured around the room, pointing a finger at the chandelier and the lamps, his raised eyebrows making it a question.

"Swept an hour ago, Mr. Mannberg."

"Ludwig, please, Colonel Wassermann," Mannberg said.

"Karl-Christoph, but I usually go with Carl, with a 'C,' " Wassermann said, and then went on. "What are a couple of nice German-American boys like us doing in this business?"

"Fighting the Red Menace?" Mannberg said.

"And how can the Vienna CIC help the DCI in that noble endeavor?"

"Why don't we have a taste of Slivovitz while I tell you?"

Wassermann said, "When I told my mother I was coming to Vienna — actually I'm a *Hungarian*-American boy, Mother is from Budapest — she strongly advised me to stay away from that fermented plum juice, but why not?"

Cronley remembered that the last time they were in Vienna, he had told Spurgeon that he was "sort of aide-de-camp" to Mannberg, and hurried to pour the Slivovitz.

Mannberg and Wassermann touched glasses.

"Does the name Ivan Serov mean anything to you, Carl?" Mannberg asked.

"If you're talking about the Ivan Serov who is first deputy to commissar of State Security Nikolayevich Merkulov, it does."

"Mr. Cronley and I are going to have dinner with Comrade Serov tonight at the Drei Husaren."

"They do a very nice *Paprikás Csirke,*" Wassermann said in German. "Just like my mother used to make. Are you familiar with that, Mr. Cronley?"

*He wants to know if I speak German. What's that all about?*

"No, sir," Cronley replied in German. "My mother is a Strasbourger."

"They simmer chicken in a paprika sauce until tender and then stir in sour cream," he went on, still in German. "You really ought to try it."

"Thank you, sir, I will."

"What Comrade Serov wants to discuss is an exchange," Mannberg said. "I'm presuming you know Colonel Mattingly's gone missing."

"General Greene called to tell me about Mattingly. He didn't tell me the Reds have him."

"He may not know," Mannberg said. "We heard from a former Abwehr Ost asset. I don't know if the chief, DCI-Europe, told General Greene."

"I have to wonder why not. Is there — how do I say this? — *friction* between Greene and the chief, DCI-Europe?"

Wassermann's eyes drifted to Cronley, then back to Mannberg.

*Why did he look at me, Mannberg's "aide"? Does he think I'll talk? Or is there something else?*

*And why the hell did he ask that?*

*Has that sonofabitch Seidel been bad-mouthing me — DCI-Europe — to this Wassermann?*

*More important, has he been successful?*

*And is that somehow going to fuck up this meeting with Serov?*

*Seidel didn't know about that.*

*Unless of course somebody I trust got on the phone and told him.*

*Shit!*

"No," Mannberg said. "I know for a fact that the chief thinks very highly of General Greene. And, as far as I know, the reverse is true."

"The speed with which gossip travels is often a function of how nasty, and untrue, the gossip is," Wassermann said. "What kind of an exchange?"

"Well, we don't know for sure — our contact didn't use names. Just that we have something they want which they wish to exchange for something they have."

"Can you tell me what we have?"

"We think Serov is talking about Polkóvnik Sergei Likharev of the NKGB, who the chief turned and moved to Argentina."

"I didn't know we — you — had Likharev," Wassermann said. "But I suppose there's a lot of interesting things I'm not told about."

"That happens to all of us, I suppose," Mannberg said.

"If you don't feel comfortable answering this, don't," Wassermann said. "But the first things that popped into my mind just now were surprise that you were — your chief was — able to turn someone as senior as Sergei Likharev. And then I wondered if he's really been turned, or whether Merkulov has misinformation, important misinformation, that he wants to feed our side through Likharev."

"That's still possible, I suppose, but everything he's given to us since the chief got Likharev's wife, Natalia, and their sons, Sergei and Pavel, out of Russia and to Argentina has been both valuable and has checked out."

"That's amazing. I hadn't heard about that, either. But now that would seem to suggest posing the very difficult question to you: Who is more valuable, Polkóvnik Sergei Likharev or Colonel Bob Mattingly?"

"You knew — *know* — Colonel Mattingly?"

"Yes, I do. He's a fine man and a fine officer."

"I don't know if exchanging Colonel Mattingly is on the table. I would judge probably not. Which brings me to the answer to your question about what you — the CIC — can do for the DCI. The chief decided — and I think he's right — that we should meet with Comrade Serov to hear what he has to say. And we will. But Mr. Cronley and I want to ensure that we'll come back to the Bristol after dinner, perhaps to have a beer and some salted peanuts in the bar."

"Well, I can certainly understand how much our Soviet friends would like to have a chat with you in the basement of that building on Lubyanka Square."

"But even better for them, wouldn't you agree, would be to have the chief, DCI-Europe, in the Lubyanka basement?"

"I don't think I understand."

"I think you do, Carl," Mannberg said.

After a visibly thoughtful moment, Wassermann nodded.

"I was wondering if you were going to tell me," he said.

"Who told you? The identity of DCI-Europe is classified. Classified, specifically, as Top Secret–Presidential."

Wassermann didn't reply.

"You can consider that an order, Colonel Wassermann," Mannberg said.

"I'm not sure you have that authority, Mr. Mannberg."

"He does," Cronley said.

"I have no question about you having that authority, Mr. Cronley," Wassermann began.

Cronley's mouth ran away with him when he saw the look on Spurgeon's face. His jaw had dropped.

"Close your mouth, Charley" — *Jesus, I just remembered your first name* — "or flies will swarm in."

Wassermann and Mannberg both chuckled.

Wassermann then said, "What happened was that General Greene came to see me —"

*Jesus Christ, and I thought Greene could be trusted!*

"And told you I'm chief, DCI-Europe?" Cronley demanded angrily.

"He did. And he told me the circumstances."

"Jesus Christ! And what did he tell you those circumstances were? And more important, why was he telling you about them?"

"To answer your second question first: He said that he knew Colonel Mattingly and I were friends, and because of that, he thought I should know what the actual circumstances of your appointment were should Colonel Mattingly come to see me. Which, shortly after General Greene came to see me, Colonel Mattingly in fact did."

"What did he want?"

Wassermann took a moment to collect his thoughts.

"What General Greene led me to believe he would: to enlist me on the side of those who believe that DCI and, specifically, DCI-Europe have to be taken over by G-2 here and in the Pentagon. And, Mr. Cronley, if General Greene had not come to see me and told me what he did, I would have enlisted. Both because Bob Mattingly is not only an old friend, but an officer for whom I have a great deal of admiration."

"Tell me what General Greene told you," Cronley said.

"In brief, or in detail?"

"In detail. Every fucking detail."

Cronley sensed Mannberg's eyes on him. When Cronley raised his eyebrow, Mannberg nodded, just perceptibly.

*Jesus! I expected an icy Gehlen-style glare.*

*But that nod means I'm doing the right thing!*

"General Greene told me he had no authority to tell me what he was about to tell me, but that he had decided because of my assignment, and because he knew Bob Mattingly and I were friends, that he was going to tell me, even if I wasn't in the loop.

"He said that he had just come from seeing General White. He said General White had told him that Admiral Souers had gone to see him at Fort Riley, just before he came back over here, bearing a letter from President Truman. The handwritten letter made it clear that Souers was speaking with the authority of the President.

"General White said Souers told him about the formation of DCI, and the command structure of DCI-Europe. The major problem DCI-Europe would face was that the OSS's movement of Germans to Argentina would be exposed. That Operation Ost would be placed under DCI-Europe. Ensuring that Operation Ost remained secret was the highest priority.

"The second most important problem facing DCI-Europe — the DCI itself — was that its formation was going to displease the Pentagon, the Navy, the State Department, and the FBI, all of whom had urged the President to disestablish the OSS and have its functions transferred to them.

"Almost immediately after disestablishing the OSS, the President realized that he had made a mistake. He — the Office of the President — needed an OSS-like organization answerable only to the President. By Executive Order, he established the DCI and named Admiral Souers as director.

"General Greene told me that General White had told him that Admiral Souers had told him that he — Souers — had been selected for two reasons. One was that the President had turned over to Souers — then assistant chief of naval intelligence — just about all of the OSS operations, including Ost, that had to be kept running when the OSS was disestablished.

"The second reason was that the President and Admiral Souers were close, longtime personal friends. He trusted him. General White said that Admiral Souers told him that he had told the President that it was to be expected that Army G-2, which had some nominal authority over the OSS — more in law than in fact — would now begin to attempt to swallow DCI, starting with DCI-Europe, and that he didn't think that should be allowed to happen.

"White told me that Souers's recommendation to keep that from happening was to make Generals McNarney and Bull aware of the President's desires and to establish a command structure within DCI-Europe which could resist the efforts of US-FET G-2 to take it over.

"It was generally assumed that Colonel Mattingly would be named chief, DCI-Europe. Souers recommended that Colonel Mattingly remain with USFET-CIC, where he and many OSS officers had been assigned when the OSS had been disestablished. Souers had met Mattingly and had come to the conclusion that Mattingly, who had applied for a regular army commission, would likely decide that his bread would be better buttered if he joined those who believed that G-2 should swallow DCI-Europe.

"White said that Souers told him he had

suggested to the President a scenario which might solve most of their problems. The President had recently met a very young OSS officer to whom he had awarded the Distinguished Service Medal and promoted from second lieutenant to captain for something he'd done in South America that remains classified."

"The DSM?" Spurgeon blurted. "What the hell did you do?"

"I just said, Lieutenant, that General White said that was classified," Wassermann said. "Button your lip, Charley!"

"Yes, sir. Sorry, sir."

"General White said that Admiral Souers had recommended to the President that for both obfuscation and to, quote, have someone to throw to the wolves should Operation Ost be exposed, unquote, newly promoted Captain Cronley could be named chief, DCI-Europe. The appointment of a junior officer to that post, when it inevitably became known, would tend to suggest that DCI-Europe, and thus Operation Ost, was not very important.

"The question of having a more senior and more experienced officer on hand to both advise Captain Cronley and to step into the chief, DCI-Europe, post should that become necessary would be solved by assigning another former OSS officer, Major Harold Wallace, who was now in USFET CIC, to command a CIC detachment in Munich. General White told me the President had also approved that scenario and it was put in place.

"That's about it, Mr. Cronley," Wassermann concluded.

"Did General Greene have anything more to say about Major Wallace?" Cronley asked.

"He said the major had been told to lean over backward to ensure that no one suspected he was in the wings."

"That's all?"

"He told me that Major Wallace is actually Colonel Wallace," Wassermann said.

"Well, I see that he's told you just about everything that no one's supposed to know," Cronley said. "Which leaves just one question: How do you feel about being drafted into the loop?"

Wassermann visibly considered his reply before giving it.

"I'm fine with it, Mr. Cronley," he said finally. "To tell you the truth, when I heard that the OSS was being shut down, I thought it was a mistake."

"Why?" Cronley asked.

"The CIC is pretty good at sensing Joe Stalin's nose trying to get under the tent flap, but it doesn't have the authority, or the assets, to stick a bayonet in his nose when he does. I'm hoping the DCI does, that it has the authority to do what needs to be done."

"And I'm hoping that the CIC does have enough assets to keep Ludwig and me safe from Joe Stalin's evil minions while we're having our dinner tonight," Cronley said. "Welcome to the loop, Colonel."

"I think we do," Wassermann said. "Let me tell you what I think we should do."

Cronley looked at Spurgeon.

"I wonder what Dick Tracy Derwin would think of you and me being here tonight under these circumstances?"

"He'd probably wet his pants," Spurgeon said, chuckling. "We heard what happened to him. He got drunk and fell under a freight train?"

"That was the conclusion," Cronley said.

He met Mannberg's eyes. There was no visible reaction.

# [Two]

*Drei Husaren Restaurant*

*Weihburggasse 4*

*Vienna, Austria*

*2010 29 January 1946*

On the way to the restaurant from the Hotel Bristol, Cronley and Mannberg walked past the ruins of the Vienna Opera and the Stephansdom — Saint Stephen's Cathedral. As they passed the latter Mannberg enriched Cronley's fund of cultural knowledge by telling him that in the cathedral were buried the bodies, or the hearts, or the viscera, of seventy-two members of the Habsburg dynasty, it being the odd Habsburg custom to bury various parts of the bodies of deceased noblemen in separate places.

"You're kidding, right?"

"Not at all. By removing the organs, they made sure they were really dead."

They were expected at the restaurant. Once Mannberg invoked the name of Colonel Serov, the elegantly uniformed headwaiter bowed them down a flight of stairs to the main dining room.

Mannberg further added to Cronley's

365

cultural knowledge by telling him the head-waiter was wearing the uniform of the Fourth Regiment of the Austro-Hungarian Hussars, which meant light cavalry.

"Surreal, Ludwig. People outside are wearing rags and this guy is dressed like a character in a Franz Lehár operetta."

"And we haven't even met Comrade Serov yet," Mannberg replied. "You know Lehár, do you?"

"My mother didn't want me to grow up to be a Texas cowboy. If there was an operetta within five hundred miles, we went to it. Actually, I learned to like Lehár."

The restaurant was in the basement of the bomb-damaged building. It was very similar to the one Commandant Jean-Paul Fortin of the DST had taken Cronley and Winters to in Strasbourg, with a high ceiling supported by massive stone arches that had been strong enough to protect the basement when the building had fallen.

The main dining room was huge. At least a hundred men were seated at candlelit tables, many of them with well-dressed and attractive women. Most, but not all, of the men were in uniform — English, French, Russian, and American.

*More surreal.*

*Somewhere in here are the six CIC special agents whom Wassermann has provided to keep us from being kidnapped.*

*And, obviously, Serov has NKGB people undercover in here, too.*

*So, at least a dozen spooks. Six good guys and at least six bad.*

*And I don't have a clue which is which.*

The headwaiter Hussar pushed open a door to a small private dining room.

"Oberst Serov, your guests are here," he announced in German, and then waved Cronley and Mannberg into the room.

Two men in Russian uniforms rose from a table.

One was about fifty, heavyset, and wore the shoulder boards of a *polkóvnik* — colonel — and the other, a blond-haired, pleasant-looking man who looked to be in his mid-twenties, wore those of a lieutenant colonel.

"Thank you for coming," the young man said in German, putting out his hand to Cronley. "It is always a pleasure to break bread with our American allies."

His smile was warm and his handshake firm.

"This is Colonel Dragomirov," the young

367

man announced. "My superior, who suggested we meet."

Dragomirov's hand was callused and his handshake turned into a crushing contest, which Cronley almost lost.

"Hauptmann Cronley," Dragomirov said, using the German translation of "captain."

"Polkóvnik," Cronley replied.

*That used up one-tenth of my entire Russian vocabulary.*

"Which must make you Comrade Serov," Mannberg said to the younger man.

"At last we meet, Oberst Mannberg," Colonel Ivan Serov said, extending his hand to him.

"All things come to he who waits," Mannberg said.

"A drink is obviously called for," Serov said. "And thanks to international cooperation, I believe I am prepared."

"Excuse me?" Mannberg asked.

"As a gesture of courtesy between friends, senior officers affiliated with the Quadripartite Commission are honorary members of the senior officers' clubs of all parties," Serov explained. "Colonel Wassermann, for example, is welcome at the Red Army Senior Officers' Club, and I am welcome at the American Club, the French Club, and so on. At the American Club, James, knowing we were going to meet, I visited the spirits store."

*"James"? We're now buddies?*

Serov snapped his fingers and a waiter, in Hussar uniform, came to the table and put a bottle of George Dickel sour mash bourbon on the table.

*What about the waiter?*

*Is he a bona fide Viennese in an operetta uniform — or an NKGB agent?*

"Actually, I'm a scotch drinker," Cronley said.

*Why did my automatic mouth come up with that?*

"Not a problem," Serov said. "With Ludwig in mind, I also stopped by the spirits store at His Britannic Majesty's Officers' Club . . ."

*With Ludwig in mind?*

Serov gestured, and another waiter rolled in a table on which was an array of bottles.

"And found Dewar's in case he had acquired a taste for it during his time in London."

*Clever! What this sonofabitch is doing is letting us know he knows a hell of a lot about Mannberg.*

"But in case he didn't, and not without effort," Serov said, picking up a bottle, "I came up with this."

He showed the bottle first to Mannberg and then to Cronley, who read the label: *Berentzen Icemint Schnapps.*

"How kind of you," Mannberg said. "That's hard to find these days."

"And not to leave out our French allies," Serov said, pointing to two towel-wrapped bottles in a wine cooler, "Veuve Clicquot champagne."

Serov smiled, and then went on, "And last but certainly not least, from the Motherland, Beluga vodka." He pointed at the table. "And to go with the Beluga vodka, Beluga caviar."

*Fish eggs. Oh boy!*

*All this while they no doubt have Mattingly sitting in some cold, damp stone cell.*

"Your hospitality, gentlemen, is overwhelming," Mannberg said.

"Not at all. I wanted this to be a night of friendship and mutual understanding that we will all remember," Serov said, and then turned to Cronley. "Do you like caviar, Jim?"

"Some of it. I don't think I've had any . . . What did you say? 'Beluga'?"

"Beluga," Serov confirmed. "From the Caspian Sea. Try some. This is the very best."

He reached to the rolling cart, picked up

the large silver bowl that held ice and a smaller silver bowl brimming with caviar. He laid it before Cronley.

*Christ, there has to be a pound of it in there, maybe more!*

With a flourish, the waiter placed a plate containing toast tips and a small ceramic spoon before Cronley, and then hurriedly opened one of the bottles of champagne.

"Unless you would prefer vodka?" Serov asked.

"I'm still pretty new to vodka," Cronley said. "Champagne will do fine."

Cronley picked up the spoon, dipped it in the bowl of caviar, and then waited for his champagne to be poured.

Then he used the spoon to deposit a thumbnail-sized amount of caviar onto the first joint of his index finger before moving it to his mouth. He chewed gently for a moment, then pursed his lips appreciatively. He then took a small swallow of champagne.

"Magnificent," Cronley announced. "Frankly, I didn't believe this could be as good as people say."

"I'm glad you like it," Serov said. "Where did you say you're from in America?"

*As if you don't already know!*

"I don't think I did. I'm from Texas. A ranch outside a little town called Midland in West Texas."

"Forgive me if this sounds rude, but I'm a little surprised that caviar — how do I say this? — that caviar has penetrated America as far as West Texas."

"Oh, we Texans aren't as — how do I say this? — *bar aller Kultur* as many people believe. We have indoor plumbing and everything. So far as caviar is concerned, the last caviar I had before this was Uruguayan. My grandfather said as far as he was concerned, it was superior to Beluga. I wouldn't go quite that far, but it was really good."

He then took another ceramic spoonful from the silver bowl.

Serov smiled, and so did Mannberg, but Colonel Dragomirov's face remained icily impassive.

"Well, why don't we order?" Serov suggested.

"We'd better," Cronley said, "before I really get into this Beluga. It's like peanuts for me — if caviar's available, I can't stop. And if I don't stop, I get what they call in West Texas 'the runs.' "

Serov raised his eyebrows, and nodded.

"They do a very nice *Paprikás Csirke* here," Serov said.

"We were talking about that before,"

Mannberg said. "That's fine with me."

"And if I may make a suggestion," Serov went on, "a bottle of Weissburgunder to go with it. It's a Pinot Blanc."

"Sounds delightful," Mannberg said.

The *Paprikás Csirke* and the Weissburgunder were both delicious, but Cronley put his hand over his glass when Serov, smiling, tried to top it off.

"I've had enough, thank you," Cronley said.

" 'Take a little wine for thy stomach's sake,' " Serov quoted. "That comes from Saint Timothy, I think."

Cronley chuckled.

"Are you a Christian, James?" Serov asked.

*Now what is this sonofabitch up to?*

"I'm an Episcopalian."

"I'm of course Russian Orthodox," Serov said. "And before we get to the subject of our meeting, there is a situation I'm hoping we can discuss as fellow Christians."

"What would that be?"

"Christian burial."

*Christian burial?*

"Of who? Whom?"

Serov took a red leatherette folder from his jacket pocket and extended it to Cronley.

"Have you ever seen one of these, James?"

It was obviously an identity document. There was a photo of Serov and a thumbprint. But it was printed in Russian, and Cronley had no idea what the Cyrillic characters meant.

It was the first one he had seen, but he lied by nodding and then handed it to Mannberg.

Mannberg took a quick look, and then, smiling, said, "So that's who you are, Senior Major of State Security Ivan Serov. I never would have guessed."

*Thank you for the translation, Ludwig!*

"At your service, Ludwig," Serov said.

*That much I know.*

*A senior major of the NKGB is the equivalent of a Red Army* podpolkóvnik, *or lieutenant colonel.*

*But Comrade Ivan, since I know you're Commissar of State Security Nikolayevich Merkulov's Number Two, I don't think you're really a lowly* podpolkóvnik, *even if you look a lot younger than I think you are.*

*I don't know what, but the equivalent of at least a brigadier general, whatever that's called in the NKGB.*

Serov reached below the table, picked up a battered briefcase, and put it on his lap.

"I have four more of these to show you,"

Serov said, and handed Cronley four red leatherette identity documents.

Cronley looked at each one. The last one had a photograph of Lazarus riveted to it.

*Jesus, I hope my face didn't give away that I recognized him!*

*What the hell is Serov up to?*

Cronley handed the folders to Mannberg, who translated them one at a time.

"Sergeant of State Security Fyodor Yenotov.

"Senior Lieutenant of State Security Iakov Mravinsky.

"Another senior lieutenant, this one named Mikhail Jidkova.

"And, finally, Major of State Security Venedikt Ulyanov," Mannberg concluded, and laid the identity documents on the table. Serov returned them to his briefcase.

*I can't positively put a name to the faces, either the photos of the corpses I saw, or these identity cards, but obviously one of them, probably Major Ulyanov, is Lazarus.*

"These associates of mine — three of them, anyway — recently died in the line of duty. I'm sure there's no need for us to get into the circumstances. The fourth, I suspect, is still alive."

"How did they die?" Cronley asked.

Serov smiled sadly.

"As I'm sure you know, James, one should never underestimate one's adversary. Or take for granted that women are unarmed."

"That's always dangerous," Cronley said.

"We're in a dangerous profession. These things happen," Serov said. "We should all be prepared to meet our maker at any time. Which brings me to what I'm going to ask you to do for me. We know the bodies of the three men who died in the 98th General Hospital in Munich were turned over to the German authorities, who probably — we don't know this for sure — interred them in the Giesinger Friedhof cemetery."

"Ivan," Cronley said, "I really don't know what happened to the bodies of these men."

"But you can find out," Serov said.

"Probably. You want to know where, is that it?"

"I want my associates to have a Christian burial, in ground sanctified by a priest, in a grave that will be undisturbed for all eternity."

"I don't think I understand, Ivan," Mannberg said. " 'Undisturbed for all eternity'?"

"I'm referring to the German custom of reusing grave sites after twenty-five, or sometimes fifty, years," Serov said.

*What?*

"Someone who has given his life in the

service of his country deserves —"

"I agree," Mannberg said. "What is it that you wish us to do?"

Serov dug in his battered briefcase again and came up with a stack of photographs. He handed them to Mannberg, who glanced at them and then slid them across the table to Cronley.

"These are photographs of the identity documents I just showed you. What I'm asking you to do is use them to identify the men now lying in 'unknown' graves in the Giesinger Friedhof — or wherever they are — and then to arrange for their Christian burial. By that I mean a Russian Orthodox priest will consecrate the ground in which they lie, and then conduct a proper burial service, which will include the blessing of their tombstones, which will have their names and the dates of their birth and death on them, and be topped by a *Suppedaneum* — Russian Orthodox — cross."

"I'm sure that can be arranged," Mannberg said.

"I thank you," Serov said. "It's important to me that they be laid properly to their eternal rest."

Cronley's mouth went on automatic: "But what will happen when the Germans want to reuse the grave site in twenty-five years?"

377

"A great deal can happen in a quarter century," Serov said. "We are talking about eternity here, James."

Cronley worked his way through the photographs and came to the last one.

"Jesus Christ!"

"Your blasphemy tells me you have come to the last photograph," Serov said. "May I suggest that we finish the Christian burial service business before turning our attention to that?"

Cronley shoved the photographs to Mannberg. He glared at Serov, but he was able to shut off his automatic mouth.

Mannberg looked through the images, then reached the last one.

It showed Colonel Robert Mattingly. He was standing with his hands handcuffed in front of him. His right upper arm held a bloody bandage. His shirt was torn and bloody. His right eye was swollen shut, and there were bruises on his face.

Mannberg met Serov's eyes.

"I thought you heard me say that what you're asking of us will be done," he said.

"I wanted to be sure," Serov said. "For several reasons. Not only is it important to me that my fallen comrades receive the rites of the Church, but that we establish a relationship built on mutual trust. I'm sure that you will agree that as time passes, we will find ourselves dealing with one another again."

Mannberg nodded.

"What is it you want, Ivan?" he then said.

"Comrade Merkulov, the commissar of State Security, feels that the defection of Polkóvnik Sergei Likharev is something we simply can't live with. It sets a very bad, wholly intolerable example for others."

Neither Cronley nor Mannberg replied.

"Especially — and I must say I admire your being able to do this, James — since you managed for his wife and children to join him. I would love to know how you made that happen."

Again Mannberg and Cronley said nothing.

"Just before we came here, Comrade Dragomirov received word that Colonel Mattingly has safely arrived in Berlin. As I am aware of your personal affection for him, let me assure you that he has received, and will continue to receive, medical attention for his wound, and the prognosis is that he will fully recover."

"Is he getting this medical treatment before or after you're beating him?" Cronley asked.

"Colonel Mattingly showed a great — and

frankly admirable — reluctance to accept our hospitality. We are not beating him. At this time, we have no reason to mistreat him in any way."

Once more neither Cronley nor Mannberg replied.

"There is a difference between Berlin and Vienna in that there is no 'Four Party Zone' in Berlin as there is here, no 'Four Men in a Jeep,' so to speak. Each of the Allies has its own area. For this reason, Comrade Merkulov has directed that the exchange take place on the border between the Soviet and American zones.

"One of the border markers between our zone and yours is the Havel River, which runs between the Wannsee district of Berlin and the German state of Brandenburg. A bridge, the Glienicker Brücke, crosses over the Havel near the Sanssouci Palace. In the center of that bridge is where we will see Colonel Mattingly and Colonel Likharev and his family returned to their respective homelands."

Neither Mannberg nor Cronley replied.

"Exactly in the center of the Glienicker Brücke is a white line," Serov went on, "marking the border. Starting the day after tomorrow, every day at nine in the morning a Soviet vehicle will back onto the bridge, stopping perhaps five meters from that line. The doors will open and you will be able to see that Colonel Mattingly is in good health, and improving.

"Fifteen days from now — to be precise, at nine in the morning of February thirteenth — the Soviet truck will again back onto the bridge, this time stopping twenty meters from the white line. Colonel Mattingly will be taken out of the truck and escorted close to the white line.

"Simultaneously, Colonel Likharev and his family will get out of the vehicle in which they have been transported to the bridge. You will escort them to the white line as our people escort Colonel Mattingly to it. Once the Likharevs cross the line, Colonel Mattingly will be permitted to cross it, and the transaction will be completed.

"Any questions?"

Neither Cronley nor Mannberg had any questions, and Cronley managed to disengage his automatic mouth a split second before it was about to ask, *Transaction will be completed? We're talking about human beings, you sonofabitch, not the swap of two jerry cans of gasoline for two cartons of Lucky Strikes!*

Serov stood up and put his hand out to Cronley.

"You'll have to excuse us now, unfortunately, as Colonel Dragomirov and I have another engagement for which we're already late. I hope our dinner pleased you, and I look forward to seeing you again soon." He paused, and then added, "On the Glienicke Bridge, at nine in the morning of February thirteenth."

Cronley took the hand. The grip was strong and warm, as if between friends.

*Why am I surprised?*

*What did I expect, that it would be cold and slimy like shaking hands with a lizard or grabbing a rattlesnake?*

Colonel Dragomirov rose and offered his hand, and again tried to crush Cronley's hand. This time Cronley was prepared for it, and the contest was a draw.

Serov and Dragomirov walked quickly away from the table.

Mannberg waited until they were out of sight, then shrugged and exhaled audibly.

"Why don't we go back to the bar in the Bristol and have the beer and peanuts we talked about?"

# [THREE]

*Suite 304*

*The Hotel Bristol*

*Kaerntner Ring 1*

*Vienna, Austria*

*2210 29 January 1946*

On the walk back to the Hotel Bristol, which again took them past the ruins of the Stephansdom and the Opera, they were solicited by three ladies of the evening — two of them quite beautiful — but Cronley could see nothing in the other pedestrians that suggested they were agents of either the NKGB or the CIC.

When they walked into the lobby of the hotel, however, there was a familiar face.

Sitting at one of the small tables near the door to the bar was a well-dressed, middle-aged woman with a fox fur cape over her shoulders. One hand raised a small coffee cup to her lips as the other stroked the head of a small — almost a puppy — dachshund in her lap.

Mannberg apparently saw and recognized the woman at the same instant Cronley did. He quickly touched Cronley's shoulder, and when Cronley turned to look at him, nodded his head — just perceptibly — toward the elevator bank.

On the elevator, with only the operator on it, they confined their conversation to raising eyebrows at one another.

When the door opened on the third floor, a man sitting in a chair in the corridor got quickly to his feet.

Cronley thought, *You, sir, might as well have CIC agent tattooed on your forehead.*

As he and Mannberg walked to their suite, he saw two more CIC agents in the corridor.

Mannberg had just put the enormous brass key to the door when Charley Spurgeon pulled the door open from the inside. His Ike jacket was unbuttoned, revealing a Colt .45 automatic in a shoulder holster. Colonel Carl Wassermann was sitting on a couch before a coffee table on which sat a U.S. Army backpack shortwave radio.

"Welcome home," Spurgeon greeted them. "How was dinner?"

Mannberg and Cronley ignored him.

"She just happened to be there," Mannberg said to Cronley.

"Or Serov or Dragomirov sent her to make sure we got safely home."

"Or Serov or Dragomirov sent her, and somebody to watch her, to see how we reacted when we saw her," Mannberg said.

"Yeah," Cronley said. "How surprised do you think we looked?"

Mannberg shrugged.

"How did it go?" Wassermann asked. "And who is 'her'?"

Mannberg handed him the photographs of the NKGB identity documents and Colonel Mattingly.

"Jesus, they really worked him over, didn't they?" Wassermann said.

"Serov said he showed a 'frankly admirable reluctance' to accept their hospitality," Cronley said.

"What's with the identity documents?" Wassermann asked.

"Three of them are of the people Sergeant Colbert blew away in the back of an ambulance when they tried to kidnap her. Serov wants us to see that they get a proper Christian burial, complete with a Russian Orthodox priest and their names on a proper Russian Orthodox tombstone."

"What's that all about?"

"I don't know," Cronley said. "But, as one Christian to another, I said I'd do it."

"There's four documents."

"Colbert missed Major of State Security Venedikt Ulyanov in the ambulance. We've got him in the chapel at Kloster Grünau.

385

We call him Lazarus."

"And Serov wants him back?"

"He suspects — knows — we have one of the four, but he doesn't know which one. He wants, obviously, whomever we have back, but what he really wants in exchange for Mattingly is Likharev. Likharev and his family. I think he thinks Lazarus is expendable."

"And?"

"We have been ordered to have the Likharevs on some bridge in Berlin . . ."

"The Glienicke Bridge, between Potsdam and Wannsee," Mannberg furnished.

". . . at oh-nine-hundred on thirteen February, when the exchange will take place. In the meantime, Mattingly will be shown to us every day to show us he's still alive."

"You're going to make the exchange?" Wassermann asked softly.

"Over, maybe literally, my dead body," Cronley said. "That exchange would take a direct order personally from President Truman. And if that order comes, he's going to have to send someone else to the bridge. I'll have nothing to do with turning Likharev or his wife and kids over to those sonsofbitches."

"A direct order is a direct order," Wassermann argued softly.

"And I knew that sooner or later I would have no choice but to disobey one," Cronley said.

There was a long moment's silence.

Wassermann finally broke it.

"Who is the 'her' you were talking about when you walked in here?"

Cronley waved at Mannberg, telling him to reply.

"When we came into the lobby, we saw an NKGB agent with whom we have a relationship having a cup of coffee at one of the tables near the bar."

"She looks like a Viennese grandmother," Cronley said.

Wassermann's eyebrows rose but he didn't say anything for a moment.

"I've got a man behind the desk with a Leica," he said. "Behind a one-way mirror. He can see the whole lobby. You want a picture of this woman?"

"Good idea," Mannberg said. "It might come in handy at the Compound."

"Call him, Charley," Wassermann ordered.

Cronley's mouth went on automatic: "No. Hold it a minute, Charley."

He immediately wondered, *Where the hell did that come from?*

Everyone looked at him in surprise.

And then he knew the reason.

"There are people in the Compound who would be interested to learn that we know Rahil, aka Seven-K."

"You're right," Mannberg said. "I should havc thought about that."

"You've got a mole in DCI-Europe?" Charley Spurgeon blurted.

"Almost certainly more than one," Cronley said. And then his mouth went on full automatic: "Colonel, what kind of a photo lab do you have? Specifically, can you copy negatives?"

Wassermann was visibly surprised at the question, but replied, "Yes, we can."

Cronley pointed at Spurgeon.

"You can take shorthand, right?"

Spurgeon nodded.

"Find something to write on," Cronley ordered.

"What?"

"Just do it, Charley," Cronley snapped.

Spurgeon took a notebook and a pencil from his jacket.

" 'Secret,' " Cronley dictated. " 'From Commanding Officer' " — he pointed at Colonel Wassermann — "whatever the CIC Detachment number is, 'to Commanding General, CIC-Europe, eyes only General Greene. By armed officer courier.' "

"Jim," Mannberg said, "what's going on?"

Cronley silenced him with a wave of his hand.

" 'Subject,' " he went on, " 'Possible Identification of NKGB Agents.'

" 'Paragraph one. The undersigned received reliable intelligence that a number of NKGB agents would be in the lobby of the Bristol Hotel and in the Drei Husaren restaurant here last night' — no, put in the date. 'It was possible to surreptitiously photograph these people.

" 'Paragraph two. Forwarded herewith are' . . . How many CIC detachments are there?"

"Nine," Wassermann replied. "Plus of course Major Wallace's Twenty-seventh, and the Twenty-third."

" 'Forwarded herewith are twelve sets of thirty-five-millimeter negatives each containing thirty-six images of persons suspected of being NKGB agents.'

"If possible, one of the shots should show Seven-K and an NKGB agent . . . for that matter, anyone walking close to her not in a U.S. Army uniform . . . in the same frame. But make sure there is one — only one — good shot of her. Understood?"

Wassermann and Spurgeon said, "Understood," on top of one another.

" 'Paragraph three,' " Cronley went on. " 'It is strongly recommended that these negatives be forwarded, immediately and with great care, to all eleven CIC detachments, in the hope that identification, or identifications, can be made.' "

"You left DCI out," Spurgeon said.

" 'I'm the commanding officer of the Twenty-third CIC detachment,' " Cronley said. "Any other comments or objections?"

"That'll solve the problem," Mannberg said.

"I have a comment, if I may," Wassermann said.

"Shoot," Cronley said.

"Those that don't think you have the experience, or the general makeup, to be running the DCI are dead fucking wrong."

"I wish I could agree, but I don't. Thanks anyway."

"There are two colonels in this room, Cronley, who have been in this business since you were in short pants. Before either of us had even considered moles in our organizations, you did, and you came up with a very clever — and very detailed and workable — solution to that problem off the top of your head. I stand by my comment."

"And I concur," Mannberg said.

"If I'm so smart, why don't I have a fucking clue how to get Mattingly back without swapping the Likharevs for him?"

"I would suggest, Jim," Mannberg said, "that that problem is almost infinitely more complex."

"Sir," Spurgeon asked, "should I get started on this?"

Cronley answered for Wassermann: "Charley, do whatever you have to do to be back here at oh-six-thirty with everything in your hands. I want to get out of Schwechat as soon as we can in the morning."

"Yes, sir, I understand."

When he had gone, Wassermann said, "I now have a question. Why do you want Charley to carry the negatives to General Greene?"

"Because when General Greene has him standing tall and demanding to know what's really going on with the negatives — and he will — Charley will tell him everything and Greene will believe him."

Wassermann nodded his acceptance of the explanation.

"And now, although I would really like the whole bottle," Cronley said, "I am going to have one small nip of Jack Daniel's and then go to bed. I want to get back to Germany as quickly as I can. Maybe General Gehlen will have an idea what we should do now."

[FOUR]

*Kloster Grünau*

*Schollbrunn, Bavaria*

*American Zone of Occupation, Germany*

*0905 30 January 1946*

Lieutenant Tom Winters and Kurt Schröder, who was now wearing ODs with triangles, walked up to the Storch as Cronley, Mannberg, and Spurgeon got out.

"I didn't expect you to be here, Tom," Cronley said.

"You said you wanted Kurt to check me out in the Storch," Winters replied. "And here we are."

"How did you get here?" Cronley asked.

"In an L-4."

"The Storch checkout is going to have to wait," Cronley said. "What you're going to do is get back in the L-4 and take Charley here — Excuse me, Charley Spurgeon, Tom Winters and Kurt Schröder."

The men shook hands.

Cronley went on: "What you're going to do, Tom, is take Charley to Eschborn. I'll call ahead and have a car waiting. He's going to the Farben Building to see General Greene. When he's finished, you'll fly him back here . . . to the Compound . . . hopefully in time for him to catch the Blue Danube so he can get back to Vienna."

"Can I ask what's going on?" Winters said.

"Charley will explain on your way to Eschborn. Charley, you can tell Tom everything. He's one of the good guys, as is Kurt."

"Got it," Spurgeon said.

"And you, Kurt, make sure both Storches are ready to go. I think we're going to need both of them."

Schröder nodded.

"How's Lazarus?" Cronley asked.

"Tom and I just fed him his breakfast," Schröder said. "His appetite's all right."

"I found out who he is," Cronley said. "Major of State Security Venedikt Ulyanov."

"How'd you find that out?" Winters said.

"Senior Major of State Security Ivan Serov told me while he was telling me how we're going to exchange Likharev and his family for Colonel Mattingly. It came out, specifically, when Serov was asking me, as a fellow Christian, to arrange Russian Orthodox burials for the three guys Claudette took out. Who he also identified for me."

"What?" Schröder asked.

"Jesus!" Winters blurted. "You're going to make the swap?"

"So," Cronley went on, "what I've been wondering about as I dodged rock-filled clouds on the way up here — keeping in mind that Serov is much smarter than me — is whether ol' Ivan just let who Lazarus is slip out, or whether he wanted me to know. And I don't know, so I guess for the moment I'm going to have to pass on getting to see the look on Lazarus's face when I call him Major Ulyanov."

He paused, and then asked, "Is there a car here, or am I going to have to go to the goddamn Compound in an ambulance?"

"There's two Fords here," Winters said.

"In that case, Lieutenant Winters, sound 'Boots and Saddles.' Let's get the cavalry moving."

"Yes, sir," Winters said.

He smiled and so did Charley Spurgeon. Schröder looked confused.

# IX

## [ONE]

*Office of the Military Government Liaison Officer*

*The South German Industrial Development*

*Organization Compound*

*Pullach, Bavaria*

*American Zone of Occupation, Germany*

*0955 30 January 1946*

When Cronley went into his bedroom to change out of the furlined flying boots he had been wearing since he put them on at Schwechat Airfield in Vienna, he found three large cardboard boxes sitting on his bed.

He took a closer look and saw that an envelope addressed to him sat atop one of the boxes. The printed return address was that of his mother.

He sat on the bed, pulled the boots off, then removed the letter from the envelope and read it:

January 20, 1946

My Dearest Jimmy:

This is a very difficult letter for me to write because, knowing if your father knew about it he would be hurt or angry or both, I am writing it behind his back. I can only hope that you will understand.

I received a letter from my nephew, your cousin Luther Stauffer, thanking me from the bottom of his heart for the food packages I sent via you to him and his family. It touched me more deeply than I imagined possible. When I thought about this, I came to decide it was because it meant that for the first time since I left Strasbourg to marry your father so long ago, I was again in touch with my family, and more important was able — with your help, of course, my darling — able to help them in a time of their need.

I have to tell you that your father went to the trouble of getting our congress-man, Dick Lacey, to send him the actual regulations — which he showed to me — which prohibit you from getting packages through the Army Postal System that contain "prohibited items" and then passing them on to what the regulations call "indigenous persons."

The last thing I want, my darling boy, is to get you in any trouble with your superiors or the Army, or anybody. But if the three packages I mailed yesterday somehow reach you — your father said I would be wasting my time, effort, and money if I tried to send my family anything else via you as the packages would almost certainly be inspected and the coffee and canned ham and other prohibited things seized — if there is any way you can get them to your cousin Luther and his family, I think God would consider it an act of Christian charity, no matter what your father and the Army think.

I will also leave up to you whether you tell your father about the packages or this letter.

*With all my love, my darling boy,*
*Mom*

"Oh, shit!" Cronley said.

He felt around under the bed until he found his Western boots. He started to pull them on, then changed his mind. The fur-lined boots had not only kept his feet warm but had made them sweat. He pulled off his socks, sniffed them, and grunted as he tossed them. He found clean socks in the chest of drawers and put them on, followed by the Western boots.

As he walked into the main room, his feet feeling refreshed, he found a large number of people — but not General Gehlen, whom he expected. Staff Sergeant Albert Finney was there, and his presence disappointed him. Cronley had hoped that the very large, very black twenty-four-year-old, after being corrupted by Cousin Luther, would be somewhere around Salzburg learning who Cousin Luther's partners in crimes were.

"Welcome home," Major Harold Wallace greeted him. "How did things go in Vienna?"

"Swimmingly," Cronley said. He put his briefcase on the table, took from it the photographs Serov had given him, and put them on the table.

"Have a look," he said. "Everybody have a look."

"Well, at least Bob Mattingly is still alive,"

Wallace said after a moment.

"So Lazarus is an NKGB major," Tiny Dunwiddie said.

"Let's start with Mattingly," Cronley began. "They want to exchange Colonel Likharev and family for him . . ."

He had just about finished when General Gehlen, Colonel Mannberg, and Major Konrad Bischoff came into the room.

"Sorry to keep you waiting," Gehlen said.

"I was just telling everybody what I presume Oberst Mannberg has told you," Cronley said.

"I found the presence of Seven-K in the Hotel Bristol very interesting," Gehlen said. "Did she have something for us, or did Serov send her there?"

Cronley said, "What I've been wondering is what Serov is up to with getting a Christian burial for the people Claudette took out in the ambulance."

"Simple answer is that he wants to know which of the four is still alive, which he will know if you go through with the burial of the others," Bischoff said.

Cronley saw on the faces of Wallace, Gehlen, and Mannberg that they agreed with him.

"General, do you think we should go

through with the burial?" Cronley asked.

Gehlen seemed to be framing his reply when Wallace said, "Anything that may help get Bob Mattingly back."

Cronley thought: *This is not the time for me to say I have absolutely no intention of swapping the Likharevs for Mattingly.*

*What I have to do is let Cletus Frade know what's going on.*

*He can arrange to get the Likharevs somewhere where they'll be safe not only from the Russians in Argentina, but from the Pentagon and USFET G-2 types who will be more than willing to swap them for Mattingly.*

*And how the hell am I going to do that?*

*If I get on the SIGABA there are people both in Iron Lung McClung's station in Fulda and at Vint Hill Farms who will fall all over themselves making sure USFET G-2 and the Pentagon hear my "hide the Likharevs" message.*

*And that will get me relieved!*

"Surely no one is actually considering exchanging the Likharevs for Colonel Mattingly," Bischoff said.

"What did you just say?" Wallace asked incredulously.

Cronley's mouth went on automatic: "That decision hasn't been made."

"Making the exchange would simply encourage Serov to kidnap somebody else,"

Bischoff said.

Cronley's mouth was still on automatic: "And returning the Likharevs would just about kill any chance we have to turn any NKGB officer in the future. Serov obviously plans to march Likharev and his family back and forth in Moscow before middle- and senior-level NKGB brass, saying, 'Take a good look at what happens to people who think they can desert to the Americans.' "

"Precisely," Bischoff said.

Major Wallace glared at Bischoff and then at Cronley.

"It had better be understood from this point that we're going to do whatever it takes to get Colonel Bob Mattingly back," he said. "Understood especially by you, Captain Cronley."

"I intend, Colonel, to do everything possible to get Colonel Mattingly back, short of exchanging the Likharevs for him."

*Two fucking mistakes. I shouldn't have said "short of exchanging the Likharevs for him."*

*And I shouldn't have called him "Colonel."*

*What the hell, everyone in here knows he's really a colonel.*

"That's not your decision, fortunately, to make, Cronley," Wallace said.

Just in time, Cronley managed to shut off his automatic mouth.

Instead, he said, "About the first thing we have to do is get somebody to Berlin. Where's Hammersmith?"

"What do you want with him?" Wallace demanded.

"He's holding down the office in the Vier Jahreszeiten," Tiny said.

"I'm presuming he has CIC friends in Berlin," Cronley said.

"He does," Wallace said.

"I want to get him there as soon as possible. I want pictures of that bridge — both ends of it — before they bring Mattingly on it tomorrow morning. I think the CIC can do that better than anyone else."

"Getting pictures of their end of it may not be easy," Tiny said.

"I have people in Brandenburg," Gehlen said. "I'll have pictures before tomorrow morning."

"And can your people find out where Serov's holding him? And learn the back-and-forth route from wherever that is to the bridge?"

"That'll probably take some more time, but eventually, yes," Gehlen said.

"You're not thinking of trying to kidnap him back from the Russians, are you?" Wallace asked.

"I'm trying to think of all our possible actions, Colonel," Cronley said. "Tiny, pick a dozen of your largest, meanest-looking troopers and get them — with full Constabulary regalia — to Berlin as soon as possible. By air. Cut orders giving them the highest priority."

"Got it," Dunwiddie said.

"And cut the same kind of orders for Colonel Mannberg, Ostrowski, and me."

"Got it."

"Correction," Cronley said. "Ostrowski and four of his people who speak German and Russian."

"Ostrowski has DCI credentials," Freddy Hessinger said. "His people don't. You probably can't get them on the Berlin airplane at all, much less with a priority that would see them bumping American officers or enlisted."

"So you suggest?"

"Have them drive to Berlin in one of the Fords. Driven by somebody with DCI credentials to get them past the MPs at the Helmstedt checkpoint on the autobahn."

"Like who? Who with DCI credentials?"

"Me," Hessinger said.

"You're needed here to cut the orders."

"I can handle that," Claudette Colbert said.

Cronley looked at her, visibly cut off what

he was about to say, and instead said, "No."

"No?" she challenged.

"Change that to three of Ostrowski's people, Freddy, and Dette. No offense, Freddy, but Dette flashing DCI credentials at the Helmstedt MPs is going to dazzle them more than you would. And you can probably find something else for her to do in Berlin. Sergeant Miller can cut the orders, et cetera, as well as you can, Dette, right?"

"Nearly as well as I can," she replied, and then added, "Thanks. I really want to be in on this."

"Okay, you and Freddy get going."

"I have something to offer of a tangential nature I think you should hear before I leave," Hessinger said.

"Won't it wait?"

"I think you should hear it before I leave."

"Make it quick, Freddy."

"It has to do with Lazarus, especially since you have identified him as Major of State Security Ulyanov."

Cronley motioned impatiently for him to get on with it.

"By now I think he has figured out that we are not going to . . . *dispose* of him. Similarly, I think it unlikely that we will be able to turn him. We could send him to

Argentina, but confining him there would be difficult. So, what do we do with him?"

"Why do I think you're about to offer a suggestion?"

"Treat him as a common criminal," Hessinger said.

"What?"

"I have researched the applicable German laws," Hessinger said. "Everyone participating in a crime of violence is equally guilty of an offense as anyone participating in said crime."

"Which means exactly what?"

"The men who attempted to kidnap Dette and Florence Miller committed not only that crime but murder."

"They didn't murder anybody. Dette murd— *took out* the three."

"Right. And so all four Russians are equally guilty under German law of the crime of murder, because the deaths occurred during their involvement in the kidnapping, which qualifies as a violent crime."

"Hessinger's onto something," General Gehlen said. "Major Ulyanov thinks we're probably not going to *dispose* of him, and I don't think he thinks we have anything on him that will cause him to turn. I submit we do: Thirty years to life in a German prison for the crime of murder is a nightmare that a major of State Security simply does not want to face. Turning may seem to be a far more attractive alternative."

"How do we get the Germans to try an NKGB major in their courts?" Ziegler asked.

"I think that Hessinger is suggesting that Ulyanov is a displaced person, not a Russian," Mannberg said. "The story Miss Johansen wrote said the would-be rapists were Polish DPs who escaped from the Oberhaching displaced persons camp."

Gehlen said, "And I can't see Lazarus standing up in court and proclaiming, 'Now just a minute, I'm actually Major of State Security Venedikt Ulyanov!' That would be tantamount to admitting the NKGB has people running around the American Zone without identification bent on despoiling innocent American enlisted women. Or with other nefarious intent, such as kidnapping American officers."

"And Lazarus would know," Cronley said, picking up the thought, "that even if admitting who he is kept him out of a German jail, he'd really be in the deep shit with Comrade Serov and all he would be doing if we gave him back to the Russians would be exchanging a cell in a German prison for one in the basement of the . . ."

". . . NKGB building on Lubyanka Square in Moscow," Gehlen picked up. "Or worse. Leaving him only one alternative, the least unpleasant of the three, turning. Freddy — what is it Cronley is always saying? 'You get both ears and the tail!' "

Cronley jumped up, walked quickly to Hessinger, wrapped his arms around him, and kissed him wetly and noisily on the forehead.

"Just as soon as we get back from Berlin," Cronley said, "we will move Ulyanov into a large room at Kloster Grünau —"

"A large room?" Mannberg asked.

"So that everybody can be there to see the look on the sonofabitch's face when he learns we've got him," Cronley explained. "But, first things first, specifically the funerals. Ziegler, do you happen to know a Russian Orthodox priest?"

"As a matter of fact, I know a bunch of them."

"One who will go along with this burial business?"

Ziegler nodded.

"Okay, you are appointed the Bury the Russian Officers. You better get a Russian speaker from Ostrowski to go with you. And get pictures of everything."

"Yes, sir."

"And now that the other Dutchman is back from Pfungstadt," Cronley went on, "take him along with you. How did it go at *Stars and Stripes,* Wagner?"

"Well, sir, I found out how they're moving people on the trucks," PFC Karl-Christoph Wagner said.

"You mean you think you have an idea how they're doing that?"

"No, sir. I mean I *know* how they're doing it."

"Well, I can hardly wait to hear that . . ."

"I think he does, Captain," Ziegler said.

". . . but I'm going to have to wait until I get back from Berlin. Right now, I need to know why you're here, Finney, instead of in Salzburg worming your way into my cousin Luther's black market operation."

"He's onto us," Finney said. "Onto you."

"Shit!" Cronley said, and gestured for Finney to explain.

" 'Herr Stauffer,' I said in my best GI German, 'I have ten cartons of Lucky Strike cigarettes and a case of Maxwell House coffee I'd be willing to sell if the price was right.' "

"And?"

"Cousin Luther said that he was really sorry but he couldn't help, and then suggested I might have better luck in Salzburg. I'm sorry, Captain, but Cousin Luther is onto us."

"Shit," Cronley said again.

"When I thought about it," Finney said, "I realized I shouldn't have been surprised. We tried to pass ourselves off to Commandant Fortin as the Mobile Kitchen Renovation Company, but he had already checked with European Command and learned that there ain't no 711th MKRC. I think Cousin Luther probably did the same thing. He's not stupid."

"Did you have a chance to talk to Fortin?"

Finney nodded.

"When I got to Salzburg, I got on a secure line and called him."

"And?"

"Then I came back here. I didn't see any point in going to Vienna. Neither did Major Wallace. He sent Kurt Schröder down in an L-4 to bring me back."

"That's not what I was asking. What did Fortin have to say?"

"He said (a) he wasn't surprised, and (b) Cousin Luther is up to something else he doesn't know what, and (c) when I saw you, I was to ask you to reconsider your thoughts about his not having Cousin Luther in for a little chat."

"What were those thoughts, Jim?" General Gehlen asked.

"Let's say I don't approve of his interrogation techniques," Cronley said. "Okay. Don't get far away, Al. There'll be something I'll need you to do."

"Yes, sir."

"And if the rest of you will kindly excuse me, I will now start to write my report of what's happened to Colonel Mattingly, which I want to get on its way before we go to Berlin."

"Your report to whom?" Major Wallace asked.

"Admiral Souers."

"With a copy to General Seidel?"

"No."

"I think you should."

"Duly noted. But I don't work for the US-FET G-2."

"So you're not going to bring anyone in USFET intelligence into this?"

"Right. Not yet."

"Not even General Greene?" Wallace challenged sarcastically. "Bob Mattingly is his deputy, and Greene does command USFET CIC."

"I strongly suspect that Lieutenant Charley Spurgeon has already brought General

Greene up to speed on what I've been doing, and even if he hasn't, I suspect that my report to Admiral Souers — which has to pass through Iron Lung McClung's ASA — will be in General Greene's hands before it's decrypted in Washington. Any other questions?"

"Just one," Wallace said. "Do you have any idea how close you are to being relieved?"

There was a long moment's silence, then General Gehlen said softly, "In my judgment, relieving Captain Cronley at this point in this scenario would be ill-advised for a number of reasons."

"It would be my call, General," Wallace snapped.

"I suggest you make your decision very carefully," Gehlen said.

Wallace glared at him and then marched angrily out of the room.

## [TWO]

*44–46 Beerenstrasse, Zehlendorf*

*U.S. Zone of Berlin*

*1810 30 January 1946*

As the Military Transport Command Douglas C-54 "Skymaster" had made its approach to the Tempelhof airfield in the

411

growing darkness, Cronley saw that what had been the capital of the Thousand-Year Reich was mostly in darkness. There were exceptions. Here and there he saw islands of light, small parts of Berlin that had somehow escaped the damage brought by one thousand-bomber raid after another. The buildings in those parts were lighted, and some of the streets, and he had even seen the red and green of traffic lights.

And one of those islands of light, he knew, was their destination: the city suburb of Zehlendorf.

The Skymaster touched down and taxied under the curved arch of the terminal. An Air Force bus pulled up to the aircraft as its door opened. Two full colonels rose from their seats and walked to the door. Both of them glared at Cronley, Mannberg, and Ostrowski as they did.

The original manifest had had another full colonel and a lieutenant colonel listed as passengers. They had been bumped by a higher travel priority given — for reasons the two colonels who had not been bumped could not imagine — by two young, and therefore obviously not senior, men whose uniforms bore the blue triangles of civilian employees of the Army.

Cronley signaled to Ostrowski and Mannberg to wait until just about all the other passengers had debarked. Then they got on the bus, which carried them farther into the terminal.

"My God," Ostrowski said, as they walked into the terminal, "this place is enormous!"

"First time in Berlin, Max?" Mannberg asked.

"First time on the ground. The last two times I was here I was an exchange pilot with the 8th Air Force flying B-17 escort in a P-51."

Cronley saw the two were smiling at one another. And then he saw something else, and said, "Well, Comrade Serov will see that we are following his orders."

He nodded his head toward two Russian officers who were standing against a counter looking at the arriving passengers.

Cronley waved cheerfully at the Russian officers as Mannberg and Ostrowski, shaking their heads, smiled.

Staff cars were available for senior officers, and Mannberg's DCI credentials got them one, an Opel Kapitän driven by a German wearing ODs dyed black.

When they got to the house on Beerenstrasse, Cronley saw a 1942 Ford with 711

MKRC bumper markings. That told him Hessinger, Claudette, and Ostrowski's men had made it to Berlin.

And then the headlights of the staff car lit up a sign, a four-by-eight-foot sheet of plywood held up by two-by-four studs. It carried the legend SOUTH AMERICAN AIRWAYS, the letters arranged in a circle around a representation of the world.

At first Cronley was amused.

*Well, why not? That sign was probably Clete's idea. This house was taken over by the OSS right after the war. When the OSS went out of business, Operation Ost didn't, and needed a place in Berlin. You could hardly put a sign reading OPERATION OST on the lawn.*

*So, why not South American Airways, whose managing director and chief pilot was Señor Cletus Frade — and who's also, or was then, the senior OSS officer in the Southern Cone of South America?*

And then he had more sobering thoughts.

*My God! I completely forgot that Berlin, not Frankfurt, is the European terminal for SAA!*

*This is where the crews rest for twenty-four hours before heading back to Buenos Aires.*

*Was there an SAA Constellation at Tempelhof? It was too damn dark to see!*

*If there is an SAA crew here and, please,*

*God, one of them is somebody I know, I can get word to Clete without anybody finding out that I have.*

When he was allowed to enter the house — after having to show his DCI credentials to a security guard armed with a Thompson submachine gun — he found the foyer crowded with what looked like a party, one that was spreading into the adjacent dining and living rooms.

More than a dozen of the men in the foyer were Tiny's Troopers, just about all of whom had beer bottles in their massive hands. There were also about eight men whose blue-triangled OD Ike jackets bulged with concealed weapons.

*CIC agents? What the hell?*

Cronley walked to the door of the living room. He saw that there were a number of Ostrowski's men, all with beer bottles, two more CIC types, and a lieutenant colonel and a major he had never seen before.

*Who the hell are they?*

He went to the dining room.

Tiny Dunwiddie, wearing his captain's uniform, was sitting at the table with Claudette Colbert, Freddy Hessinger, and Jack Hammersmith. They were all wearing pinks and greens with triangles. There were also seven men wearing parts of SAA aircrew uniforms at the table.

*Pilot,* Cronley thought, as he searched for a familiar face among them, *copilot, flight engineer, radio operator/navigator, and three stewards.*

*SAA doesn't have stewardesses.*

And then he found whom he was looking for seated at the head of the table.

A handsome blond-haired man in his late twenties was refilling his glass from a bottle of Haig & Haig Pinch Scots whisky. He looked up and saw Cronley.

The man cheerfully called, "Hey, look who's finally showed up!"

Cronley went to him.

"Hansel, you have no idea how glad I am to see you!"

Former Luftwaffe major Hans-Peter Freiherr von Wachtstein, now Captain von Wachtstein of South American Airways, stood up.

Cronley wrapped his arms around him and kissed him wetly on the forehead.

At that moment, the lieutenant colonel and the major whom Cronley had seen in the living room approached. Both looked confused or disapproving or, more precisely, confused *and* disapproving.

"Mr. Cronley?" the lieutenant colonel asked.

"Guilty."

"My name is Ledbetter, Mr. Cronley. I command the Twenty-sixth CIC. This is Major Rogers, my deputy."

Cronley shook their hands. "What can I do for you, Colonel?"

"That shoe's on the other foot," Ledbetter said. "General Greene called and ordered me to get in touch with you and provide whatever assistance you require."

Cronley looked into Colonel Ledbetter's eyes.

*Are you really here, Colonel, to provide whatever assistance I require?*

*Or are you here so that you can tell General Greene and he can tell General Seidel and the USFET intelligence establishment what the loose-cannon young captain who has been given more authority than he can be expected to handle is up to?*

*General Gehlen told me that the one thing intelligence officers should always remember is to trust no one.*

*But, as my mother told me, there is always an exception to every rule.*

*My gut tells me I can trust General Greene, and thus this cold-eyed colonel.*

*Supporting that argument is that Hammer-*

417

*smith is here. If Greene wanted someone to report to him on me, it would be Hammersmith.*

*Should I go with my gut feeling, or listen to Gehlen's Trust No One?*

*Yet another factor bearing on this problem is that until I'm relieved — and Major Harold Wallace more than likely is working hard on that right now — I'm chief, DCI-Europe.*

*And, as such, I'm supposed to make decisions without — what did Patton say? "Do not take counsel of your fears" — immediately deciding that the worst-case scenario is the one most likely to bite me on the ass.*

"In that case, Colonel, I'm very glad you're here," Cronley said.

"So, what can I do for you?"

"Did General Greene tell you why I'm interested in the Glienicke Bridge?"

Ledbetter nodded.

"I'd like to have a look at it as soon as possible. How far is it from here?"

"Not far, but you're not going to be able to see anything at this time of day."

Hessinger and Claudette stepped closer.

"There's not much to see, Mr. Cronley," Hessinger said. "Miss Colbert and I took a look before we came here."

"And?"

"Girder bridge, two lanes."

"What about Russians?"

"There were maybe half a dozen Russian soldiers at their end of the bridge," Claudette said. "Just standing around."

"And on our end?"

"Two MPs sitting in a jeep."

"Colonel," Cronley asked, "has this — a prisoner swap or, for that matter, any interaction between us and the Russians — ever happened at the bridge before?"

"Just the return of Red Army soldiers who got drunk and locked up in our zone," Ledbetter said. "Or GIs who got drunk and locked up over there. Nothing like this."

"What I would like to do tomorrow," Cronley said, "after they put Colonel Mattingly on display on the bridge, is to try to see where they take him afterward. Any ideas how we can do that?"

"I'm already working on that," Mannberg said. "There are two possibilities. One is the Cecilienhof Palace in the Neuer Garten —"

"Where they held the Potsdam Conference, right?" Cronley interrupted.

Mannberg nodded. "Comrade Serov might be staying there. As it was good enough for Crown Prince Wilhelm Hohenzollern, he may have decided it's appropriate quarters for Commissar of State Security Nikolayevich Merkulov, his deputy, and a visiting American."

"And possibility two?"

"They're holding Mattingly someplace else, God and Serov only knowing where."

Ledbetter looked at Mannberg and said, "I gather you're no stranger to Berlin, Mr. . . . ?"

"Sorry," Cronley said. "Colonel, this is Mr. Ludwig Mannberg of the DCI. And Claudette Colbert, Fred Hessinger, and Max Ostrowski, ditto."

Everybody shook hands.

"Why are you smiling, Jack?" Ledbetter asked.

"You asked if Ludwig was a stranger to Berlin. Is it all right if I tell him, Cronley?"

*In for a penny, in for a pound!*

"In a previous life, Colonel, Mr. Mannberg was Oberst Mannberg of Abwehr Ost," Cronley said.

"Really?"

"Under Admiral Canaris, in whose dining room we are now gathered," Mannberg confirmed.

"I'd heard this was his house," Ledbetter said. "He must have been a fine officer."

"Why do you say that?" Mannberg asked.

"Because of what the Nazis did to him. I saw his rotting corpse still hanging from a gallows when we liberated the Flossenbürg concentration camp."

"And Captain von Wachtstein of South American Airways," Cronley said, gesturing toward him, "who is also DCI, was Major von Wachtstein of the Luftwaffe."

"And Mr. Ostrowski? Also ex-Luftwaffe?" Ledbetter asked softly.

"Ex–Free Polish Air Force," Ostrowski said. "The last time I was in Berlin I was flying an Eighth Air Force North American P-51."

"Magnificent airplane!" von Wachtstein said.

"I know it's not polite to ask questions," Ledbetter said, "but . . ."

"For example?" Cronley replied.

"How is an Argentine airline connected with the DCI?"

Cronley visibly thought it over before replying.

"If I have to say this, Colonel, just about all of this is classified Top Secret–Presidential and I probably shouldn't tell you and Major Rogers any of it. But some of it may — probably will — come into play in the next week or so, and you should know who the players are.

"So, to answer your question, SAA is a DCI asset, inherited from the OSS when OSS was shut down. It was started up at

President Roosevelt's order by the Southern Cone OSS station chief, Lieutenant Colonel Cletus Frade, USMCR."

"When I met Frade, he was Captain Frade of SAA," Ledbetter said.

"Well, the DCI does have its little secrets, Colonel," Cronley said.

"There are rumors going around that the DCI has been shipping Nazis to Argentina —"

"Scurrilous and absolutely untrue," Cronley said, smiling.

"I wondered how," Ledbetter said, smiling back.

"Very few Nazis," Cronley said. "Lots of relatives of former members of Abwehr Ost whom our Russian allies wanted to chat with. The deal Allen Dulles struck with Gehlen was that Gehlen would turn over to us all his assets, including agents in place in the Kremlin, in exchange for us keeping his people, and their families, out of the hands of the Russians."

Ledbetter nodded.

"Well, the official story is that Dulles never told Donovan about the deal. That it was kept secret from Donovan because if he knew he would have felt obligated to tell President Roosevelt, who probably would have stopped it and/or told Mrs. Roosevelt, who would have promptly told her Soviet friends.

"Clete thought that story smelled. He thought Donovan knew about Operation Ost from the beginning and that Donovan knew that the OSS was going to need a means to get Gehlen's people — especially the Nazis among them — out of Europe to Argentina. What better way to do that than with an Argentine airline that the OSS controlled?"

"What comes to mind is that phrase 'Oh, what a tangled web we weave when first we practice to deceive,' " Ledbetter said.

"There were other scenarios," Cronley went on. "One was that the Air Force had bet on the Douglas C-54 and the later C-56. Both were Air Force designs, and production was in full swing. Then Howard Hughes had come up — on his own, at his own expense — with the Constellation. It was superior in every way to the Douglas airplanes. It was faster, had a longer range, and carried more.

"And there was another scenario that was either part of that one or stood alone. Roosevelt was not fond of Juan Trippe, who owned Pan American Airlines, which had a commercial monopoly on international/intercontinental passenger service. Trippe was operating his Clippers — seaplanes — from Miami to Argentina, for example. And from New York, via the Azores, to Europe. And from the West Coast to the Pacific.

"Trippe could be taken down a peg if somebody started flying Constellations across oceans. They were much faster and had a greater range than Trippe's Clippers. So, since the Air Force didn't want them, Lockheed was free to sell the Constellations. But, to keep them out of the hands of Pan American/Juan Trippe, and out of the hands of Transcontinental and Western Airlines — which Howard Hughes owned although he wasn't supposed to, and everybody knew he wanted to start across oceans with the Connies — Roosevelt ordered that the nine that Howard had sitting at the Lockheed factory couldn't be sold to either.

"They could be sold to others. Clete's grandfather, Cletus Marcus Howell, of Howell Petroleum, got to buy one to fly around his petroleum empire. And Roosevelt had no objection to their being sold to neutral Argentina, which he had heard was thinking of starting up an international airline."

"Fascinating," Ledbetter said.

"We'll probably never know the real story," Cronley said.

"That happens, from time to time, in our line of business," Ledbetter said.

"Anyway, that's how come Clete and Hansel are flying SAA Constellations," Cronley said.

"It doesn't explain how you got from being a second lieutenant in the CIC in Marburg to . . . where you are now," Ledbetter said. "Is that question off-limits?"

"Yes, sorry," Cronley said. "I can tell you this: A decision was made by a very senior government official that a good way to divert attention from Operation Ost and DCI was to put it under a very junior captain. If such an unimportant young officer was running it, it couldn't be very important, could it?"

"Clever," Ledbetter said.

"Just between you and me, Colonel, not to get any further, General Seidel and Company are right. I am just about totally unqualified to be head of DCI-Europe —"

"I challenge that," Mannberg said.

"And so do I, Jim," Tiny Dunwiddie said. "We've had this discussion, and you're still wrong."

"And I, Captain Cronley," Ledbetter said, "know General Greene well enough to know he wouldn't have ordered me to do whatever you ask if he thought —"

"And as an example of that," Cronley interrupted, "the distinguished head of DCI-Europe, after due consideration of the problem of getting Mattingly back from the fucking Russians, has come up with a brilliant plan to do so."

"Which is?"

"Tomorrow morning I am going to go out to the Glienicke Bridge so that Comrade Serov can see me and see that I am obeying his orders, and then I am going to fly back to Munich and bury three of Comrade Serov's comrades according to the rites of the Russian Orthodox Church as he ordered me to do."

"And?" Tiny asked.

"That's it. I don't have a fucking clue how to get Mattingly back from the fucking Russians. That's why I shouldn't be chief, DCI-Europe."

There was a moment's silence.

Then Cronley added, "Herr von Wachtstein, would you be so kind as to slide the Haig & Haig down this way?"

# X

## [ONE]

*Glienicke Bridge*

*Wannsee, U.S. Zone of Berlin*

*0625 31 January 1946*

Colonel Ledbetter offered them the choice of a Ford staff car or a jeep for what Cronley had dubbed "Our oh-dark-hundred look at the bridge."

"A jeep, I think, will attract less attention," Cronley said.

"In that case, you'll need parkas. It's snowing. Miserable conditions."

Ledbetter had then provided them with the bulky cotton garments, which were olive drab on one side and white on the other. They had hoods, ringed with what Cronley thought could have been fur.

"The last time I wore one of these was in the Battle of the Bulge," Dunwiddie announced, as he pulled on his parka. "It didn't keep me warm then, but maybe we'll get lucky today."

"We're going to need all the luck we can get," Cronley said.

A jeep "comfortably" held four people. Into the one Ledbetter provided went five

427

— Hessinger, driving because he knew the way, plus Cronley, Mannberg, Dunwiddie, and Ostrowski.

Snow fell heavily as they drove up to the bridge, obscuring its far end. The half-dozen men there were recognizable as Russian soldiers, but their faces and rank insignia were lost in the white-out blur.

The snow, Cronley saw, coated the canvas roof of the MP jeep sitting to one side of the bridge, and made invisible the white line that marked the center of the bridge.

When they got close to the bridge itself, the MP jeep came suddenly to life and moved to block their way. A sergeant got out of the jeep and walked around the front of their jeep to the driver's side.

"Sorry," he said to Hessinger with monumental insincerity, "I got to write you up for five in a jeep. Let me have your trip ticket, driver's license, Russian Zone authorization, and the ID card of the senior guy in there. He's responsible for the violation."

"That would be me," Dunwiddie, sitting beside Hessinger, announced. "Let's start with this, Sergeant: Don't the MPs in Berlin salute officers?"

The sergeant was visibly surprised, but he saluted and said, "Sorry, sir. Your parka covers your bars. I didn't see them. But I still got to write you up."

Dunwiddie said, "What you still got to do, Sergeant, is get back in your jeep and forget you ever saw us. This is CIC business."

Dunwiddie fumbled around under his parka, and then turned in his seat and asked, "Has anyone got their CIC credentials with them?"

Cronley, laughing, produced his, and they had the expected reaction on the sergeant.

"But I still got to see your Russian Zone authorization," the sergeant said. "Nobody gets to cross the bridge without a Russian Zone authorization. Orders is orders."

"Not a problem, Sergeant," Cronley said. "We're not going over there."

He reached between his legs and came up with something wrapped in a blanket.

"Here you go, Sergeant," he said, handing it to the sergeant. "Keep up the good work."

"Sir? What's this?"

"A thermos of coffee," Cronley explained. "Which I brought along thinking we might be here long enough to need it. Take us home, Freddy."

The sergeant saluted crisply as Hessinger spun the jeep around and drove away from the bridge.

# [Two]

*44–46 Beerenstrasse, Zehlendorf*

*U.S. Zone of Berlin*

*0715 31 January 1946*

Hans-Peter von Wachtstein and the other SAA crewmen were in the process of loading themselves into a Chevrolet station wagon with an SAA logo on its doors when Hessinger drove the jeep into the parking area.

Cronley jumped out of the jeep.

"Hansel, what's going on?" he demanded.

"Air Force Weather said the snow's going to stop in the next hour, but they don't know for how long. As long as it's stopped, I'll have the half-mile visibility I need to take off. Which means I've got to get out of here as soon as the snow stops."

"I needed to talk to you. I told you that."

"Jimmy, I have to get out of here," von Wachtstein said.

"I was going to give you a letter to give Clete . . ."

"Something wrong with the SIGABA?"

". . . saying something I didn't want anybody with SIGABA access to see. I ran out of time, so I need you to pass it verbally."

430

"Jesus! What the hell are you up to?"

"As soon as you get to Buenos Aires, get Clete alone and tell him this. Tell him exactly this. Memorize it."

"I'll write it down."

"No. Just memorize it."

Von Wachtstein's eyebrows went up as he nodded.

"Okay. What's the message?"

"That I am not going to obey any order to turn over the Likharevs to the Russians, even if that means I'll have to spend the rest of my life in Leavenworth."

"What's Leavenworth?"

"The Army prison. It's in Kansas."

"*Mein Gott,* you're serious, aren't you, Jimmy?"

"Yeah. I'm serious. I'm just not going to do it."

"So they'll get somebody else to do it. Have you considered that?"

"Another sentence for you to repeat to Clete: 'And I will do my best to fuck up any transfer by anybody, and I mean anybody, else.' "

"I don't know if you're stupid or noble. My father did the noble thing and got himself hung from a butcher's hook."

"As far as I know, the intelligence community doesn't use butcher's hooks."

"You do something like this, they'll come up with something."

"Just do what I'm asking, Hansel, please."

Von Wachtstein looked into Cronley's eyes for a moment.

"How long are you going to be at the Glienicke Bridge?" von Wachtstein asked.

"I don't know. Serov said he'd show us Colonel Mattingly at nine o'clock."

"After that, you're going back to Munich?"

"On the eleven-o'clock courier flight to Rhine-Main. Presuming the weather lets the plane get out of here. Otherwise, I'll have to drive."

"All of you?"

"Just me. Mannberg and Ostrowski need to be here in case I can't get back in time for Serov to put Mattingly on display tomorrow. The sonofabitch will expect to see at least one of us."

"When you finish at the bridge, get to Tempelhof as quick as you can. I'll hold off taking off as long as I can. With a little bit of luck, you can ride with me to Rhine-Main."

"What's that all about?"

"Between here and Rhine-Main, I will try to talk you out of your noble plan to go to prison for the rest of your life."

Von Wachtstein then quickly got in the Chevrolet station wagon.

## [THREE]

*Glienicke Bridge*

*Wannsee, U.S. Zone of Berlin*

*0850 31 January 1946*

The Air Force weather briefing had been accurate. The heavy snow had stopped, the clouds cleared, and the sun had come out.

Three Ford staff cars, the lead one bearing MP insignia and a fender-mounted chrome siren, rolled up to the bridge and stopped.

Immediately, a dozen of Tiny's Troopers — all wearing white parkas, glossily painted helmet liners with Constabulary insignia, gleaming leather Sam Browne belts, and all armed with Thompson submachine guns and .45 ACP pistols — filed out of the two three-quarter-ton "weapons carriers" that had brought them to the bridge.

They immediately formed into two six-man squads, were called to attention, and with the Thompsons at the port arms position, marched to the bridge, six men on each side. When they were in position, Tiny Dunwiddie, also in Constabulary regalia, got out of the third staff car, marched to the men at the bridge, came to attention, and bellowed, "Sling Arms. Parade Rest!"

As Dunwiddie assumed that position, his troops slung their Thompsons from their shoulders and assumed the position.

As this was going on, two jeeps with pedestal-mounted .50 caliber Browning machine guns, and each carrying three similarly uniformed troopers, drove up and parked facing the bridge. The canvas covers were removed from the machine guns, and ammo cans put in place.

All of this was Cronley's idea.

"I don't want us to show up there as beggars," he had said. "So we'll stage a little dog and pony show for Comrade Serov."

He had then gone on to explain the details of the dog and pony show.

He thought Mannberg and Ostrowski had agreed that it was a good idea, and he was sure Colonel Ledbetter, Jack Hammersmith, and Freddy Hessinger had not.

Ledbetter, however, did arrange for the other things Cronley thought they should have. These included the MP staff car and photographers, a motion picture cameraman and two still photographers, one with a Speed Graphic Press camera, the other with a Leica mounting an enormous lens.

The photographers were standing on a platform on the roof of a Signal Corps mobile film laboratory, which was mounted on a six-by-six truck chassis.

When everyone was in place, Cronley and Mannberg got out of the MP staff car. Cronley was in Class A uniform, wearing a trench coat with his captain's bars pinned to the epaulets and a leather-brimmed officer's cap. Mannberg wore a fur-collared overcoat and a fur hat.

Max Ostrowski, wearing Class A's and a trench coat, got out of the second car, as did a second man, wearing ODs. Three more men got out of the car in which Tiny Dunwiddie had been riding. All the men were CIC agents, one of them Jack Hammersmith.

Cronley and Mannberg marched up to the edge of the bridge, stopping where the metal structure of the bridge began. Ostrowski and Hammersmith marched up to six feet beside them and stopped.

Cronley could now see all the way across the bridge. He saw that the white line marking the middle was clearly visible. Someone — probably the Russian — had swept the snow from it.

There were about twenty Russians, some of them officers, on the far end of the bridge. Cronley did not see Ivan Serov among them.

*I'm sure he's here, that he's seen the cameras and doesn't want his picture taken.*

*Or doesn't want to be seen, period.*

For what seemed like a very long time, nothing happened.

Cronley made an exaggerated gesture of looking at his wristwatch. He saw that it was almost exactly nine.

"Jim," Mannberg said softly.

Cronley looked at him. Mannberg nodded just perceptibly down the bridge.

Cronley saw that an enormous truck, with a body as large as the trailers on what he thought of as "eighteen wheeler" tractor trailers, was beginning to slowly back onto the bridge.

Along the truck body's left side was an officer walking backward, occasionally looking over his shoulder while giving hand signals to the driver. Immediately behind him were eight Red Army soldiers, in a file, each carrying a PPSh-41 submachine gun across his chest. Another eight similarly armed soldiers marched on the other side of the truck body.

Mannberg put his fist to his mouth, coughed, and then softly observed, "Dog and pony show, Serov version."

The truck continued to slowly back up until it was within ten feet of the white line marking the center of the bridge. It stopped with a squeal of brakes.

The officer who had been giving instructions to the driver signaled for a soldier to unlock the rear doors of the truck body. When the soldier had done so, the officer turned and looked toward the American end of the bridge. He folded his arms across his chest.

A moment later, the left rear door was pushed open by a soldier inside.

It was dark inside the body. Cronley couldn't see anything beyond the soldier.

Then the right rear door swung open.

And interior lights came on.

They illuminated Colonel Robert Mattingly, who was sitting on a wooden chair. He was wearing his trench coat.

The officer then turned and ordered both doors quickly closed.

"What the hell?" Cronley exclaimed.

The truck didn't move.

"Now what?" Cronley asked after ninety seconds, which seemed longer.

The truck doors then again were opened.

Colonel Mattingly now was standing, naked except for his white jockey shorts. A chain circled his waist, to the front of which his hands were handcuffed. His ankles were shackled. There was a clean white bandage on his upper right arm.

*Well, at least they changed his bandage.*

Somewhat awkwardly, Colonel Mattingly began shuffling his feet to turn counterclockwise. He stopped when he was back to where he was looking at the American end of the bridge.

The officer signaled for the rear doors to be closed. As soon as they had, he signaled to the truck driver, who began to slowly drive off the bridge. The soldiers followed alongside.

Cronley watched until the truck reached the end of the bridge, where it turned and he could no longer see it.

"Those sonsofbitches!" he said.

"Comrade Serov said he would provide proof that they would treat Colonel Mattingly's wounds and not physically abuse him," Mannberg said. "It looks as if he's done that." He paused, then added: "You're going to Frankfurt with von Wachtstein?"

"Yeah," Cronley said. "I'll try to get back for our nine o'clock dog and pony show tomorrow, but if I don't get back, we do the same show. Okay?"

Mannberg nodded.

Cronley went to the MP staff car, got in

the front seat, and told the CIC agent behind the wheel, "If that siren will get us to Tempelhof any quicker, turn it on."

Cronley arrived at Tempelhof in time to see the SAA Constellation begin its takeoff roll.

## [FOUR]

*The South German Industrial Development*

*Organization Compound*

*Pullach, Bavaria*

*American Zone of Occupation, Germany*

*1730 31 January 1946*

The flight on the Air Force C-54 from Tempelhof to Rhine-Main — some 240 miles that took almost two hours — put Cronley on the ground in Frankfurt at 1300. There had been time to call the house in Zehlendorf and tell Claudette Colbert to call Lieutenant Tom Winters in Eschborn to have him meet Cronley's flight.

Cronley used the time on the C-54 to consider the problem of what Hans-Peter von Wachtstein was going to do in Buenos Aires. There was absolutely no question he would give Clete the message verbatim. What was not clear was what Hans-Peter, or Clete, or most likely both, would do to keep Cronley from spending the rest of his life in Leavenworth.

Cronley also considered at length how stupid it had been of him to tell Dette to have Tom meet him at Rhine-Main. Winters had one of the Storches. The Air Force did not like Storches with U.S. ARMY painted on their fuselages. The way things were going, there would be a flap at Rhine-Main, which would see the Storch impounded, sending him and Tom rushing to the Hauptbahnhof in Frankfurt to — just in time — catch the Blue Danube train to Munich.

Things began to look up when Winters met him in the Arriving Passengers Terminal.

"I hope I did the right thing," Winters said. "I left the Storch in Eschborn. Freddy Hessinger told me landing one here might cause problems."

They drove to Eschborn and boarded the Storch.

In the Storch, which raced through the skies at about eighty miles per hour, the approximately 190-mile flight from Eschborn to Pullach should have taken no more than two and a half hours. But the snow, which had left Berlin, had moved south. The flight took three and a quarter hours, leaving the fuel gauge needles indicating empty tanks when Cronley touched down at the Compound.

From the look on Winters's face, Cronley saw he was unimpressed with his argument that experience had taught him that even when the needles indicated empty there was still "several" gallons of avgas remaining.

Announcing, "Looks like we cheated death again," after shutting down the engine did not exactly help.

Cronley pushed getting to Pullach because he needed to see General Gehlen as soon as possible. He wanted to tell him what had happened in Berlin and see if he had ideas how to get Mattingly back without swapping the Likharev family for him.

Thus, when First Sergeant Abraham Lincoln Tedworth met them, Cronley was less than pleased to hear Honest Abe report that the general was taking dinner at the Vier Jahreszeiten hotel with several of his officers and had said he probably would spend the night there because of the snow.

Making matters worse, the ex-ambulance in which they then drove from Pullach to Munich had both a malfunctioning heater and a missing windshield wiper, which made the drive on the snow-covered cobblestone road slow, uncomfortable, and more than once terrifying.

## [FIVE]

*The Lobby Bar*

*Hotel Vier Jahreszeiten*

*Maximilianstrasse 178*

*Munich, American Zone of Occupation, Germany*

*1840 31 January 1946*

"My friend will have a Shirley Temple," Cronley greeted the bartender. "And I will have a little taste of that Johnnie Walker Black. Make it a double."

Lieutenant Winters gave Captain Cronley the finger.

"I'll have the same," Winters announced to the bartender.

"Excuse me, sirs," the bartender asked. "Is the Herr Captain and the other gentleman aware this is a senior officers' establishment?"

*Shit,* Cronley thought, *I'm wearing my captain's bars.*

*What the hell else can go wrong?*

"Yes, the Herr Captain and the other gentleman are," Cronley replied. "Where's

442

the regular bartender?"

"It's all right, Franz," a female voice said. "These junior officers are with me. You can serve them."

*"Es wird mir ein Vergnügen, gnädige Frau,"* the bartender said, and reached for glasses.

Cronley and Winters looked down the bar.

"Well, if it isn't Miss Janice Johansen, of the Associated Press," Cronley said. "You know Miss Johansen, don't you, Lieutenant Winters?"

"I have that pleasure," Winters said.

"Fuck you, Jim," Janice said. "And you, too, Winters."

"Why do I suspect I have in some small way offended you, Miss Johansen?" Cronley asked.

"Our deal, and you know it, you sonofabitch, was that I was to be in on everything."

"That's our deal as I remember it," Cronley said.

"So how come I didn't get to go to Vienna with you? Or Berlin?"

"Who told you about Vienna or Berlin?"

"I'm a journalist. I find things out. Maybe I should give lessons to you spooks."

"Janice, we shouldn't be talking about any of this in here."

"Okay. So when the drinks I got you are served, you pay for them, and carry them into the dining room."

"That's no better than the bar."

"Unless we go where General Gehlen is, in a private dining room."

When First Sergeant Tedworth had told Cronley and Winters that General Gehlen was having dinner at the Vier Jahreszeiten with several of his officers, Cronley naturally had presumed that these would be maybe a half dozen of the former Abwehr Ost lieutenant colonels and majors now in the Compound.

But when Gehlen's Polish bodyguards passed him, Janice, and Tom Winters into the private dining room off the main dining room, Gehlen had only two Germans sitting at his table, Major Konrad Bischoff and Kurt Schröder, the ex- and present Storch pilot, and two Americans, Major Harold Wallace and Lieutenant Colonel John J. Bristol.

Everybody at the table rose when they saw Cronley, Janice, and Winters approaching the table.

*It would be nice to think that was a gesture of courtesy to me as chief, DCI-Europe.*

*But it wasn't.*

*They stood up as a Pavlovian reaction to Janice, even though Wallace and Bischoff*

444

*clearly are unhappy to see her.*

"Well," Gehlen said, "I see I was wrong, Miss Johansen, when I told you I thought there was no chance at all of Jim being able to get here before the Blue Danube arrived at eleven. Please sit down."

"You flew from Frankfurt?" Kurt Schröder asked incredulously as chairs were pulled to the table.

"He flew," Winters replied, "while I prayed watching the fuel gauge needles bang against the empty peg as we went through the blizzard."

"I need something to eat," Cronley said. "I haven't had anything since breakfast."

"And when he's finished," Janice said, "or preferably *while* he's eating, he's going to tell us all about Vienna and Berlin."

Wallace's face showed he strongly disapproved of that idea.

"Is this one of those occasions where I should be asked to be excused?" Colonel Bristol asked.

"No," Cronley said firmly. "Colonel, this is one of those occasions where I'll be more comfortable knowing you know everything, rather than wondering what you know and what you've intuited."

"Same question, Herr Cronley," Kurt Schröder asked.

"Same answer, Kurt."

A waiter approached, and Cronley ordered a New York strip pink in the middle, fried eggs with running yolks, and *pommes frites.*

Winters said, "Just the steak and the French fries for me, please."

Ten minutes later Cronley concluded: "Colonel Ledbetter promised to have the film processed and to send it with one of his people as soon as that can be done. And so, there being nothing more for me to do in Berlin, I came home to bury the Russians Claudette shot."

He met Gehlen's eyes, and thought, *And for your advice on getting Mattingly back without swapping the Likharev family.*

"Interesting," Gehlen said, as if he read Cronley's mind. "This will require some thought."

"And I get the pictures of Mattingly in the truck on the bridge, right?" Janice asked.

"With the understanding you can't use any of them until this thing is resolved one way or another."

"No offense, Miss Johansen," Wallace said, "but I'm more than a little worried that unless we have only our hands on that photography, it's likely to get out."

"No offense taken, Harry," Janice said. "I

understand your concern. But Jim promised me I could have a look at the photos. And he's a man of his word. You're just going to have to trust me."

*Your face, Colonel Wallace,* Cronley thought, *suggests you trust her only about as far as you can throw her. Or maybe halfway as far as you could throw Tiny Dunwiddie.*

"I don't suppose anybody knows where Augie Ziegler is," Cronley said.

"At the Munich NCO club," Janice said. "After he decided you wouldn't be coming back tonight — you weren't on the Blue Danube, and you, quote, wouldn't be dumb enough to try to fly in this weather, close quote — he took Wagner there."

"That was nice of him."

"He had an ulterior motive."

"Which was?"

"To punch holes in Wagner's theory about how the *Stars and Stripes* trucks are moving the bad guys around."

"Wagner has a theory?"

"Augie calls it a theory. Casey says he knows."

"Who the hell is Casey?"

"PFC Wagner's Christian name is Karl-Christoph. You know, K dash C. Casey?"

"Now you've aroused my curiosity. Who is he?" Colonel Bristol asked.

"He's an enormous seventeen-year-old Pennsylvania Dutchman who works for Ziegler. Translator. Janice has a Press Office jeep. So we sent . . . *Casey* . . . to the *Stars and Stripes* plant at Pfungstadt to see what he could see."

"He's *seventeen* years old?" Bristol asked.

"He looks older," Cronley replied. "He could pass for eighteen, maybe even nineteen."

"And he speaks fluent Hessischer Deutsch," Kurt Schröder offered. "Not many Americans do. He could pass as a Frankfurter."

Cronley chuckled and then looked at him questioningly.

"I took an L-4 and picked him up in Pfungstadt," Schröder explained. "And on the way back here he told me — in fluent Hessischer Deutsch — about what he learned about the *Stars and Stripes* trucks."

"And?"

"I think he's onto something," Schröder said.

Cronley considered that a moment.

"I'm tempted to have you share that, or go hear it from him, but it can wait until morning. Augie can tell me when he reports how he's coming with the funerals, or reburials, whatever the hell it is."

"Ziegler," Bristol said, "came to me early this morning to ask if I could put him onto a stone cutter for the tombstones. I did." Bristol then added, "He had a photographer with him."

"Good," Cronley said. "To prove to Comrade Serov that I'm a fellow Christian obeying his orders, I want to give him pictures of everything connected with reburying those bastards."

"Major Wallace is taking Kurt and me to the Gloria Palast," Gehlen said. "They're showing *Gilda* with Rita Hayworth and Glenn Ford."

*Wallace is taking Gehlen and Schröder to a Rita Hayworth movie?*

*Gehlen doesn't seem in a hurry to discuss how to get Mattingly back . . .*

"And Tom and I are going to meet our wives there," Bristol said. "At seven-thirty. Which means we're going to have to leave now. You want to come, Janice? Jim?"

"I saw it in Frankfurt," Janice said.

"And I'm so tired I'd fall asleep in five minutes," Cronley said. "But thanks."

"Does that mean we can go back in the bar?" Janice asked.

"Janice, I love you, but if I went back to the bar and had another drink, you'd have to carry me to my room."

449

"I don't think I could carry you, but I'm sure we can get a wheelchair somewhere."

Gehlen, Schröder, Wallace, Winters, and Bristol chuckled and smiled as they rose from the table.

"I'll see you in the morning, Jim," Gehlen said. "Get a good night's rest."

*Does he know Janice isn't kidding?*

*Do any of them?*

# [SIX]

*Suite 507*

*Hotel Vier Jahreszeiten*

*Maximilianstrasse 178*

*Munich, American Zone of Occupation, Germany*

*0830 1 February 1946*

PFC Karl-Christoph Wagner was wearing ODs bearing the blue triangles identifying civilian employees of the Army when he and Augie Ziegler walked into the office.

Cronley's mouth went on automatic: "Where'd you get the triangles, Wagner?"

Wagner's face reddened.

"My idea," Ziegler said. "We went to the NCO club last night. Neither of us belonged there. We stood out like —"

"Ladies of the evening in church?" Janice asked.

"Something like that. And since I think we should move him in here, I think we better get him CIC credentials."

Ziegler read Cronley's face.

"He can't go on living in the MP *kaserne*," he went on. "And wait till you hear what he came up with at *Stars and Stripes.*"

Cronley thought: *If I issue this kid CIC credentials, Wallace will go through the roof.*

General Gehlen, in German, said: "Mr. Schröder has been telling me, young man, that you learned something interesting when you were at Pfungstadt. Why don't you tell us what that was?"

Wagner looked between Gehlen, Cronley, and Ziegler in confusion.

*He's wondering who the guy in the seedy suit is, and what he's doing here.*

Schröder picked up on Wagner's confusion at the same time.

"Karl-Christoph," he said in German, "this is General Gehlen. You can tell him."

Wagner nodded, and then began, in German, to tell them what he had learned in Pfungstadt.

Cronley had just heard enough to conclude, *I'll be damned. He did find something,* when Wallace suddenly jumped to his feet and stood at attention. A moment later, Augie Ziegler looked where Wallace was looking and jumped to his feet.

Cronley looked where Ziegler was looking and jumped to his feet when he saw that Lieutenant Colonel William W. "Hotshot Billy" Wilson was holding the door to the office open for Major General I. D. White.

White, who was wearing ODs and highly polished tanker's boots, marched into the office. His uniform was crisply pressed, but there were no ribbons on his breast.

"As you were, gentlemen," he ordered conversationally. Then he saw Janice.

"Good morning, Miss Johansen. I really am glad to see you."

"Why don't I think that's because of my feminine charms?"

White laughed. Genuinely, not to be polite.

"Because of your feminine charms, and also because you're at about the top of the list of people on my See As Soon As Possible List."

"Not at the top? I'm crushed. Who is?"

"General Gehlen," White replied.

Then he smiled at General Gehlen, and said, "General, I'd ask for a few minutes of your time right now, but I'm getting the impression that I just interrupted something interesting."

Gehlen smiled and chuckled.

"What?" White demanded. "Is it important?"

"Just as you came through the door, General, the Eighth Psalm came to mind," Gehlen said.

White considered that a moment.

" 'Out of the mouth of babes . . .' " he quoted.

"I believe this young man has," Gehlen said, nodding at Wagner, "uncovered how the Odessa organization is moving people we're looking for around Europe."

"How?"

"On *Stars and Stripes* delivery trucks."

"General Greene told me his CIC people had looked into that and —"

"Mr. Hammersmith, whom General Greene describes as his best CIC agent, told me — told us — the same thing. That's why, listening to this young man, the Eighth Psalm came to mind."

"This, I have to hear," White said, and turned to Wagner. "Who are you, son?"

Wagner, looking very uncomfortable, popped to attention.

"PFC Wagner, Karl-Christoph, sir."

"You can stand at ease, son. Despite what

you might have heard, I really don't bite off the heads of enlisted men."

"Yes, sir," Wagner said, and changed his posture from Attention to the nearly as rigid Parade Rest.

White smiled. "Even those who don't know the difference between Parade Rest and At Ease."

Wagner smiled sheepishly and relaxed.

"Sorry, sir," Wagner said, and then blurted, "I'm a little nervous. I've never talked to a general before."

White chuckled.

"Well, son, there's a first time for everything. And I'll let you in on a little secret. General officers put on their pants just like PFCs. So why don't you tell me what you've learned?"

"Yes, sir," Wagner said. "What Mr. Hammersmith — and I guess the others — missed is that the six-by-sixes aren't the only trucks, only vehicles, that *Stars and Stripes* uses to deliver the newspapers every day."

"Excuse me?"

"The *Stars and Stripes* motor pool sergeant, his name is Master Sergeant Gallant, they call him 'Red Ball,' he told me about the other vehicles."

"Why did he do that?" White asked.

454

"Sir, Mr. Ziegler told me to find out everything I could, so I figured the best way to do that was to get close to the motor sergeant."

"Who is Mr. Ziegler?"

Wagner pointed to him.

Ziegler popped to attention.

"August Ziegler, sir. Former CID agent. Now in DCI. When I came in, I brought Wagner with me. Before that, he was an interpreter for the MPs."

"And you sent this young man to *Stars and Stripes*?"

"No, sir. That was Mr. Cronley's idea."

"And did you think that was a good idea, Mr. Ziegler?"

"Yes, sir, I did. I just didn't want to take the credit for it. It was Cron— Mr. Cronley's idea."

White looked at Wagner. "Go on, son. How did you get close to Master Sergeant 'Red Ball' Gallant?"

"I bought him a couple of beers in the Stars and Stripes Club and asked him why they called him 'Red Ball.' "

"And?"

"He told me because he'd set up the *Stripes* delivery system like the Red Ball Express. Do you know what that is, sir?"

"If we're talking about the same Red Ball

Express that rushed supplies from the ports in Normandy to the front during the war?"

"Yes, sir. That's it. Red Ball told me how he'd started as a corporal in a Quartermaster truck company and wound up with six stripes as the battalion operations sergeant."

"Sounds as if he's a good soldier. Smart."

"Yes, sir. He's a good soldier. But I wouldn't call him smart."

"Why do you say that?"

"I don't think he has a clue what's going on."

"And what's that, son?"

"He told me that the motto of the Red Ball Express was *Keep the Supplies Moving, No Matter What,* and that's what he was doing with the *Stars and Stripes* delivery system."

"Tell me how that works," White said. "From the beginning."

"Yes, sir. Well, when the papers come off the press, most of them are bundled in packages of a hundred."

He held his hands about two feet apart to show the size of the bundles.

"Then they're put on pallets — wooden things that can be picked up with a forklift?"

White nodded to indicate that he knew about pallets and forklifts.

"Then, for example, the papers coming

here to Munich. They send twenty-six hundred papers here. So they load thirteen packages on two pallets, label them 'Munich,' then pick them up with a forklift and load them onto a six-by-six. You can get two pallets in a row."

He paused. "It gets a little complicated here, General."

"So far I'm with you, son."

"Yes, sir. Well, on the way to Munich there are — I don't know — say, twenty places that get newspapers. The QM gas stations, for example, along the autobahn, get one, maybe two bundles. So they lay tarps on top of the Munich pallets, and then put the single bundles, or two bundles tied together, on top of the tarp, with signs saying, for example, 'QM Gas Station, Mile 45' or whatever."

He looked questioningly at General White.

"Got it," White said. "And?"

"Well, that's how it works, all the six-by-sixes are loaded the same way, no matter if they're going to Munich, or Naples, or Cherbourg, in France."

"Now I'm a little confused," White said.

"Well, sir, Master Sergeant Gallant told me he kept the *Stars and Stripes* delivery trucks rolling the same way he'd kept the original Red Ball trucks rolling. Or the supplies, in this case, the newspapers, moving when the trucks broke down, had a flat tire, et cetera."

"And did he tell you how he was doing this?"

"Ycs, sir. By doing what the Red Ball did."

"Which was?"

"By stationing a wrecker and an empty truck every fifty miles along the delivery routes. If a truck gets a flat tire, or breaks down, the driver, or the assistant driver, hitches a ride to the wrecker. The wrecker and the empty truck then go to the broken-down truck, carrying spare wheels, gasoline, and a mechanic."

"I'm not quite following you now, son."

"Well, what I think happens, General, is that one of the trucks carrying the Nazis we're looking for, quote, breaks down, unquote, near the border. Borders. Between Germany and Austria. Between Austria and Germany. Between Germany and France. Those borders. The driver then hitches a ride — maybe from one of the Constabulary jeeps patrolling the highway — and goes to the wrecker. The wrecker then goes to the, quote, broken-down, unquote, truck —"

"Carrying spare wheels, gasoline, a mechanic, *and* one or more of the people the CIC is looking for," Hotshot Billy Wilson said. "Who then hide behind the pallets. The truck then drives across the border. How the hell did the entire CIC miss that?"

"Pray let PFC Wagner continue, Colonel," White said icily.

"That's what I think, General," Wagner said. "Except the way it's set up, they could take people from the trucks, as well as putting them on."

"And do you think Master Sergeant Red Ball knows what's going on?"

"No, sir. He's not smart enough to figure it out himself. What I think is that one or two of the drivers, maybe more, are the people smugglers."

"You have any idea who they are?"

"One of them got Red Ball an apartment for his fräulein. I know that."

"You didn't say anything to the sergeant about Odessa, did you, son?" White asked.

"No, sir. My orders from Captain Cronley were to keep my eyes open and my mouth shut."

"Do I have to tell you that you have to continue keeping your mouth shut now?"

"No, sir. I know I'm not in DCI, but Mr. Cronley made me understand how important it is to keep what goes on around here a secret."

Cronley's mouth went on automatic:

"You're in DCI now, Casey. And just as soon as Mr. Hessinger gets back from Berlin, he'll cut orders making you a sergeant."

White looked at Cronley.

"I was about to make a suggestion along those lines, Captain Cronley," he said, then put his hand on Wagner's shoulder. "Well done, son. Very well done."

PFC Wagner blushed.

"And now back to my list of things to do," White said. "Cronley, is there somewhere General Gehlen, Colonels Wallace and Williams, and you and I could have a private conversation?"

## [SEVEN]

*Suite 527*

*Hotel Vier Jahreszeiten*

*Maximilianstrasse 178*

*Munich, American Zone of Occupation, Germany*

*0855 1 February 1946*

"Would it surprise you, Captain Cronley," General White asked as soon as everyone had found chairs in Cronley's sitting room, "to learn that in addition to feeling that you're wholly unqualified to hold your present position, General Seidel feels — and has told General Bull — that you're the last man he would choose — the phrase he used was 'any rational senior officer would choose' — to be in charge of getting Colonel Mattingly back from the Russians?"

"No, sir," Cronley said. "It would not."

"Then you will probably not to be surprised . . ."

*Well, the ax ending my brilliant intelligence career didn't take long to fall, did it?*

*What comes next?*

*"You will probably not be surprised to hear that Admiral Souers has decided that you are to be relieved as chief, DCI-Europe, effective immediately, and that Colonel Wallace will assume that position."*

". . . to learn that both General Bull and I are interested to hear what precisely you said to General Seidel that made him splutter like that."

Wallace laughed.

"When the best-laid plans of mice and men gang aft agley," Wallace said, "the planner often splutters."

"What plan was that, Harry?"

"General Seidel demanded that Cronley come to that meeting so he could sandbag him. If Seidel had his way, Cronley was going to agree to permit the FBI to snoop around the Compound and Kloster Grünau, in which case the FBI would find not only Lazarus —"

"Who?"

"Four NKGB agents were involved in the attempted kidnaping of Miss Colbert and Technical Sergeant Miller. Colbert killed three of them at the site, and we — actually Cronley — decided to report that the fourth man died in the hospital. He's actually alive, under medical attention, in a cell at Kloster Grünau. Code name Lazarus. We have subsequently learned that he is Major of State Security Venedikt Ulyanov."

"Go on," White said.

"As I was saying, sir, General Seidel thought he was in a win-win position with Cronley. Either Cronley would agree to let the FBI into the Compound and Kloster Grünau, in which case they would find Lazarus —"

"And the secret graves alleged to be there?" White interrupted.

Wallace nodded. "And other things which would bolster the argument that DCI, under Cronley, is out of control and has to be taken over. Or, Cronley would deny the FBI access, same result. What possible reason but having something terribly illegal to hide would cause Cronley to refuse to accept the help of the saintly FBI?

"Cronley then sent General Seidel's plan *agley* by not only telling him that the only way he was going to let the FBI nose around the Compound was with the okay of Admiral Souers, and if the general had nothing else to ask him, he had things to do.

"By the time this happened, I think you should know, General Seidel was already on the edge of spluttering because the parts he had planned for Generals Schwarzkopf and Greene to play in the sandbagging had also *gang agley.*"

"Explain that," White said.

"He and the FBI guy, Special Agent in Charge Preston, had come up with really off-the-wall theories that General Gehlen was involved in the deaths of the Schumanns and Major Derwin, and was possibly, even probably, involved in Bob Mattingly's disappearance. This was, I'll admit, before we learned that Serov and Company had Bob.

"Schwarzkopf bluntly called the theories nonsense and Greene backed Schwarzkopf. Which meant that Seidel couldn't take them to General Bull to support his position."

White considered that for a moment, grunted, and then said: "Let's take a look at where we — and by we, I mean everybody — are. Let's start at the top: What I think is going on is Pentagon/Washington politics at its worst."

He considered that for a moment, and then went on: "The assistant chief of staff–Intelligence, the chief of Naval Operations, the State Department, and the FBI are all pressing the chief of staff to take over DCI and then — since none of them can have it — to shut it down. That's a turf war. The only difference between a Washington turf war and, say, Waterloo is that turf wars are much nastier.

"As chief of staff, Eisenhower has several problems dealing with that situation. The DCI was set up by Truman — and he picked his good friend Admiral Souers to head it — primarily to keep Operation Ost from becoming public knowledge. Operation Ost was set up by Allen Dulles of the OSS to bring General Gehlen and Abwehr Ost and all its assets under our tent.

"Eisenhower could see the enormous value of what General Gehlen offered but — wisely, I believe — sought and got Truman's permission to go ahead with it. In great secrecy, of course, under the OSS. If it became known that Operation Ost involved moving Gehlen's Nazis and their

464

families to Argentina, Truman's opponents — not only the outraged Jews — would have called for his impeachment and Eisenhower's court-martial.

"That threat is very much still there. Very few people recognize the threat the Soviet Union presents, so the argument that what General Gehlen has done — and will do in the future — justifies Operation Ost simply will not hold up in the court of public opinion.

"The problem was then compounded when Truman — under enormous pressure from J. Edgar Hoover, George Marshall, the State Department, and the Navy — disestablished the OSS. He thought he would be able to hide Operation Ost within the Office of Naval Intelligence if he had someone he trusted completely there. So he promoted Souers to rear admiral and gave him Operation Ost.

"Whether or not Eisenhower told him this was not a long-term solution, I don't know. Truman, as most people have learned by now, is much smarter than anyone thought. He replaced the secretary of State, Stettinius, who he didn't trust, with James Byrnes, another crony he knew he could. Byrnes could have told him Souers in the ONI was not a long-range solution. Or he figured it out himself.

"Anyway, by Executive Order, Truman established the DCI and gave it — and Operation Ost — to Souers. Appointing Captain Cronley as chief, DCI-Europe, was pure Truman. My personal view is that it was very clever. The President had just stumbled across, as a result of what Cronley had done finding the U-boat with the uranium oxide in Argentina, a young officer who was much smarter and more competent than the average second lieutenant. Said young officer already knew all about Operation Ost. The FBI knew what he had done in South America, so they weren't surprised when Truman promoted him to captain, and gave him a little bonus, command of DCI-Europe. Truman thought people would think if he gave DCI-Europe to Cronley, it couldn't be very important.

"What Truman and Eisenhower apparently didn't see, which surprised me, was that Seidel here, and the intelligence establishment generally, would decide that Cronley's appointment would make it easier for them to do what they were determined to do, take over DCI. And they immediately began to try to do just that.

"The disappearance — later to be determined to be the kidnapping by the NKGB

— of Colonel Mattingly gave them what they saw as that opportunity. They took it, but Cronley didn't let them get away with it. So where does that leave them? And us?

"They went to General Bull with their complaints and theories, obviously in the hope that Bull would take it to General McNarney. Instead, Bull sent for me. He began the conversation by saying we had a mutual friend, Admiral Souers. I was surprised to hear this, as the admiral had said nothing to me about Bull being in the loop. But when Bull went on to tell me that General Seidel and Mr. Preston had come to see him, and why, and what he suggested was the best way to handle the problem, I knew he was in the loop."

"What was General Bull's suggestion, General?" Gehlen asked.

"That we act promptly on Mr. Schultz's suggestion that we come up with proof that the Joint Intelligence Objectives Agency blatantly defied the President's order not to bring any Nazis into the United States in connection with Operation Paperclip. That was proof that Bull is in the loop. And, apparently acting as good chiefs of staff act, shielding their general as much as possible.

"It was clear to me that his suggestion was in the nature of an order, and that Bull was relaying that order from General McNarney. So I suggest, Captain Cronley, that you take the suggestion."

"Yes, sir," Cronley said.

"General Bull," White went on, "will, I think, accept my belief that relieving you and turning the recovery of Colonel Mattingly over to General Seidel and the FBI would be counter-productive at this time. And so inform both General McNarney and General Seidel. But I think we can count on General Seidel not giving up. And neither will the FBI man, Preston.

"So, Captain Cronley, I further suggest that you have — that DCI-Europe has — two priority objectives. The first is getting Colonel Mattingly back —"

"Sir," Cronley said, "I don't have a clue how I'm going to do that."

"I have learned over the years, Captain, that there is always a clue. What you have to do is go over the facts again and again and again until you find it. Let's do that, starting with Fact One: The Russians — Serov — want to exchange Mattingly for Colonel Likharev and his family on the Glienicke Bridge at nine in the morning of February twelfth. That gives us eleven days. Is that correct?"

"The *thirteenth,* sir, which gives us not

quite twelve days."

"I don't like to think what will happen to Bob Mattingly if we don't get him back in twelve days, but I suggest that General Seidel and Company are going to start crowing something along the lines of 'If only young Captain Cronley had accepted the assistance that I and the FBI offered, poor Colonel Mattingly would be free.' "

"Yes, sir, I've thought of that."

"And?"

"For the time being I decided the thing to do is what Serov asked me to do. I showed up at the bridge, as ordered, and today I'm going to rebury the Russians."

"That's all?"

"I've been hoping, sir, that Lazarus might somehow be useful in getting Colonel Mattingly back but —"

"Swapping him for Colonel Mattingly, you mean?"

"Yes, sir. But, General, I was going to say I don't think they'll swap Colonel Mattingly for a major. What the Russians want — what they specifically have told me they want — in exchange for Mattingly is Polkóvnik Likharev and his wife and children."

"Do the Russians know you have this Lazarus?" White asked.

"Sir, I think somebody who knows has

told them we have him."

"You have a mole, is that what you're saying?"

" 'Moles,' plural, General," Wallace said. "We're working on it."

"Good luck. Moles are notoriously difficult to eliminate," White said.

"But eventually, it has been my experience, if one keeps one's eyes open," Gehlen said, "they pop their heads out of the ground, permitting them to be eliminated."

White met Gehlen's eyes, and nodded. Then he said, "Why do you think the Russians know you specifically have this man?"

Cronley took a moment to frame his reply.

"Sir, prefacing this by saying I'm a beginner in the business of dealing with senior NKGB officers, I had the feeling that Serov was much more interested in getting him back than he let on. I came out of our meeting feeling that there was more to this reburial business than Serov's devotion to his religious faith."

"According to Oberst Mannberg, Jim," Gehlen said, "you did very well in your dealings with Comrade Serov."

"That's two compliments from people I respect, Cronley," White said. "So why don't you tell us how you thought you might use Lazarus — Major . . . Whatsisname?"

"Ulyanov, sir. Major of State Security Venedikt Ulyanov."

"How might you use Major Ulyanov to get Colonel Mattingly back?"

"My idea didn't work, sir. What I thought might work was to infiltrate the Odessa organization, grab one or more of the Nazis it's moving around, and offer them, plus Lazarus, to Serov in exchange for Colonel Mattingly."

"How had you planned to infiltrate Odessa?"

"The head of the DST in Strasbourg, Commandant Jean-Paul Fortin, is after Odessa with a vengeance, sir."

"How did you come to know this Fortin?"

"That's a long story, sir."

"Let's have it," White said.

"My mother is a Strasbourgerin, sir," Cronley began. "A war bride of the First World War. She received a letter from her nephew there, my cousin, a man named Luther Stauffer . . ."

Five minutes later, Cronley finished: ". . . but when I returned from Berlin, Sergeant Finney told me that Cousin Luther made no move to corrupt him, and that Commandant Fortin later told him that Luther himself had disappeared into Odessa. So that idea didn't work."

"You say your cousin was an SS officer?" White asked.

"Yes, sir. According to Commandant Fortin, he was an SS-*sturmführer* when he deserted in the last days of the war."

"According to my information, so did SS-Brigadeführer Ulrich Heimstadter and his deputy, Standartenführer Oskar Müller. I think we may be onto something."

"I don't understand, sir. I never heard those names before."

"Wernher von Braun's rocket operation at Peenemünde required much labor support," Gehlen said. "Slave labor, to put a point on it. Heimstadter was in charge of the labor force, and treated these people very badly. And then when it initially appeared that the Russians would reach Peenemünde first, before the Americans, he had all of them shot and buried in a mass grave, so they wouldn't be able to tell the Russians what they had seen. And then SS-Brigadeführer Ulrich Heimstadter and his deputy, Standartenführer Oskar Müller, deserted and disappeared."

"Why did they desert?" Cronley asked.

"They thought it might be a defense when they fell into Russian or German hands. 'Just as soon as I could, after learning for the first time what terrible things the SS had done, I deserted . . .'

"Then came Operation Paperclip. Every one of von Braun's people who could be passed through one of the 'kindly' denazification courts that General White mentioned had been 'denazified' and sent to the United States. In the process, the scientists professed shock and indignation about what Heimstadter and Müller had done to the poor slave laborers —"

"Which meant," White picked up, "that Heimstadter and Müller didn't get to go to America, but instead have been on the run from both the Allies and the Russians. They are trying to make their way — assisted, as Good Nazis, by the Odessa organization — first to Italy or Spain, and finally to South America."

"Sir, you don't think these two — Heimstadter and Müller — have so far made it out of Germany?" Cronley asked.

White shook his head and said, "No."

Gehlen said, "I would be very surprised if they've made it to South America. Spain, perhaps, but not South America."

"Why do you say that?" White asked.

"Niedermeyer would know."

"Who's he?"

"The man I have in Argentina to keep an

eye on the Nazis we sent there. Former Oberst Otto Niedermeyer."

"Going off at a tangent," White asked, "what's ultimately going to happen to the Nazis? Where are they now?"

"Full details, or a synopsis?" Gehlen asked.

"Try to strike a reasonable compromise between the two, if you please, General," White said, smiling.

"Originally," Gehlen said, "they were all confined on an estancia in Patagonia. The estancia had passed to Cletus Frade on the death, the murder by the SS, of his father. Their confinement was supervised by General de Brigade Bernardo Martín of BIS —"

"Which is?" White asked.

"The Argentine intelligence service. Martín is its chief. The Nazis were — are — guarded by BIS men who in turn supervise the actual guards who are soldiers of the Húsares de Pueyrredón, a cavalry regiment which el Coronel Frade had commanded. Niedermeyer told me Martín had told him that what the Húsares wanted to do with the Nazis was disembowel them.

"Martín himself hates Nazis. But, realizing that the people we sent there could not be held forever, they set up what could be called their own denazification program.

Once they had impressed upon the Nazis that while they would eventually be released, what they should be considering was the conditions on which they would be released, and that the Argentine government did not consider itself bound by the deal struck between Mr. Dulles and myself. That, in other words, should they misbehave, they would be sent back to Germany to face trial."

"How did you feel about that?"

"General, my insistence on including the Nazi members of my organization in my arrangement with Mr. Dulles was not out of concern for the Nazis, but rather their families. I knew what the Soviets would do to them."

White was silent a moment. Then he nodded and said, "I had to ask, General Gehlen."

"I understand. Well, to shorten this. General Martín and Otto Niedermeyer have released some of our Nazis, starting with those they agree will pose the least threat to Argentina. Some have been released within Argentina, where the BIS keeps an eye on them. Others were released to Paraguay and Brazil. With regard to the former, the president is Major General Higinio Morínigo, who until we lost the war and the horrors of the death camps became known, was an unabashed admirer of National Socialism, generally, and Hitler, in particular.

"The same is true of one of his colonels, Alfredo Stroessner, with whom Martín has had a relationship over the years, and has come to believe that Stroessner has not lost his admiration for National Socialism but believes the Nazis were responsible not only for the death camps and other atrocities but for what he calls the 'perversion of National Socialism.' "

"That's absurd," White said.

"Of course it is. But Stroessner apparently not only believes it, but has managed to bring President Morínigo around to believe it's the case. Going off on a tangent, Martín believes that Stroessner intends to depose Morínigo as soon as he sees the opportunity so that he can bring 'True National Socialism to Paraguay.' "

"General Buckner," White said, "General *Simón Bolívar* Buckner, who was killed on Okinawa, once told me that the man for whom both he and his father had been named wrote that South America is ungovernable."

"One sometimes does get that impression," Gehlen said. "In this case, this plays

476

to our advantage. Martín and Colonel Niedermeyer — with the concurrence of Colonel Frade — have been sending 'True
National Socialists' to Paraguay after making it clear to them that Stroessner will
execute them out of hand if he even suspects
they were part of the evil Nazi cabal that
caused the downfall of National Socialism."

"Incredible," White said.

"So far, I understand, Colonel Stroessner
has only had to do this twice. And since
then, the others have been diligently trying
to be good Paraguayan National Socialists.
As far as the Nazis released in Argentina
are concerned, General Perón has made
them conditionally welcome. I don't think
they'll cause him, or us, any trouble."

"I've heard that he had — has — Nazi
inclinations?"

"According to Oberst Niedermeyer, he
was a great admirer of Mussolini Fascism.
Oscar Schultz told me Perón sees himself as
the future Il Duce of South America."

"Speaking of Schultz, how much does he
know of what's going on with Colonel Mattingly?"

Gehlen nodded toward Cronley, who
replied: "Sir, I sent him — DCI sent him —
a report of what happened in Vienna as soon
as I got back and, at oh-dark-hundred this

morning, I sent a report of what happened in Berlin, and told him I was going to go through with the Russian Orthodox funerals and then go back to Berlin."

*And I also sent a message via Hansel to Clete saying I will scuttle any attempt to swap the Likharevs for Mattingly.*

*But I don't think this is the time to mention that.*

"Then the ball is in their court," White said. "Whether to exchange Bob Mattingly for the Russian or not. I'm glad I don't have to make that call." He paused thoughtfully for a moment, and then went on: "Well, we should know soon. In the meantime . . . what do we do, Cronley?"

"As I said, sir, I'm going to go ahead with reburying the Russians, and then go back to Berlin."

"You don't think there's any chance of resurrecting your idea of getting into Odessa through Commandant Whatsisname, the Frenchman, in Strasbourg?"

"Fortin, sir. Commandant Jean-Paul Fortin. Anything's worth a try, sir."

"Your cousin — that relationship — would not pose a problem for you?"

"No, sir."

"How did Winters get along with Commandant Fortin?"

"Very well, sir."

"Then do you think it would be a good idea if he flew you — before or after the re-interments of the Russians, but before you return to Berlin — over there to have a shot at that . . ."

*Is Cousin Luther going to cause me problems if Tom Winters flies me over there?*

*Have I just ever so tactfully been reprimanded for flying down here in the bad weather last night?*

*You bet your ass I have.*

". . . and, in the meantime, I was thinking that General Gehlen, Colonel Wallace, Colonel Wilson, and myself can get together with that marvelous Pennsylvania Dutchman PFC of yours and see what we can come up with about getting into Odessa through the *Stars and Stripes* trucks. Does that make sense to you, Cronley?"

"Sir, I would suggest you include Augie Ziegler in that."

*And now I have just been ordered, with great tact, so as not to antagonize the enormous — and wholly unjustified — ego of the chief, DCI-Europe, to have DCI do something I should have thought of myself, involving Wallace and Hotshot Billy Wilson, with the Stripes trucks.*

*This man is amazing!*

*No wonder Wallace, Hotshot Billy — and, come to think of it, Mattingly and Tiny Dunwiddie — think Major General Isaac Davis White walks on water.*

"I should have thought of that," White said. "I am afraid PFC Wagner really still thinks I bite off people's heads. Thank you for that suggestion, Cronley. And for what I think of not only as a profitable meeting, but one which will permit me to put General Bull's concerns at rest when I tell him about it."

Cronley's mouth went on automatic: "General, that 'thank you' shoe unequivocally belongs on my foot, not yours."

White stood up, looked at Cronley intently for a moment, and then smiled at him.

"Have fun at the burials and in Strasbourg," he said.

# XI

## [ONE]

*Glienicke Bridge*

*Wannsee, U.S. Zone of Berlin*

*0855 1 February 1946*

The small convoy of vehicles — an MP jeep, a Chevrolet staff car, and two former ambulances — drove up to the bridge and stopped.

The rear doors of the ambulances opened and six men in Constabulary regalia — all black soldiers, all six feet tall or better, and all armed with Thompson submachine guns — got quickly out of each. A Constabulary sergeant got out of the front seat of one of the ambulances and formed the men into two six-man squads. He then marched the soldiers up to the staff car, where he opened the rear door.

Captain Chauncey L. Dunwiddie got out. The sergeant saluted crisply and Dunwiddie returned it. DCI Special Agents Max Ostrowski and Ludwig Mannberg then got out of the car. None of them appeared to be armed. All were wearing pinks and greens, trench coats, and leather-brimmed uniform caps.

When Dunwiddie, with Ostrowski and Mannberg following, walked to the head of the column of soldiers, Dunwiddie towered over all of them.

The three started to walk toward the bridge.

The sergeant quietly ordered, "Port H-arms! Forward, harch!" and the soldiers fell in behind them.

As this was happening, an enormous

481

truck, apparently the same one the Russians had used in their first meeting on the bridge, began backing onto the bridge, again guided by a Red Army officer walking backward. Red Army soldiers marched on either side of it as they held PPSh-41 submachine guns across their chests.

The truck stopped ten meters from the white line marking the center of the bridge. The officer who had been walking backward did an about-face and came to attention on the left side of the truck.

Senior Major of State Security Ivan Serov appeared on the right side of the truck. He gestured with his right hand, and the doors of the truck opened. Colonel Robert Mattingly was sitting on a wooden chair about ten feet inside. He was wearing a trench coat and a leather-brimmed cap.

Dunwiddie, Mannberg, and Ostrowski walked onto the bridge and stopped when they were ten meters from the white line marking the center.

Dunwiddie saluted crisply. Serov returned it casually. Mattingly, in a reflex action, tried to return it, but handcuffs and a waist chain stopped the movement of his hand when it was halfway to his chest.

Serov made another gesture, and the truck

started to drive off the bridge as the doors closed.

He then walked right up to the white line.

Dunwiddie, Mannberg, and Ostrowski walked up to it.

"I rather expected to see Captain Cronley," Serov said in English.

"He's arranging an interment in Munich," Dunwiddie replied.

"When you're in touch, please tell him that I'm living up to my side of our arrangement, too. You can see that Colonel Mattingly is in good health."

"I'll tell him, Ivan, that you had him chained to a chair," Mannberg said.

Serov smiled.

"You find that amusing, Ivan?" Mannberg asked.

"Not what you said. What I find amusing, Ludwig, is to see you and your Polish associate in American uniforms."

"Just a convenience, Ivan. Like your wearing a *podpolkóvnik*'s shoulder boards rather than those of a major general. Or have you been demoted since the last time I checked?"

Serov's smile froze for a moment, and then brightened.

"It's always a pleasure to play mental chess with someone of your caliber, Ludwig," he said.

Then he came to attention, saluted, and marched back down the Russian side of the bridge.

"Colonel," Dunwiddie asked, as they drove away from the bridge, "can I ask what that rank business with Serov was all about?"

"Serious answer?"

"Please, sir."

"Usually, it's better that your adversary think you have less knowledge than is the case," Mannberg explained. "Sometimes, when dealing with Russians, it's better to challenge their superiority. He let us know he knows Max is Polish — which also meant he wanted us to know he has a mole in the Compound. So I let him know I knew more about him than he thinks I did."

"How did you know he's really a major general?"

"I don't *know*. I do know that it's highly unlikely the NKGB would have a lieutenant colonel running an operation like this. So I took a chance with major general, which seemed to be a realistic rank for someone serving as first deputy to Commissar of State Security Nikolayevich Merkulov. And I think my dart struck home."

Ostrowski chuckled.

"Another question from an amateur," Dunwiddie said. "We now have pictures of Colonel Mattingly sitting chained to a chair in that truck. So why don't we just go to the Allied Commandantura with them. 'Here's proof you have our officer chained to a chair. Now let him go.' "

Mannberg considered his reply for a moment before making it.

"The Communists have one advantage over us in any confrontation," he said finally. "We enter such proceedings weighed down by Exodus 20:1–17, and Deuteronomy 5:4–21. *'You shall not bear false witness against your neighbor.'* The Russians enter a meeting expecting to lie through their teeth to get what they want.

"If we went to the Commandantura with this, the most likely thing that would happen is that they would first deny any knowledge of anything. Then if we pressed them — with photos of poor Mattingly in that chair, for example — they would accuse us first of lying and then of provocation. And then — unless they had something important they wanted from the Commandantura — they would storm out of the meeting in righteous indignation, and stay out until they wanted something from the Commandantura. And then, when the question of

Mattingly came up, they would say that was in the past, and, for everyone's mutual benefit, there should be a fresh start with a new slate."

"In Russia," Max Ostrowski said, "the state religion is Communism, Tiny. Officially, there is no God."

"Then what's this business about giving Christian burials to the guys Claudette put down?"

"I don't really know," Mannberg said. "It could be that Serov is really a Christian. Or not."

" 'Russia is a riddle wrapped in a mystery inside an enigma,' " Ostrowski said, obviously quoting. " 'But perhaps there is a key. That key is Russian national interest.' "

"He does have a way with words, doesn't he?" Mannberg said, chuckling.

"Who does?" Tiny asked.

"Winston Churchill," Ostrowski replied. "He said that in a speech in 1939."

"I suspect this burial business has a meaning," Mannberg said. "We have no choice but to play along with it until we find out what that is."

"Do you suppose it might have something to do with Russian nationalism?" Max asked drily.

# [Two]

*München-Ostfriedhof Cemetery*

*St.-Martins-Platz*

*Munich, American Zone of Occupation,*
  *Germany*

*1050 1 February 1946*

"Augie," Captain James D. Cronley Jr. inquired of Chief Warrant Officer August Ziegler as the Ford staff car entered the gates of the cemetery, "is this the right place? Comrade Serov said 'the Giesinger Friedhof cemetery.' That plaque — brass sign, whatever — read MÜNCHEN-OSTFRIEDHOF."

"I can only surmise," Ziegler replied, "that no one elected to tell Comrade Serov that the establishment — opened in 1821 as the Giesinger-Friedhof cemetery and designed to provide approximately thirty-five thousand burial plots within its nearly forty hectares — which is just shy of a hundred acres — was renamed München-Ostfriedhof, or Eastern Cemetery of Munich, in September 1929, when the crematorium was opened. Rest assured, Captain Cronley, sir, that I would never take you to the wrong boneyard."

"Did anyone ever tell you, Mr. Ziegler,

that you're a smart-ass?'"

"Often, sir. How about you?"

"Where'd you get all that historical data? And how did you remember it all?"

"In a previous life, you will recall, I was a CID agent. And before that I was a cop who wanted to be a detective. I learned to memorize things so I could write them down later. Sometimes stuff like that sticks in my mind for a while. I got it while praying the 98th General Hospital didn't send the corpses right to the crematorium."

"What?" Cronley asked.

"I was afraid that might happen, considering the Kraut rule of After Twenty-five Years, Pay Up or Into the Crematorium."

"The what?" PFC Karl-Christoph Wagner inquired from the backseat.

"It's sort of a Rent-a-Grave system," Ziegler explained. "After a quarter century, unless the family pays for another twenty-five years, they exhume the bodies, cremate what's left, and then rent the grave to somebody new."

"Jesus Christ!"

Cronley said, "If they'd cremated those bastards, we'd be fucked with Serov. Are you sure they didn't?"

"We're about to find out," Ziegler said as he pulled up before a large building with a round roof. "The crematorium also houses the grave-locating office."

"What the hell does that sign mean?" Cronley asked.

"For the captain's edification, 'Det 7, AGRC' means 'Detachment 7, American Graves Registration Command.' I can only surmise we're burning our dead. That would be cheaper than buying them a coffin and then flying them home."

"Or they're looking for the bodies of still-missing American POWs," Cronley said.

"I didn't think of that," Ziegler admitted.

When they were halfway up the steps to the door of the building, an American voice called out, "Mr. Ziegler?"

A short, muscular first lieutenant trotted up to them, saluted Cronley, and said, "Lieutenant McGrory, sir. Munich Post Engineers. Colonel Bristol sent me to do whatever Mr. Ziegler requires."

He pointed to the side of the building where an Army backhoe sat on a trailer attached to a three-quarter-ton truck. Half a dozen GIs sat on the fenders and running boards of the truck and on a jeep next to it. "Is that you, sir?"

"Guilty," Ziegler said. "Welcome."

"What can we do for you, sir?" Lieutenant

McGrory asked.

"Presuming we can find their graves," Cronley said, "we are going to exhume the bodies — which may or may not be in caskets — of three recently buried men . . ."

McGrory's face showed he didn't like this information at all. But he said nothing.

". . . and then we're going to take them to the morgue at the 98th General Hospital."

"Sir, I can't get three bodies, with or without caskets, on that three-quarter-ton."

"Four bodies," Cronley said, as if to himself.

"Sir?" Ziegler and McGrory asked.

Before Cronley could reply, a Chevrolet staff car drove up beside them. Three men, all in ODs with triangles, got out. One of them carried a Speed Graphic press camera and had a Leica 35mm camera hanging from his neck. Another had an Eyemo motion picture camera.

"Ziegler, what the hell is going on here?" the man who did not have a camera asked.

"Mr. Cronley, this is CID Agent Walt 'Hollywood' Thomas, of the CID photo lab. Hollywood, this is Mr. Cronley of the DCI."

"I heard you got transferred there. What the hell is the DCI?"

"I'm surprised Colonel Kellogg didn't tell you not to ask questions," Ziegler said.

"Yeah, he did," Thomas said, and, turning to Cronley, added, "If I'm out of line, sir, I'm sorry. My orders from the provost marshal were to do whatever Ziegler asked. And not to ask questions."

"We need pictures, still and movie, of digging up some bodies, of the bodies in the morgue of the 98th General Hospital, and then of them in caskets, and then of their reburial here —"

"Which will take place as soon as we get the caskets," Ziegler interjected. "And the tombstones. Which hopefully will be tomorrow but will probably be the day after tomorrow."

"Can I ask what this is all about?" Thomas asked.

"No," Ziegler said. "Classification, Top Secret. You'll develop the film, immediately, make prints of the stills, give everything to me, and then forget everything. Got it?"

"You get that, Lieutenant?" Cronley asked the engineer officer.

"Yes, sir."

"Make sure your men get it."

"Yes, sir, I will."

"I need a quiet word with you, Mr. Ziegler," Cronley said.

"Yes, sir," Augie replied.

Cronley led him up the stairs and into the

crematorium.

"Serov knows three of his guys were killed," Cronley began. "Janice wrote that the fourth guy died in the hospital. He knows, I think, that the fourth guy is Lazarus, Ulyanov. And I don't think he thinks Lazarus is dead. I think this whole reburial process is because it's important to Serov to know that he's dead. Why is he so important? I don't have a fucking clue. But I want to play with that."

"I don't know what you mean," Ziegler replied.

"You're the expert on this place. What do they do with the ashes of somebody who gets cremated?"

"For all I know, they use them for fertilizer. Maybe into a mass grave of ashes."

"What if somebody rented a grave? Then what?"

"That I know. They put the ashes into what looks like a flower pot with a lid and the deceased's name on it, on a little bronze strip, and then bury it."

"They dig a six-foot hole for a flower pot?"

"They dig a hole maybe two feet deep."

"You just made my day," Cronley said. "Get one of these flower pots. And put on a bronze strip: MAJOR OF STATE SECURITY VENEDIKT ULYANOV. When we open the three graves and get pictures of the caskets and bodies, we will open, right next to it, a fourth grave, maybe two feet deep, from which we will exhume and take pictures of a flower pot with no name tag on it. Later, we put the name strip on it, take a picture of it, and then of it being reburied."

"And you're thinking that will convince Serov that Lazarus is dead?"

"I don't know. What I want to see is his reaction. Is he pissed? Relieved? What?"

"How about 'unbelieving'?"

"I have a gut feeling this should be done, so we're going to do it."

"By 'we,' you mean me and Wagner."

"You're going to do it. I'm going to take Wagner to see General White. Have a nice day, Mr. Ziegler. I'll see you at the hotel at the cocktail hour."


# [THREE]

*München Ostbahnhof*

*Haidhausen, Munich*

*American Zone of Occupation, Germany*

*1205 1 February 1946*

The locomotive was pulled nose first into the left platform of the station. An American flag and a red flag with two silver stars —

indicating the presence of a major general — hung limply from poles mounted forward of the boiler.

"Relax, Casey," Cronley said to PFC Karl-Christoph Wagner. "He really doesn't eat people alive."

"Actually, I sort of like him," Wagner replied. "He reminds me of my grand-father."

"When he's through with you, call the office and they'll send a car. Got the number?"

"Yes, sir."

They walked past the locomotive, which was lazily puffing steam from under its boiler onto the platform, and then past the car immediately behind the locomotive. A very crisply uniformed Constabulary sergeant stood guard at the door of the next car. He was armed with both a Thompson submachine gun and a .45 ACP pistol. He wore a glistening helmet liner and had a yellow scarf puffing out of his Ike jacket.

He looked to be a little younger than Wagner, and Cronley recalled another lecture from Freddy Hessinger, in which Freddy had reported that the average age of enlisted men in USFET was eighteen-point-something years, that ninety-something percent of them were high school graduates with an average Army General Classification Test score of 113, which would have qualified them for officer candidate school had they been old enough — twenty-one — to become officers. Seventy-something percent of them had taken advantage of the Army's desperate need for troops by accepting the offer to enlist for eighteen months, which made them eligible for college under the GI Bill.

"Sergeant, this is Mr. Wagner, who has an appointment with General White," Cronley said to the eighteen-point-something-year-old sergeant.

"Yes, sir," the sergeant replied. "We've been given a heads-up. If you'll come with me, Mr. Wagner?"

The sergeant did not seem at all surprised that another eighteen-point-something-year-old was wearing the triangles of a civilian employee of the Army or that he had an appointment with the major general who commanded the U.S. Constabulary.

Wagner, who was not supposed to salute another civilian wearing triangles, saluted Cronley, who returned it.

As Cronley opened the door of the staff car, he was still considering the surreal aspects of the situation, which included himself having become a captain while his A&M classmates were still waiting for their automatic promotion to first lieutenant after eighteen months of service and his being in charge of an operation attempting to get a full bull colonel back from the Russians who had kidnapped him.

He was abruptly brought out of his reverie when a voice barked, "Sir, Lieutenant Douglas, sir. Aide-de-camp to Major General White, sir. General White's compliments. Sir, it would please the general if you would attend him at your earliest convenience."

Cronley turned and found himself looking at a second lieutenant whose Constabulary uniform bore the lapel insignia and aiguillette of an aide-de-camp to a major general and who looked to be about as old as PFC Wagner.

"Lieutenant, how long have you been in the Army?"

"Sir, about seventeen months. I'm Norwich, '45."

"When you were at Norwich, did you know a great big black guy named Dunwiddie?"

"Yes, sir, as a matter of fact I did. Tiny Dunwiddie was my first sergeant, and then he dropped out of school. There was a rumor he enlisted. I've always wondered what happened to him."

*Well, right about now he's a captain stand-ing on the Glienicke Bridge in Berlin, dealing with NKGB Senior Major of State Security Ivan Serov, trying to get a colonel the Russians kidnapped back.*

*Surreal!*

"Lead the way, Lieutenant."

"Yes, sir. If you'll come with me, I'll take you to the general."

Cronley stepped inside the third railcar. Seated at a map-covered conference table were General White, Lieutenant Colonel Hotshot Billy Wilson, PFC Wagner, and a lieutenant colonel and a major, all of whom Cronley had sort of expected. Also seated at the table was Miss Janice Johansen of the Associated Press, which really surprised him.

"Come on in, Cronley," General White said. "I'm glad Lieutenant Douglas caught you."

"Good afternoon, sir," Cronley said. "Miss Johansen."

"How did the funeral go, sweetheart?" she asked.

"Cronley, this is Colonel McMullen, my G-2, and Major Lomax, his deputy," White said.

The men shook hands.

"Sit down, and tell us how the funeral went, sweetheart," General White said.

Colonel Wilson laughed. Colonel McMullen and Major Lomax chuckled. Lieutenant Douglas and PFC Wagner tried hard to do neither.

*Sonofabitch!*

*His two G-2 officers and the aide aren't cleared for any of this.*

*Do I ignore that and answer the question or say something and piss General White off?*

*And what the hell was him calling me "sweetheart" all about?*

*Just being funny, or is he letting me know he knows I've been screwing Janice and letting me know he disapproves?*

"I hope you were paying attention, Greg," White said. "And you, too, Wagner. Although I suspect you're already aware of what you should do in a situation like the one I just put Captain Cronley in."

"Sir?" Lieutenant Douglas asked, visibly confused.

"Cronley doesn't know any of you are in the loop," White replied, pointing at McMullen, Lomax, and Gregory. "So when I asked him — coupled with something I hoped would upset him — questions about the funeral, the answers to which would have been Top Secret–Presidential, he did the right thing. He kept his mouth shut and gave me a really dirty look. Get it?"

"Yes, sir," Gregory said.

White added, "Even if he had said, politely, 'General, that's classified,' he would have been letting you know that there was something secret about the funeral. You get that, Greg?"

"Yes, sir."

"Cronley, Admiral Souers gave me permission to bring anyone into the loop I thought necessary. Will you take my word on that?"

"Yes, sir. Of course."

"After Billy and I talked with Wagner yesterday, I decided that the contributions Dick McMullen and Fred Lomax could make toward solving the problem justified bringing them into the loop. I brought Greg into the loop as part of his education. Aides should do more than pass canapés. They should learn how things work at the higher echelons of the Army. Does my bringing Lieutenant Gregory into the loop pose a problem for you, Cronley?"

"No, sir."

"He's Norwich. Same class, '45, as a mutual friend of ours. Speaking of whom?"

"Sir, Captain Dunwiddie is, or was at oh-nine-hundred, on the Glienicke Bridge in

Berlin, dealing with NKGB Senior Major of State Security Ivan Serov, trying to get Colonel Mattingly back from the Russians."

"Wipe that expression of shock and disbelief off your face, Greg," White said. "An officer needs to have a poker face."

There were chuckles at Gregory's visible discomfiture.

"If something other than what you expected had happened, I presume you would have heard by now?" White asked.

"Yes, sir."

"Which brings us back to the funeral. How's that going?"

"Sir, when I left the cemetery just before coming here, a backhoe that Colonel Bristol sent over was about to open the graves. He also found somebody to make the tombstones."

"Greg, he's Norwich, too, '40, I think," White said. "Engineer. Good man. I suspect — but don't know — that Captain Cronley has brought him into the loop."

"Yes, sir. I did."

"How long is this exhumation/reburial process going to take?" White asked.

"It depends on how soon we get the tombstones. Augie Ziegler found a Russian Orthodox priest —"

"An archiereus," Wagner interjected.

"That's like a bishop."

"I stand corrected," Cronley said. "An *archiereus* who will conduct the burial."

He turned to Wagner and asked, "Does this guy have priests under him? I mean, can we get priests, brothers, whatever to participate?"

"There was a price. Augie said he thought you'd be happy to pay it."

"And I will be. I want this done right."

"My question was," White said, "how long is this going to take?"

"Colonel Bristol said he's been promised the tombstones by the day after tomorrow, but not to hold my breath. I'm working with the day after the day after tomorrow. That would be February fourth."

"And since Serov wants the exchange to take place on the thirteenth, that would leave nine days."

"Yes, sir,"

"Mr. Cronley," Colonel McMullen said, "General White said something about you having a relationship with Commandant Jean-Paul Fortin of the DST?"

Cronley nodded.

"In connection with SS-Brigadeführer Ulrich Heimstadter. I hope, I hope?"

"If you're talking about the guy from Peenemünde, his name never came up when

I was with Fortin."

"Damn," McMullen said.

"Can I ask what you were doing with Fortin?" Major Lomax asked.

"Trying to get into Odessa by . . ." Cronley paused, then said, "Bottom line is that my clever idea didn't work."

"What didn't work?" McMullen asked.

"It's a long story, Colonel."

"My wife and the other ladies won't be back for an hour and a half," White said, after looking at his watch. "Will that give you enough time?"

"Yes, sir. Well, my mother is a Strasbourgerin, a World War One war bride . . ."


". . . Finney said he's sure my cousin Luther was onto our little scheme," Cronley concluded. "And Finney is a very clever guy."

"Chauncey speaks very highly of him," White said. "Do you think it would be useful if you raised the question of this chap Heimstadter with Fortin? McMullen suspects Heimstadter and the other Peenemünde Nazi . . ."

White looked at McMullen, who furnished, "Standartenführer Oskar Müller."

". . . *Müller* are high on the list of people Fortin doesn't like."

"I'll certainly bring it up to him when I

see him, sir."

"It would mean you would have to pass on a late luncheon with the ladies, but you could have Tom Winters fly you to Strasbourg now."

"Fortin's not in Strasbourg, General. I was going to see him while the exhumation was going on and called to make sure he would be there. His sergeant told me he won't be back until the day after tomorrow."

"Did he say where he was?" McMullen asked.

"The Spanish border. He wouldn't say — and I asked, pressed — why, which makes me suspect he's looking for my cousin Luther."

"He could be looking for Heimstadter and Müller," McMullen said. "We're starting to think the Odessa route, or at least one of them, is Germany-France-Spain and then to Brazil, Argentina, Paraguay, wherever."

"So we're back to two days from now until you can see Fortin," White said.

"Three, sir," Cronley said. "I want to hand Serov — or have Tiny hand him — pictures of me burying the Russians."

"That's important?"

"I have a gut feeling that it is, sir."

"So three days until you can see Fortin."

"Yes, sir."

"So, sorry, it looks like luncheon with the ladies," White said. "No offense, Miss Johansen."

"None taken, darling."

"Would you be offended if I say you've been remarkably quiet during all this? Most reporters, I think, would have been asking all kinds of questions."

"Most reporters, darling, don't know how to listen. I'm getting the picture. But now that you mention it, I do have a question."

"Shoot."

"I know why Jim wants these two Krauts. But I don't know why you and McMullen are so hot to get them. Same reason?"

"I don't know why Mr. Cronley wants to get them," McMullen said.

"Why do you?" Cronley asked.

"Do you know Major General Harmon, Mr. Cronley?"

"No, sir."

"He commanded Hell on Wheels — 2nd Armored Division — before he turned it over to General White. He now commands the Constabulary, which will be turned over to General White."

"I said I didn't know him. I do know who he is," Cronley said.

"He was at Peenemünde when we found the mass graves in which Heimstadter and

Müller had buried . . . Actually, more accurately where they had forced the slave laborers to dig a mass grave and then lined up the slaves and mowed them down with Schmeissers, and dumped them into it.

"It was a scene straight from hell. Some of them still had been alive when the grave was closed. About a third were women. General Harmon turned to me — I was then G-2 of 2nd Armored — and told me, 'McMullen, from this moment on your priority is to find the bastards who did this, so we can hang them.' I've been looking for them since."

"Jesus Christ!"

"When I assumed command of Hell on Wheels," White said softly, "one of the reasons I wanted to get to Berlin quickly was that McMullen had heard that Heimstadter and Müller were there. I learned that they had been. What we thought then was that Russians had them. The Reds wanted to know what they knew of Peenemünde. The Russians accused us of having them, which was predictable, I suppose. Now McMullen has learned that they're still on the loose."

"Courtesy of Odessa," Colonel Wilson said.

"When I brought these people into the

loop, Cronley," White said, "I didn't get into why DCI is interested in Heimstadter and Müller. The political reason. I thought that should be your call. I think I should tell you that General Seidel is Colonel McMullen's brother-in-law."

*His brother-in-law!*

*Shit!*

"Sir," McMullen said to White, "what's that got to do with anything?"

"I thought you might be aware that Captain Cronley is not high on the list of junior officers whom General Seidel thinks are making substantial contributions to the Army." White paused, then added, "Actually, I can't tell you what he thinks about Captain Cronley in the presence of a lady."

"Aren't you sweet, darling?" Janice said.

"My wife told me that if I get into another brouhaha with her brother about the DCI, she'll . . . She said I'll spend the rest of our marriage sleeping on the couch."

"And what do you think of the DCI, Colonel?" Cronley asked.

"I had a lot of respect for the OSS during the war. That's where I met Bob Mattingly, when he was running OSS-Forward. I thought President Truman made a mistake when he shut it down. And I was delighted when I heard he'd established DCI."

"Why?" Cronley asked.

"I'm tempted to say because my brother-in-law thought it was absolutely the wrong thing to do. But the truth is because I don't think the Army can — or for that matter, should — do the things of questionable legality that sometimes have to be done in order to accomplish things like getting Bob Mattingly back. It takes an agency like the OSS — like the DCI."

"You're aware, Colonel, that General Seidel is trying to either take over DCI or shut it down?" Cronley asked.

"That's hardly a secret, Mr. Cronley."

"My priority is to see that doesn't happen."

McMullen looked between Cronley and General White.

"How can I be of assistance?" he asked.

"My boss believes the one way we can get the intelligence community off our backs is with Operation Paperclip. You know about Paperclip?"

"General Seidel has told me a great deal about his role in getting the German rocket establishment to Alabama. He believes it was a triumph of Army intelligence, and frankly I'm prone to agree with him."

"Including his role in running the Nazis who ran Peenemünde through, quote, sympathetic, unquote, denazification courts? Thus going directly against Truman's order than no Nazis be taken into the States?"

McMullen, after a moment's reflection, said: "He never mentioned anything along those lines. But frankly, so what? We have von Braun and his scientists and the rockets. And the Russians don't."

"Which would you say gave the United States the best deal? Paperclip, which gave us von Braun and his people, or Operation Ost, which gave us everything General Gehlen had, including agents inside the Kremlin?"

"Tough call," McMullen said, nodding thoughtfully. "Isn't it the same kind of a deal? Paperclip let some Nazis dodge getting tried and got them to the States. Operation Ost let them escape to Argentina. If that was the price that had to be paid, so be it."

"The difference is that Operation Ost had Truman's approval," Cronley said.

McMullen nodded again. "Point taken."

"And to keep Seidel and Company from taking over or shutting down DCI, I have been authorized to take whatever action is necessary."

"I don't think I understand."

"The reason I want to find Heimstadter

and Müller — who are probably feeling very sorry for themselves because every other Peenemünde Nazi but them is safe in the States and they're in hiding from both the Russians and us — is to get them to make statements — before movie cameras — about everything they know about Peenemünde and Operation Paperclip."

"To what end?"

"I think Admiral Souers might call on the assistant chief of staff–Intelligence or the chief of Naval Intelligence, and say something like, 'I'm going to show you a movie that I plan to show to the President unless you get off the back of DCI right now. And stay off.'"

"You're going to blackmail them," McMullen said, almost incredulously.

"Not ninety seconds ago you were saying something about 'things of questionable legality' that sometimes have be done," General White said.

McMullen met White's eyes, then looked at Cronley.

"Well, then I suggest, Cronley, that we pool our talents and assets and find those two bastards."

White said: "I was going to suggest Cronley take you with him to see Commandant Fortin when he goes there in three days."

"Yes, sir," Cronley said. "Good idea."

"How well do you get along with Fortin?" McMullen asked.

"Very well," Janice said, "after Jim gave him two refrigerators and a trailer full of photo lab supplies. Fortin is French, you know."

"You gave him two refrigerators, Cronley?" White asked. "Where did you get them?"

"I'd rather not say, sir."

"What were we just saying about things of questionable legality?" White said, then chuckled. "Well, that's it. Wagner can start on giving us details of the *Stars and Stripes* delivery system. Until lunch. Which brings us to that. Miss Johansen, what we're having for lunch is clam chowder. You're familiar with New England clam chowder?"

"Of course."

"Clams, potatoes, a little tomato, all in a milk broth. Served very hot?"

"I said I was."

"Miss Johansen, if you refer to me or Colonel McMullen with a term of endearment, such as 'darling,' in the presence of my wife or his, you will shortly thereafter enjoy a lap full of clam chowder. Do we understand one another?"

"General, darling, I never get guys I really

510

like in trouble with their wives. You and the handsome Irishman have absolutely nothing to worry about."

## [FOUR]

*München-Ostfriedhof Cemetery*

*St.-Martins-Platz*

*Munich, American Zone of Occupation, Germany*

*1050 5 February 1946*

It had begun to snow and the shoulders and hats of the archiereus and the priests who had conducted the service began to be covered as they watched cemetery workers pat the dirt over the graves into neat mounds with shovels.

Finally, the workers finished and looked at the archiereus for his approval.

He answered by making the sign of the cross, mumbling a final prayer, and then brushing the snow off his ornately embroidered vestments.

He then looked at Cronley and Ziegler, who, wearing Class A uniforms, stood across the graves. He blessed them, mumbled something to the priests and brothers, and then turned away from the graves and started to walk toward the Ford staff car that had brought them to the cemetery.

CID Agent Walter Thomas, of the CID photo lab, followed the procession for fifteen seconds with an Eyemo 16mm motion picture camera. Then he panned to Ziegler and Cronley for five seconds and then put the camera down.

"I fully expect to get an Academy Award for this," Hollywood announced. "Category, Weird Funerals in a German Snowstorm."

"Just develop that film, Hollywood, and get his" — Ziegler pointed to another CID agent who had been photographing the funeral with a 35mm Leica still camera — "film developed and printed and over to the Vier Jahreszeiten, like, ten minutes ago. This is important."

"I hear and obey, Master. Give me two hours."

"I'm going to hold you to two hours," Ziegler said.

"You know what I was thinking when all that was going on?" Ziegler asked as they drove through the cemetery toward the gate.

"No," Cronley said. "But I guess you're going to tell me."

"Munich got pretty well screwed up during the war. It doesn't look like it used to, I mean."

"A sage observation, Mr. Ziegler."

"This place," Ziegler said, gesturing at the gravestones, tombs, and trees they were passing through, "hasn't changed hardly at all. Today, we buried some Russians who got themselves shot while doing their duty to their country. Two years ago, some Germans who got themselves shot doing their duty to their country got buried here, probably ten yards from where we buried the Russians. A couple of years before that, the Nazis used this place to hide the ashes of three thousand nine hundred and ninety-six Germans they'd killed in Dachau, Auschwitz, and Buchenwald —"

"Three thousand nine hundred and ninety-six? Where'd you get that number?"

"After that — I guess they ran out of space here — they just buried them in Dachau, et cetera," Ziegler said.

"Is there a point in this history lesson?"

"I was thinking that pretty soon, at some cemetery in Berlin, or maybe Moscow, some NKGB guys are going to stand around watching guys with shovels pat the earth over Mattingly's grave into a neat pile."

"We don't know that's going to happen," Cronley said.

"You don't think we're going to get him back, do you?"

"What we're trying to do now is just that."

"They won't give him back unless we give them the Likharevs, and you know — or should — that we're not going to do that."

"I don't know that, either. Somebody may decide that we need Mattingly more than we need the Likharevs."

"We can't do that, and you know it. That would encourage the bastards to kidnap somebody else whenever they want something from us."

"I tried to make that point to Schultz and the admiral."

"What did they say?"

"They didn't say anything."

"Figures. They want to make the swap."

Cronley let slip: "I'm not going to let that happen."

"What the fuck did you just say?"

"Nothing. Forget what I just said."

"How the hell can I do that?" Ziegler asked. "You really think you can stop them from swapping the Likharevs for Mattingly?"

"Change the subject, Augie. Please."

"If you fuck up a swap like that, and I don't see how you could — but if you even try to fuck up a swap, you'll find yourself in Leavenworth."

"I wasn't suggesting you change the

subject, Mr. Ziegler. That was an order."

Ziegler looked at him for a moment, exhaled audibly, and said, "Yes, sir."

## [FIVE]

*Suite 507*

*Hotel Vier Jahreszeiten*

*Maximilianstrasse 178*

*Munich, American Zone of Occupation, Germany*

*1110 5 February 1946*

Colonel Richard P. McMullen, DCI agents Karl-Christoph Wagner and Albert Finney, Major Harold Wallace, Lieutenant Thomas Winters, and Miss Janice Johansen were filling all the chairs in the outer office when Cronley and Ziegler walked in. Technical Sergeant Florence J. Miller, now wearing blue triangles on her uniform, was sitting at the desk usually occupied by Claudette Colbert.

"Good morning, sir," Cronley said.

"How went the funeral?" Miss Johansen asked.

"If you had gone out there, you would know."

"I knew you would be giving me pictures,"

she said. "And I don't like standing around in the snow. Did anybody else show up?"

"Like who?"

"Maybe the mole you've got around here. To see if you were going to bury them, or just tell Serov you did."

*Jesus, I didn't think about that!*

*Was there somebody from the NKGB peering around a tombstone?*

*Well, if there was, he can tell Serov I'm being a good boy.*

*No harm.*

*But what good, either, is that charade I just staged going to do about getting Mattingly back?*

"Not that I saw," Cronley said. "Anything else new?"

"I called Fortin to make sure he'll be there for you and Colonel McMullen," Finney said.

"And will he be? He's back from the Spanish border?"

"Capitaine DuPres said he's back from the Spanish border —"

"Who's Captain DuPres?" Janice asked.

"He works for Fortin," Cronley said. "Little guy. Young, but one tough sonofa . . . officer and gentleman."

"My kind of guy. You'll have to introduce me," Janice said.

". . . but not yet back in Strasbourg," Finney continued. "He's apparently been following your cousin Luther all over, and right now he's in Wissembourg."

"Wissembourg?" Colonel McMullen asked.

"I looked it up, Colonel," Finney replied. "It's a little *dorf* about forty miles north of here, on a little river called the Lauter, which is the international border between France and Germany."

"So Wagner has been telling us," McMullen said.

"Excuse me?" Finney asked.

"Tell the nice man what you told us about Wissembourg, Casey," the colonel ordered.

Wagner said, "Yes, sir." Then he stood up and visibly collected his thoughts before going on.

"We have Americans all over France. In Paris, for example, on an island called — I forget what — and in places like Carentan, which is near Cherbourg —"

"I know it well," Ziegler offered. "I was there for a month. It's where we're building a permanent cemetery for our guys who bought it on the invasion beaches and as we broke out of the beachhead."

"I just have to know," Cronley said. "What the hell were you doing in a cemetery for a month?"

"You really want to know?"

"I really want to know," Colonel McMullen said.

"And curiosity seems to have overwhelmed me, too," Major Wallace said.

"Okay. Two days after the invasion on D-Day, Graves Registration started burying the people who had bought it on the beaches. Among whom, incidentally, was President Roosevelt's son — President *Teddy* Roosevelt's son — who was a buck general who bought it on the beach."

"Mr. Ziegler is," Cronley said, "in case anyone is wondering, the DCI's unquestionable expert on cemeteries."

"Carry on, Mr. Ziegler," McMullen said. "You've caught everyone's attention."

"Okay," Ziegler said. "As I was saying, right after the invasion, Graves Registration started burying bodies — most often in ponchos, but sometimes without anything. There was a lot of bodies. And then after the breakout, they opened another cemetery, this one overlooking Omaha Beach, near a little *dorf* called Colleville-sur-Mer.

"After the war the families of the guys buried there were offered the choice of having their dead returned to the States, or having them reburied in what was to be the

Normandy American Cemetery and Memorial. Nine thousand three hundred and eighty-seven families said bury them where they got killed. About that many, a little more, said, 'Send him home.'

"This started one hell of an operation. The guys to be returned not only had to be dug up, but embalmed, and then put in caskets. Freighters loaded with nothing but caskets began to arrive in Cherbourg, and the Military Air Transport Command began flying in planeloads of licensed embalmers. They put these people up in another little *dorf*, Carentan."

"Why did they need embalmers?" Major Wallace asked.

"Because in some places in the States, you can't be buried unless you've been embalmed," Ziegler clarified. "So they had to embalm all the bodies going home before they put them in caskets. And then somebody decided that it was only fair that the guys not going home get the same treatment. Before they could be buried in the permanent cemetery, they had to be embalmed and put in caskets. Which came, by the way, with silk linings, silk pillows for their heads, and silk sheets to wrap the bodies in. Which is why I spent a month in Carentan."

"Embalming bodies?" Cronley asked.

Ziegler shook his head. "Making a case against the Frogs who broke into the warehouses where the caskets were stored and stole the silk and sold it to dressmakers and brassiere makers in Paris. We got one hundred and two of them put in the Frog slam, some for stealing the silk and some for receiving stolen property."

"I have to confess that I never heard anything about this before," Colonel Mc-Mullen said.

"The ambassador — our ambassador to France — got the whole investigation classified Secret. He said it 'would impair Franco-American relations unnecessarily,' and the French government kept it out of the French newspapers. I got a Green Hornet for 'good work in a classified investigation.' "

"A Green Hornet?" Janice asked.

"The Army Commendation Medal. The ribbon is green with white stripes. Anyway, that's what I was doing in Carentan. Casey, what's with you and Carentan?"

"The way they deliver *Stripes* in France is to send a truckload of them to Paris, to that island in Paris I can't remember the name of — it's some sort of depot — where they unload. The *Stripes* is then taken by the depot's trucks to the American bases all over France, like Carentan, for example, when they make their regular daily runs carrying supplies or whatever.

"When I was looking at the maps, I started wondering why the *Stripes* trucks went that way to Paris. It's not the direct route, and it's not a major highway. There is a Constabulary checkpoint at Wissembourg, because it's an international border. But then I started thinking, since *Stripes* trucks go by them every day, the Constab guys aren't going to take a real close look at them.

"And then when I kept looking at the maps, I saw that there's nothing much on both sides of the border around Wissembourg. It's in the middle of nowhere. And there's not much traffic on the road. So no one would see the truck stopping, and a couple of guys coming out of the woods and getting on the trucks, and then getting off, with nobody seeing them, on the other side of the border."

"And," McMullen said, "Commandant Jean-Paul Fortin has followed Cousin Luther — what's his name, Cronley?"

"Stauffer, Luther Stauffer. My mother's maiden name is Stauffer."

"So Commandant Fortin of the Direction de la Surveillance du Territoire has followed Herr — or is it Monsieur? — Stauffer to

521

Wissembourg," McMullen said. "Does anyone else find that fascinating?"

Before anyone could answer, the telephone on Florence Miller's desk rang.

Cronley looked at her impatiently as she answered, and then curiously as she gestured to Tom Winters that it was for him.

Winters jumped out of his chair and went to her and took the telephone.

His face brightened as he listened.

"I'll be right there," he announced after a moment, handed the telephone to Florence, and looked at Cronley.

"Sorry, I have to go," he said.

"You have to go where?"

"The stork is about to land at the Compound."

"Where the hell was the Storch?" Cronley demanded, and then understood. "Oh! Christ, she can't have a baby in the Compound."

"That's why I have to go. To take her to the 98th General."

"Calm down, Tom," Cronley said. "Get on the horn to Bonehead. Have him take Barbara to the hospital. You meet her there."

"Bonehead is already there. He took Ginger there at about five this morning. I didn't have the chance to tell you."

"Well then, what the hell are you waiting

for?" Cronley said. "Get going! Tell the ladies good luck."

"Talk about timing!" Winters said, and headed for the door.

After a moment, Ziegler said, "Well, I guess Tom won't be going with us to Wissembourg. He and Bonehead will be holding hands in the waiting room of the maternity ward."

That triggered laughter and chuckles.

"There's no point in anybody going to Wissembourg," Cronley said.

"I thought you and the colonel had to see Fortin," Major Wallace challenged.

"We do," McMullen said. "But I'd be surprised if there's an airfield there. So we'd have to drive. Forty-odd miles on bad roads. And when we get there, then what? We wander around what Wagner describes as a little *dorf,* stopping people and asking, 'Excuse me, Madam — or Gnädige Frau — we're looking for a senior officer of French intelligence named Fortin who's chasing a chap named Stauffer. Can you point out either of them to us, please?' "

"Ouch!" Wallace said. "I will try to atone for that stupid suggestion, Colonel, sir, by suggesting that I stick around here until we get the stuff from the photo lab. I will then have someone fly me to Frankfurt, where I

523

will catch the Air Force courier flight to Berlin. Meanwhile, you and Cronley can fly to Strasbourg and wait for Fortin to return from Wissembourg."

He paused long enough for that to sink in, then asked, "How's that sound to you, Cronley?"

*That wasn't an announcement. He's asking my permission.*

*What's that all about?*

"That's fine with me, if it's all right with you, Colonel McMullen."

"It's either that, or go over to the 98th and offer our moral support to the fathers-to-be."

"Thank you," Wallace said. "I'd really like to get a feel about what's going on in Berlin. And I've been thinking that if I show up at the Glienicke Bridge with the film of the funeral, Serov will accept that I'm simply your messenger. And it might help Bob Mattingly's morale if he sees me there."

"How does Colonel Mattingly feel about attractive women?" Janice asked. "Would seeing me on that bridge do anything for his morale?"

Cronley shut off his automatic mouth just in time. He was about to say, *You're not going anywhere near that goddamn bridge!*

Instead, he asked, "Colonel, do you think

Comrade Serov would shoot our Janice if she walked out onto the bridge, taking pictures with her Leica, beside Major Wallace?"

McMullen considered that for five seconds, which seemed longer, before replying.

"Possibly, but unlikely," he said. "We haven't paid a lot of attention to public relations in this, have we?"

"Just Janice's *Stars and Stripes* slash Associated Press stories," Wallace said.

"I was thinking it couldn't make anything worse than it already is," Cronley said. "And it might shake up Comrade Serov a little. *Where's Cronley? What's he doing? And what's the role of Janice Johansen of the Associated Press in this?*"

McMullen granted his approval of that scenario with a grunt.

"Your call, Jim," Wallace said.

*He's asking me. Again. Not telling me.*

*What's going on?*

"Florence, call the Military Air Transport Service and make reservations for Major Wallace and Miss Johansen on every Berlin courier flight starting at fifteen hundred."

"If they give you any trouble," Wallace said, "get Colonel Aaron of MATS on the line, and tell them the reservations we're asking for are for me."

"Yes, sir."

"And, Florence, call the Maison Rouge hotel in Strasbourg and make reservations for Colonel McMullen and me," Cronley said.

"Yes, sir."

"And nobody but General Gehlen, Colonel Mannberg, and, if he calls, Mr. Schultz is to know where we are."

"Keeping the mole in his hole?"

"Well, I don't think the mole is either Gehlen or Mannberg. So maybe this will make him stick his head out to see what's going on, and we can lop it off."

He looked at McMullen.

"Let's have a late lunch in Strasbourg, sir."

"Why not? The food's probably better there than it is in the Vier Jahreszeiten," he said, and stood up.

"Which one of us is going with you?" Ziegler asked.

"Everybody's going," Cronley said. "Florence, find Kurt Schröder. Tell him we're on our way and to have both Storches ready."

"And call that hotel and make sure we get rooms, too," Ziegler said.

# [Six]

*Hotel Maison Rouge*

*Rue Des Francs-Bourgeois 101*

*Strasbourg, France*

*1620 5 February 1946*

Commandant Jean-Paul Fortin and Sergeant Henri Deladier walked into the alcove off the main dining room in the basement of the hotel.

Seated at a long table on which were several bottles of Crémant d'Alsace and an impressive array of hors d'oeuvres were Lieutenant Colonel McMullen, Captain Pierre DuPres, Sergent-chef Ibn Tufail, and DCI agents Wagner, Finney, Ziegler, Schröder, and Cronley.

The Frenchmen and Wagner stood up.

"Clever fellow that I am," Fortin greeted them, "when I saw those illegal airplanes at the airfield, I intuited that you, Cronley, would be here trying to subvert my staff. But I didn't expect to see you, Mon Colonel."

He walked to McMullen and shook his hand, and asked, "Whatever is a fine officer such as yourself doing with these disreputable people?"

"Well, I figured the food would be better

here than in Wissembourg," McMullen said. "How are you, Jean-Paul?"

"Fine, and at the moment both hungry and thirsty, both of which hungers I will be delighted to satisfy at the expense of Jim Cronley."

He sat down at the head of the table and reached for a bottle of the Crémant d'Alsace.

"Capitaine Big Mouth here told you I was in Wissembourg?" Fortin said, pointing at DuPres.

"Only after I gave him a heads-up that I was thinking of going there," Finney said.

Fortin raised his champagne flute in salute.

"Looking for Cousin Luther?" he said.

"Actually, no. I wanted to have a look at the place. Wagner" — Finney pointed at Wagner — "thinks it's Odessa's preferred point to smuggle people across the border into France."

"While I am wholly convinced that great minds travel the same roads, frankly I'm surprised to be walking along with someone so young. May I ask how you came to this conclusion, young man?"

Wagner told him.

"General Gehlen, Jean-Paul, referred to this as 'wisdom from the mouth of babes,' "

McMullen said.

"How old are you?" Fortin asked.

"Seventeen, sir."

"When I was seventeen, I was in my first year at Saint-Cyr," Fortin said. "Well, gentlemen, I have reached the same conclusion about Wissembourg, but I reached it not by logical conclusion but by following your cousin Luther there, Jim, from the Spanish border. Which brings us to him. Or which has brought him to us."

"Brought him to us?" Cronley asked.

"I have him confined here. I'm about to have to turn him over to Capitaine DuPres and Sergent-chef Ibn Tufail for interrogation."

Cronley thought: *And when you're through, are you going to shoot him in the knees and elbows before you throw him in the Rhine, like you did with the priest?*

"But I wanted to talk to you before I started that, Jim."

"Because he's my cousin?"

"Because he knows who you are."

"I don't think I understand."

"When I arrested him, he tried to reason with me. He asked if I thought he and I couldn't come to some sort of arrangement. He was offering, I thought, to change sides. I told him I wasn't interested. He then suggested I think his offer over carefully. For one thing, he knew he could be useful to me, and for another, he asked if I thought it would be wise of me to endanger my present cordial relationship with DCI-Europe by refusing the chief of DCI-Europe's cousin's offer to realize the error of his ways and change sides."

"The sonofabitch!" Cronley said.

"Of course he was — is — desperate, but I thought it interesting that he knew you were the head man of DCI."

"Well, we knew he knew I wasn't Second Lieutenant Cronley of the 711th Mobile Kitchen Renovation Company when he gave Finney the cold shoulder, but . . . Jesus!"

"Sergent Deladier found that out with a simple telephone call," Fortin said. "But I wonder who told him who you really are. I didn't think you or Finney let that slip."

"No," Finney said. "He didn't get that from me."

Cronley's mouth went into high gear: "What I suggest you do, Jean-Paul, is let Finney help Captain DuPres and Sergent-chef Ibn Tufail in their interrogation of Herr Stauffer. He can ask him who told him about us, a name I'd really like to have, and he can ask him if the next people he hoped to help across the border, and across France to the Spanish border, are two people we're really looking for, SS-Brigadeführer Ulrich Heimstadter and his deputy, Standartenführer Oskar Müller."

This time, unusually, Cronley did not regret hearing what had come automatically and without thought out of his mouth.

"Who are they? Why do you want them?" Fortin asked.

Cronley told him.

"Interesting," Fortin said.

"And I just had one of my famous inspirations, based on a number of if's. *If* Cousin Luther planned to get these two bastards across the Wissembourg border . . ."

"I'm sure, with Finney's help, DuPres and Sergent-chef Ibn Tufail can find that out," Fortin said.

". . . and *if* we can lay our hands on them . . ."

"Place your faith in the U.S. Constabulary in that regard, Jim," McMullen said.

". . . and *if* we take them to one of the cells at Kloster Grünau and let them consider their plight overnight, and the next morning Captain Pierre DuPres and Sergent-chef Ibn Tufail interview them before movie cameras about their knowledge of who was what in Operation Paperclip, they will sing like the canaries we hear about."

"Why DuPres?"

"Particularly, if they are now being guarded by half a dozen men — Ostrowski's Poles — who chatter in Russian, and half a dozen of the largest and most menacing of Tiny's Troopers," Cronley continued, and then added, "DuPres because the people in the Pentagon who get to see the movie will then wonder how much our French allies know about Paperclip and how much they might tell the press if the press start asking questions."

"Don't let this go to your head, Cronley," McMullen said, "but I don't think you're really as much of a joke as an intelligence officer as General Seidel thinks. You are really one devious sonofabitch."

"Thank you, sir," he said, and then pointed. "And *if* that champagne bottle isn't empty, would you slide it this way?"

# XII

## [ONE]

*The Glienicke Bridge*

*Wannsee, U.S. Zone of Berlin*

*0900 6 February 1946*

Right on schedule, the huge-bodied Red Army truck started backing onto the bridge.

When it was halfway to the white line marking the center of the bridge, Ostrowski, Mannberg, Dunwiddie, and Wallace started walking onto the bridge. Janice Johansen, with two Leica 35mm cameras hung around her neck, followed them.

When they stopped fifteen feet from the white line, Janice moved to within thirty feet of the line and started taking pictures.

The truck stopped and its rear doors opened, revealing Colonel Mattingly sitting handcuffed in a chair with his shackled ankles chained to the floor.

Janice moved closer, one of her cameras to her eye.

The Russian officer who had directed the truck as it backed up to the line marched off and Serov appeared. He walked almost to the dividing line. The Americans did the same.

Serov saluted. Dunwiddie returned it.

"Good morning," Serov said.

"At least it's not snowing," Mannberg replied.

"Who's that woman?" Serov demanded.

"I understand she's from the Associated Press," Mannberg replied.

"I don't like her being here," Serov said.

"I hear that all the time," Janice said. "What's your name, handsome?"

Serov's face tightened but he didn't reply.

"Where is Cronley?" he asked finally.

"Occupied elsewhere," Wallace said. "He asked me to give you these."

He handed Serov three cans of motion picture film and a large manila envelope.

"What is this?" Serov asked as he opened the envelope.

"Still and motion pictures of the reinterment of your people," Wallace said.

Serov pulled several 8×10 photos halfway out of the envelope, looked at them quickly, and then slid them back into the envelope.

"Please tell Cronley I will look at these carefully."

"I'll do that," Mannberg said.

"And please tell him that a week from today, at this hour, I look forward to seeing him and Polkóvnik Likharev and his family here."

He saluted again, waited for Dunwiddie to return it, and when he had, did an about-face and marched away. The doors to the truck closed as it drove off.

The Americans turned and walked off the bridge.

## [Two]

*U.S. Constabulary School*

*Sonthofen, Bavaria*

*The American Zone of Occupied Germany*

*1100 8 February 1946*

Major General I. D. White, trailed by his junior aide-de-camp, Second Lieutenant Gregory Douglas, walked unannounced into his conference room. Before any of the officers sitting at a twenty-foot-long conference table could rise — jump — to their feet, he made a waving gesture and said, "At ease, gentlemen."

He then slipped into the ornate high-backed leather-upholstered chair at the head of the table and announced, "The major problem as I see it is that the people we are looking for will learn, either through the mole, or moles, we feel we are infected with, that we will be looking for them at Wissembourg, or they will learn because we do

535

something stupid, especially in and around Wissembourg.

"If this problem has not been a factor in your planning, which would deeply disappoint me, then go back, so to speak, to your drawing board. If it has, let's hear what you've come up with."

McMullen stood up.

"Here's where we are, sir," he began. "Commandant Fortin's interrogation of Luther Stauffer was only partially successful. He was in fact at Wissembourg to arrange the movement for Odessa of two men across the Franco-German border, then across France to the Franco-Spanish border."

"He admitted this?"

"Ol' Pierre — Captain DuPres — General, began questioning him by asking what seemed to be an innocent question," DCI agent Finney said. " 'How's the Gasthaus Zum Adler, Luther? Comfortable? Good kitchen?' When he saw the question made Cousin Luther uncomfortable, he sent Sergeant Deladier to the gasthaus to search his room."

"How did he know this fellow had a room in that particular gasthaus?" White asked.

"It's the only gasthaus in Wissembourg, sir."

"Dumb question," White admitted. "Go on, please."

"That took about thirty, forty minutes. During which we left Cousin Luther alone with Sergent-chef Ibn Tufail."

"Who is?"

"A Berber, sir, from Morocco. Great big mean-looking sonofabitch."

"I don't think I want to hear what this man did to Mr. Stauffer," White said. "Do I?"

"Probably not what you're thinking, General," Finney said. "What he did was let Cousin Luther know that he found him . . . very attractive."

"Clever!" White said after a moment.

"Yes, sir. I thought so. Captain DuPres and Ibn Tufail make a very effective interrogation team. I don't think the CIC School at Holabird will start teaching the 'I think I'm in love with you' technique, but they should."

Second Lieutenant Douglas's eyes widened as comprehension dawned on him.

White saw this and, failing to suppress a smile, said, "Get on with it, Mr. Finney."

"Yes, sir. Well, Sergeant Deladier came back with two Nicaraguan passports."

"Here you are, sir," McMullen said, and walked down the table to White and handed him the passports.

White examined them carefully.

"It's not what it says in here," he said. "But the real names of these two are Heimstadter and Müller."

"SS-Brigadeführer Heimstadter seems to have grown a mustache," McMullen said.

"Not a Hitler mustache, but a real soup-strainer," Cronley said. "The rest of his disguise is probably lederhosen and one of those green felt hats with a feather."

"Well, whatever it is, so far it's worked," McMullen said. "This is as close as we've ever gotten to the bastard."

"What else did you learn from Herr Stauffer?" White asked.

"That they plan to cross the border on a *Stripes* truck on February tenth, two days from now. Stauffer will meet them a couple of miles inside France with the passports and a car. They will then drive to the Spanish border."

"Sir, the *Stripes* truck will leave Pfungstadt about three in the morning," DCI agent Karl-Christoph Wagner said. "That should put them at the border at daylight."

Cronley saw that Wagner was no longer uncomfortable being in the presence of the august General White.

"Anything else about the trucks we should

consider, Wagner?" White asked.

"I think I told you where these people hide on the trucks?" Wagner asked.

"Tell me again," White said.

"Yes, sir. Up in front of the truck bed. They make a place for them by laying planks between stacks of *Stripes.* Five or six stacks. They bundle *Stripes* in packages about so big."

He demonstrated the size of the packages with his hands, and then went on: "They make sort of a cave, in other words."

"I get it," White said. "And?"

"The trucks are pretty full of newspapers. Which means that when they put these guys in the cave, first they have to unload stacks of papers to get to the back, then make the cave, and then load the newspapers back on. I don't think they can do that in less than ten minutes, maybe fifteen."

"Unless they have a lot of people doing it," White said.

"You can't get a lot of people on the truck," Wagner argued.

"Point taken," White said. "So tell me what you've come up with, Dick."

"Yes, sir," McMullen said. "If the general will have a look at the map?"

White got out of his high-backed chair and walked to where several maps were laid out on the table.

"This is the highway, General, Route B38, which runs from Bad Bergzabern through Oberotterbach to Wissembourg," McMullen said, pointing it out with a pencil. "We think Heimstadter and Müller will attempt to get themselves on the truck here, somewhere along the five-kilometer stretch between Oberotterbach and Wissembourg."

"Why there?" White asked.

"It's woods most of the way on the north side of the road," Wagner answered for him. "We figure these guys will either have spent the night in Oberotterbach or maybe be driven there in the wee hours. If they've been in Oberotterbach, they'll sneak out of wherever they've been in the dark and walk far enough down the road so they can't be seen and then duck into the woods and wait for the *Stripes* truck.

"Or, whoever — somebody from Odessa — has driven them from wherever they've been will drive through Oberotterbach and down the road far enough not to be seen when they drop these two guys off."

White considered that for a moment.

"It would be nice," he said, "if, in the latter case Wagner suggests, we could lay our hands on whoever drove these people from wherever they were."

"Sir, we considered that possibility in planning Operation Bag the Bastards," McMullen said.

"Tell me."

"We're going to hide six four-man teams of men in jeeps in the woods along this stretch of road, beginning here, near Oberotterbach. Between them, they can surveil the entire stretch of road. Each team will be in sight of the team on either side of it, and they will be radio-equipped. And they will be armed with Thompsons, Garands, and pistols."

He pointed with his pencil at the map where the jeep teams would be stationed.

"The first thing they will look for is any vehicle that comes out of Oberotterbach headed for Wissembourg and then turns around and heads back toward Oberotterbach. The occupants of that vehicle will be detained.

"The next thing they will look for is the *Stars and Stripes* truck. They will keep it under observation until it stops, and goes through the unloading/reloading process Wagner described. It will be allowed to proceed for a kilometer or so, and then it will be stopped by one or more of the jeep teams.

"When the newspapers have been unloaded and former SS-Brigadeführer Ulrich Heimstadter and his former deputy Standartenführer Oskar Müller have been removed from their cave, they will be trussed up like Christmas turkeys and loaded aboard Storch aircraft, which will have landed while the foregoing was going on, and flown to Kloster Grünau, where, Cronley tells me, there are sufficient cells, once used by monks, in which they can be conveniently incarcerated."

McMullen and the others waited thirty seconds for General White's reaction.

It was not what they expected.

"Dick, maybe Cronley can be excused, but you should know better. This is not Leavenworth and the Command and General Staff School where you can stand around a sand table and play war games for a couple of hours and then head for the O Club for a couple of martinis. Grabbing these bastards is for real, and it's pretty goddamned important."

McMullen's ruddy face whitened.

"Would the general be kind enough to show me where I went wrong?" he asked in a very soft voice.

"I was about to do that, Colonel. You didn't have to ask. Let's start with these six four-man teams who are going to be responsible for carrying out this complex plan of yours. Where, knowing as you should that the average Constabulary trooper is eighteen-point-something years old, and has been in the Army less than a year, are you going to get them? And how do you plan to adequately train them to have any chance of accomplishing this complex operation you're asking them to do in the time we have available?"

"General . . ." Cronley began.

"My questions were directed at Colonel McMullen, Captain Cronley," White said coldly.

"With all respect, sir," Cronley said. "This is my — the DCI's — operation, not the Constabulary's. Any questions about it should be directed to me."

Thirty seconds later, Cronley thought, *To judge by the look in his eyes, I am going to die a painful death right here and right now.*

"Would you be kind enough, Mr. Cronley, to answer the questions I posed to Colonel McMullen?" White asked.

"Yes, sir. No reflection on the Constabulary, sir, but I thought it would be better to use Tiny's Troopers for this operation. The only things I need from the Constabulary are the jeeps, someone to drive them, and the radios. I don't have such equipment, and I don't have the time to try to get it."

"And the training? How are you going to arrange that in the limited time we have?"

"Colonel Wilson and Honest Abe Tedworth are in the process of doing that now at Kloster Grünau, sir."

"Who the hell is Honest Abe Whatever you said?" White demanded angrily.

*He's pissed because I was right, and I'm a captain, and he's a two-star general, and he knows he was wrong to jump on McMullen.*

"First Sergeant Abraham Lincoln Tedworth of Company C, 203rd Tank Destroyer Battalion, sir. DCI's security force. Company C is on detached service from the Constabulary and wear Constabulary insignia."

"I asked who he was, Mr. Cronley," White snapped. "What are his qualifications for doing something like this?"

"I don't think there's anybody around who's qualified to do something like this. But Honest Abe comes highly recommended."

"By whom?"

*Gotcha! You're probably going to go back to Highly Pissed on the Edge of Apoplexy, but I got you!*

"By Captain Dunwiddie, sir. Tedworth and Tiny — and Mr. Finney, now that I think of it — were in Charley Company when it got nearly wiped out in the Battle of the Bulge. Tiny made Abe first sergeant when he took his commission. There's no doubt in my mind that Colonel Wilson and Honest Abe can train Tiny's Troopers to carry this off."

"I wondered where the hell Hotshot Billy was," White said, in almost a mutter. Then he raised his voice. "Greg, have you been paying attention to all this?"

Second Lieutenant Douglas replied, "Yes, sir."

"Pay close attention to this. It doesn't happen very often. General officers too often tend to think of themselves as all wise and incapable of making a mistake."

"Sir?"

"Colonel McMullen and Mr. Cronley, please accept my sincere apology for underestimating you. Wagner and Finney, you can include yourself in my apology."

"General, no apology is necessary," McMullen said.

"If I didn't think an apology was necessary, Dick, I goddamn sure wouldn't have offered one. Accepted or not?"

"Accepted under duress, sir."

"Cronley?"

"Unnecessary, but accepted, sir. Thank you."

White grunted and then said, "Now that we're back to being pals bubbling all over with mutual admiration and comradely affection, I've got a couple more questions, Jim, if you don't mind."

"Yes, sir?"

"What did the Frenchmen get out of Stauffer vis-à-vis the mole we suspect is in your organization?"

"Nothing, sir," Finney said.

"Anything about how he found out that Jim is head of DCI?"

"No, sir. When I called off the interrogation, he was still saying he knew nothing about either subject."

"Why did you call off the interrogation?"

Finney hesitated a moment before replying.

"Sir, I didn't want to have to tell Mr. Cronley that his cousin had passed away after falling down in the shower."

"If the mole we suspect — hell, know — is around here learns about this operation, it's dead," White said.

"Yes, sir," Finney said. "Well, we're going to try again when we have Stauffer at Kloster Grünau."

"You took him there?"

"Captain DuPres suggested that we take away what comfort Stauffer was taking from being in familiar surroundings by moving him somewhere where he would be uncomfortable," Finney said. "And we wanted to give him time to think."

"And recuperate a little so that he doesn't fall in the shower?"

"Yes, sir. That too. And I thought we'd give Major Bischoff a shot at him, and we could do that in the monastery."

"Who's he?"

"General Gehlen's interrogator, sir," Cronley furnished. "He was the Sicherheitsdienst's mole in Abwehr Ost until the general turned him."

"Do you think one of Gehlen's people is the mole?"

"General Gehlen considers that a strong possibility, sir."

"Under the circumstances, I suggest, all we can do is hope that the mole doesn't find out what we're doing here."

"Yes, sir. That seems to be it," Cronley agreed.

"Or that we find the mole," Finney said.

"Presuming you can carry off getting Heimstadter and Müller off the *Stars and Stripes* truck alive, you're going to move them to Kloster Grünau, is that right?"

"Yes, sir."

"In your Storch airplanes?"

"Yes, sir. We can get them onto and off that road without a problem. And then it's a short flight to the monastery," Cronley said.

"Who's 'we'?"

"Colonel Wilson and myself, sir."

"Pay attention, Greg," White said.

"Yes, sir," Second Lieutenant Gregory Douglas said.

"There is a lamentable tendency among officers senior enough and/or bright enough to plan an operation such as this to hear a bugler sound 'Charge' and involve themselves personally in its execution. This often has disastrous results."

"Sir," Cronley said. "I suggest it's a question of the pilots best qualified to accomplish the mission."

"I suggest that the pilot . . . what's his name, Kurt Schröder? . . . who flew General Gehlen all over Russia in a Storch could probably —"

"Colonel McMullen," Cronley interrupted. "Change in our manning table: Colonel Wilson out of Storch number one, replaced by DCI agent Kurt Schröder."

"Good idea," McMullen replied. "The Army can ill afford to lose such a distinguished leader by his crashing an illegal airplane onto a country road on the Franco-German border."

"I further suggest that Tom Winters," White went on, "could also probably fly an illegal airplane onto —"

"General, Tom just had a baby. A boy. He's going to name it Thomas Halford Winters —"

"Is that a miracle? Or did *Mrs. Winters* just give birth to a male child?"

"The latter, sir," Cronley said.

"Then, if you were so inclined, Captain Cronley, you could tell Colonel McMullen to make another change in your manning table, to wit: chief, DCI-Europe, out of Storch number two, replaced by Lieutenant Thomas Halford Winters the Third, correct?"

"Please do so, Colonel McMullen," Cronley said.

"Good idea," White said. "That will serve two purposes. When I next see Major General Thomas Halford Winters Junior I will be able to congratulate him on the arrival of his grandson, and also tell him that his son was selected by the chief, DCI-Europe, personally to fly an important mission because of his unusual skill in flying illegal airplanes."

McMullen laughed.

"And the changes you and McMullen have just made to the manning table, Cronley, may save two officers who, in the probably failing wisdom of my dotage, I believe will make substantial contributions to the Army in coming years, providing they stop listening to the bugler blowing 'Charge.' "

He paused, and then went on, "Greg, if you think you will have trouble remembering all this, write it down."

"Yes, sir," Second Lieutenant Gregory Douglas said.

"And now that we are apparently through here, Mr. Cronley," White said, "I presume you will get back in your illegal airplane and fly off to your monastery, and deliver a message to Hotshot Billy to get his tail back here?"

"Yes, sir," Cronley said. "But not today. That will have to wait until tomorrow. I have things to do at the Compound, and I don't want Colonel Wilson to think I'm looking over his shoulder while he sets up the operation."

"You know, I know that we're pressed for time. Having said that, I'd be pleased if you — all of you — would join me at lunch."

"Very kind of you, sir. Thank you very much."

# [THREE]

*Kloster Grünau*

*Schollbrunn, Bavaria*

*American Zone of Occupation, Germany*

*1355 9 February 1946*

"Everything seems to be in order," Lieutenant Colonel William W. Wilson said to Captain James D. Cronley Jr. "That worries the hell out of me."

First Sergeant Abraham Lincoln Tedworth laughed.

"The best-laid plans of mice and men . . ." Wilson began.

"Gang aft agley," Tedworth finished for him. "But I think we have everything covered, Colonel."

*Me too,* Cronley thought.

He was impressed with what Wilson and Honest Abe had set up in so little time.

There were six Constabulary jeeps lined up. Each had a BC-654 Radio Receiver Transmitter mounted in it. It would permit communication not only between the jeeps, but with Kloster Grünau, where he and Hotshot Billy would be during the operation.

The jeeps were also stuffed with sleeping bags, which Honest Abe had told them, based on his experiences in the Battle of the Bulge, were about the best way to keep warm when one was "standing around in the woods in the middle of winter with a thumb in one's anal orifice waiting to see what was going to happen next."

Tedworth and Wilson had also come up with stoves burning jellied gasoline — which gave off no smoke — on which the men could heat rations and reheat previously brewed coffee during the long hours they would be hiding in the forest waiting for what they were looking for to appear.

"Boots and saddles time, Colonel?" Tedworth asked.

Wilson had decided the best way to avoid suspicion about half a dozen Constabulary jeeps driving through Oberotterbach was to send the first one as soon as possible, with the others following at staggered, long intervals.

"Why not?" Wilson said, and then put his fist to his mouth and mimicked the bugle call.

Tedworth smiled, and then put his fingers in his mouth and whistled shrilly.

Two of Tiny's Troopers and the Constabulary trooper who would drive the jeep trotted up to them.

"Load up," Tedworth ordered. The men

began to load themselves and their weapons into the first jeep in the line.

The plan was that Tedworth would go to the road between Oberotterbach and the Franco-German border first, and find a place to hide the jeep about halfway down the road. He and his men would then find the best places for the other jeeps to hide, marking them by doing something to the kilometer markers along the road — putting a rock on them, or overturning them, or sweeping the snow away from them. When the arriving jeep teams were off the road, they'd contact Tedworth by radio, and then he or one of his men would meet them and show them the best place to hide.

When the others had finished cramming themselves into the jeep, Tedworth got into the front seat. He saluted and then gestured for the driver to get going.

"I guess it's time for Schröder to fly me to face the wrath of ol' I.D.," Wilson said.

"I don't think he's pissed."

"He's always pissed," Wilson said, offered Cronley his hand, and then walked to where the Storches were parked.

"And I suppose it's time for me to have a chat with Cousin Luther," Cronley said, although there was no one within earshot.

# [Four]

Technical Sergeant James L. Martin, who was six feet three, and weighed 235 pounds, led Luther Stauffer into the room that had once been the office of the father superior of the monastery. Sergent-chef Ibn Tufail followed him.

"Put him in the chair," Cronley ordered.

Martin guided Stauffer into the chair with a massive hand on his shoulder, and then stood behind and to the left of him.

*He doesn't seem to be badly beaten up.*

*Well, I suppose if you're as skilled as Sergent-chef Ibn Tufail and DuPres are, you can cause a lot of pain without leaving too many marks.*

"So we meet again, Luther," Cronley said in German.

"Tell your mother about it, the next time you write her, Cousin James," Stauffer said.

Martin slapped him with the back of his hand.

"But if you don't feel like writing, don't worry. When my wife learns what you've done to me, and she will, Ingebord will let her know."

Martin slapped him again, harder.

*What the hell is that? Audacity?*

"Luther, you're really not in a position to

threaten me. And sarcasm is not nice."

"What position am I in, Cousin James?"

Martin slapped him hard again.

"You heard the captain," Martin said in German. "Sarcasm is not nice."

*I didn't know Martin spoke German until just now.*

"I'd say a pretty difficult one. You're in trouble, and you're going to be in deeper trouble if you don't tell us who told you that I'm not really a Quartermaster second lieutenant who repairs potato-peeling machines."

"A little bird told me and then flew away, Cousin James."

*You arrogant sonofabitch!*

Martin slapped him again, this time causing blood to run from his nostrils.

*What the fuck is wrong with him? Does he like getting slapped?*

*Maybe he figures DuPres or Fortin, when we're finished with this, is going to shoot him in the knees and elbows with a .22 and then throw him in the Rhine like he did the priest. The sonofabitch has certainly heard about that.*

*Or maybe he thinks he's still Sturmführer Stauffer and is holding up the honor of the Schutzstaffel while being interrogated by the enemy. Name, rank, and serial number only, even if you pull out my fingernails.*

And then when the epiphany came, Cronley said, "Oh, shit!"

"Sir?" Sergeant Martin asked.

"Martin, take my cousin Luther out somewhere where . . . No, put the sonofabitch back in his cell. For the time being, I'm through with him. And then make sure that Captain DuPres and I are not disturbed while we have a chat."

"Yes, sir," Martin said.

"He's not going to give us the mole, Jim," DuPres said, when Martin closed the door after him. "Or anything else unless I let Ibn Tufail loose, and Commandant Fortin said I was not to do that without your permission."

"Pierre, I have noticed that when Frenchmen give people a gift, the person gifted gives the giver a kiss on the cheeks. True?"

"Excuse me?"

Cronley motioned for DuPres to come closer, and when he did, Cronley grabbed his shoulders and kissed him wetly on both cheeks.

And when he turned him loose, he wiggled a finger at Sergent-chef Ibn Tufail to come close and kissed both of his cheeks.

"Jim?" DuPres asked. "What —"

"I have just had one of the famous James D. Cronley Junior epiphanies."

"A what?"

"I have just had a sudden and striking realization vis-à-vis my cousin Luther that I should have figured out — or at least suspected — a long time ago."

"Jim, I don't understand what you're talking about."

"And come to think of it, Jean-Paul and you have been as blind as I have."

"Blind to what?"

"Cousin Luther is not just the low-level flunky running errands for Odessa that we all thought him to be. That's why I kissed you," Cronley said. "You have given the DCI what we have been looking for — without any success at all — a high-ranking member of Odessa. The sonofabitch has been in Odessa — in the inner circle of Odessa — from the beginning."

"What?"

"Think about it, Pierre. Where did Odessa start, where was that organizational meeting held?"

"You mean, the meeting in the Maison Rouge hotel in Strasbourg?"

"Right. So let's start with that. Why Strasbourg? Why not in Köln or Munich, or for that matter, Berlin?"

"So it wouldn't come to the attention of the SS?"

"That, and because they knew as soon as they lost the war, Strasbourg would be returned to France. All a Nazi — either a businessman or a senior SS officer — would have to do to avoid getting bagged after the surrender was get across the Rhine into what again would be *French* Strasbourg.

"And in the beginning, it was called *Die Spinne,* right? It had nothing to do with the SS. In fact, they didn't even want the SS to know what they were up to."

"That's true."

"But there was a senior SS officer at the meeting . . ."

"SS-Obergruppenführer Wilhelm Kramer," DuPres said. "Who we haven't been able to catch."

"And the SS never heard about *Die Spinne,* right? If they had, Himmler would have had all those businessmen hung in the Flossenbürg concentration camp where they hung Admiral Canaris. So why didn't the SS learn about *Die Spinne*? Because a very senior SS officer . . ."

"SS-Obergruppenführer Wilhelm Kramer," DuPres interjected.

". . . killed any investigation," Cronley concluded. "Now, these people couldn't just paddle across the Rhine in a rowboat to Strasbourg when the time came unless they had somebody there to take care of them. But who?

"There was an interesting man in the SS . . ."

"Sturmführer Luther Stauffer."

". . . who was from Strasbourg. And had been awarded the Iron Cross. So SS-Obergruppenführer Whatsisname . . ."

"Kramer."

". . . looks up Cousin Luther, tells him what they want him to do, hands him a lot of money — and probably documents that will allow him to get through the SS checkpoints looking for deserters — and sends him off to Strasbourg."

"That doesn't explain how he found out you're DCI," DuPres said.

"Let's say Kramer is still around," Cronley said. "Maybe still in Germany, maybe in Switzerland, but still running things. By things, I mean what has become Odessa. He has been watching General Gehlen, for the obvious reasons. He has a mole in the Compound, or Kloster Grünau, or both. The mole learns that the South German Industrial Development Organization is now under the DCI, and that the guy really running it is a young captain named

James D. Cronley Junior. This word is passed to Cousin Luther.

"The name rings a bell. His aunt Wilhelmina had been kicked out of the family for marrying an American with that name. Long enough ago to have produced a son who could now be a young captain. Cousin Luther decides — and Kramer, whoever is running Odessa — agrees that a relationship with the chief, DCI-Europe, could prove valuable."

"Set him up for blackmail, for example."

"But how to establish contact? He could hardly walk up to me and say, 'Howdy, I'm your cousin Luther, and I'd like you to meet this nice fräulein . . .' "

"Who will give you a blow job while we take moving pictures . . ."

"But he could get me to come to him, his poor starving cousin, if he wrote a begging letter to my mother. He'd set me up in the black market and use that to blackmail me. Or use the fräulein you mentioned."

"But then you showed up at his door pretending to be a Quartermaster Corps second lieutenant, and since he already knew you were DCI, he thought, *My God, the DCI is onto me.*"

"And so he gave Finney the cold shoulder when Finney went there to let your cousin corrupt him."

"Yeah," Cronley said. "It all fits, Pierre and I just had another pleasant thought. If Serov knows as much about Odessa as I think he does, he'd probably like to have a long chat with someone high up in Odessa. What I'm thinking is that he might be willing to swap Colonel Mattingly for Cousin Luther."

"He'd have to be convinced that Luther really knows all of Odessa's secrets. How are you going to do that?"

"I don't know. Maybe just tell him what Luther has told us."

"He hasn't told us anything."

"That brings us back to Sergent-chef Ibn Tufail."

"You're willing to . . ."

"Yeah, I am," Cronley said.

The door opened and Florence Miller walked in.

"Goddammit, I told Sergeant Martin we didn't want to be disturbed," Cronley exploded.

"So he said," she replied. "But I told him you'd think this was really important."

She handed him a SIGABA printout.

Priority

Top Secret Lindbergh

Duplication Forbidden

From Polo
via Vint Hill Tango Net
2210 Greenwich 7 February 1946

TO Altarboy
Copy to El Jefe

Meet Saa flight 744 ETA Tempelhof
1730 9 February with blackened
window school bus or similar
vehicle to securely transport
one adult male, one adult female, two adolescent males and
eight man security detail to
secure location.

Polo

End

Top Secret Lindbergh

*Oh, shit!*
*Admiral Souers has decided to swap the*
*Likharevs for Mattingly.*
*I should have known that the minute things*

*seemed to be going well enough for me to pat myself on the back, things would really fuck up!*

*Well, that swap just is not going to happen.*

*How I'm going to stop it, I don't know.*

*But I am going to stop it.*

"Florence, get me a seat on the next Air Force flight to Berlin."

"I've already done that, sir. You couldn't make the last flight today . . ."

*Which means I won't be able to meet the SAA flight!*

". . . so you're on the first flight tomorrow at 0715, ETA Berlin 0810. And I called Mr. Dunwiddie to tell him about the bus. I thought you'd want me to."

"Florence, you're a jewel," Cronley said. "Have somebody meet me at Tempelhof."

"You'll be met, sir."

"Pierre, I'm going to try to convince Comrade Serov that Luther is valuable enough to swap for Colonel Mattingly."

"I don't think that will work, but good luck."

# [FIVE]

*44–46 Beerenstrasse*

*Zehlendorf, U.S. Zone of Berlin*

*O835 10 February 1946*

There were three staff cars, their exhausts showing they were anticipating passengers, lined up in the drive when Cronley arrived in the staff car that had picked him up at Tempelhof.

He was out of the car before it came to a complete stop, and ran into the building.

There were four men in the foyer, all of whose clothing indicated concealed firearms. One of them was large and burly, and the other three were small and wiry, almost delicate.

*Part of that fucking "security detail" in the SIGABA message.*

*Who are they?*

*Doesn't matter.*

"Where's Colonel Likharev?" Cronley demanded.

"Excuse me?" one of them asked.

*That's a Spanish — Argentinian — accent! What the hell?*

Cronley whipped out his DCI credentials and held them in the face of the large man.

"I am James D. Cronley, chief of DCI-

Europe, and unless you want to find yourself in deep shit, you better tell me where Colonel Likharev is!"

"Given the time difference between here and Mendoza," a voice said, "I'd wager the guess that at this hour he's snuggling up against Señora Likharev in their bed at Estancia Don Guillermo."

Cronley snapped his head toward the speaker.

"That was your cue, Little Brother, to say, 'What a pleasant surprise! What in the world are you doing here?' " Cletus Frade said.

"You sonofabitch!"

Frade opened his arms.

"Come to Big Brother, Chief of DCI-Europe," Frade said.

Cronley did so. They embraced.

When they finally broke apart, Cronley asked, "What the hell are you doing here?"

"At the moment, waiting for Ludwig Mannberg to find his shoes. When he finally does we're going out to the Glienicke Bridge so that I can have a look at Senior Major of State Security Ivan Serov. Would you like to tag along?"

*Oh, shit!*

"That's what I'm here to do, Clete. But right now, I'm wondering if I should let you go with me."

"You're taking that chief, DCI-Europe, title seriously, aren't you?"

"Yeah. I am. And unless you came here to tell me I've been relieved, I'm calling the shots."

"What El Jefe said to me, Jimmy, was, 'I think it would be useful if you went to Berlin to see how you can help Cronley. Maybe between the two of you, you can pull a miracle and get Mattingly back.' "

Cronley didn't reply.

"El Jefe meant 'get Mattingly back even though there's no way we can swap the Likharevs for him.' "

Again, Cronley didn't reply.

"Yeah. Hansel told me you were thinking of going to Leavenworth. Noble of you, Jimmy, but unnecessary. There was never any thought of swapping the Likharevs for Mattingly. The admiral said it would set a very bad precedent."

And once more, Cronley didn't reply.

"So do you have any miracles in your back pocket, Jimmy?"

Mannberg, Dunwiddie, and Ostrowski came out of the dining room and walked up to them.

"No miracles," Cronley replied. "I've got a couple of things going. *If,* repeat *if* any of them work, maybe . . . I'll tell you what I have in the car on the way to the bridge."

"Okay."

"Who are these guys?" Cronley asked, nodding toward the four men.

"BIS guys. Bernardo Martín loaned them to me."

"What for?"

"El Jefe's idea. Serov's people will be watching to see if we sent the Likharevs here from Argentina. We obviously don't want Serov to know they're not coming. So when we landed at Tempelhof, they saw us hustle Major Fernandez — Colonel Likharev" — Frade pointed to the large man — "and his wife and the boys" — Frade indicated the others — "bundled to the ears against the cold, off the plane and into the school bus."

"You're sure they were watching at Tempelhof?"

"If your mole read the SIGABA Polo sent, which El Jefe is sure he did, we think it reasonable to presume they were."

"It's quarter to nine," Mannberg said. "We better get going."

## [Six]

*The Glienicke Bridge*

*Wannsee, U.S. Zone of Berlin*

*0900 10 February 1946*

When the Red Army truck began to back onto the bridge, Cronley led the procession — Frade and Mannberg immediately behind him, and Dunwiddie and Ostrowski immediately behind them — onto the bridge to meet it.

When the truck stopped and opened its doors, revealing Colonel Mattingly sitting chained to a chair, Serov appeared and walked to the line marking the center of the bridge.

"Well, James," Serov said, "how nice to see you. I've been wondering where you were."

"Busy doing the Lord's work, Ivan. You know how it is."

"And who is this gentleman?"

"Lieutenant Colonel Cletus Frade, U.S. Marine Corps, at your service, General Serov."

"It's Senior Major Serov, Colonel . . ."

"If you say so."

"And your role here?"

"Surely a senior officer of the NKGB

knows what General Sun Tzu said about the wisdom of knowing one's enemies."

"But James and I are not enemies, Colonel. We are professional officers engaged in a transaction that benefits both of us."

"I'm not surprised that's the way you look at it," Frade said.

"So tell me, James, how is the movement of Polkóvnik Likharev and his family going? Everything going according to schedule?"

"Ivan, I have a new friend," Cronley said.

"Really?"

"You've heard of Odessa?"

"Something."

"Well, my friend is high up in the Odessa organization and has been telling us how it works."

"Actually, we know how it works. And what does this have to do with anything?"

"I thought you might like to talk to my friend."

"What did you say his name was?"

"I didn't."

"James, you disappoint me. You didn't really think I would entertain the notion of this friend of yours being a substitute for the Likharevs, did you?"

"It ran through my mind."

"Why should I think he's of any value at all?"

"Well, he allowed us to bag two Nazis I know you've been looking for."

"Who would that be, James?"

"SS-Brigadeführer Ulrich Heimstadter is one of them."

"Never heard of him."

"And Standartenführer Oskar Müller is the other."

"Never heard of him, either. Why were you looking for them?"

"What we were thinking, General . . ." Frade began.

"You don't listen very well, do you, Colonel? Either that, or you're trying, and succeeding, to be very rude. I've told you my rank twice. Enough!"

". . . is that Heimstadter and Müller plus Jimmy's friend in Odessa certainly would be more valuable to you than Colonel Mattingly."

"You're a fool, Colonel!"

"Now who's being rude, General?"

"Pay close attention to me, Colonel," Serov said, coldly furious. "I'm not going to exchange Mattingly for Heimstadter and Müller! Have the Likharevs here on Thursday!"

"I politely suggest, General," Frade said, "that you don't have the authority to make a decision like that. So why don't you ask

Commissar of State Security Nikolayevich Merkulov what he thinks of my offer and let us know on Thursday?"

Serov, white-faced, glared at Frade but said nothing.

"I don't see any point in meeting tomorrow," Frade said. "For one thing, it will probably take Comrade Merkulov, who we both know is a little slow, longer than twenty-four hours to make up his mind, and for another, you're not going to do anything to Colonel Mattingly without his permission. So we'll see you here same time on Thursday." He paused and then raised his voice. "See you on Thursday, Mattingly!"

"You will come to regret this, you arrogant sonofabitch!" Serov exploded.

He turned and marched quickly away, gesturing impatiently for the truck to start moving. The doors remained open and swung back and forth as the truck drove off.

When the truck turned right at the end of the bridge and disappeared from sight, Cronley turned and, with the others following him, walked off the bridge.

"Well," Cronley asked, when he, Frade, Mannberg, Ostrowski, and Dunwiddie were crowded into the staff car, "has anyone got anything to say except Clete really pissed off Serov?"

"How about *the die has been cast*?" Mannberg said.

"Pissing him off was the idea, wasn't it?" Dunwiddie said. "And Colonel Frade really did that."

"Well, as soon as we get back to the house, we can find out what happened at Wissembourg," Cronley said. "I think we should all start praying."

Frade and Ostrowski chuckled.

"That's what I have been doing," Mannberg said, obviously dead serious. "I think we're at the point where we need a little help from the Almighty."

"Vatican, Altarboy for Top Kick. The line is secure," the ASA operator said.

"Put him through," First Sergeant Tedworth said.

"Honest Abe?" Cronley asked.

"Sir, it went off so smoothly I didn't believe it."

"Praise the Lord! Both of them?"

"Both of them."

"Where are they now?"

"In separate cells under the chapel. And . . . you may not like this, Captain. Wearing GI blankets."

"What's that all about?"

"Major Bischoff was here when we flew in. Said General Gehlen had sent him to find out how things had gone. He wanted them naked in the cells. I didn't think that was what you wanted. So we compromised on taking their clothes and giving them blankets. It's cold as a witch's teat in those cells, and I didn't think you wanted them catching pneumonia."

"Good call, Abe," Cronley said. "But keep Bischoff away from them until we get there."

"Yes, sir. And when will you get here?"

"As soon as we can get on the Air Force courier flight to Rhine-Main. Have Winters and Schröder waiting for us at Rhine-Main. Tell them to leave now."

"Yes, sir."

"Is Sergeant . . . *Miss* Miller there?"

"Yes, sir. You want to talk to her?"

"Ask her if she takes shorthand."

Cronley could hear Tedworth posing the question.

"Yes, sir," Tedworth reported,

"Tell her to get out her notebooks and sharpen her pencils. First order of business is to get Heimstadter and Müller talking. Are the photographers there?"

"Yes, sir. I haven't told them what for."

"Tell them. Get them all set up."

"Yes, sir."

"Unless you have something else, I think that's it."

"I don't have anything else, sir."

"Break it down, Fulda," Cronley said, and then turned to Frade and asked, "You heard?"

"I heard. The Good Lord, thanks to Ludwig, seems to be on our side."

"Now all we have to do is get seats on the courier flight," Cronley said. "Start praying, Ludwig."

"For the moment, until el Coronel Perón finally gathers the courage to face my wrath by seizing it, SAA is still a DCI asset," Frade said. "If the chief, DCI-Europe, wants to commandeer the SAA Constellation aircraft sitting at Tempelhof, I would have no choice but to comply. And everybody could go."

"Consider it commandeered," Cronley said. "Thanks."

"There's a caveat," Frade said. "Everybody would include the eight gentlemen from BIS. I promised General Martín to give them a tour of DCI-Europe."

"Which means you want me to let them into Kloster Grünau? What would El Jefe think about that?"

"Let me put it this way, Jimmy: When the executive assistant to the director of the

DCI was in Argentina, the director of the BIS called him 'Oscar' and Schultz called General Martín 'Bernardo.' "

"The director of DCI-Europe accepts your kind offer, Colonel Frade. How soon can we leave?"

"As soon as we get to Tempelhof."

## [SEVEN]

*Kloster Grünau*

*Schollbrunn, Bavaria*

*American Zone of Occupation, Germany*

*1505 10 February 1946*

CIC Supervisory Special Agent John D. "Jack" Hammersmith walked into one of the cells under what had been the monastery chapel.

Former SS-Brigadeführer Ulrich Heimstadter, naked under a blanket, was sitting on a wooden chair.

He looked up questioningly at Hammersmith.

"I would like to apologize for taking your clothing, Herr Heimstadter," Hammersmith said. "The DCI doesn't follow the procedures of the Counter Intelligence Corps when it comes to the treatment of prisoners. I'll see what I can do about at least get-

575

ting your underwear and your trousers back immediately. And I guarantee that when you're placed in my custody for transfer to the Russians, you will be fully clothed."

"Transfer to the Russians?" former SS-Brigadeführer Ulrich Heimstadter asked. "I thought that when I was . . . detained . . . I would be sent to Nuremberg. I want the chance to prove my innocence of the unfounded accusations made against me."

"Well, what's happened is that the Russians have put in a strong request to USFET that you be transferred to them."

"Why are the Russians interested in me?"

"I've heard they want to ask you about Peenemünde and the rocket work that went on there. That was the reason General Bull said he had no objection to your being transferred, as we know all about Peenemünde."

"What do you mean, you know all about it?"

"I don't know why I'm even discussing this with you. But after how badly the DCI has treated you . . . I thought you would know that the scientists, from Dr. Wernher von Braun down, whom the Nazis had pressed into service at Peenemünde were so happy to be freed from what amounted to Nazi imprisonment that they not only told us everything we wanted to know, but volunteered to go to America to help us with our rocket program. Just about all of them are now in Huntsville, Alabama. You didn't know this?"

"I would say, sir, that you have your facts wrong."

"What facts?"

"Wernher von Braun was not a 'Nazi prisoner,' for one. He held the rank of *sturmbannführer* in the SS."

"I find that hard to believe."

"And I can't think of one senior scientist at Peenemünde who wasn't a member of the Nazi Party."

"Give me the name of one who was."

"I can give you the names of just about everyone who was. I suggest, sir, that you have been taken in by dozens of 'anti-Nazis' who were in fact members of the Nazi Party."

"Give them to me."

"Not if you're going to turn me over to the Russians."

"Frankly, I think you're making all this up to keep from being turned over to the Russians."

"I swear to God! I swear on the grave of my mother that I'm telling you the truth!"

Hammersmith considered that for fifteen

seconds.

"Would you be willing to be interviewed by a French officer with whom the CIC has been working on Peenemünde — he has no connection with the DCI — about the Nazis you say were in Peenemünde, give him the names of the Nazis who are now in the United States?"

"If you do not hand me over to the Russians, I would be pleased to tell the whole world about these Nazis who you believe are now your friends."

Hammersmith paused thoughtfully for a long time.

"The interview would have to be done immediately," he said. "And it would have to be filmed. People in Washington would have to hear what you say. I can keep you from being handed over to the Russians, but I can't have you sent to the States, at least until I know you're telling the truth."

"I swear to God I will tell you the truth," Heimstadter said fervently.

"Well, let me see what I can set up," Hammersmith said.

He then left the cell and walked down the corridor to the cell that held former SS-Standartenführer Oskar Müller and had essentially the same conversation, with the same results, with Müller.

# [EIGHT]

*Kloster Grünau*

*Schollbrunn, Bavaria*

*American Zone of Occupation, Germany*

*0815 12 February 1946*

The screen — a sheet stapled to the wall of Cronley's office — went white as the film running through the projector ran out.

"Great job!" Cronley said. "Thanks, guys. This was really important."

"If you want, I can make up a title board for it," CID agent Walt "Hollywood" Thomas, of the CID photo lab, who had photographed the interviews, and then had done a rush job overnight of processing the film, said.

"Saying what?" Cronley asked.

" 'German Canaries Sing.' Both of those bastards were really trying to stick it to the Peenemünde Krauts, weren't they?"

He heard what he had said, and quickly went on. "No offense, General."

"None taken, Mr. Thomas," General Gehlen said. "I've heard the phrase before."

"What did you think, General?" Cronley asked.

"I think it will splendidly serve the intended purpose," Gehlen said.

"I don't suppose you're going to tell us what that is?" Thomas asked.

"Correct. You win the cement bicycle and an all-expenses-paid tour of downtown Pullach," Cronley said.

"Can I ask what you are going to do with those two . . . German gentlemen?"

"Nice try, Thomas," Ludwig Mannberg said. "But while they are German, they're not gentlemen."

"At 0900 tomorrow, we're going to try to swap them with the Russians for Colonel Mattingly," Cronley said. "And if that doesn't work — and I don't think it will — I'm going to turn them over to Military Government for trial at Nuremberg. If anybody deserves the hangman, those two do."

"If you had let me interrogate them," Konrad Bischoff said, "I'd have had them singing like canaries about what they did to the workers at Peenemünde."

"But if I had," Cronley said, "then Thomas would have had movies of two guys with broken noses, black eyes, and lots of bruises. That would have been counterproductive to our purpose of the film. And besides, don't take offense, Konrad, but I think Captain DuPres is a better interrogator than you are."

Bischoff didn't say anything, but he looked at Gehlen, obviously hoping Gehlen would defend him.

"I have to admit, Captain DuPres," Gehlen said, smiling, "that your handling of those two Peenemünde Krauts was beyond reproach."

"Thank you, sir."

"Please give my regards to Commandant Fortin when you see him," Gehlen said, as he got to his feet.

"Mon General, I will be honored to do so."

"How did you do, ladies?" Cronley asked Claudette Colbert and Florence Miller, who had both recorded the filmed interview in shorthand.

"A couple of corrections," Colbert replied. "We can have it all fixed in an hour."

"Great!"

Gehlen said: "Before I go back to the Compound, Jim, if it would be all right with you, I'd like to have a look at Lazarus."

"And so would I," Mannberg said.

"I'll walk you over to the chapel, sir," Cronley said. "Can I ask . . ."

"Why? I don't know why. Simple curiosity, perhaps. Or one of those . . . what do you call them? 'Feelings in the gut.' "

■ ■ ■ ■

One of Tiny's Troopers pulled the door to Lazarus's cell open and motioned Gehlen to go in.

Cronley saw Lazarus sitting on a wooden chair as Mannberg followed Gehlen into the cell. He was examining what was obviously a just-changed bandage on his shoulder.

"*Ach, du lieber Gott!*" Mannberg exclaimed softly.

Lazarus rose from the chair, came to attention, and snapped a bow.

"The Herr General will understand that I am not at all happy to see him," Lazarus said.

"Franz," Gehlen said, "isn't the attempted kidnapping of two American enlisted women a bit beneath the dignity of an SS-*brigadeführer*?"

"One does, Herr General, what one must to survive. May I suggest the Herr General knows that?"

"Forgive my bad manners, Jim," Gehlen said. "May I introduce former SS-Brigadeführer Baron Franz von Dietelburg?"

"I'll be a sonofabitch!" Cronley said.

"I have the privilege of Captain Cronley's

582

acquaintance," von Dietelburg said.

"The last we heard of SS-Brigadeführer von Dietelburg, Jim," Mannberg said, "he had been marched off to Siberia with General von Paulus after the debacle at Stalingrad."

"To judge by that suit of clothing, Ludwig," von Dietelburg said, "you have not only survived the collapse of the Thousand-Year Reich, but seem to have prospered. You're now Number Two in the Gehlen Organization. Very impressive!"

"Actually, I'm Number Three," Mannberg replied. "Then as now, Oberst Otto Niedermeyer is the general's deputy. He's now in Argentina."

"Have you forgotten, Ludwig, that at one time I had the privilege of serving as the Herr General's deputy?"

"I stand corrected, Herr Baron. I do recall that," Mannberg said. "That was before the Herr General decided your primary loyalty was to Himmler and had Admiral Canaris have you transferred to the Sixth Army."

"I suppose I should be expected to say something like this," General Gehlen said, "but I have had a . . . gut feeling . . . all along that you didn't perish at Stalingrad. Did you turn, Franz, before or after General von Paulus surrendered?"

"I began to realize that the Soviets were going to win when, because of the Fuhrer's incompetent interference with the Oberkommando der Wehrmacht, we failed to take not only Stalingrad, but the oil fields . . . et cetera. So I used my contacts to —"

Cronley's mouth went on automatic: "This is fucking surreal."

"Excuse me, Jim?" Gehlen said.

"This conversation, this standing around, pretending you're all gentlemen politely discussing things of mutual interest, like a bunch of fraternity guys discussing how to get laid, is . . . fucking surreal."

"What we are, if I may, Captain Cronley," von Dietelburg said, "are professional intelligence officers. Are we gentlemen? Yes, I would hope we fit that term, but primarily professional intelligence officers. As such, we see a situation for what it really is, rather than what we would prefer it to be."

"And what would you prefer this situation to be?"

"What it was before Herr General and Ludwig walked in here. I was close to thinking everyone accepted me to be Major of State Security Venedikt Ulyanov. As Major Ulyanov, I could see several ways out of my then uncomfortable position."

"What rank did the Reds give you?" Mannberg asked.

"At first the NKGB equivalent of my SS rank. I have subsequently been promoted."

"And do you see a way out of your now changed situation?" Cronley interrupted angrily.

"Just two. One is that, after interrogation, you will dispose of me here, and maintain the polite fiction that you had no idea that Major Ulyanov was actually Commissar 2nd Rank of State Security Ulyanov."

"You now have a Russian name?" Gehlen asked conversationally.

"Or," von Dietelburg went on, ignoring Gehlen's question, "you can take me to wherever you're dealing with Ivan Serov and see who the NKGB thinks is more valuable to them, me or your Colonel Mattingly."

"If they would take you back, Franz," Gehlen said, "you would probably wind up in the execution cell in the basement of that building on Lubyanka Square."

"But 'probably,' Herr General, I'm sure you will agree, is a more pleasant word than 'certainly,' which would apply to my being buried in an unmarked grave here, or spending the rest of my life in a prison cell here in Germany."

## [NINE]

*Glienicke Bridge*

*Wannsee, U.S. Zone of Berlin*

*0855 13 February 1946*

The huge Red Army truck backed onto the bridge as usual. When its doors opened, Cronley saw that Colonel Mattingly was again sitting chained to a chair.

"Go," Cronley ordered, and Jack Hammersmith put the Ford staff car in gear and drove onto the bridge, stopping twenty feet from the white line marking the center of the bridge.

When Ivan Serov appeared, Cronley got out of the front seat of the staff car and walked to within a few feet of the white line.

Janice Johansen trotted onto the bridge with two Leica cameras hanging from her neck and started taking pictures.

"Good morning, James," Serov said. "Presumably the Likharevs are delayed?"

"They're not coming, Ivan," Cronley said. "But there's a consolation prize."

He raised his right hand, balled in a fist, above his shoulders and moved his arm up and down. It was the standard U.S. Army hand signal for "Join me."

Ludwig Mannberg got out of the left rear

of the staff car and walked around the rear and opened the right rear door. Captain Chauncey Dunwiddie got out and then turned to help former SS-Brigadeführer Franz von Dietelburg out. When he was standing beside Dunwiddie, a shirt draped over but not concealing the massive bandage on von Dietelburg's shoulder, Mannberg reached into the car and came out with a U.S. Army officer's trench coat, which he draped around von Dietelburg's shoulders.

Dunwiddie put a massive hand on the trench coat over von Dietelburg's good arm and marched him to the white line.

Serov's face showed no expression.

"Turn Colonel Mattingly loose, Ivan," von Dietelburg said. "The operation didn't go quite as we planned it."

Serov didn't move, and his face remained expressionless.

"Get Colonel Mattingly out of the truck now," von Dietelburg ordered coldly.

"You know how it goes, Ivan," Cronley said. "You win some and you lose some."

Serov flashed him a furious glance.

Then he turned and started barking orders.

Mattingly was unchained from his chair and then helped to his feet and off the truck.

As he approached the white line, Dunwiddie took his arm off von Dietelburg.

"It was good to see you, Ludwig," von Dietelburg said.

"Good luck, Franz," Mannberg replied.

"And I would be remiss not to thank you, Captain Cronley, for not only my treatment but your courtesies."

"You're welcome," Cronley said.

As Mattingly and von Dietelburg passed each other at the white line, they nodded at one another.

Dunwiddie took Mattingly's arm and guided him to, and then into, the staff car, and then got in beside him. Cronley and Mannberg walked to the car. Just before he got in, Cronley turned to Janice Johansen and made an obscene gesture that would guarantee the photographic image she was making of him would never appear in a newspaper.

"Wiseass!" she said.

Hammersmith started the car, made a tight U-turn, and drove off the bridge.

## [TEN]

Page 1, above the fold, *STARS AND STRIPES* 14 February 1946.

# CONSTABULARY ENLISTED MEN NAB WANTED SS BIG SHOTS

## Constabulary Commander Lauds Three Constabulary Troopers for "Great Work"

By Janice Johansen
Associated Press Foreign Correspondent

**Sonthofen February 13 —**

Major General Ernest Harmon, Commanding General of the U.S. Constabulary (left in photo) congratulates (left to right) Constabulary troopers 1st Sgt A. L. Tedworth, Sgt Homer B. Kelly, and Pfc Peter J. Foster for their capture of SS-Brigadeführer Ulrich Heimstadter and SS-Standartenführer Oskar Müller as Major General I. D. White (far right) looks on.

The long-sought SS officers were arrested by the Constabulary troopers at a remote Constabulary checkpoint on the Franco-German border very early in the morning of February 12.

The two Nazis, who headed the CIC's Most Wanted list, were carrying false identification papers and attempting to cross into France when Tedworth became suspicious.

"I wondered why a butcher from Dresden

and a tailor from Kassel were going to France on a remote road at that hour, so I checked the CIC's list, and bingo, there were pictures of them in their SS uniforms," Tedworth said. "But the real credit for catching these guys goes to Pfc. Foster. He came to me and said, 'First Sergeant, there's something about these two that smells. Why don't you take a look?' If he hadn't done that, they'd probably have gotten through."

General Harmon said that the two SS officers would be turned over to the War Crimes Tribunal in Nuremberg, which has already indicted them *in absentia* on a number of charges.

Page 7, *STARS AND STRIPES* 14 February 1946.

## WAYWARD OFFICERS GO HOME TO FACE REPRIMAND

### What Could Have Been an International Incident Turns Out to Be Too Much Booze in Wrong Place

By Janice Johansen
Associated Press Foreign Correspondent

## Berlin February 13 —

What at first appeared to be an international incident in the making turned out to be nothing more than two officers, one Russian and the other American, drinking too much in the wrong places.

The issue was resolved at nine o'clock this morning in Berlin, when the Russian officers marched Colonel Robert Mattingly, of USFET headquarters, to the center of the Glienicke Bridge while simultaneously American officers marched Major of State Security Venedikt Ulyanov, of the Allied Commandantura, to the same place.

A white line in the center of the bridge over the River Havel marks the dividing line between the Russian and American zones of Berlin. Once the two officers reached that line, Russian officers released Col. Mattingly into the custody of an American captain, probably a military policeman, who in turn released Major Ulyanov into the custody of a Russian major, also probably a military policeman.

This reporter has learned exclusively that despite early reports that Colonel Mattingly was missing and kidnapping was suspected, and that Major Ulyanov had been kidnapped in retaliation, the truth seems to be that prior to their exchange on the Glienicke Bridge

Colonel Mattingly was sitting in a jail cell in Thuringia, in East Germany, after his arrest for driving under the influence, and Major Uly-anov was sitting in a West Berlin jail after his arrest for public intoxication on the Kurfürsten-damm.

Both headquarters, Berlin Command and the Allied Commandantura, refused to confirm or deny what this reporter had learned, but a U.S. Army spokesman said "the incident is under investigation."

## [ELEVEN]

*Westminster College, Fulton, Missouri*

*1330 5 March 1946*

"From Stettin in the Baltic to Trieste in the Adriatic, an iron curtain has descended across the continent," Sir Winston Leonard Spencer-Churchill said.

# ABOUT THE AUTHORS

**W.E.B. Griffin** is the author of seven bestselling series: The Corps, Brotherhood of War, Badge of Honor, Men at War, Honor Bound, Clandestine Operations, and Presidential Agent. He has been invested into the orders of St. George of the U.S. Armor Association and St. Michael of the Army Aviation Association of America, and is a life member of the U.S. Special Operations Association; Gaston-Lee Post 5660, Veterans of Foreign Wars; the American Legion, China Post '1 in Exile; the Police Chiefs Association of Southeastern Pennsylvania, Southern New Jersey, and the State of Delaware; the National Rifle Association; the Office of Strategic Services (OSS) Society; and the Flat Earth Society (Pensacola, Florida, and Buenos Aires, Argentina, chapters). He is an honorary life member of the U.S. Army Otter-Caribou Association, the U.S. Army Special Forces Association, the U.S. Marine Raider Association, and the USMC Combat Correspondents Association. Griffin lives in Alabama and Argentina.

**William E. Butterworth IV** has been an editor and writer for more than twenty-five years, and has worked closely with his father for over a decade on the editing and writing of the Griffin books. He is coauthor with him of more than a dozen *New York Times*-bestselling novels. He is a member of the Sons of the American Legion, China Post '1 in Exile; the Office of Strategic Services (OSS) Society; and a life member of the National Rifle Association and the Texas Rifle Association. He lives in Florida.

The employees of Thorndike Press hope you have enjoyed this Large Print book. All our Thorndike, Wheeler, and Kennebec Large Print titles are designed for easy reading, and all our books are made to last. Other Thorndike Press Large Print books are available at your library, through selected bookstores, or directly from us.

For information about titles, please call:
  (800) 223-1244

or visit our Web site at:
  http://gale.cengage.com/thorndike

To share your comments, please write:
  Publisher
  Thorndike Press
  10 Water St., Suite 310
  Waterville, ME 04901